The

ROYAL GAME

The

ROYAL GAME

A NOVEL

LINDA KEIR

**BLACK
STONE**
PUBLISHING

Printed in the United States of America
Originally published in hardcover by Blackstone Publishing in 2024

First paperback edition: 2024
ISBN 979-8-212-63107-5
Fiction / Romance / Royalty

Version 1

Blackstone Publishing
31 Mistletoe Rd.
Ashland, OR 97520

www.BlackstonePublishing.com

A crown Golden in show, is but a wreath of thorns. Brings dangers, troubles, cares, and sleepless nights . . .

—John Milton

Part One

THE ROYAL TREATMENT

Chapter One

GIRL WITH GUITAR

Life was a mystery—hers, anyway.

Day three in another half-full club and Jennie Jensen was already questioning the magical numbers her manager had conjured to justify sending her on a solo acoustic tour of the Mediterranean. The opening night had gone as well as expected: a short opening set for DJ Spikeymau5 on Ibiza in front of seven thousand raving fans, all of them pumped to hear her sing "I Can't Even," a four-year-old song given new life thanks to the DJ's sample of Jennie singing those three words in his club hit, "Girl Said Goodbye." Even though the crowd was obviously just waiting to heave to the headliner's sick beats and massive drops, they roared with approval for Jennie and her acoustic guitar— almost as though they'd known she was only scheduled to play a handful of songs.

Spikeymau5—whose real name was Eugene Rosencranz— had invited her to the after-party when his set wrapped at two in the morning, but after only a few minutes she'd decided to leave: the VIP lounge where Eugene held court was packed with pretty young things and the whole scene was beyond gross.

The rest of her shows were booked in cabarets and clubs, usually as an opener for another indie folk artist, in front of audiences that had, so far, been hard to predict. The crowd tonight in Mallorca wasn't bad: some of them knew some of her songs, almost all of them listened respectfully, and no more faces than usual were lighted from below as they scrolled on their phones.

Actually, it was probably two-thirds full tonight. And the only open tables were in the back. It was a beautiful May evening, with a warm, dry breeze flowing through the large, open street windows, past the patrons at the bar, all the way to the stage where she faced the audience barefoot, her toes curled into a plush Persian rug. Stage lights always made it hard to see, but she could be sure the audience was tan, fit, happy, and well-heeled.

Jennie knew lots of people probably thought her career was trending downward. Her mother, Karen, fretted about her unpredictable finances. Leaving out this latest spike of interest, it had been four years since "I Can't Even" was featured on the soundtrack of an indie rom-com of the same name that suddenly blew up, allowing Jennie to take a full band on a hastily planned world tour in which they opened for bigger acts in midsized venues from LA to Sydney to Vienna to Stockholm to London. The merch sales alone allowed her to pay a year's rent in advance on her one-bedroom apartment in Bed-Stuy, and soon afterward, she licensed the song to Volkswagen for five figures. She'd used that money to pay down her student loans and open a small retirement account.

Since then, however, not much had happened. She spent a year writing and recording another album for a small indie label, did a solo US club tour, and listened as her loyal manager obsessed about ways to help her break big. The Mediterranean tour was part of that.

Just look at your itinerary, he insisted. *It's* cool. *These* places *are cool. Play these places and people will realize you're cool, too. You can work it like crazy on Instagram, and then we'll pitch you for some festivals after you get back.*

Jennie, willing to try his approach even though the label's budget put her in questionable Airbnbs, signed off. She had a secret she didn't dare tell the man whose job it was to make her rich and famous: she had already accomplished more than she'd ever dared to dream while growing up in suburban Peoria, and still couldn't believe she got to make music for a living. She was young, single, and had the privilege of singing songs she'd written onstage. Tomorrow, she had a half day to sit on the beach and play tourist until catching the ferry to Barcelona. *Barcelona!*

What she couldn't tell her manager was that she was already living her dream.

———————

Her set was almost over when four square-shouldered men came into the room and stationed themselves near the exits. Then, in a slick move Jennie had only ever seen in a movie about fifties mobsters, the nightclub owner physically carried a table onto the floor and ushered two men to their newly created front-row seats.

The whole production was unusual, but she didn't think too much of it. Strange things happened in the playgrounds of the rich and famous, and the men had arrived so late that they'd obviously come to see the headliner. She had learned long ago to play through any distraction.

Then she broke a string—the B string, to be precise. Maybe she actually was distracted and strummed too hard. Maybe she should have changed the strings that morning. Or maybe it was simply fate. When she'd toured after The Movie, she'd had her own guitar tech, but now, on the "Girl with Guitar" tour, it was just her and her favorite acoustic. All she could do was apologize and change the string onstage.

"We now interrupt your regularly scheduled programming," she joked as she snaked the silver string out of its wrapper, crumpling the paper, and dropping it on the stage. "Sorry for the delay. My roadie's getting drunk at the dive down the street."

"Are you going to play 'I Can't Even'?" asked one of the guys up front, the one on the left, his English accent as upper class as polished silver.

Why was he asking about The Song? Was he actually here to see *her*?

She shaded her eyes against the lights and saw a handsome man with tousled brown hair and a week's growth of beard. He and his friend were both wearing suits with loosened ties.

He looked slightly familiar. Maybe he was an actor in something she'd seen—or maybe he was just another rich, handsome man who traded on his British accent and well-cut wardrobe.

Jennie refocused on the head of her guitar, trying to find the hole in the tuning peg.

"I already played it," she told him, her amplified voice filling every corner of the room. "You should have been on time."

A slight hush, followed by a rising murmur, gave Jennie the feeling that, even though she didn't know who this guy was, every one of the two-hundred-odd concertgoers did.

"I'm so sorry!" he protested. "I truly am. The traffic from the airport was horrendous."

She had to admit, his voice was warm and appealing. Not that clipped, dead-lipped sound produced by some snobby Brits. But it was time to call his bluff.

"So you're saying you flew in just for my show?" she asked.

"I did."

In the back of the room, a woman gasped. Jennie tightened the string, its twanging, rising timbre like an avant-garde film score foreshadowing danger.

"And I was hoping to hear that song in particular."

"Oh, you were, were you?" Jennie shot back.

"Cross my heart and hope to die."

The audience's breathless anticipation was almost audible as Jennie used her electronic tuner to finish restringing.

Feeling a strange flutter in her chest, she waited a beat before grinning at the man and asking the audience, "Do you all mind hearing it again?"

The applause was the loudest she'd heard all night.

———

The two well-dressed men disappeared before the house lights came up, escorted out by the four security goons. Jennie knew she would eventually file their encounter away as just another funny thing that happened on tour, a good story to tell her friends when she got back home. She finished her set—no encore required—then sat on the lip of the stage to chat and sign merch while the headliner's officious roadie began moving microphone stands into place behind her.

Twenty minutes later, she was closing her guitar case and getting ready to leave when she heard someone say, "My friend wants to meet you."

Jennie looked up. It was one of the men who'd been seated up front. Not quite as handsome as the one who'd requested The Song.

"Did your friend break his leg on the way out?"

He blinked, confused. "I'm sorry?"

"I'm just wondering why he sent you."

Jennie stood up and slipped her feet into her sandals. Pulling on her small backpack, she picked up the guitar and hopped off the stage.

"I suppose one could say it's not easy for him to meet people," said the wingman.

"He seems outgoing enough to me."

"It's not that at all." Working to cover his frustration, the guy checked his watch, a Rolex that seemed as big as a tuna can. "My name's Nigel Courtenay. My friend is an honorable man, a truly delightful fellow—"

"I'm sure he's a prince of a guy," interrupted Jennie, enjoying his discomfort.

"He is." Nigel finally smiled. "I vouch for him."

"And I can trust you?"

"Implicitly," said Nigel.

Jennie had been propositioned by people who claimed to be many things, usually film, TV, or music executives, but also sometimes heirs to fortunes from grocery chains or pharmaceutical empires. She would have written off these apologetic Englishmen if there wasn't something so awkward about them. Jennie trusted her instincts, and nothing at all was telling her to run.

And she had to give the guy credit: he knew how to make a girl curious.

But, of course, he wasn't waiting on the sidewalk out front. Nigel wanted her to accompany him, in a chauffeured Mercedes, on what he insisted would be "a short drive."

Jennie knew her mom would have been horrified to see her climb into a stranger's car, and she probably wouldn't have if Nigel hadn't told her that the bodyguard in the front seat had been sent for her protection. Maybe she *was* being kidnapped and would never be heard from again, but she just didn't believe kidnappers wore suits, ties, and Rolexes with such impeccable style.

"So are you going to tell me your friend's name?" asked Jennie, after the chauffeur had stowed her guitar in the trunk.

"You honestly didn't recognize him?" asked Nigel.

She shook her head, starting to wonder if this was some kind of hidden-camera prank show.

He chuckled. "We've been friends since boarding school, and there we all used to call him Honks."

The car rolled smoothly out of town, followed a winding coastal road, and entered an enclave of walled villas, where they passed through an ornamental iron gate and stopped on a circular cobbled driveway. Nigel led her through a huge, baroque mansion to French doors that opened onto a flagstone patio.

"He's out there," said Nigel, turning back into the house.

She was relieved she hadn't been asked to bring her guitar with her: at least this wasn't a rich fan wanting a free private concert.

As she walked outside, stars glowed on the mirrorlike surface of the motionless pool. Beyond it, lights twinkled from the houses lining the rocky cliffs. Far off in the distance, a single ship's light glided across the horizon. The man from the club was taking in the scene from a table topped with a candle, an iced bottle of wine, and two glasses.

"Nice house," she said as she approached.

Hearing her, he turned. "It belongs to an old family friend. I'm not sure I'd go for quite so much red velvet and gold filigree."

"Your friend said to call you Honks."

He tossed his head back and laughed. "He harbors a grudge because no one ever calls him Nigel. He's been Courts for ages."

Her host stood up, pulled out her chair, and poured her a glass of wine. Her inability to place his face bothered her. Now

that she'd seen him up close, she *knew* she'd seen him somewhere and was starting to feel like an idiot for not matching it
with a name.

"Thank you so much for coming," he told her.

"It's all very mysterious," she said.

"Regrettably necessary. Then again, royals have been playing cloak and dagger for centuries, so you might say it's in our
blood."

Royals.

It clicked. She knew. She'd seen him dozens and dozens
of times . . . on the covers of magazines her mom habitually
brought home from the grocery store.

She almost spat out her wine. "You're Prince Hugh!"

He looked startled. "You didn't know? I'm so terribly sorry.
I'm actually mortified. My mum would have slapped my fingers
if she'd caught me using such poor manners."

*His mother, Princess Penelope, who died in a private plane
crash when he was a teenager.*

Jennie put down her glass using both hands. She would
have expected a prince to have a golden aura. At least they could
have played trumpets when he walked in—*something* to alert
clueless Americans.

"I'm embarrassed it took me so long. Should I bow or something? I don't know what the protocol is."

He grinned. "You should most definitely *not* bow. But let's
meet properly. I am Hugh 'Honks' Windsor, who shouldn't presume his reputation precedes him. Very pleased to make your
acquaintance."

"And I'm Jennie 'Guitar' Jensen, also very pleased to make
your acquaintance."

They shook hands. When his soft, strong fingers encircled
hers, she felt an undeniable tingle.

"That's not seriously your nickname, is it? Guitar?"

"No! When I was in seventh grade, I really wanted it to be, though."

Prince Hugh laughed. "I wanted to be in a band, too! Unfortunately, the King of England told me I had to be Prince of Wales instead. But I will always love music. After I heard your voice in that Spikeymau5 song, I listened to everything you've recorded. I knew I had to meet you."

"Well, I *never* wanted to meet you," said Jennie, smiling.

"With my manners, I couldn't say I blame you," said Hugh.

Chapter Two

THE COMFORTS
OF HOME

Jennie's stomach lurched as the pilot banked away from the Thames. Her first-ever trip in a helicopter and it had to be a *royal* helicopter, piloted by a combat-hardened RAF captain who'd missed his true calling as a tour guide. She sat alone in the luxuriously appointed cabin, buckled into one of the six buttery soft leather seats, while the pilot noted every point of interest between Heathrow and Kensington Palace. So far, they'd flown over the Royal Botanic Gardens at Kew, the King's House Sports Ground, and Charing Cross Hospital—to name the three landmarks she could remember.

"And that's the Royal Albert Hall directly ahead," the pilot informed her through the cabin speaker.

As interesting as it was to view London from the air, Jennie was only fixated on one point of interest: Hugh. She hadn't seen him for almost a month.

A month during which her life had, in Hugh's words, "gone completely pear-shaped."

Even though their public encounter last spring had triggered a brief cycle of tabloid stories ("Music-Lover Hugh Scolded from Stage by Singer"), Hugh's precautions in keeping their first meeting private had paid off: no one outside of their closest friends had any idea they were seeing each other. For nine blissful months, they'd fallen in love long distance and in absolute secrecy, spending time together every few weeks in some of the unlikeliest places, from a British military base to an Italian villa owned by another one of Hugh's "family friends" to Disneyland, where they waited in line wearing hats, sunglasses, and wigs. For New Year's, Hugh flew her to Finland so they could watch the Northern Lights nestled beneath fur blankets in a glass-domed "igloo." Their encounters were too infrequent, but they were both busy: Jennie's Mediterranean tour had indeed generated more buzz and more bookings as she continued to write and record songs for what she hoped would be a new album, and Hugh was even busier, with a relentless schedule of ribbon-cuttings and troop visits and state dinners. But every moment spent together was electric, charged even more by the need to treat their romance like it was a dangerous secret.

Jennie had quickly come to realize just how much a future king's relationship status meant to not only England and the United Kingdom but to all the countries of the Commonwealth. Shortly before meeting Jennie, after years of an on-and-off relationship, Hugh had finally broken things off with Imogen Banfield-March, the aristocrat many people had speculated he'd marry. The lack of news since then only seemed to make some reporters even more determined to get the scoop on who he dated next.

Jennie's name had popped up in a few speculative gossip columns, but nothing had come of it until some unnamed source in Kensington Palace—they still didn't know who—told a reporter that Hugh was "the happiest I've ever seen him" and "absolutely smitten with Jennie Jensen, the American singer."

Within hours, Jennie found the street outside of her Brooklyn apartment building besieged by so many reporters and TV trucks that NYPD officers were forced to clear the snarled street. Watching it all on her phone from behind her locked door was the closest she'd ever come to an out-of-body experience, especially after some rando gave a completely fictitious interview saying he'd "definitely seen that Prince Hugh sneaking in and out the building, wearing, you know, like a fake beard, sunglasses, and a Yankees cap." Hugh had never been to her block, much less inside her apartment. It just seemed too risky.

After sneaking out at 4 a.m. in a hoodie, Jennie had first sought refuge in the loft of her longtime friend and bass player Diego, until Hugh apologetically reminded her that "it might be taken the wrong way" if she were to be discovered living under another man's roof, even if that man was gay. From there she was smuggled to a guesthouse on the Hamptons estate of a married music producer Hugh happened to know, where she tried and failed to write songs. But when her host's twelve-year-old daughter spotted men with long camera lenses hiding in the bushes at the edge of the property, Jennie fled home to Peoria. That worked for a few days, until the other families on her parents' quiet cul-de-sac started sharing on social media that the now-famous Jensen girl was visiting home. Reporters smelled blood in the water and swarmed yet again.

Hugh's public plea to the media to leave her alone seemed to do the opposite of what he intended. Not only did it confirm that they were seeing each other, the British public began to debate whether an American royal would be a breath of fresh air or a breach of tradition. When one intrepid journalist dug up the "shocking" fact that Jennie was adopted, it seemed to add a further possible insult to the bloodline. Who knew who her ancestors were?

Come to England, Hugh texted, as even more reporters flocked to downstate Illinois. *We may as well weather this storm together.*

Crossing the Atlantic on a private jet, Jennie had felt like she was flying into the eye of the storm. Would Hugh have second thoughts about whether she was worth the trouble? Did she have the guts to keep going? Her butterflies only flapped their wings more furiously when she was ushered to a landing pad to board the luxuriously appointed "King's Flight," a burgundy helicopter with the royal crest of the House of Windsor painted on the side.

Sorry, but it's the safest way to sneak you in, Hugh had explained.

Now, as the aircraft descended over the February-brown expanse of Hyde Park, Kensington Palace loomed closer and closer in view. She had visited several times before, and nothing about Hugh's world had been like she pictured. Kensington Palace was a rambling, red-brick compound where various royals lived in "apartments" and assorted outbuildings. And although Hugh was now the most important royal after his father, King Edmund, he didn't even live in the palace but behind it, in the small but charming Nottingham Cottage, or "Nott Cott," as Hugh called it. While she had learned that many countryside "cottages" were actually mansions, Hugh's bachelor digs were indeed cozy—and about a third the size of the beige McMansion where she'd grown up.

The helicopter touched down and the door slid open. The prop wash buffeted her like gale winds as a man in a suit helped her down the steps and across the soggy ground into a waiting car. Outside the roped-off area, she could see several tourists raising their phones to document this unexpected spectacle— hopefully from too far away to take identifiable pictures. After her suitcases were stowed in the trunk, they drove several hundred yards to the palace grounds, around the back of the palace proper, and into the gravel court in front of Nott Cott.

Hugh was waiting on the front step, wearing jeans and a thick crew-neck sweater that showed off his muscular torso. He grinned widely but waited until they were safely inside—royal protocol prohibited PDA, and eyes and cameras were everywhere—before crushing her in a ravenous hug. She melted into him, savoring his scent of plain soap and . . . pizza?

"Hungry?" he asked.

"Words cannot describe how hungry."

She followed him to the kitchen, smiling as he ducked under its low doorway, and accepted the inevitable mug of tea.

Hugh slipped on oven mitts, opened the oven, and carefully removed a steaming deep-dish pizza with a golden crust.

"Oh my God, that looks just like Lou Malnati's!" said Jennie. The Chicago-based pizza chain was a Jensen family favorite.

"It required only the smallest bribe to have an acquaintance in our embassy package one for overnight international delivery," he said, rummaging in drawers for a knife and spatula. "My good lady, may I present one spinach-and-veggie, gluten-free, Chicago-style deep-dish pizza. All the comforts of home."

Jennie planted a kiss on his cheek, yet again amazed at his thoughtfulness. Hugh had been waited on by a small army of servants since the day he was born, and yet he seemed to take continuing delight in discovering that he could wait on her, too.

"We never drink tea with our pizza back home, but I'll let that slide," she said. "The only thing that could make this more perfect would be a box of Thin Mints."

Completely deadpan, Hugh maintained eye contact while he opened a cupboard and removed a box of the Girl Scout treats.

"No pudding until after supper," he stated as he set them on the countertop.

Grinning, Jennie snatched the box and tore it open, dancing out of his reach before he gave up and started cutting a slice of pizza.

After they had eaten, sitting cross-legged on the rug in front of a small but crackling fire, Hugh set the dishes aside and helped her to her feet.

"I want to show you something," he said.

They crossed the gravel court and entered the palace through a very ordinary back door, then walked down an empty, ornate hallway until they reached heavy plastic sheeting that walled off the work going on behind.

"My father, the King, has decreed that I shall live like one, too, by moving into the palace proper," he told her, holding back a flap so she could enter. "An order I can only accept if it no longer looks like a museum."

"You're remodeling?"

He chuckled. "Practically demolishing. They've been at it for months. Most of the rooms were done in early Victorian, but others had 1950s updates and even shag carpets. My aim is to balance the required amount of palace pomp with something contemporary and even comfortable."

The ground floor looked finished except for sheets over the furniture and stray pieces of painter's tape on the walls. It was formal and elegant but not at all old-fashioned. It seemed a tiny bit like a grand hotel, but she reasoned that Hugh would undoubtedly have to do a lot of entertaining. After they climbed the stairs to the second floor—what Hugh insisted on calling "the first floor"—they navigated an obstacle course of ladders, sawhorses, drop cloths, and carefully stowed toolboxes.

"Looks like a bomb went off, I know," said Hugh. "Did

you know this place was actually bombed in World War II? Not badly. In fact, it's possible we dropped one ourselves, just so we could show the punters we were all in the same boat."

As they passed through room after room—with two floors still above them—Jennie felt overwhelmed by the size and splendor of the "apartment." She had recorded an album in an old mansion that had been converted into a recording studio in Tennessee, and she'd stayed at a slightly moth-eaten château while performing at a music festival in Normandy, but when she wasn't at her one-bedroom apartment in New York, she lived mostly out of hotel rooms, tour buses, and vans.

"Hugh, I don't know if I'll ever be able to wrap my head around the fact that you live in this place."

"If it makes you feel any better, it hasn't always been the finest address. A century ago, it housed so many unwed eccentrics that people referred to it as the 'Aunt Heap.' Oh, and we have ghosts! A king, a princess, and some sort of feral child, although I don't recall the details."

She gave him a playful shove. "Still too much like something out of a storybook."

"Sorry, darling," he said, kissing her.

Turning a corner, they entered what looked like a torn-up living room. The wallpaper had been removed, revealing patched plaster walls. Built-in cabinets and bookcases had been scraped and sanded awaiting new coats of paint. As elsewhere, the ceiling was so high it made Jennie feel tiny.

"This was Mum's favorite sitting room," said Hugh. "I'm going to freshen it up but otherwise leave it basically as is. It holds a lot of good memories—she taught me to read sitting on a sofa right over there."

Jennie still hadn't quite gotten used to his personal stories about Princess Penelope. She'd grown up hearing gossip about

Penelope's drinking problem and affairs from her royal-obsessed mom, but Hugh's version of her was nuanced and affectionate. To him, his mother was vulnerable, kind, and sometimes corny, but also far more intelligent than history gave her credit for.

Hugh's eyes had grown misty while he talked about his mother. She loved that about him: though he was strong enough to bear the burden of expectation his family and country had placed upon him, he also wasn't afraid to show his emotions. Losing his mother at the age of thirteen was a wound that clearly hadn't healed.

In a way, Jennie had lost her mother, too. Abandoned as an infant, she was adopted from foster care by Karen and Dave Jensen and their ten-year-old son Daniel. And although she truly thought of Karen as her mom and the Jensens as her family, she was sometimes still surprised by unexpected aches to know her birth mother, or at least to understand what had caused her to endure pregnancy and childbirth only to leave her daughter in front of a fire station.

"No need to tramp through all twenty rooms," Hugh said. "Come outside and I'll show you the garden."

The acre-size traditional English garden would be breathtaking in spring. Even better, a walled perimeter made it perfectly private, so they could hold hands as they strolled the flagstone path between the trimmed-back and leafless vegetation. Clouds had mostly kept the sun in check since she'd landed at Heathrow, but wider gaps showed more blue sky, and the warm sunshine was welcome on the chilly winter day.

"Well, I don't know how you'll ever keep all those toilets clean," she kidded him, "but I think you'll be very happy here."

"I hope you will be, too." Hugh squeezed her hand, let go, and took a ring box out of his pocket as he dropped to one knee. "Call me old-fashioned, but it just seems like this sort of thing ought to be done while one's knees throb in agony."

"Hugh . . ."

She had no idea how to finish the sentence. It had crossed her mind that this might be a possibility, but not seriously. Girls from Peoria didn't marry princes . . .

He opened the box. The ring was an enormous oval sapphire, surrounded by a glittering halo of diamonds.

"My father proposed to my mum with this ring. I know their story didn't end as planned, but it's time we changed the family luck."

"It's too much," Jennie whispered. "It belongs in a museum, not on my finger."

"I can't think of a more deserving hand in the world," said Hugh intently. "I can't offer you the world—the empire's not what it used to be. But I can offer you my whole heart, forever."

She felt dizzy. His eyes seemed to sparkle in the sunlight.

"Jennie Jensen, will you marry me?"

"Yes," she whispered. "Yes, yes, yes."

HRH The Princess of Wales

24 JULY 1982

"Princess, will you lift me up?" Anabelle Osborne-Webb, the youngest and most precocious of her four flower girls, tugged on Penelope's wedding gown. "I want to touch the sparkly ceiling."

"I don't think I'm quite tall enough for that, sweetheart," Penelope told her, gazing up at the sunlit, etched-glass dome two stories above Buckingham Palace's Grand Staircase.

Confusion clouded the girl's cherubic face. "But you're a *princess*."

It had been little more than an hour since Lady Penelope Maxwell walked down the aisle carrying a sprig of myrtle in her bouquet. She'd exchanged vows with her prince—resplendent in his Royal Navy commander's full-dress uniform—before God and 750 million earthly souls. A band of Welsh gold now nestled beside her sapphire engagement ring.

And yet, Princess Penelope still felt like an actress—Jane Seymour or maybe even Diana Rigg—playing a part in the world's grandest production.

"Rumor has it there's a porcelain frog somewhere in the Green Drawing Room," she told little Anabelle as they climbed the final steps and proceeded toward the Throne Room. "If you find him and kiss him gently, he may just turn into a prince."

"Is that how you met Prince Edmund?"

"Something like that." A better explanation for a three-year-old than years of appearing at all the right places, at the most opportune times, playing her part in her parents' plot to beguile the heir to the throne. "I did have a poster of him on the inside of my wardrobe as a girl."

"Did you kiss it?"

Penelope giggled for the first time all day. "I thought about it once or twice."

"And Prince Edmund realized you loved him and came and found you?"

While she'd definitely harbored a girlhood crush on the broad-shouldered prince with the dreamy brown eyes—who didn't?—she'd gone along with what she secretly called Operation Penny for Princess largely to appease her titled, but often overlooked, parents. Plus, the parties, which inevitably orbited His Royal Highness, were loads of fun.

And then Edmund really, *surreally*, did take notice.

She'd been tumbling around in his gravitational pull ever since.

"We found each other," Penelope said, glancing behind her and hoping to catch her husband's eye as he accepted congratulations from various members of the extended bridal contingent.

His scent—bergamot, cypress, and fresh citrus—lingered on her sleeve from their arm-in-arm walk down the aisle and their open-topped carriage ride from Westminster Abbey to Buckingham Palace. So far that day, they'd spent exactly zero minutes alone together.

Her heart raced at the thought of tonight.

"Your Highness, the photographer needs to take your portrait now if we're to stay on schedule," said Jeremy Legrand, Edmund's pinch-faced private secretary, appearing at her side to usher her through the doors to the Throne Room. "And we're already behind schedule."

The photographer, a round fellow who was already sweating through his shirt, smiled nervously as he indicated where she should stand. "I'll try to make this as painless as possible, Your Highness."

Penelope had been primed, prepared, admonished, instructed, and told exactly what was expected of her for months. Years, really, given that the countdown started when Mr. Crowden brayed a fateful, gin-fueled compliment to Mum and Dad at her good friend Kitty Crowden's end-of-summer pool party.

If you're smart, you'll lock that one up and throw away the key until Prince Edmund is ready to find a bride.

And yet, every adjective Her Royal Highness the Princess of Wales might use to describe the experience—*magical, surreal, magnificent*—fell hopelessly flat.

Thankfully no one had actually asked. All that had been required of her was to follow directions—where to sit, stand, and walk, even how to emote and to whom—delivered by the small army tasked with ensuring she sailed through the most celebrated and revered event in the British monarchy. Aside from a coronation, of course.

"Your Highness, please tilt your head slightly," the photographer said. "Now look up and smile."

Princess Penelope did exactly as instructed, looking into the camera and not daring to glance past the photographer or his lens at the pair of thrones on the raised dais. Not allowing any thoughts of the dusty-rose seat cushion that would someday bear her initials. Knowing her parents, standing across the way and watching her every move, had that very thing on their minds.

Legrand's surprisingly deep voice rumbled through the room. "Flower girls and page boys, please join the bride."

As the various royal offspring began to gather around her, Penelope watched Eleanora Osborne-Webb bribe little Anabelle with a treat from inside her clutch.

The photographer arranged the four wiggling flower girls and two bored page boys around her with expertise that belied his nervous demeanor.

When he was finished, Anabelle opened her fist, revealing two wine gums. "My mum said I had to wait until after the photo."

"Your mum is a clever woman."

"Would you like one, Princess?"

"Aren't you dear," Penelope said. "But they're for you."

"I'm good at sharing."

Less dubious about the sticky sweets than the state of her breath, Penelope accepted a piece and popped it into her mouth. She loved sweets and the raspberry flavor was surprisingly soothing. Familiar in a way nothing else around her was.

"We will now require all members of the bridal party, please," announced Legrand.

Penelope tried to prolong the fleeting sense of normalcy by telling herself that this wedding portrait session wasn't really all that different from any other—assuming one could book Buckingham Palace as a venue, that the bride's parents weren't destined to be the grandparents of a future monarch, and that the bridal party didn't include the Queen of England.

People were taking their places around Penelope when her dashing prince strode into the room.

Her *husband*.

How long would it be until his mere presence—his charm, steady gaze, and supremely confident gait—didn't make her catch her breath?

"I see the world's most celebrated bride is holding up beautifully," Edmund said, kissing her cheek and standing beside her.

She willed herself not to muck up the group photo by blushing beet red.

With brusque diplomacy, Legrand helped the photographer arrange his subjects by height, family association, and in the case of Princess Alice, to obscure her sturdy ankles.

"If everyone would be kind enough to remain in place until the photo has been taken," he said.

"Fat chance," Queen Alexandra whispered after taking her place one step down and to the right of Edmund. "My dogs keep still better than Princess Stuart."

Penelope and Edmund shared a quiet laugh. The day had been such a blur that she was looking forward to watching a rebroadcast of the whole glorious event, from beginning to end, wanting both to relive her favorite moments and to reassure herself she had actually been there.

She wanted to see herself wave from the Rolls-Royce on the way to Westminster Abbey looking like a blushing bride-to-be—even though her rosy cheeks were caused by the hothouse heat of mounds of fabric, nervous perspiration, and sunbaked, enclosed glass.

She wanted to remember the words Dad had whispered in

her ear just before the door to the car was opened with cameras from all over the world trained on her.

You are perfect, Penny.

Never mind that his touching sentiment came in response to her question, *Do I have anything on my face or hanging from my nose?* and that his certainty was misplaced because he'd been too vain to wear his glasses.

Penelope wanted to hear all the commentary on her dress and to confirm that no one spotted the blotted bloodstain on the veil—she'd pricked her finger on an unexpectedly sharp prong of the old, borrowed Maxwell family tiara.

"Prince Edmund, might you lift the Princess's hand and bring it to your lips?" the photographer asked uncertainly, as though this standard wedding pose might somehow be considered inappropriate.

Edmund complied without hesitation. His cool lips sent a jolt of warmth up her arm. And her thighs, too.

He was all hers now. When she rewatched her three-and-a-half-minute march down the aisle, Penelope knew she would scan the pews for Edmund's old flames. Would their faces betray regret for the indiscretions that rendered them unsuitable, or judgment about how they'd have worn it better?

Jeremy Legrand appeared beside the photographer, looking slightly less pinched now that most of the photographs had been taken. "Everyone but the prince and princess may now proceed to the Centre Room."

Penelope's parents, whose practiced poise had so far masked their boundless elation, were visibly giddy to be accompanying their new royal in-laws to the celebrated chamber. Known for its Chinese embroideries and a peculiar glass chandelier resembling a flower, it served as a gathering area ahead of official appearances on the famed balcony outside.

Penelope was content to see them go. She craved a few minutes of almost-alone time with her new husband, regardless of how staged and official.

"Let's do one with a more somber expression," the photographer said, firing off his final shots. "Excellent. Now a smile . . . This time look into each other's eyes . . . Marvelous. Truly regal."

"I couldn't agree more," Edmund said, his eyes still locked on hers.

"This doesn't feel at all real," she admitted.

"Hopefully things will feel less imaginary tonight."

Penelope felt a rush of heat in her cheeks and, once again, elsewhere. "I'm serious, Edmund."

"I'd be more surprised if you didn't feel a little out of sorts."

"So, you're saying it's normal."

"Nothing about this life is normal," he said. "If it helps you, I'm feeling nerves myself."

"But you—"

"Got married today," he said. "In case you weren't aware."

"Who's the lucky bird?" she teased.

"Just a beautiful brown-haired, blue-eyed beauty who embodies all the qualities required of a princess. And, eventually, queen."

"She sounds perfect."

"She's certainly made me proud so far." He gave her hand a squeeze. "Ready for the next royal milestone?"

"Depends on which one you're referring to." She couldn't help but giggle.

He smiled wryly and looped his arm through hers for their stroll across the palace to rejoin the bridal party. "All in good time."

As they entered the Centre Room the footmen opened the doors to the balcony, letting in the deafening roar of the crowd she knew spanned the length of the mall and beyond.

Edmund winked. "I believe the world awaits our kiss, Princess."

Chapter Three

SNAKES AND LADDERS

"I meant to tell you, you've got the most enormous piece of kale stuck between your two front teeth," Hugh said under his breath as they turned their backs on the gaggle of reporters.

It was all Jennie could do not to snort and give him a firm elbow in the ribs, but with the cameras still clicking away behind them, she didn't want that image to be the one that defined their engagement announcement. Instead, she kept her arm wrapped around his, reaching across her body to hold his hand, and remained focused on keeping her stiletto heels out of the cracks between the flagstones as they walked away from their "photo call" at the budding Sunken Garden and back toward Kensington Palace.

"Well, your fly is down, and your *willy* is hanging out of your *trousers*," she told him just as quietly, emphasizing the key words in her worst English accent.

"Completely intentional," he deadpanned. "Royal prerogative."

She laughed and leaned into him, trying to match his long strides, grateful that her future husband never took himself as seriously as everyone around him did.

Since Hugh's proposal six weeks ago, there had been a steady, carefully stage-managed rollout engineered by Jeremy Legrand, King Edmund's longtime private secretary. Hugh had wanted to make the announcement immediately, but Jeremy pushed back, insisting, "Many will feel you've moved too quickly as it is. There are steps we must take to ensure the public takes to your American the way the royal family is certain to."

Which didn't make Jennie feel exactly *taken to*, but she surrendered herself to the process. It was like being caught in a riptide or carried by a wave. She knew she loved Hugh—that was the one thing she knew—and any fleeting fears she had about her new life were tempered by the sobering realization that it would never be the same again, no matter what. She did her best to smile brightly through the intimidating private audiences required for King Edmund and Queen Consort Eleanora's official approval of the marriage; a charity polo match where Hugh galloped on the field and she sat in the stands, being careful not to cheer too boisterously; and a visit to a battered women's shelter where she helped prepare the evening meal. Though she enjoyed helping and the women's stories touched her deeply, Jennie felt utterly unqualified to be the spokesperson at the center of the reporters' and photographers' attention.

As Legrand had outlined, everything was building inexorably to this morning's joint announcements. First, Buckingham Palace released an official statement on its impressive regal letterhead:

HIS ROYAL HIGHNESS PRINCE HUGH OF WALES AND
MS. JENNIE JENSEN ARE ENGAGED TO BE MARRIED

*His Majesty the King of England is delighted to announce the
engagement of Prince Hugh to Ms. Jennie Jensen.*

The wedding will take place in the summer. Further details about the wedding day will be announced in due course.

His Royal Highness and Ms. Jensen became engaged in London last month. In addition to the King and the Queen Consort, Prince Hugh has also sought and received the blessing of Ms. Jensen's parents.

The couple will live at Kensington Palace.

Immediately following the initial announcement, another press release, this one on Kensington Palace letterhead, announced her parents' support:

STATEMENT ISSUED ON BEHALF OF

MR. AND MRS. DAVID JENSEN

On the announcement of their daughter Jennie Jensen's engagement to His Royal Highness Prince Hugh of Wales, Mr. and Mrs. David Jensen said:

"We are so amazingly overjoyed for Jennie and Hugh. Like all parents, our daughter's happiness is the most important thing in the world to us, and we couldn't be more thrilled that these two kind and caring people have found each other.

"We know they will have a long and wonderful marriage!"

Jennie had laughed at the use of *amazingly overjoyed*, surprised some royal press person hadn't translated it to a more dignified descriptor. Even in the context of a royal wedding, her mom still sounded like her mom, even if Karen's first name hadn't made the cut. Jennie knew *Mr. and Mrs. David Jensen* drove her nuts, but Hugh had promised she would receive a "positively medieval-looking" official wedding pronouncement "with wax seals, ribbons, and indecipherable calligraphy," which Jennie hoped would make up for the slight-by-protocol. As for *David*, her mustached, heavy equipment sales supervisor dad had never, *ever* been anything but a Dave.

The carefully choreographed "press availability" they were now walking away from had lasted less than two minutes. They'd walked out and stood on a chalked X on the opposite side of an ornamental pond—both a symbolic and literal moat—from a hand-selected pool of royal journalists. Then, while cameras clicked and whirred (why did digital cameras still make the shutter-clicking noise?), the designated interviewer had, after congratulating them, asked, "How are you both feeling?" "How did you propose?" "Was it romantic?" Finally, a photographer shouted, "Will you show us the ring, please?"

As coached by Legrand's assistant—*Keep your hand low. Simply hold it over the Prince's hand and, for God's sake, don't hold it up and wiggle your fingers!*—Jennie had shown them the ring.

The split-second pause in photography felt like the media equivalent of a gasp. Then the interviewer's final question was nearly drowned out when the photographers furiously resumed shooting.

"Was that Princess Penelope's?"

Hugh nodded and said, "I know my mum, if she could be with us today, would be absolutely delighted to see Jennie wearing her ring."

And that was it.

Engagement announced.

Having left the Sunken Garden and snaked their way up a

winding path, they now approached a side door of the palace, which two footmen deftly and deferentially opened for them.

"Now for the hard part," said Hugh, his voice tightening.

"What do you mean?" asked Jennie. "Your family is *lovely.*" Her British accent, one part Monty Python and two parts Spinal Tap, usually made Hugh laugh.

But not this time.

"You haven't met them all in a group," he said.

———————

"I hope we passed the audition," Hugh called cheerily as they entered the Privy Chamber, a wood-paneled room hung with tapestries that was, like many of the historic spaces in the palace, also available for events.

The assembled members of the royal family—King Edmund and Queen Eleanora, Edmund's younger siblings Prince Freddie and Princess Alice, Freddie's wife Cecilia, as well as various other spouses, offspring, and cousins—did not turn around quite as quickly as she expected. Apparently, Edmund had been in the middle of an anecdote.

He broke it off, though, answering Hugh drily: "I was told the two of you were all but snogging."

Everyone seemed to think that was *terribly* funny.

"Didn't realize we'd stumbled into Madame Tussaud's," Hugh said, gently urging her into the room and accepting two flutes of champagne from the liveried footman who appeared at his elbow.

King Edmund, still dashing if slightly doughy, raised his glass. His famous brown eyes twinkled. "I think you all know why we're here. A toast to the happy couple."

There were a couple of quiet "hear, hears," as the two dozen or so assembled royals tilted their glasses. Then conversation quickly resumed.

Jennie felt hurt, not for herself, but for Hugh.

"That's it?" she whispered.

"Trust me, that was an absolute outpouring of emotion," he said.

"What did he mean about us snogging?"

"Someone must have told him we were holding hands."

They had been holding hands, but she was the one who'd laced her arm through his and held on tightly, leaning her head on his shoulder—so she was apparently the true offender.

"Come on, charm offensive, into the fray," he said, leading her forward.

Hugh had explained that having a champagne reception at Kensington Palace was a breach of protocol in itself. According to the unwritten rules of royalty—Or who knew? Maybe they were written down somewhere—the monarch didn't travel to *you*, you traveled to *him*. And Edmund, in particular, liked having things his way. So, they should have been at Buckingham Palace. But Hugh had cajoled his reluctant dad into it, saying, "We want to have you round to *our* house, a housewarming of sorts." Never mind that their twenty-room, four-story apartment still wasn't quite finished, Jennie thought the symbolism was appropriate, because Kensington Palace would be Prince Hugh's "house."

Their house.

Even though King Edmund had agreed to come, it sounded like he might be holding a grudge.

Hugh took Jennie right over to King Edmund and Queen Eleanora. Dave and Karen would have wrapped Jennie and Hugh in warm hugs, but Hugh, his father, and his stepmother all regarded each other from a respectful distance. Jennie curtseyed awkwardly.

"How's that pony of yours?" asked the King, asking about Hugh's favorite polo horse, Villan, who had been injured by a trainer the previous week, as if nothing could be more important at the moment.

Hugh's skin reddened behind his ears, an obvious sign he was frustrated, but he did his best not to show it and gamely offered his father an update on the animal's condition.

"I love your dress," Jennie told the Queen, realizing it was really just the two of them.

The older woman appeared to consider the compliment before discarding it. "My dresser chooses wisely. Are you still dressing yourself? You always look quite smart."

Jennie had seen Eleanora lampooned as long past her prime by the media, probably because she refused to resort to fillers and a facelift. But in person, she exuded an appealing alertness and charisma. Jennie's mom had shown her pictures of a pretty, vibrant young Eleanora. Did Edmund hold that image of her in his mind after all these years?

"Thank you, Your Majesty," said Jennie. "I'm doing my best. There's a lot to learn besides what to wear."

"Sink or swim," said Eleanora. "Show me the ring."

Jennie lifted her left hand and Eleanora took it, inspecting the ring intently, holding on long enough that Jennie began to flush. According to her mother, there were rumors that Eleanora had always had a crush on Edmund, like so many other women in his circle. After all, who wouldn't want to marry a handsome and charming Prince? Of course, it wasn't until Penelope's passing that she got her wish. Edmund and Eleanora's wedding was less splashy than his wedding to Penelope but still made headlines the world over. The overwhelming realization that Jennie was now part of the story almost wobbled her on her feet.

"Crook your finger or she'll slip the ring off and pocket it," said Prince Freddie, sliding up to them. His breath was boozy and sweet from champagne.

"The wise and witty prince," said Eleanora tartly, finally releasing Jennie's hand.

"Congratulations, Jennie," said Prince Freddie. "I mean it. You've obviously made Hugh very happy. And never mind the rest of this lot. They only smile when someone falls off a horse."

"Thank you," said Jennie gratefully.

"Do you know Princess Stuart of Gloucester?" said Prince Freddie, bringing a passing woman into their conversation. "You're practically flatmates."

Jennie shook her head but smiled and curtseyed. Hugh was being pulled farther away.

"You don't curtsey to *her*," said Eleanora, sounding irritated.

"Her husband, Prince Stuart, is a first cousin of our late Queen," said Freddie. "Seventh in line to the throne when he was born . . . what is he now, Betts?"

"Forty-seventh," said Princess Stuart, or, apparently, *Betts*.

"As you see, it's a game of Snakes and Ladders," said Freddie. "One day you're up, the next you're down. You've got a firm grip on the rungs yourself."

For now, Jennie was still just Miss Jensen. After saying, "I do," she would magically become Her Royal Highness, and people would be worrying about whether to bow, curtsy, or grovel and scrape when they met her. She understood now why so many people used the words *fairy tale* to describe what was happening to her—it was as strange as anything she'd ever read in a children's book.

Princess Stuart of Gloucester, whom Jennie would never dream of calling Betts, smiled.

"It's true! We're neighbors," she said. "Prince Stuart and I live in apartment 10, but we're often abroad."

"I'm sorry we didn't meet each other sooner," said Jennie.

"Is it true you were a foundling?"

It took her a second to process the archaic word. It was accurate enough—she had literally been found on a doorstep, after all.

"Yes, I was adopted," she confirmed after a beat.

"It's so terribly exciting, almost Dickensian," said Princess Stuart. "I imagine it will give the royal genealogists fits."

"They can just draw a new leaf on the family tree, right?" said Jennie, trying hard not to show her annoyance.

"Betts" beamed vacantly at Jennie. "We are all but twigs on the sturdy oak of the House of Windsor. Some of us greener than others."

Jennie leaned forward and caught Hugh's eye, sending him a telepathic plea for help.

Her message was received. He broke off his conversation, strode toward her, and touched Princess Stuart on the elbow. "I'm terribly sorry, but may I borrow my fiancée for a moment?"

They moved away, nodding and smiling.

"It's like she thinks I'm going to steal the silverware," Jennie told Hugh, once they were out of earshot. "I was almost afraid she was going to ask if I was still a virgin."

After checking to make sure nobody was looking, he gave her a dangerously long kiss.

"Thank God those days are over," he said. "Shall I take you home?"

She grinned. "I'll race you there."

Hugh obviously thought Jennie was kidding, but the instant the door closed behind them, she took off running, leaving him in her dust. He only caught up with her at an intersection of hallways where she had forgotten which way to turn.

"Cheeky," he teased her.

"I'm in a hurry," she said.

They settled into a speed walk, side-eyeing each other, daring each other to go for it. When the footman opened the final door, Jennie hip-checked Hugh and sprinted across the gravel court. Both of them were laughing so hard they could barely breathe. She kept the lead all the way to Nott Cott, where she burst through the door and scrambled upstairs.

"I let you win," he said, panting, as he finally caught up with her on the bed.

She kissed him. "Nobody likes a sore loser."

They stopped talking. Melting into his arms, she forgot all about their awkward evening.

Chapter Four

PRINCESSES WEAR PANTYHOSE

Jeremy Legrand rested his elbows on his ornate wooden desk, steepled his fingers, and arched an eyebrow at Jennie. The office suite of King Edmund's gaunt, gray-haired private secretary looked like a museum to his years of service: the fussy wallpaper was tiled with plaques, certificates, commendations, and photos of himself with royals and foreign dignitaries. With no idea why she'd been summoned to Buckingham Palace, Jennie was grateful to have Hugh's assistant private secretary, the soft-spoken Ian O'Rourke, on her side of the desk.

"Thank you for meeting with me, Miss Jensen," said Legrand.

"What's going on?" she asked.

"I've received reports of some . . . errors of protocol." Legrand consulted a handwritten list, then cleared his throat before continuing. "At last night's engagement reception, there was a too-deep curtsey toward the Queen Consort and it was said you touched the King on the arm. You are not to touch either unless they initiate contact."

Realizing she was here to receive a lecture, Jennie felt embarrassed but also incredulous. "So you're saying I can never hug my future father- and mother-in-law?"

Legrand glanced up. "Only if they hug you first. But I can assure you, the royal family does not hug."

"I'll remember that," said Jennie.

"Furthermore, you should never walk in front of Prince Hugh or exit a car first. And . . ." Legrand's cheeks colored. "You must wear panty-hose. Several members of the royal household shared their concern that you appeared at yesterday's photo call with bare legs."

"*Pantyhose?*" she repeated. She hadn't worn them since a middle school drama production.

"Female members of the royal family shall wear pantyhose with dresses and skirts without exception," said Legrand, letting his list fall to his desk and meeting her eyes again.

Jennie was speechless as she tried to wrap her head around the fact that someone had been monitoring her manners—and her legs—reporting everything back to the King's private secretary.

"She couldn't possibly have known all this," said Ian flatly.

"I quite agree," said Legrand. "Which is why the Queen Consort has suggested Jennie take on a social secretary to advise her on correct protocol, including etiquette and dress."

"If Miss Jensen agrees, I'll be happy to gather a selection of candidates," said Ian.

"The Queen Consort has put forward Prudence Banks, Her Majesty's fill-in dresser. Miss Banks is a trusted member of the royal household who knows the key names and faces, as well as which hats to wear."

"What do you think?" Jennie asked Ian, feeling pressure to

decide on the spot. Even though she wanted to hire her own assistant, she also had no idea who was qualified.

Legrand glanced at his watch. "The intention here is really only to make your life easier by removing the difficulty of countless small decisions."

"I know Poppy, actually," said Ian. "She's quite nice and I agree she'll be helpful."

"I guess it's fine, then," said Jennie.

"Excellent," said Legrand, making a note with a fat-barreled fountain pen. "And by the way, we will be assigning you a seasoned personal protection officer, Rodney Whyte, to supplement the security you are already receiving."

"Is that really necessary?" Jennie asked.

"It's standard procedure."

Jennie had a sudden urge to leave before Legrand assigned her a whole entourage, so she pushed back her chair and stood up. "And that's all?"

"Yes, that is all," said Legrand. "For now."

———

When she got back to Nott Cott—Hugh was traveling, watching his beloved Aston Villa "football" team play a game at someplace called Turf Moor—Jennie called her mom.

"You looked absolutely beautiful at the announcement!" said Karen, instead of hello.

"Thanks, Mom. But do you want to know what the palace thought? That I should have been wearing pantyhose."

"I did notice that. Royal women always wear pantyhose."

"I have now been duly informed. I just got back from Buckingham Palace, and it was like going to the principal's office. I knew my life would change, but I didn't think I would be climbing into a time machine. Honestly, it's like living in the nineteenth century. They also chewed me out for touching the King's arm, if you can believe it."

Her mom giggled. "I'm sorry, but did you hear yourself? *Touching the King's arm?* Pinch me."

Jennie had to chuckle. "I don't think this will ever seem normal. It's not just the crazy rules: everybody has nicknames like Skippy and Poppy even though they're actually Lord and Lady Such-and-Such, the Duke of Earl von Baron Something-or-Other. They call their country homes cottages or farms, even though they're mansions and estates, and give them names that sound like storybook houses for talking animals: Frogmore Cottage and Shrewsbury Hall. Sometimes I think I woke up in *The Wind in the Willows.*"

"Are you sure you should be saying this over the phone?" asked her mom, who had stopped laughing.

"Why shouldn't I?"

"Penelope believed they listened in."

"And who are *they*, exactly?" she asked, rolling her eyes.

"I don't think we should talk about this right now."

"This isn't going through the switchboard. I'm on my cell."

"That's just as bad! They definitely have the technology."

"They're snobs, Mom, not Bond villains!"

"I'm just saying, there were rumors that her death was no accident."

Jennie groaned, then laughed. It was funny how, even when no one was listening, she could still feel embarrassed by her mother.

"Mom, *please*. Look, the etiquette is annoying but I'll deal. Eleanora is actually sending someone to look after me—the Poppy I mentioned—so I'll just follow her lead."

"Good idea. Now keep your chin up and enjoy your time

with Hugh. You only get to be engaged once! When I get there at the end of the month, we'll go pantyhose shopping together."

Princess Penelope

4 NOVEMBER 1983

If there was one thing on which Penelope and Edmund completely agreed, it was that a princess could not be seen eating a Curly Wurly. The same went for a Starbar, Coffee Crisp, or Blue Riband, *the biscuit to beat the blues.*

Not that Penelope was sad.

In fact, she felt downright happy as she chewed and swallowed the last piece of her chocolate bar, dropped the wrapper in the footwell, and steered her silver BMW up the long gravel drive toward Highgrove House, where Edmund had retreated for what he had told her would be "a few relaxing days of reading and shooting."

Her high spirits were owed partly to her new PPO, Rodney Whyte, who shared her sweet tooth and was only too glad to stock up for both of them at Tesco, Boots, or any of the other shops she couldn't possibly pop round herself. Unfortunately, Rodney was most likely in a state of panic, afraid of losing his job—which of course he wouldn't since she'd already begun to depend on him—after he discovered she'd given him the slip today.

It couldn't be helped.

If she had told him, he'd have been obliged to report her whereabouts to the head of security, who would have in turn alerted the Highgrove staff, defeating the purpose of her romantic subterfuge.

Penelope smiled as she caught sight of the Prince's Standard fluttering in the breeze above the balustrade encircling the slate roof. Their marriage, just over one year old, was like everything and nothing she had expected. Living in London at Kensington Palace, treated like the royalty she had become, was heady, to say the least. If only she were able to spend more time with Edmund. When they weren't pulled apart by competing engagements, Edmund was retreating to the country, where he claimed to be most himself. In her mind, the key to their happiness would be to carve out special time together whenever possible. With the Queen's recent heart scare, it was hard to forget that her husband's responsibilities could be infinitely multiplied at any time, making the present much more precious.

Taking the service road to avoid the front of the house, she parked her silver BMW in a spot near the barn so it was out of view of Edmund's library windows, but not so far away that she'd muck up her trainers trudging through horse manure. She sprayed mint Binaca in her mouth to cover the sweets on her breath and headed for the kitchen entrance.

———

"Welcome, Your Royal Highness," said Mr. Ratliff, the head butler, as the kitchen staff all paused their work to bow.

When Princess Penelope came to Highgrove, which was far less frequently than the prince and typically only on weekends, she preferred to enter through the kitchen, giving her a chance to say an informal hello and inquire about all that transpired since her last visit. Due to the relaxed atmosphere at the country house, she encouraged them to forgo unnecessary formality—a position tolerated but not necessarily endorsed by the prince.

She had clearly caught them off guard, just as she'd planned. What Penelope didn't anticipate was the unusual hustle and bustle in the kitchen. A sizable meal was being prepared; she hadn't even considered the possibility that Edmund might be entertaining.

"No Rodney?" asked Mrs. Morris, the longtime head housekeeper.

"I'm afraid I've thrown him for a bit of a loop," she said, adding, "And apparently everyone else. Let me guess, pheasant for dinner?"

"With wild mushroom dressing," answered the cook, who had hurried back to the stove.

"And?" Penelope asked, seeing the pastry chef putting the final touches on a chocolate ganache cake.

"Brussels sprouts with sliced almonds and mustard glaze, and potatoes Dauphinoise with nutmeg and Irish cheddar."

"Lovely," she said, hoping she sounded more cheerful than she suddenly felt. "The prince must have enjoyed a very successful day of shooting."

"It's a fox hunt, but not until tomorrow," blurted Mrs. Morris's twelve-year-old grandniece, who served as a junior assistant on occasion.

What was the occasion?

Lionel, the footman, entered the kitchen holding a crumb-strewn silver hors d'oeuvres tray.

Penelope tasted acid and chocolate in the back of her throat. "I assume the prince is in the drawing room?"

Penelope pushed through the butler's door and emerged into the large front room, which was filled with FOEs—her pet name for the callous, snobby, and highly insular Friends of Edmund, many of whom kept country homes nearby. All of his inner circle were dressed for cocktails and had drinks in their hands. Arriving from the rear, she obviously hadn't seen the forecourt packed with cars.

The prince stood in the doorway to the entry hall, greeting pockmarked Digby Clifford. Although Edmund spotted her immediately, his only discernible reaction to Penelope's sudden appearance was to comb his fingers through his neatly groomed hair. It transformed her own confusion into outright infuriation.

"You look like you've just finished a riding lesson," said Anne Claxton-Murray, noting Penelope's jeans and button-down blouse as she beelined toward her husband. "Does this mean you'll be joining us for this weekend's hunt?"

"We'd best put the local foxes on high alert!" enthused a boozy, red-faced Lord Clark Thompson, one of Edmund's oldest polo chums.

Penelope's lack of poise in the saddle was a long-standing source of amusement to all of Edmund's friends.

"And I've warned the village publicans to lock their doors," she said, forcing a smile.

Anne guffawed, looking very much like one of the equines of which she was so fond. "You get cheekier every time I see you, dear girl."

Girl.

And there it was in a nutshell. To them, she was the pretty, pliable girl whose job it was to bear the royal heirs while making as few demands on Edmund's time as possible.

Penelope grabbed a Tanqueray and tonic from Lionel's silver tray as he reentered the room.

She could only imagine the conversation going on in the kitchen.

Can you believe the princess had no bloody idea the prince was throwing a party?

Edmund appeared beside her.

"Darling, I'm so glad you're here," he said, as though her

unexpected arrival was all part of his plan. "I'm quite sure you'd like to get changed for dinner."

As he gently but firmly took her elbow and ushered her into the hallway, Penelope whispered, "You didn't tell me you were hosting a party tonight."

"A *dinner*, for Felix Hill's birthday," the prince replied with his customary cool.

"Felix's birthday was two weeks ago, if I'm not mistaken."

"This was the only weekend that worked for everyone's schedules."

"Everyone's but mine, apparently."

"We'll discuss this later," he said.

As he left her at the base of the main staircase and returned to the party, the blond, beautiful, buxom Vivienne Hill sashayed up to Edmund, wearing a sparkly spaghetti-strap dress.

Perhaps the worst FOE, Vivienne had not only given Penelope the nickname Penny Dreadful at boarding school, but she had dated Edmund—at least until the tabloids unearthed a sexual past that rendered her unworthy of his affections.

Judging by their friendly kiss hello, his interest in her hadn't waned entirely.

As if reading her mind, Eleanora Osborne-Webb plucked two fresh gin and tonics from Lionel's tray and brought one over to her.

"You look in need of a refill."

Eleanora was the one FOE she found tolerable—even likable. When Penelope and Edmund first started dating, while the others found ways to remind her how much closer they were to Edmund, Eleanora had been the only one to make overtures of friendship. The only one to offer little tips, such as: *Don't smother him* and *Remember, he absolutely* hates *surprises.*

Why hadn't she heeded that sage bit of advice today?

"How is your darling daughter Anabelle?" Penelope asked Eleanora, trying to ignore Edmund not ignoring Vivi's ample cleavage.

"Precocious as ever. She's quite insistent we give her an elephant for her upcoming birthday."

"Only one?" said Penelope, gulping her cocktail.

Eleanora looked concerned. "Are you feeling all right?"

"Yes, of course. It's just that I can't believe—"

"Vivienne Hill would show up looking like such a slag?"

Penelope couldn't help but giggle. "That she's here at all."

"She *is* the sister of the birthday boy," Eleanora said.

"Isn't it just my luck that she's my husband's oldest mate's little sister," Penelope said, hoping she didn't sound as jealous as she felt. "Does she turn up regularly for hunting weekends?"

"She's hunting for a husband."

It wasn't quite the unqualified *no* Penelope had hoped for.

"I thought she'd set her sights on becoming the next Lady Banfield-March," continued Eleanora, "but maybe that was just at the last party. So much can change in a week."

"Does Edmund have parties often when I'm at Kensington Palace?"

"Princess, you needn't worry," Eleanora said. "Certainly not about that girl."

"You looked especially pretty tonight," Edmund said from bed as Penelope came out of her dressing room. "I like you in lavender."

"I've repeated that dress one too many times."

"I'm sure no one noticed."

"Not after I turned up in jeans." Standing beside the bed, she listened for any creaks or footfalls outside their suite before continuing. "Why didn't you tell me about tonight?"

"I was under the impression that you had an important event scheduled in London tomorrow. As this was simply a dinner with my oldest friends, I didn't want you to feel conflicted about which event to attend."

"How very considerate."

"Penelope," Edmund said. "Not only do you find my group stuffy and dull, but you hate hunting and riding, which, I'm afraid, is how we plan to spend the weekend."

"I'm willing to learn," she said, fighting tears. "But I can't if you don't give me the chance."

"There'll be plenty of time for you to muck about with horses."

Meaning, *after* she produced the requisite heir and spare.

"Come here," he said, patting the silk duvet cover.

Tears ran down her face as she sat down on the edge of the bed.

"Let's not row," he said as he caressed her hand, which was as close as he ever came to apologizing. "I realized at dinner that I hadn't asked what brought you here today in the first place."

Penelope tried to collect herself. "We don't see each other nearly enough. I thought it would be nice to surprise you with a few days together. I had some foolish notion of you and me in front of the fireplace."

"A truly romantic gesture."

"In theory."

He kissed her. "In actuality."

"I should never have surprised you."

"And yet," he said as he began to kiss her neck, "you do so continually."

Maybe they didn't have as much in common as he did with his old pals, but they definitely had chemistry. And even though they wouldn't have the weekend alone like she'd imagined, he was all hers right now.

And hadn't that been the point?

Chapter Five

A NOTE OF DANGER

Living in a palace wasn't all it was cracked up to be. Jennie supposed it was better than a castle—which had fortified walls to keep you in—but in addition to the wrought iron fence guarding its perimeter, Kensington Palace was carved into tiny fiefdoms by dozens of other boundaries, visible and invisible. Though she had pictured herself roller-skating down endless corridors, exploring to her heart's content, the reality was a lot more complicated and a little bit less fun.

For starters, Prince and Princess Stuart had their own apartment, as did Hugh's cousin Rex, Prince Freddie's son, who lived in Ivy Cottage with his new wife. Not everyone living there had royal blood, either: other tenants included members of the military, courtiers, staff, and even a few private citizens who paid a princely sum for a bragworthy address. That brought the total number of residents to roughly fifty people, almost as many as in Jennie's small Brooklyn apartment building.

And even these residents had access to only a portion of the palace: like the White House, Kensington Palace offered daily tours. Tourists had a choice of four different routes through the complex and had access to most of the beautifully maintained grounds, too. Both groups were separated by an elaborate system of scheduling, secured doors, and windows whose distorted glass cleverly blocked all views into private living areas.

Confined to Nott Cott until the renovations on apartment 1A were complete, Jennie felt more captive than cosseted. She wouldn't complain—even if she did, who would listen?—but as her face and story became known all over the world, the part of the world she could roam freely had shrunk to the size of a postage stamp.

Immediately after their engagement announcement, Hugh had been called away for two weeks on a tour of British military bases in Asia and Africa. His itinerary was so extensive she'd joked about enlisting so she could spend more time with him. But the tone of their phone call the day before had been somber, with Hugh feeling reflective after visiting three soldiers in Somalia who'd been badly injured when their vehicle was destroyed by an IED. Jennie's whole body ached to see him when he finally returned tonight.

After spending an hour walking as slowly as possible through their beautiful private garden, now blooming and buzzing with happy bees, she felt a sudden urge to inspect the apartment. She'd only peeked in a couple of times since Hugh left for his impromptu tour, and although Sidney Reddy, Hugh's private secretary, had assured them both the work was nearly done, she wanted to see for herself.

She pushed through the plastic curtain, surprising two workmen conferring over a clipboard, both of them wearing boilersuits and paper booties. One of them seemed so startled to see her that he dropped his phone.

"Good morning, miss," said the phone dropper at the same moment the other one said, "Good morning, ma'am."

"Good morning," she said, resisting the urge to add, *Please call me Jennie.* Hugh had apologetically explained that while informality was well-intentioned, it actually put servants and others in an awkward position, pressuring them to disregard their training and remember exceptions. "Can I look around?"

"Of course, ma'am," said the one holding the clipboard. "I would be very pleased to show you our progress."

"I don't want to interrupt. Can I just wander?"

"Certainly."

"Should I put on paper booties, too?"

Both men looked horrified.

"Oh no, miss—ma'am," said the phone dropper. "These are for . . . us."

Apparently free to track in as much dirt as she wanted, she thanked them and walked on, hoping her new role as the bride-to-be of the next King of England didn't mean she'd make people nervous for the rest of her life.

The work appeared nearly complete. In one room on the ground floor, both wallpaper and a chandelier were being hung simultaneously, but elsewhere, most of the workers were applying finishing touches. As she made her way down the hall, she saw a man buffing a parquet floor by hand, a painter touching up a doorway, and heavy furniture being placed by burly men who moved with the graceful choreography of dancers.

Upstairs, everything looked ready for moving day. The sounds of activity faded into the background as she poked into room after room, including some she'd never seen before. On the fourth floor, Jennie glanced through a doorway and stopped in surprise. She was looking at a small music studio: guitars lined one wall opposite a baby grand piano, and an array of microphone stands stood next to a small mixing board and editing suite. Under a skylight at the center of the room, an armless upholstered chair sat on a Persian rug, bathed in natural light.

Jennie blinked away tears. Hugh had never said anything about this—obviously, he intended to surprise her with a safe, tranquil space to compose and play music in their home. Every detail was so perfect that she wondered whether he'd been talking to Diego or another one of her musician friends.

She closed the heavy door and drank in the silence, noting that there were even discreet acoustic baffles on the walls to deaden the reverb. She picked up a gleaming Martin acoustic and strummed a G chord, then winced. It was badly out of tune. Sitting down on the chair, she tuned by ear and started to noodle.

It was ironic that, to the public, "I Can't Even" had become Jennie and Hugh's song. Once their relationship had gone public, internet sleuths had quickly traced their first meeting to Hugh's request at her concert. Not that his asking her to play the song made him unique: its brief ubiquity had made it her most requested number. Jennie was grateful for all the song had given her, from a big career boost to her fiancé, but she did not think of it as "their song." She'd written it at a low point after a bad breakup and its world-weary lyrics just reminded her of a time when she felt too tired to even get out of bed.

She had tried repeatedly to write a love song for Hugh without success because every new line sounded like a bad greeting card. Was true love bad for artistic growth?

Now, over a simple, stately chord progression, a verse arrived from nowhere:

I've got a prince, he's a heck of a guy
They don't know that I'm going to steal him
I've got his heart and the rest of him, too
Says the note that I'm holding him for ransom

The lyric came out so perfectly it made her laugh—*this* would be their song, because she knew it would make him laugh, too. And it perfectly captured her true feelings. She wished she could steal him away, even though she knew that was impossible.

For obvious reasons, she wouldn't record and release it. Because England would not get the joke.

When the news broke about them, even touring got put on hold for Royal protocol and security concerns. Her long-suffering manager told her she was in such high demand that she'd been asked to play Carnegie Hall, a mind-blowing invitation she'd reluctantly had to decline. Even harder to accept, the timeline for her return to live performances now extended beyond the horizon. She missed performing. Would that ever happen again? The album she had been trying to finish during her secret months with Hugh seemed further from completion than when she'd started. That was due both to all the time they were spending together and the whiplash changes that came along for the ride. How could she write relatable lyrics now that she traveled on private planes?

After playing a while longer and roughing out a chorus, she left the music room feeling serene and satisfied. Even though the only tour on her itinerary was the rest of the apartment.

Something drew her back to the second floor, to what Hugh had said was Penelope's favorite sitting room. The decor had not been modernized as extensively as the rest of the place. Yes, it was freshly painted, and several new pieces of furniture matched Hugh's preference for a clean and simple design. But there were also several of what her mom would call "conversation pieces": an expensive but worn and dated-looking couch, an ugly area rug, and a half dozen throw pillows embroidered with inspirational messages.

Hugh had told her that his mom had a surprisingly cheesy sense of humor, and Jennie could see for herself it was true. The messages were straight out of a mall novelty store: *Good girls go*

to heaven, bad girls go everywhere; You have to kiss a lot of frogs
before you find a prince; I feel sorry for people who don't drink be-
cause when they wake up in the morning that is the best they are
going to feel all day.

Jennie felt a bittersweet ache at these reminders of Hugh's determined effort to remain connected to his mother. She pictured the two of them reading on the couch and wrestling on the rug.

The empty mantle, shelves, and sideboards cried out for family photos. Thinking it would be sweet to surprise Hugh by making it even homier, Jennie started opening cabinets and cupboards, wondering whether Hugh had had any old pictures delivered along with the furniture.

In a closet, she found a stack of boxes, each one labeled *HRH Penelope Personal Effects.*

Jennie put the topmost box on the floor and paused with her hands on the flaps. Was she overstepping? Maybe, but the boxes weren't even sealed: if workmen had been allowed to handle them, presumably so was she.

The box contained framed family photos just as she hoped. Sitting cross-legged, she looked through them one at a time, finding picture after picture of Hugh, from adorable cowlicked toddler to gangly tween—Penelope had died before he became a dashingly handsome young man. She was in many of them, looking just like the attentive mother Hugh had described. The only one featuring Edmund was a casual snapshot of the family walking toward the camera on the midway of a fair or carnival: Edmund smiling faintly, Hugh wild with joy, and Penelope wearing an expression that could have been either a scowl or a squint.

Jennie arranged the photos around the room, then returned to the closet for another box. This one was a mix of odds and

ends, from appointment books to rubber-banded stacks of letters
to a gray plastic cell phone that looked more like a walkie-talkie.
Jennie opened one of the books and fanned the pages, watching a year's worth of lunches, dinners, and international travel
pass in seconds. Was this how her own existence as a princess
would be tallied?

A piece of paper fluttered out and fell in her lap. Jennie
unfolded it and saw a note written in a neat, masculine hand.

> Penny, I need you. To touch you. Despite the danger,
> we must find a way to be together.

———————

That evening, after Hugh returned—and after a quick romp
in bed that proved he had missed her every bit as much as she
missed him—they went outside.

"After ten hours in a bloody airplane, I'm desperate for some
fresh air," Hugh told her.

Pulling on sweatshirts, they crunched along the gravel
garden paths Jennie had prowled only that morning. Now that
he was with her, everything was absolutely perfect.

He looked tired. She knew that flying so many thousands
of miles and shaking so many hundreds of hands took its toll.
But she had never heard him complain about it other than to
say, slightly wearily, "It's my job." Hopefully, she could share the
load after they were officially allowed to travel together.

"Sidney texted me, by the way," Hugh said with a sly smile.
"The tradesmen told him you'd been inspecting their work."

"I was going to tell you!" she said, wrapping him in a hug
and planting a big kiss on his lips. "Thank you so much for the
music studio. I absolutely love it."

"I'd intended it to be a surprise, Miss Nosey Parker."

She snaked her arm through his as they continued walking. "Sorry for jumping the gun. The whole thing looks wonderful. The idea of living in such a grand place used to intimidate me, but you've made it feel like home. To return the favor, I took the liberty of putting out your childhood photos."

Hugh groaned. "Then you've truly seen me at my worst: spots, trendy haircuts, and orthodontics."

"All completely adorable," she said. "I wish I'd paid more attention to Prince Hugh when I was a little girl."

"I'm glad you didn't! If you had, I'd never have been able to sneak up on you."

"I also found this," she said, handing him the mysterious note.

Hugh read it quickly, shoved it into his pocket, and turned back toward Nott Cott, his expression darkening. When they passed several people climbing into a car, one of them greeted Hugh, but he didn't reply.

"I'm sorry," she told him. "I thought you'd want to see it."

"Things were horrible between my parents for years before she died," he said distantly. "It was all an absolute mess. I was too young to understand what was happening."

"Do you have any idea who might have written it?" Jennie asked, even though she had *some* idea who might've been sending love notes to Penelope before her death: retail mogul Scott Corbyn, Penelope's close friend and reported lover. She had been on his private plane when it crashed, ending the Princess's life at age thirty-eight, though Corbyn himself wasn't with her.

"I'm not about to start excavating my mother's emotional life," he snapped.

As they crossed the gravel court between the palace and Nott Cott, Jennie squeezed Hugh's hand. "I'm sorry. I know it's hard. The word *danger* just got to me."

Hugh let go of her hand as they stepped through their gate but didn't take it again on the other side.

"Danger can mean many things," said Hugh as he hung up his coat. "The danger of discovery. The danger to one's reputation."

"Do you think we should show it to someone?" she suggested.

"There is quite enough evidence of my mum's private business in the world already, Jennie. I don't know what that would accomplish, other than fueling further tin-pot conspiracies when it is inevitably discovered by the general public. Let's both forget we ever even saw it."

Pulling it out of his pocket, he ripped the folded note in half, then in half again, dropping the four pieces into a nearby wastebasket before stalking off to their bedroom.

Jennie felt sick to her stomach as she watched him go. She'd never seen Hugh like this. But as much as she'd been hurt by his sharp, authoritarian tone, she also realized she couldn't possibly understand the depths of the pain caused by the rumors about his mother, and her tragic and untimely death. She resolved not to mention it again.

Still, she couldn't help retrieving the torn note from the otherwise spotlessly clean wastebasket, smoothing out the pieces, and hiding them inside the biggest book she could find in the living room: Winston Churchill's *Into Battle*.

From Princess Penelope's Private Diary

18 DECEMBER 1983
It is past midnight. I am exhausted but too exhilarated to sleep. Instead, I am sitting across the room at a writing desk lit by the glow of the full moon whilst Edmund snores softly beneath the floral canopy of the four-poster bed where his parents and grandparents also enjoyed romantic assignations.

It is a tradition I appreciate, even if I don't care to think about it too much.

As for tradition, the Queen chronicles the events of her day before she retires for the evening. Edmund does the same—when he remembers. I realise my own thoughts won't have the same historical importance, but I've decided to chronicle days, events, and thoughts I don't want to slip from memory. And this is a particularly momentous day.

Ever since Hellgrove weekend (where I didn't ride or hunt but did manage to distract Edmund from our other houseguests once we'd retired for the evening), things have been different—happier and brighter. Initially, I attributed this newfound improvement to Edmund realising that his high jinks hurt me badly. In the aftermath, he arranged for our schedules to be better synchronized. As a result, we've spent more time together, enjoying joint appearances at the National Ballet's Christmas performance of The Nutcracker and the Prince's Trust Awards but also workaday events such as the opening of a centre for pensioners at Percy Circus and a private reception for members of the Glamorgan County Cricket Club. (Edmund would never have brought me along to a sport-related event had I not spoken up.) I believe I've shown myself to be more than a pretty, pliable girl, one worthy of standing at my husband's side. I finally feel like a princess.

But that isn't all.

For the past month, I've felt more present than ever before. Yet also oddly off. It started with my sense of smell—tracking unusual odors to the kitchen only to discover it was simply chicken and broccoli. And then retching at the sight of raw poultry.

One by one, the tell-tale signs began to present themselves. Today Dr. Smythe confirmed my suspicions.

A royal heir is due in August!

Edmund is delighted, and I am utterly beside myself with joy. Neither of us can wait until it is safe to announce our news to the Queen.

To the world!

Chapter Six
PRINCESS DRESS

Jennie watched Karen chuckle as Poppy Banks topped off her glass with Dom Perignon and then offered her a silver platter covered with an assortment of perfectly cut finger sandwiches.

"This is literally the royal treatment!" her mom said, probably giddier from jet lag than the champagne.

Poppy grinned. "I'm glad you think so, Mrs. Jensen. But just wait until you're dining at Buckingham Palace with thirteen pieces of cutlery!"

Eleanora's former dresser had wasted no time in teaching Jennie which fork to use, what she should wear, and whose hand to kiss, but this was her biggest job yet: guiding Jennie through the process of selecting her wedding dress.

The setting was anything but elegant. After parking by a loading dock in a nondescript neighborhood just south of the Thames, Jennie, Karen, Poppy, and Rodney Whyte, the stocky, middle-aged PPO who was now her constant companion, had entered through a back door and taken a freight elevator three floors up to an empty, skylit room whose plank floor and brick walls dated to the Victorian era.

Saskia Wainright, Britain's hottest fashion designer, had been waiting, accompanied only by her executive assistant, Adalberto, and eight dressmaker's dummies, each one draped with a different, stunning wedding dress. After Sidney Reddy's reminder that every additional person posed a possible security breach to this top-secret mission, they'd limited it to the six of them, with Rodney doubling as chauffeur and Poppy cheerfully volunteering to serve food, even though it wasn't her job. Hugh was touring "the most charming paint factory in all of Lancashire"—not that the groom would have been included in this process under normal circumstances—and her dad had been relieved to be dismissed, opting instead for the Battle of Britain bunker and a walking tour of historic pubs.

Their snacks sorted, Jennie and Karen were enthroned on comfortably padded folding chairs while Saskia, all business beneath a dark slash of bangs, fiddled with the beadwork on the bodice of one of the dresses.

"Under ordinary circumstances, of course, we'd have live models," she explained. "But the last thing we want to do is ask those girls to keep a secret like this. If you see an element you like or don't particularly care for, be sure to let me know. I would encourage you to try all of these on so I can see how they hang on you. That will give us a good starting point."

"I'm sure any of these would work perfectly," murmured Jennie, looking at each of the stunning dresses in turn.

"Yours has to be one of a kind," pronounced Karen. "After all, it will be in the history books—and then a museum."

Her mom had been an enthusiastic armchair observer of the royal family while Jennie was growing up, sharing the latest gossip and speculation despite her daughter's indifference. Jennie remembered almost none of what she'd learned. Back then, her response had been to put in her earbuds and turn up the volume.

"Poppy, can I please have some more champagne?" asked Jennie, wishing her mom didn't have such a knack for making her nervous.

Her new Girl Friday practically bounded over with the bottle. "Of course. And, gentle reminder, you don't ask or even say *please*."

"I had no idea I was raising her wrong, making her say *please* and *thank you*," her mom told Poppy.

How politeness could be a breach of protocol was completely beyond Jennie, but she was past the point of questioning anything.

Other than being immaculately white, the dresses were all very different, from an elegant column to a full-blown princess gown. Saskia talked through the virtues of each, meanwhile appraising Jennie's figure as if she were a mannequin herself.

When she got to the billowing princess gown, the designer stopped. "Now that I've seen you in person, I don't even want to talk about this one, because I think you'll simply disappear in it. What are you, five foot four?"

"Five-five," said Jennie. "Almost."

"Eight and a half stone?"

"I have no idea how much that is, but the last time I weighed myself, I was one-eighteen."

Saskia nodded. "We'll want to emphasize the vertical, and bear in mind, whatever we settle on will be accented by the veil, your tiara, and a jaw-dropping train."

After standing up and twirling for Saskia and Adalberto, and some back-and-forth with her mom, who favored a mermaid-style fit and flare, Jennie agreed with Saskia that the two strongest shapes for her figure were the column and a body-hugging silhouette. Stepping into a temporary changing booth constructed of rods and curtains, she undressed and allowed Adalberto to help her into the most finely brocaded dress she had ever seen in her life.

When she stepped out, her mom gasped. "Oh my God, Jennie."

"That good, huh?"

Karen's tearful nod said it all. "You look . . ."

"Like a princess, right?" laughed Jennie. "I think I might even be starting to feel like one."

Karen pulled her sparkle-cased iPad mini out of her purse. "Your dad is going to die!"

Rodney was halfway across the room before she could aim it. "No phones, please. No pictures."

Her mom looked genuinely wounded. "They're for her father's eyes only."

"I'm sorry, Mrs. Jensen," said Rodney gently. "The tabloids have been known to hack people's phones. We can't risk any kind of a leak. The bookies are already giving odds on who the dress designer's going to be. If this gets out, some punters are going to lose their shirts, and I'm going to lose my job."

They left the secret location without drawing any attention, and soon Rodney was piloting the car smoothly through the crowded streets. Saskia would deliver a full set of sketches for her proposed dress soon. Jennie was surprised to learn that the final dress would require at least half a dozen fittings; the designer seemed lost for words when Jennie asked how much the dress would cost. Fortunately, Poppy rescued both of them by explaining the bill would be "taken care of."

"What's next, Poppy?" asked Karen, who apparently loved the thrill of a minute-by-minute itinerary.

"I think you've both done enough wedding work for one day. It's time for you to enjoy some pampering and go shopping just for fun."

"How can we possibly go shopping?" asked Jennie. "I thought those days were over."

Poppy smiled mischievously. "A friend of the royal family has made arrangements for you to visit his store in complete privacy. He calls it his engagement gift to the future princess."

"And who is this generous gentleman?" asked Jennie.

"I'm not at liberty to say," said Poppy. "He wishes to remain anonymous for now."

"I like that girl," her mom whispered as Poppy lifted her phone and listened to a voicemail. "She's got spunk and you can tell she knows how to keep a secret."

Jennie had also been pleasantly surprised by Poppy. Hearing the name, she'd pictured an elderly Mary Poppins who would constantly be scolding her, but not only was Poppy friendly, funny, and thirtyish, she wore her designer eyeglasses so well that Jennie half wished she were nearsighted herself.

Still, she couldn't get used to the fact that, no matter where she went, other people went with her. It was starting to feel downright rude to act as though Rodney wasn't driving the car.

"What did you think of the dresses, Rodney?" she asked, trying to bring him into the conversation. "Princess worthy?"

"I should say so," he answered, signaling left and checking his mirror. "But I'm the last person you should be consulting. Princess Penelope asked my opinion on hers, and after I gave it, she told me I was obviously a blind man."

As a round-eyed Karen mouthed *wow*, Jennie said, "I didn't know you'd worked for her."

Rodney nodded. "I spent some time with your prince, too, when he was just a wee scamp."

Spotting the legendary Mayfair department store Selfridges through the windshield, Jennie at first assumed they were merely en route to some easily reserved boutique, but Rodney circled the block, entered a narrow alley behind the building, and drove into the garage entrance at the back. On the fourth floor, he double-parked at a door with a prominent *Out of Service* sign and sent a text. Moments later, a slender young man strode out of the store and relieved him behind the wheel. Rodney escorted Jennie, Karen, and Poppy into the store, where they were met by an authoritative man wearing a blue suit and holding a walkie-talkie.

"Welcome to Selfridges," he said. "The salon has been reserved for your exclusive use for ninety minutes. Please don't hesitate to let me know if there's anything at all you require."

They followed him in astonishment to the hair and beauty salon, which was completely empty except for a dozen expectant hairstylists, manicurists, pedicurists, and aestheticians. Shaking their heads at the absurdity of the whole situation, Jennie and Karen settled in to enjoy the carefully choreographed experience while Poppy disappeared to check her email. After receiving massages and facials, mother and daughter were snipped, styled, filed, and painted. The busy hubbub of a crowded store was clearly audible, but the blazer-wearing security guards didn't let a single soul past the velvet ropes. Jennie couldn't even imagine how much the treatment would cost. She barely remembered the last time she'd touched money since entering Hugh's orbit, but somehow, she was spending more than she ever had in her life.

The salon was only the beginning. Rejoined by Poppy, they were whisked into a private suite for twenty minutes with a perfumer who had curated what he called "the royalty of scents." Karen loved it, but Jennie had a fragrance sensitivity that made her prone to headaches—a potentially awkward moment that was expertly finessed by Poppy. Even so, Jennie felt relieved when the man with the walkie-talkie led them away toward the women's designer galleries.

As the men in blazers cleared a path to the escalator down to the second floor—that was, the third floor—then cleared the escalator itself, a murmur of curiosity rippled through the crowd.

"We don't run and we don't dawdle," Rodney explained as heads began to turn. "Just move steadily and don't make eye contact, but don't duck your head. If you act as though you don't want to be recognized, you will be."

Several sections of the sales floor had been cordoned off in the women's designer galleries, but the well-heeled shoppers seemed closer and more curious. In the distance, Jennie could see people raising phones like periscopes, hoping a lucky shot would reveal who was keeping the rest of them out.

Jenny felt increasingly on edge but did her best not to show it, wanting her mom to enjoy this waking dream. And Poppy was truly in her element, expertly rifling through the racks to suggest just the right blouse, belt, or handbag.

"Perhaps the lady would like something more?" asked the solicitous man in the suit after every selection.

In the end, Jennie chose a cute Junya Watanabe coat and a perfectly matching Prada leather clutch—totaling about five thousand pounds—while Karen went for a Valentino handbag, a Celine scarf, and Bottega Veneta earrings that somehow looked very midwestern, despite their London price.

And, yes, two dozen pairs of Wolford hosiery.

To Jennie's relief, their mysterious benefactor, a distinguished man in an immaculately tailored chalk-stripe suit, finally appeared as they finished making their selections. She had been wondering whether they were supposed to simply waltz past the checkout or tell them to put everything on the royal tab. He looked vaguely familiar.

"Oh my God," whispered Karen. "It's Scott Corbyn."

"Please accept these gifts with my compliments and my sincerest congratulations on your engagement," he told Jennie, bowing slightly.

"You're too kind," Jennie said as she offered her hand to Penelope's former lover, wondering if her words were a suitably royal replacement for *thank you*. She didn't know for sure if it was proper protocol to accept the gifts at all, but Poppy had signed off on everything, so she assumed she was handling herself correctly.

The man took her hand and kissed it, his dry lips barely grazing her knuckles.

"It was so unbelievably nice of you to open the store to us—well, close parts of the store—for us!" gushed her mom.

He smiled and kissed her hand, too. "I do hope your lovely daughter will prosper in England."

As they headed for the exit, her mom bubbling with excitement over their celebrity encounter, Jennie didn't know what to think. Corbyn must have truly adored Penelope if he was showering Hugh's bride-to-be with gifts.

Their car was waiting on the other side of the door. Jennie sank into her seat and sighed with relief as the locks clicked and they began to roll down the ramp. The outing had been fun but a little intense.

Suddenly, in the front seat, Poppy's phone began to buzz with waspish insistency. She looked at the screen, frowned, and unlocked it.

"What is it?" asked Jennie.

Poppy looked pale. "Rodney, please take us to Kensington Palace as quickly as possible."

The PPO nodded as he accelerated into the alley.

"Please tell me what's happening," said Jennie, feeling sick. "Is Hugh okay?"

"Hugh's fine," said Poppy.

"Then what is it?"

"I'm forwarding you the link now," Poppy said without looking up. "I'm so very, very sorry."

———————

It felt as though the champagne bubbles were bursting one by one as they rode back to Kensington Palace in grim silence, all three of them staring at their phones.

I HAD A THREESOME WITH PRINCESS JENNIE, the headline screamed.

"Do you know what this is referring to?" asked Karen quietly, as if hoping Poppy couldn't hear her.

Jennie didn't respond. She started reading, then scrolling quickly, unable to focus but wanting to know how long it went on.

Sentences jumped out at her: *Jennie knew what she wanted, and we both went along . . . For such a petite girl, she's a tiger in the sack . . .*

Jennie forced herself back to the beginning, hating the way her mom kept looking up at her, eyes asking, *Is this true?*

The romantic past of hunky Prince Hugh has been well documented, even before his shocking engagement to an American singer who, admit it, you've never heard of. (OK, you know her only hit single, "I Can't Even," but could you pick her out of a lineup?)

With royal fanpeople (who apparently exist) desperate to know more about the girl who made the score of the century, I'm here to report that the princess-to-be is no blushing bride. And clearly, the House of Windsor has come a long, long way since Princess Penelope's vaunted virginity was job requirement one.

And how do I know Jennie Jensen likes to get her freak on? Reader, I was there . . .

The article's author, Lindsey Peters, had been Jennie's roommate during their junior year at the University of Michigan. While Jennie double-majored in music and sociology—thinking she might try social work if the whole musician thing didn't pan out—Lindsey studied communications and media, hoping for a career as a journalist. An exposé on questionable perks for big donors earned her the joking nickname "Scoop," but Jennie couldn't recall anything else Lindsey had published at the time.

Jennie *did* remember the drunken night off campus at the Blind Pig when an innocuous game of Would You Rather turned into a competition. At closing time, Lindsey and Jennie had stumbled home with the guy in tow, then flanked him on the couch as they listened to music and drank what was supposed to be the last beer of the night.

She still couldn't remember who kissed him first, why they started taking turns, or how everyone's shirts had come off, but it hadn't gone much farther than that. Jennie liked sex and had it when she wanted to, but she wasn't really into casual hookups, either.

She hadn't really kept in touch with Lindsey after graduating but remembered from Instagram posts that her former roommate was now living in Chicago. The pictures of tall buildings, street art, and a rescue puppy had offered no clue if she was pursuing her journalistic dreams.

Apparently, she was.

In Lindsey's written account of the drunken night, Jennie came across as pushy, horny, and uninhibited. The word *skank* wasn't used but it was definitely implied.

"Do you know the author?" asked Poppy, looking over her shoulder.

Jennie nodded.

"Can you think of any reason she'd be doing this?"

Jennie shook her head. "It really wasn't like that."

"The palace communications team is already meeting to discuss a response."

Most of the media attention Jennie had received since the engagement announcement had painted her and Hugh as an unlikely but exciting match. There had been several unflattering profiles of her family—London tabloids depicted her parents as hicks, lavishing attention on Dave's bushy chevron mustache and calling him "He-Man Dave"—and several snooty suggestions she was too "common" for the role, but nothing like this.

Jennie couldn't have felt more exposed if Lindsey had shared actual pictures of the event. Which, thankfully, did not exist.

———————

Back at Kensington Palace, in Penelope's old living room, Poppy opened her laptop on the coffee table while Karen flopped down on a fainting couch and Jennie paced, unable to organize her thoughts.

"What was Lindsey thinking?" she asked nobody in particular.

"You know, these English newspapers pay a lot," said her mom, staring off into the distance. "They even made us an offer for your baby pictures!"

"It's published on Medium, so even if it goes viral, it won't make her a fortune," said Poppy. "Perhaps the author sees this as a résumé builder."

Karen sat up suddenly. "Why don't you call her and ask her to take it down?"

Jennie pictured the conversation. If Lindsey had thought

so little of her to write it in the first place, she was unlikely to delete it.

"I'd advise against making contact," said Poppy with a grimace. "Anything you tell her could end up online again."

Jennie couldn't hold back the tears that started to flow. Her mom sat down next to her and pulled her close.

"This is so fucked up, Mom. How could she do this?"

"For all we know, she's having money problems or mental health issues," said Karen.

Jennie laughed bitterly. "That's just a little too understanding for me right now, Mom."

"I'm doing my best. I could have happily lived my whole life without knowing about this particular college adventure."

"Let's let the professionals advise us," said Poppy. "We've got a call with Jeremy Legrand, Sidney Reddy, and Hugh in fifteen minutes."

Jennie felt her heart stop. "Oh my God—Hugh."

"Call him right now," said Karen firmly. "You don't want to have your first conversation about this be during a conference call."

Jennie fumbled for a tissue, wiped her eyes, gave her nose a good, long blow, and picked up her phone. For all her daytime TV and self-help books, sometimes her mom was right on the money.

She was still walking out of the room when he answered.

"I love you," he said by way of a greeting.

Did he know yet—or didn't he?

He answered her question immediately by telling her, "Listen, Jennie. We've both been with other people, and we've both done things we might regret, but it's all in the past. Attacks like this come with the territory, I'm afraid. But we've got each other. We'll face them together."

Her tears this time were those of relief.

Princess Penelope

14 JANUARY 1985

Penelope had managed to sneak past the permanent encampment of paparazzi outside the gates of Kensington Palace, only to discover two snappers awaiting her arrival on Harley Street with cameras at the ready. Luckily for her, it was the same pair she'd spotted having a pee break on the Sandringham lawn last Christmas.

As Rodney slowly rolled past them in his Vauxhall—their go-to decoy vehicle—she lowered the passenger side window.

"Anyone need to take a wee?" she called out.

The shorter, pot-bellied one blushed crimson, while the other simply looked mortified that the Princess might have seen more than they'd realized that day. They'd been bested and they knew it, which she would attempt to use to her advantage by dispatching Rodney to barter for a photograph of her exiting her dentist's office two buildings down, rather than where she was actually headed.

She could only hope the plan worked. If it didn't, she'd be swarmed by photographers in an hour.

The pregnancy should have brought Edmund closer to her, but if anything, it had had the opposite effect. Blaming her increasing moodiness, he began spending more and more time away. Now, three months after she had given birth to Hugh Arthur Edmund Windsor, the most beautiful blue-eyed baby boy she could have imagined, her moods had gone from bad to worse. Despite the baby's sunny disposition and ready smile, all she ever wanted to do was weep.

And now, by royal decree, she had been ordered to share her problems with a stranger.

"I'm glad you managed to maintain your sense of humor, Your Royal Highness," said Dr. Thomas Ward once she was safely inside and had related the encounter. "But I can't say I find crude banter with paparazzi quite so amusing."

"I would prefer if you just called me Penelope," she said, settling into a paisley print armchair—the fussy decor more like a sitting room in Buckingham Palace than a therapist's office.

Judging by his Etonian demeanor, three-piece suit, and framed *By Royal Appointment* certificate, Dr. Ward was not going to suggest she call him Tom in return.

"Very well," he said.

"I've grown as accustomed as one can to having the paps about. After all, they've hounded me since day one," Penelope continued. "But heaven forbid I'm not wearing the right style or color, or I show too much leg—then the fashion press is out for blood along with the rest of them."

"It must be overwhelming."

"And annoying, intrusive, and sometimes even insulting. But at least I understand their motivations."

Determined to maintain her composure despite the lump forming in her throat, Penelope tried to picture herself as the seated woman gazing peacefully at the water in the Seurat oil painting on Dr. Ward's back wall.

He was clearly waiting for her to continue, so she did.

"You must know that I went into this with so much love in my heart. I truly believed that once I produced an heir everything would get sorted. But although I now have the most beautiful, perfect son in the world, I still feel as though I'm trapped in a fairy tale gone Grimm."

"Much of what you are going through could simply be temporary and biological. Depression after giving birth is, unfortunately, a far too common problem."

"Not for the mother of the future king. *Never complain, never explain*, and all that rot."

"Are you experiencing any mood swings, new or unusual feelings of apathy or sadness, or thoughts of self-harm?"

"Not where motherhood is concerned. Hugh brings me nothing but pure joy and I am entirely confident in my abilities as his mum."

"What about other realms of your life?"

"Realms, indeed. If only those in the Firm weren't so keen to spread the news I've gone crackers since giving birth."

Dr. Ward narrowed his already birdlike eyes. "You don't really think someone in the royal family tipped off the press about our appointment this morning?"

Her nose burned with the pins and needles of impending tears. Since giving birth to the heir to the throne, it had been made quite clear by her husband's family that she needed to pull herself together and get on with it. Her recent troubles had become a subject of speculation and sport.

"Everything is overheard and gossiped about by the royal family and their staff. Not to mention those eager to do the prince's bidding."

As the scratching of his pen filled the otherwise silent room, Penelope wondered if there was anyone in her world, including Edmund himself, who wasn't operating out of pure self-interest or ulterior motive.

"Before we continue, I think it's important you know that whatever is said here is completely between us," said the doctor.

"*Us* meaning you, me, and Edmund?"

"Your Hi— Penelope," he said, looking insulted. "I can assure you I adhere to the highest ethical standards in my practice."

"I am under no illusions. This therapy was set up not *for* me, but to help manage me."

"Whatever the intent, please trust that our time together is for you."

She might have apologized if that were an option. There were so few people she could trust.

"I can't help but notice you are fidgeting with your engagement ring," Dr. Ward finally said.

"It's unwieldy and spins around my finger," she said, her voice cracking. "You know, people say I picked this ring because it had the biggest stone."

"And did you?"

"It was fashioned after a brooch Edmund's great-grandfather commissioned as a gift for his future wife, Queen Margaret. Edmund recognized the design at the House of Garrard and thought the symbolism was perfect."

"As did you?"

"I preferred an emerald-cut diamond that was already part of the royal collection and wouldn't have set the coffers back a penny. But I was touched by Edmund's apparent sentimentality."

"In other words, you made the choice to please him?"

"That and countless others since," she managed to say before she began to sob.

Dr. Ward handed her the tissue box, allowing her to weep until she'd collected herself enough to wipe away the mascara running halfway down her face.

"In every marriage there is give and take," he said.

She'd done everything asked of her, even maintaining *her virtue* at her parent's insistence during the years when the prince was entirely unaware of her existence. That was easier said than done, given the abundance of handsome, more than willing prospects. And yet, she was ultimately glad she had stopped Oliver Jones—so good with his hands—given the satisfying compatibility she and the prince shared during intimacy. She'd even produced a male heir without complication. Why wasn't that enough?

Why wasn't *she* enough for him?

"When you're married to the future King of England, you give and he takes," she said, tears flowing anew. "From whomever he pleases."

Chapter Seven

GENNIE WITH A G

"I imagine they're excited to see you," said Hugh, as their three-car motorcade made the final turn.

The shrieking, which had been audible a block away, now rose in pitch and volume until it was concert level. The sidewalks on both sides of the street were thronged with people holding up phones and signs and pressing against the barricades. Among the placards she spotted PRINCESS CHARMING, which was nice; WE LOVE YOU JENNIE!!! which was even nicer; and I'LL DO HUGH WITH YOU, which made her feel suddenly short of breath.

Jennie gripped Hugh's hand more tightly. The May charity gala, a benefit for the Birmingham Youth Arts Centre, was their first official joint public appearance—and the first time they'd gone out in public together since Lindsey had decided to humiliate Jennie. She had been eagerly looking forward to the end of the arms-length protocol they'd been forced to endure until their engagement was announced and formally sanctioned, but she wished they could have faced the public under different circumstances. Although the highbrow British papers had quickly moved on from the story, tabloids, blogs, and social media had kept it in play through the month-long cooling-down period mandated by the palace. Some of the wording was coded (*Easy, Jennie!* winked one headline) and some of it simply unfamiliar slang (she regretted ever looking up *slapper*).

Hugh had told her not to worry, that people would always find reasons to take potshots at the royal family, which only made her wonder how many more ambushes were waiting. But she was truly reassured by the way he'd shrugged off the incident at the heart of the story.

When she'd apologized again, he simply laid his finger on her lips and shushed her.

Now, in the car, he lifted her hand and kissed it. "Don't worry about a thing. Let's enjoy ourselves and pretend it's a proper party."

As they entered the event in carefully choreographed stages, Jennie realized it had been a few years since her fiancé attended a *proper party*. First, they had to get out of the car. Hugh was always supposed to go first, but the red carpet was on the right-hand side, where she was sitting, so they both agreed it was best to avoid the spectacle of Hugh climbing awkwardly over her.

"Bugger Jeremy," muttered Hugh.

But when the door opened and the cameras started firing, she realized she had no idea how hard it was to keep her knees together while climbing out of a car, because she rarely wore skirts. On the sidewalk, they paused and smiled for pictures, fifteen seconds in each direction.

Then, as the front doors of the building swung open, they moved forward flanked by a phalanx of PPOs and event volunteers. Inside, they were greeted by the executive director and advisory board, who then stood aside so Hugh and Jennie could enter a side room for "one-on-ones" with twelve terrified teens.

The kids, a multicultural rainbow of skin, hair, and accents, took turns showing selections from their art portfolios and explaining how the art center had helped keep them off the streets. Twenty minutes later, after official photos with the official photographer and selfies with the teens, Hugh and Jennie were whisked into an already packed auditorium and ushered to front row center seats for a forty-minute show.

Throughout the program of beatboxing and rapping, breakdancing, slam poetry, a dramatic monologue, and a short two-actor play, the talent on display ranged from not bad to simply amazing. Jennie kept stealing glances at Hugh, wondering if she'd catch him checking his watch or his phone, but he remained focused on the performers, his eyes alert and alive, his expressions reflecting back at the performers exactly what they would have hoped to see.

Even though Jennie sometimes couldn't believe there were still kings and queens in the world, she was sure Hugh would be the kind of king every subject would want.

———

"I'm still waiting for the party," she teased him as they waited in a banquet room lavishly decorated with flowers.

He grinned. "*Now* we party. Princes have to sing for their supper these days."

Hugh had led the audience in a standing ovation for the performers, cheers and applause that somehow refocused on the two of them. Everyone had waited at their seats as Hugh and Jennie were led back up the aisle and out of the auditorium. Now the crowd was beginning to filter in.

Hugh ordered a pint of brown ale from a passing waiter and Jennie asked for a glass of sparkling rosé. They were situated at a high-top table at the edge of the room, any illusion that they were just two more partygoers dispelled by the fact that they were still visibly cordoned off by four PPOs, Sidney Reddy, and several arts center volunteers. As the room began to fill up, a reception line formed for those who wanted an audience with the star couple.

"I guess this is as close as we get to mingling?" asked Jennie.

"It's not so bad," he assured her. "I've some friends who are here tonight."

And some who aren't, thought Jennie.

Despite his long friendship with Hugh, and the key role he'd played in their first encounter, Courts had noticeably cooled toward her since word of their engagement went public. Hugh theorized he was simply hurt not to have been told the top-secret news in advance, but Jennie couldn't help wondering if he had something against her. When an unnamed "palace insider" told a gossip columnist, "I honestly thought she'd be just another one-night stand," it sounded all too much like Courts. Had he also been the source of the very first leak about their relationship? Whatever the reason, they hadn't seen much of him lately.

Although Jennie could see some younger people clustered around the bar, the donors who began to approach them were older, conservatively dressed, and completely in awe. The first man, who identified himself as the owner of a local Vauxhall dealership, pumped Hugh's hand like he was trying to jack up a car.

The woman following him was a classic cougar, pretty but caked in makeup and strapped into a form-fitting dress that looked like it was about to burst. Jennie could tell Hugh was making an effort not to meet her gaze as the woman curtseyed; when Jennie had first explained the Americanism to him, he'd been delighted and unable to stop what he called "cougar spotting."

"It's an honor to meet you, Your Hughness," said the flustered woman.

They both heard it, but her fiancé showed his impeccable training by not even batting an eye.

"And I am very pleased to meet you," he told her. "I hope you have a wonderful evening."

As the woman walked off, Jennie locked eyes with Hugh.

"Don't you dare," he said out of the side of his mouth.

"If you think I'm letting this go, you're sadly mistaken, Your *Hughness*," she told him, trying hard to emulate Hugh's elegant nonreaction.

Then Imogen Banfield-March came through the line.

"Imogen!" said Hugh, leaning forward and politely kissing her on both cheeks. "Lovely to see you."

Imogen's fingers grazed Jennie's in what passed for a handshake.

"Delighted to meet you, Jennie," said Imogen, her gaze returning to Hugh.

Jennie's first thought was that Imogen was more beautiful than she appeared in photos, where she was already clearly prettier than Jennie. With golden blond hair, sun-kissed skin, and a tiny but appealing gap in her teeth, she looked like a country-girl supermodel. Hugh and Imogen had dated on and off for seven years, and while Hugh assured Jennie he was single when she met him, some tabloids had printed stories claiming Hugh had unceremoniously dumped Imogen for Jennie. Long considered The One for Hugh—her parents were the pedigreed Lord and Lady Banfield-March—Imogen's patience through multiple breakups had earned her the nickname "All-in Imogen." Hugh had told Jennie he thought he loved Imogen at first, until he gradually began to suspect she was a little too hung up on the idea of becoming a princess. Or in his words, *She finds the crown my most attractive feature.*

His multiple reconciliations with her, he'd confessed, were motivated both by his own guilty feelings and pressure from his father to find a suitable match. And Imogen was more than suitable: not only did she know how to navigate Hugh's world in a way Jennie doubted she'd ever be able to learn, but she had never, ever embarrassed the royals with a tabloid scandal.

As if on cue, Lady Banfield-March appeared from behind Imogen. Hugh appeared delighted to see the willowy, ash-blond woman.

"Vivienne!" he exclaimed, giving her a warmly reciprocated hug. "I didn't expect you here."

"We were spending the week at the farm and thought we'd pay you a visit. It just so happens that we are benefactors of the BYAC."

Hugh turned to Jennie. "I'd like to introduce you to my fiancée, Jennie Jensen. Jennie, this is Vivienne Banfield-March."

"I'm pleased to meet you," said Jennie, hoping it sounded like she really was.

Somehow, Jennie and Hugh found themselves separated by Imogen and Vivienne.

"So you're Hugh's new Jennie," said the older woman with a throaty chuckle. Seeing Jennie's eyes widen, she added, "I see he didn't share his pet name for Imogen—Gennie, with a G."

Jennie shook her head and tried to keep smiling. She wished Hugh had mentioned it, even though she thought she understood why he'd chosen not to.

Vivienne eyed her closely as she continued, as if watching to see how she'd react. "The press has given you quite the introduction, haven't they? Do be careful. Once they stick a label on you, it can be quite hard to remove."

"I keep trying to tell myself that part is out of my control," Jennie managed to reply.

"We can't control what they report, only what we do," said Vivienne. "I've come to love that boy like a son, and his happiness is more important than anything that could have existed between him and my daughter."

"I'm sure this is hard for her," said Jennie, trying to redirect the conversation to safer ground. "They were in each other's lives for a very long time."

Lady Banfield-March waved dismissively. "Imogen will win her prince eventually. It's much harder for people my age to move on."

———————

After his second beer, Hugh told Sidney they were ready to go, and his private secretary informed the protection officers. The reception was in full swing—Jennie had noticed the crowd by the bar getting downright sloppy—but she was more than ready to go, already exhausted by dozens of bright, brittle conversations. She knew from Hugh that he'd formerly been the one to close the party, sometimes mock-ordering people to keep boozing with him, and she was glad those days were over. She'd never been a big drinker, and too many late nights playing small clubs had turned her off to the sweaty, boisterous last-call crowd.

Their quick exit received less fanfare than their entrance, but there was still a sizable crowd waiting outside. As they crossed the sidewalk to the waiting car, a hoarse male voice called from the crowd.

"Hey, Jennie!"

She turned, grinning, lifting her hand to wave.

"If you'll shag anyone, why not me, too? Slag!"

Jennie felt like she'd been slapped—then literally lost her balance when she caught a heel in the red carpet and stumbled.

Time seemed to speed up as Hugh charged forward, vaulted

a barricade, and plunged into the crowd. She saw two PPOs race toward him as he raised a balled fist. Then Rodney grabbed her from behind and practically threw her into the backseat before standing in the open door, shielding her with his body.

The shouts and confusion lasted less than a minute. Then, without a word, Rodney scrambled out of the way as Hugh slid in. Doors slammed and tires screeched as the car raced away.

Jennie wrapped her arms around Hugh and held him tightly, feeling his heart pounding beneath her cheek. Her own heart was racing just as fast.

"Are you okay?" she asked.

"I only wish I'd hit him harder," he said, his voice thick with anger.

She let go and inspected his hand. His knuckles were split and bleeding.

"Your Highness," said Rodney, offering a white handkerchief from the front seat.

Hugh wrapped the cloth tightly around his knuckles. Little red spots quickly showed through. He kicked the seat in front of him.

"How *dare* they speak to you like that!" he fumed.

"Who was it?"

"Some bloody photographer."

Jennie was confused. "A photographer? But why would—"

"They used to say things to Mum," says Hugh, turning to look out the back window. "Call her *bitch* or *harlot* or worse. Then they'd snap pictures of her angry face. Better sales that way."

"That's horrifying," Jennie said, picturing poor Penelope hunted by paparazzi while a young Hugh stood by helplessly.

And feeling shocked by the revelation that a furious princess could be worth more to the world than one who was happy.

Chapter Eight

NEVER COMPLAIN, NEVER EXPLAIN

"With all due respect, Your Royal Highness, what on *earth* were you thinking?"

Jennie felt a sense of déjà vu as Jeremy Legrand rested his elbows on his wooden desk, steepled his fingers, and fixed his gaze on Hugh.

In the eighteen hours since Hugh had punched the photographer, news of the incident had circled the world. The story sparked on English Twitter and then, as Britons went to bed, simmered to a boil in the US and other earlier time zones, as well as Asia, where it was already tomorrow. By the time England rubbed its eyes and poured its morning tea, the newspapers had printed front-page headlines ranging from PHOTOGRAPHER AL-LEGES ASSAULT BY PRINCE HUGH to ROYAL BEAT DOWN to RAGE MONSTER! HUGH SNAPS, SLAPS SNAPPER. By afternoon, columnists were condemning, defending, and demanding investigations into his actions while Tik-Tok stars reenacted the scrap or edited the video to fit into scenes from classic films. As one pundit put it on a radio talk show, "Prince Hugh has been memed and themed, but not yet redeemed."

Jennie, following the coverage in a state of near panic, couldn't help but notice that most of the stories focused on either Hugh's fury or his security detail's failure to stop him—not the taunt that made him lose control. She'd been slut-shamed and nobody but Hugh seemed to care.

Now they had been summoned to Buckingham Palace by King Edmund—who was *regretfully unable to attend*—for a meeting with not only Legrand but also Grant McCutcheon, the head of the Metropolitan Police Royalty and Specialist Protection Branch. Legrand had placed a seat for the broad-shouldered, paunchy McCutcheon behind his desk, making the whole thing feel like an interrogation. Hugh was flanked by Jennie and Sidney Reddy, who he'd brought along for advice and support.

"Well, if I'm being quite honest, I wasn't thinking, Jeremy," said Hugh. "The man said something disgusting about the woman I love."

"Can you imagine the King responding to provocation in the same manner?" asked Jeremy.

Hugh chuckled. "Well, I doubt he'd get over the barricade as quickly as I did. His hip gives him some difficulty."

As Jeremy's eyes flashed in irritation, it occurred to Jennie that he was the first person she'd seen who wasn't deferential to Hugh—outside of Hugh's blood relations. "This is hardly a laughing matter. And you're being willfully obtuse. But I'll rephrase: Is this the behavior of a king?"

"I'm not King yet. But you should note that it's only the pundit class chastising me. Our *subjects* seem to support my actions."

McCutcheon tapped a manila folder on his thigh and smiled unhappily. "Our detectives have completed initial interviews of eyewitnesses. None of them heard the photographer say"—glancing in Jennie's direction, he appeared to rethink his phrasing—"the offensive remark."

Hugh frowned. Jennie squeezed his arm.

"Then who did?" asked Sidney.

Opening the folder, McCutcheon scanned the top sheet of paper. "Witnesses described a man with close-cropped hair wearing a Birmingham City Football Club top as the one who made the comment. We have CCTV video of him and believe we are close to making a positive identification. However, insulting a public figure is not a chargeable offense unless it threatens bodily harm. Did either of you fear for your safety?"

"No," Jennie told him, remembering the shock of the insult.

Hugh slumped in his chair and shook his head. "Christ."

Legrand put on reading glasses, peered at his computer monitor, and started clicking his mouse. "This evening, the *Sun* will publish online an exclusive interview with the photographer—who, in a convenient turn of events, is employed by them. I was able to obtain a draft copy. I will read you a representative quote: 'I pleaded with him to stop, but it was clear the red mist had descended. The raging prince struck me with his fists again and again as he screamed a torrent of obscenity.'"

"I hit him once—twice—and told him if he ever came near Jennie again, I'd have him arrested," said Hugh indignantly.

"The article claims you threatened to kill him," said Legrand.

"Does he wish to prefer charges?" asked Sidney. "Is he threatening a civil suit?"

"My source informs me he is 'considering his options.'"

All five of them fell silent. Legrand watched Hugh, McCutcheon resumed tapping the folder on his thigh, and Sidney checked his phone, which seemed to have been vibrating continuously. Hugh turned to Jennie, his pained expression telling her that, for once, he didn't know what to do.

"I think you should apologize," she told him. "As soon as humanly possible."

"When he's about to publish these . . . *lies?*"

"It's standard PR in America. Admit you were wrong before the story gets even bigger. People will take your side if you honestly say you're sorry."

Legrand smiled condescendingly. "While I appreciate your perspective, Miss Jensen, you are not here in an advisory capacity. And the rules and traditions surrounding royalty are quite different from any minor *celebrities* you may have encountered."

Hugh rolled his eyes as he spoke to Jennie: "Never complain, never explain."

"A king—or a prince or a princess—does not dignify even the most outrageous accusations by acknowledging them," continued Legrand. "*Especially* the most outrageous ones. A royal does not offer comment to tabloids, much less apologize to a Fleet Street hack who is no doubt quite happy to have stumbled into the story of a lifetime."

"But Hugh did hurt him," she insisted, wishing it wasn't true.

Legrand dropped his reading glasses on his desk. "The purpose of this conference is not to discuss an apology the Prince will not make but to establish some ground rules. Due to the unconventional nature of your union, it's quite likely you will face further provocation, and it is imperative that we are united in our response."

"What do you mean, *unconventional?*" demanded Hugh.

Legrand shrugged. "Miss Jensen's background has not provided the ideal preparation for the role she is about to assume."

"So, our response is to do nothing at all and just let this play out?" asked Jennie, seething at the royal secretary's suggestion that she was a problem Hugh had brought on himself.

All day, Jennie had found herself thinking about Princess Penelope and the harassment she'd endured in the press over the rumors of her infidelity. Karen claimed Edmund was a serial philanderer but strangely, *that* had never made the papers. While Hugh's bachelor days had been heavily covered in the tabloids, the tone was always one of winking approval.

"Buckingham Palace and Kensington Palace will coordinate a response to any legal matters, and I'm confident we will reach an understanding with the photographer," said Jeremy. "We are already working to restore public acceptance of Jennie, and we will continue to do so. We will keep Sidney apprised."

His phrasing—*restore public acceptance*—made Jennie feel like she was a defective product.

"I don't need everyone to love me," she told Legrand. "I have spent years of my life onstage, and I've gotten my fair share of bad reviews. People have the right to form their own opinions."

"The public's opinion of the royal family has nothing to do with your feelings," he sniffed. "It is, in fact, a matter of national security. Speaking of which, it is essential that you both allow your security details to do their jobs. Mr. McCutcheon will explain."

Legrand nodded at McCutcheon, who stopped tapping his folder and placed it on the desk.

"We've received threats to Miss Jensen's safety," said the policeman.

Jennie felt a hot flush and shivered. The room felt suddenly smaller.

"Why haven't we been made aware of this before now?" demanded Hugh.

Every day, a courier from the palace media center delivered a packet of letters, mostly fan mail. Jennie had always done her best to read all of them but had never seen anything to worry about.

"As you know, your family occasionally receives messages of concern, which are routinely transferred to Director McCutcheon's office for further investigation," said Legrand. "The increase in such correspondence since the article about Jennie appeared has been handled in exactly the same way."

"I have a right to see them for myself," she told him, feeling sick even as she said it.

Hugh put his hand on her arm. His knuckles were still bandaged with white gauze and medical tape. "Perhaps it's best if you don't."

"It makes me feel less safe to know people are keeping things from me."

Legrand raised an eyebrow at McCutcheon, who said, "Some of these threats require time to investigate."

"And then when you're done, you can share the threats and your findings with me," said Jennie.

Hugh looked so sad that she almost regretted taking such a hard line. "If that's what Jennie wants, then I must insist," he said.

"Of course, sir," said Legrand, smiling tightly. "I will personally direct the effort."

————

Poppy rapped on the doorway and entered Penelope's old sitting room with a laptop under her arm. Jennie had been sitting on the couch and watching a mug of tea grow cold while a maid dusted on the other side of the room.

"Maybe I don't belong here," said Jennie disconsolately.

"Was it that bad?" asked Poppy.

"Not only did Hugh hit the wrong man, but the palace has also been receiving threatening letters since I showed up."

Poppy nodded sympathetically but didn't seem particularly surprised, making Jennie wonder whether her Girl Friday had known about the threats or if they were merely par for the course.

"Sometimes I think none of us belong here," she said. "Even those who sit on the throne ultimately arrived through accidents of history. It's not an easy job, and it's not often fun."

Jennie grabbed one of Penelope's silly pillows—*Live in the moment*—and clutched it for comfort. "Is this what passes for a pep talk here?"

Poppy smiled. "What I'm getting around to saying is that I think you have as much right to be here as anyone, and I think you'll make a perfect princess, once you figure out the forks."

"Thank you."

"It's my sincere pleasure. Let us handle the hard things and you'll do just fine."

As Poppy opened her laptop on a writing desk facing the wall, Jennie gave the pillow one last squeeze, preparing to set it aside—and heard a crinkle of paper in the back.

Thinking it was only a tag, she turned the pillow over without finding anything. But when she pressed on the fabric, she heard the sound again. Slipping her hand inside the cover, she found a folded, slightly yellowed envelope tucked inside. It was addressed to a Kitty Crowden in a neat, feminine cursive.

The words almost made her gasp out loud.

I must be very careful or they will kill me, too.

I am a distraction. A nuisance. I am in the way.

I don't know who I can trust. The men in grey despise me. They say I don't know my place, that I cheapen the brand, that I attract too much attention.

I'm not crazy, no matter what they leak to the press.

My so-called delusions have proven to be entirely accurate, at least where my ex-husband is concerned.

The prince cannot marry again until I'm gone.

Jennie slipped the envelope and note back into the pillow and quietly zipped it shut.

As she got up off the couch, she felt herself wobble and reached for a nearby chair to steady herself. She felt as confused as the time she'd gotten concussed on a volleyball court and struggled to make sense out of ordinary sentences.

"Jennie, what's wrong?" asked Poppy, turning in her seat. "You look like you've seen a ghost."

All Jennie could do was nod mutely. Maybe she had.

Chapter Nine

THE ROYAL MAIL

"What was Penelope like when it was just the two of you, Rodney?" Jennie asked from the back seat as the car inched through midday London traffic.

Beside her, Poppy looked up from her phone, curious to hear the answer.

"And what has you thinking about the princess?" asked Rodney in reply.

What indeed? After discovering Penelope's terrifying prediction in her own living room, Jennie had panicked, not knowing who she could turn to. She disguised her shock by telling Poppy it was a wave of anxiety about, well, everything. Once she had finally found herself alone and able to think, none of her options seemed good. Telling Hugh would have further aggravated a freshly reopened wound. Sharing a Windsor family secret with Poppy was out of the question. And actually mailing the letter to its intended recipient was downright insane.

Penelope was obviously afraid of something.

After wrestling with different scenarios for most of the evening, Jennie had finally decided to call her mom and tell her about both the anonymous note to Penelope, which she'd since taped together, and Penelope's paranoid-sounding unsent letter.

I don't know what to do, Jennie had said. *I've already brought so much trouble into his life with that article that I can't bear to hurt him anymore.*

Karen had seized on the mystery. *I wonder which one of her lovers wrote the note, the riding instructor or Corbyn? The press always made a huge deal out of the fact that she had two little affairs, but they were conveniently quiet about Edmund's philandering.*

I wish I'd never found either of these.

Maybe Penelope wanted you to find her message, said her mom. *Maybe you're the one who's supposed to find out what happened to her.*

Mom, Jennie groaned. *I can't deal with any woo-woo stuff. Just tell me what to do with the letters.*

Keep them somewhere safe. Don't tell anyone until we find someone who can help.

But even hiding the papers presented problems. She couldn't keep them in their apartment, because after all, that's where they'd been discovered. Shuddering at the thought there could be even more of them, she had searched Penelope's pillows, personal effects, and picture frames without finding anything else.

When Jennie asked where she could keep "personal items" safe and private, Poppy informed her that members of the royal family had safe deposit boxes available to them deep in a subbasement at Buckingham Palace, "where the King keeps the jewels they don't display at the Tower of London." Not wanting to arouse Poppy's suspicions, Jennie said nothing about what the "items" were. Maybe she was learning to be a royal, after all.

Now, looking at Rodney in the rearview mirror, with the

note and the letter in her new clutch giving off so much heat she half expected them to burst into flame, she told him, "Since we put out some of Penelope's old knickknacks, I've found myself wondering what kind of person she was. I have to admit, I was surprised by her sense of humor."

Her PPO completed a lane change before easing to a stop at a traffic light. He was a careful driver: she had never seen someone check all three mirrors so frequently.

"She certainly loved those silly pillows," he said, smiling as he glanced at her in the rearview. "And sweets from the corner shop. I think of her every time I eat a Mars bar."

Hearing his wistful tone, Jennie and Poppy grinned at each other. The tough and usually taciturn policeman's warm feelings for Princess Penelope were obvious.

"There was a side to her the cameras never captured," he continued, warming to his topic. "Sometimes she was . . . let's just say it's very difficult to be in constant demand. She wanted to be the best wife, queen, and mum she could be. Chocolate came in a close fourth."

That made them all laugh. Poppy looked like she was dying to ask for specific examples, but Jennie was content to let any further secrets remain unsaid.

"It sounds like she used humor to deal with the pressure," Jennie said.

"Yes," said Rodney, checking his mirrors yet again as the car moved forward. "But there were times she told me she didn't think she could walk through the door to face yet another crowd. Everyone wanted to get close to her, which added to the challenge of protecting her."

Jennie watched a bicyclist weave in and out of cars before jumping the curb and nearly running over a tourist with a wide-brimmed hat and an aluminum trekking pole.

"It had to be so hard when . . . after she died," Jennie said, feeling awkward for bringing it up.

"The worst part was feeling I might have done something to help," said Rodney. "The people who put her on the plane that night didn't know their arses from their elbows, if you'll excuse my language."

Penelope, afraid for her life, had died in a mysterious plane crash . . .

Okay, Karen! Jennie silently chided herself. Small planes crashed all the time. She had certainly been terrified the only time she had flown in one, feeling its fragility as it bucked and bounced on invisible currents of air.

"Well, the good news is that I should be a lot easier to protect than Penelope because I'm not nearly as popular," she said, hoping to lighten the mood.

"Give it time," said Poppy. "I know you'll come into your own."

Despite the heavy traffic, they were already circling the gleaming gold Victoria Monument and threading the crowd of tourists at the gate of Buckingham Palace. The guards recognized the black Audi as a royal vehicle and lowered the road blocker before waving Rodney in.

Rolling through a crowd during broad daylight hardly felt like a secret mission, but that's exactly what this was. Still, it was still impossible to keep dozens of people from learning her destination, from the footman who brought the car to the security officers who approved the itinerary to the many people who saw her leave Kensington Palace and arrive at Buckingham Palace. Jennie could only hope no one found a reason to mention the short trip to Hugh. Neither the King nor the Queen was in residence—not that Jennie would have expected them to pop out and say hello.

———

"The Yeoman of the Gold Plate will be with you shortly, Miss Jensen," Rodney informed her, after conferring with the palace guard at an elevator deep inside the palace.

"The . . . *what?*"

Jennie tightened her grip on her clutch.

Rodney smiled, amused at her reaction. "The chap who looks after the King's baubles. You don't think they let just anyone pop round to have a look, do you?"

"Of course not," said Jennie. "I just thought he'd have a more modern title."

The Yeoman of the Gold Plate turned out to be a polite middle-aged man, with a combover, whose name was Ellis Swainscott. He carried a metal box large enough to hold a dozen pairs of shoes.

"We can protect any item you require, Miss Jensen," he said. "You can place your valuables in this box and I will be happy to retrieve them for you at any time."

"I was hoping to put it away personally," she told him.

"I can certainly understand your wish, but access to the chambers is limited to the King himself or, with his written permission, senior members of the royal family."

Jennie hesitated. Was she supposed to lift the lid and drop her envelope inside like she was sending a letter via Royal Mail?

"Is there somewhere I can be alone for just a moment?"

"Yes, of course, Miss Jensen."

As Ellis showed Jennie into a small sitting room nearby, she had to admit the lack of privacy was only part of her disappointment. Despite herself, she couldn't help picturing the royal treasure room as a massive heap of gold coins, bejeweled silverware, and other plunder—quite possibly guarded by an elderly dragon.

Ellis set the box down on a polished wooden table,

straightened the lapels of his blazer, and left, closing the door behind him. Jennie removed Penelope's letter and note from her purse and dropped them inside the metal box. The box itself seemed comically oversized for two pieces of paper but was still probably too small for the size of the secrets they held.

As she pushed down the lid, Jennie realized the box didn't have a lock. Apparently, royals were supposed to rely upon the honesty and discretion of the Yeoman of the Gold Plate as he carried their secrets underground.

She had no choice but to trust him, too.

———————

When she returned to Kensington Palace, Jennie found her daily mail waiting on the polished sideboard in the entry hall. She had planned to play guitar for a while before taking a bath and getting ready for Hugh's return from up north but decided instead to read her letters first. Carrying the large red leather pouch to the library—a room where her books and Hugh's books took up only a fraction of the shelves, the rest of them filled with an impressive array of vintage, leather-bound volumes—she opened it, pulled out a three-inch-thick stack of papers, and started to read.

On the very top, an assortment of hand-drawn cards from little kids had been flagged with a note from Ian O'Rourke, who sorted her mail: *You will absolutely adore these!*

It was true. As Jennie leafed through the crayoned and penciled messages she felt as warm and gooey as one of the Fry's Chocolate Cream bar squares Rodney tried to pass off as a breath mint. She found her bodyguard's sweet tooth endearing.

The first card was just a drawing of two stick figures wearing crowns, with a heart over both their heads.

Congratlatons on yor weeding!!! read one.

You are so beautiful, read another.

Some day I will be a princess to, read a note from a little girl named Ming Mei, age eight.

The royal family did not accept unsolicited email, which Jennie had to admit was a brilliant move. Any idiot could spam you with a few quick keystrokes, but the small amount of work required to write, stamp, and send a letter undoubtedly made the volume of correspondence more manageable.

There were lots of letters from adults, too. Most had been composed on a computer and printed out, but many were handwritten: quite a few elderly correspondents congratulated her on her engagement in difficult-to-read cursive. Some people asked for photos of her; some included photos of themselves. Others pleaded for help with everything from environmental causes to criminal cases. It would have taken hours to read every word, so she skimmed and scanned, setting aside a handful for personal replies.

Even though she knew any hate mail or threats had been held for investigation, she was pleased to see that most of what she received was positive. One man from Chippenham opened by saying he felt the royal family should be abolished and *forced to get proper jobs like everyone else* but also seemed to feel it represented some kind of progress if they were now accepting *rebels from the colonies.* Though his remark had clearly been intended as an insult, she decided to take it as a compliment. Maybe she would title her next album *Rebel from the Colonies.*

At the very bottom of the stack was a handwritten note with no corresponding envelope. The block letters had been formed with a red marker.

PENELOPE COULDN'T SURVIVE HERE AND NEITHER WILL YOU.

Jennie's fingers opened involuntarily and she let the paper fall as if it had cut her.

Penelope's desperate warning may have been more than paranoia. And if so, her death was no accident.

Just as her mom had implied.

She searched the pile for the envelope, looking for some clue of who could have sent this to her, but found none. It had simply been slipped in with the pile. Which meant . . . it hadn't come in via the mail.

It had come from inside the palace.

Part Two

DRAMA QUEEN

Chapter Ten

TAKE NOTE OF YOUR SURROUNDINGS

The black bag over her head was loose but Jennie still found it hard to breathe. As the car hurtled down the road, she took deeper and deeper breaths, trying to draw in more air and convince herself she wouldn't run out.

The men had spoken only simple commands after they suddenly appeared as she stepped out of the little shop onto the sidewalk. Now that she was tightly wedged between two of them in the back seat, they weren't speaking at all. She could feel their bodies on high alert, just as she could feel the car rising and falling as they raced along at what felt like a hundred miles per hour.

She tried to tell herself it was somehow better *not* to see, to take comfort in her cocoon of darkness, but it didn't work. For all she knew, they could be heading straight for a brick wall.

Jennie tried to remember her training. It had gone by so quickly, and so much of it seemed to stress not doing anything: *If escape is not immediately possible, follow your captors' commands and do not physically resist or antagonize them.* There was no way she could *take note of your surroundings.*

Humanize yourself, one of the instructors had repeatedly stressed.

But how, exactly, was she supposed to do that? It was like a question in a college philosophy class she would have dropped once the boys started arguing with each other about artificial intelligence.

"My name is Jennie Jensen," she said, her voice strange to her own ears. "I'm twenty-seven years old and I am from Illinois, in the United States."

One of the men grunted in response. Then the car began a sweeping turn, lifting on its suspension. Her stomach dropped. She needed to steady herself, but with her hands zip-tied in front of her and fastened to a longer tie that went around her waist, all she could do was bobble helplessly.

"I'm adopted," she chanted, spitting out fabric after a fold of the bag entered her mouth. "Which I've always known, but most people didn't realize because I kind of look like my parents anyway."

The car went over a small hill, and she could tell it had left the ground because of how hard it hit when they landed. Suddenly she was on the verge of tears. Someone who was kidnapping you didn't care that you were human. Your humanness was what made you valuable.

"My fiancé will be worried about me," she choked out.

"Keep your mouth shut!" barked the driver.

Jennie reached out for a happy memory. One from before the world knew about their romance and it was still their special secret. When she was still safe.

Botswana. Hugh leading her out of the "tent"—a five-star hotel room with a canvas ceiling—to a jeep. Driving her through a green fringe to the Makgadikgadi salt pans, the sunbaked and stunningly flat remains of an inland sea. Not at all her stereotype of an African safari with birds and animals flocking to a watering hole. Apart from the jeep full of armed bodyguards that parked at a discreet distance, it was just the two of them at the edge of nowhere, with two chairs, a picnic basket, and a bottle of champagne to savor as the sun went down.

Hugh saying, *I love you, Jennie.*

Heat rising from the earth. Their glasses sparkling in the red light.

I love you, too.

She grabbed the memory tightly and held on. If she was going to die, she would want to remember that. Hugh's face. Kissing him.

Tires squealed as the driver braked and skidded into a turn. Jennie heard sirens in the distance and the low thud of a helicopter.

They were coming to rescue her.

Suddenly, wind whipped through the car. The men had lowered their windows. The pressure on both sides eased as they shifted their bodies and turned away from her and began firing at the pursuers. Her ears were stung by the gunshots, but she couldn't raise her hands to cover them. Engines whined as the pursuit vehicles drew closer. Commands were barked through a bullhorn and carried away on the wind.

In the darkness, Jennie pressed her eyes tightly shut. She bounced back and forth as the car swerved, left the road, and bumped wildly over grass before reversing direction on pavement again.

The men reloaded and kept firing, and the rescuers shot back. Jennie hoped they were aiming for the tires. Then there was an impossibly loud BANG, then another, and another as the car fishtailed, bounced, and came to a halt.

"Shit shit shit!" she heard herself screaming in terror.

The doors flew open and she could feel the men bailing out. She pictured them crouching behind open doors as the gunfire rattled like a midwestern hailstorm on the metal roof of the patio of the house where she grew up.

Then it trickled to a stop.

In the brief moment of silence, Jennie felt as alone as she ever had in her life.

Boots clomped on the road as shouting men ran to the car. Hands gripped her and pulled her out, helping her upright. Her legs were cut free, then her hands, then finally the bag came off, leaving her blinking in the bright gray light of a late spring day, surrounded by smiling SAS commandos.

"We've got you, princess," said the nearest one, who was rocking a retro pencil-thin mustache.

"I'm not princess yet," she told him after she'd caught her breath.

He winked. "That's princess with a small p."

Her knees were suddenly so wobbly she could hardly stand up.

"Cup of tea?"

———————

Minutes after being pulled from the car, Jennie found herself seated on a folding chair under a small canopy, where, shaded from the clouds, she watched Rodney pour milky tea from a thermos.

"Here you are, Miss Jensen," said Rodney, handing her a battered tin cup.

He watched intently while she took a thirsty gulp. The tea was too strong and too sweet and too milky and absolutely delicious.

"How are you feeling?" he asked.

"Pretty shaken up."

"You'd be stupid—excuse me—if you weren't scared. We

control the danger, but even make-believe car chases can end in all-too-real accidents."

Jennie shivered as he excused himself and joined a small team of officers who were supervising the cleanup. Watching dozens of soldiers clear away the chase vehicles, sweep up debris, and hose dirt off the asphalt reminded Jennie of a *Mission Impossible* reveal, when the masks came off and nothing was exactly as it had seemed. And Stirling Lines, as the Herefordshire base was called, did resemble a movie set, even despite the deadly threats defining its existence. In addition to the obstacle course and shooting range, it contained an explosion-scarred city block, various bunkers, and even a miniature village with the "sweet shop" where she had been "abducted"—all of it laced with a surprisingly extensive network of roads.

For now, at least, Jennie had decided not to show the threatening note to Hugh. The pain she'd caused by showing him the note from his mother's lover was still fresh, and after his response to the heckler in Birmingham, she didn't want to add any additional pressure unless it was absolutely necessary. That time, he'd lashed out and gotten it wrong. When he saw a more direct threat, what would he be capable of? She hated to keep anything from him and didn't want to go through it without him, but she was starting to understand the weighty pressure of his role. When she shared the letter with Rodney, her PPO had grimly assured her they'd get to the bottom of it and then promptly hand-delivered it to Jeremy Legrand. Forty-five minutes later, she had been summoned to yet another meeting with Jeremy and Grant McCutcheon. Jeremy managed to infer the note was somehow her fault for having the audacity to experiment sexually in college. Grant was more practical and simply suggested it was time for Jennie to undergo the intensive SAS training required for all working royals.

Today's "abduction scenario" was the final part of the two-day course, and as the knot of uniformed SAS soldiers and plainclothes Metropolitan Police Service officers approached the canopy, trailed by Ian O'Rourke, her minder for the weekend, Jennie felt as though she were about to receive her final grade. She had already forgotten everyone's names and was still confused by the ranks of the men overseeing the exercise—the fact that they pronounced *lieutenant* as "leftenant" made her want to giggle.

Major Somebody led the group in a round of applause that struck Jennie as neither enthusiastic nor overly sincere.

"Bravo and well done, Miss Jensen. Other than some rather," he cleared his throat, "fruity language, you kept your composure wonderfully."

"I was so scared I could hardly think," she told him. "Besides giving your men a chance to scare me, and I think they enjoyed that, I still don't see how this will help me if something like this really happens."

"All the lectures in the world will be of no use if you haven't tried to think when the world is blowing up around you," said Leftenant Something or Other.

"The only decision I made was not peeing my pants. And I'm holding you directly responsible for the end of my musical career if I go deaf from all those guns going off in my ear."

Chuckling, a few of the men exchanged looks.

"And what if you all aren't here to rescue me?"

Major Somebody looked at her soulfully. "Miss Jensen. The Crown has faced countless threats over the years and yet we have managed to keep the royal family safe for generations."

Maybe it was his careless choice of "countless threats," but his words didn't make her feel any better. Or maybe it was the fact that she couldn't unsee Penelope's frantically scrawled words: *I must be very careful or they will kill me, too.*

As Jennie's anonymous correspondent had reminded her, Penelope *hadn't* survived.

Would she?

Chapter Eleven

THE WRONG BRAND

As soon as she had settled into the back of the discreet black car for her trip back to London, Jennie texted Hugh a funny picture she'd sweet-talked the soldiers into taking with her. After removing the blanks from an assault rifle and triple-checking to make sure it wasn't loaded, they had assumed sheepish poses, their hands in the air, while she fiercely pointed the rifle as if she had just captured them at gunpoint. She was sure Hugh would approve. He had served as a helicopter pilot in the Royal Navy, after all, and although his status as heir to the throne kept him out of combat, he had trained as a soldier and flown in real-life rescue missions. She followed it with a smiling group photo, her arms around the soldiers' shoulders, just to prove there were no hard feelings.

Once upon a time—twelve months and a lifetime ago—she'd shared any image that caught her eye on Instagram, dashing off posts without even checking her spelling. After the news broke that she was seeing Hugh, she went from fifteen thousand followers to almost a million in twenty-four hours. As the media's excitement rose to a fever pitch, reporters relentlessly dissected every single image and word in the search for clues, and she quickly gave up on reading and responding to the thousands of comments and DMs. When old posts with old boyfriends started making the rounds online, she scrambled to delete them, and long before their engagement was officially announced, she went dark entirely and deleted her account. Jeremy Legrand assured her she would be able to resume "Tweeting on Instagram" after the wedding—from a palace-vetted account already reserved under the handle @kensingtonroyal—but she was in no hurry.

The only way she shared photos now was by texting.

Taking Stirling Lines by storm, Hugh answered with a laughing emoji. *I believe they say "Attagirl" in the States?*

Jennie sent him a kiss emoji. He sent back two kisses, a wink, and an eggplant. She laughed and put in her earbuds. In the left-hand front seat, Ian O'Rourke was hunched over his phone, typing furiously with two thumbs, making her panic for a moment—*Watch the road!*—but in the right-hand front seat, Rodney was alertly steering the car down a narrow, two-lane highway flanked by flat green fields with gentle hills in the distance. With three hours to kill before they reached London, it was as good a time as any to check in with Karen. She opened her favorites and touched *Mom*.

"Hello?" Her mom was panting slightly, and a metallic clatter in the background told Jennie she had just returned her shopping cart to the corral at the Hy-Vee on North Orange Prairie Road.

"Mom? I just got abducted," said Jennie, trying to keep the smile out of her voice.

In the rearview mirror, Rodney's eyes crinkled as he got the joke.

"WHAT!?" Karen screeched, no doubt turning every head in the parking lot.

"Kidding!" Jennie reassured her. "I'm headed home from this crazy training exercise where they did a mock kidnapping and shot off a bunch of guns. I guess the idea is that I won't panic if something really does go wrong, but honestly, they just made me realize how many different things I have to worry about."

"I still can't believe you scared me like that," said Karen. "You almost gave me a heart attack."

"Sorry. But at least now you've had some practice at getting bad news, right?"

Jennie heard a *ding ding ding* before Karen's car door slammed and the background noise cut out. There was a jingle of keys as she started the car.

"You know, Princess Penelope had to do the same thing," said Karen, her voice sounding like it was coming through a long cardboard tube. "All the royals did, except King Edmund, who got a note from Queen Alexandra—he was only a prince then—saying he didn't have to do it."

"Mom, I can barely hear you!" Jennie practically shouted, before mouthing an apology to Rodney. "You're not on Bluetooth or even speaker."

Karen talked on for a moment before getting her audio straightened out. "Sorry, hon. Is this better? Can you hear me now?"

"For better or for worse, yes."

"Penelope's training went wrong, you know. They set off some kind of a hand grenade, which was supposed to explode without hurting anybody, and it set her hair on fire."

"Well, I still have all my hair," Jennie reassured her.

How did her mom's mind have room for all this stuff?

"I'm surprised the royal family wanted you to do it before the wedding," said Karen while a nearby car honked, hopefully not at her. "Penelope didn't have to do it until afterward."

Jennie watched the Herefordshire countryside rolling past

her window, impressed by the way the carefully cropped hedge between highway and field seemed to stretch for miles. Then she decided to tell her.

"They moved mine up because I got a sketchy note. Apparently hand-delivered."

For once, Karen didn't say anything right away. Then she asked, "What did it say?"

Jennie told her.

Again, Karen fell silent. Jennie pictured her rolling up 91 toward Dunlap, hands at ten and two, leaning forward as she scanned the side streets and driveways, ready to stomp the brakes the second she saw a car nosing out. Due to her excessive caution, she had been rear-ended three times—that Jennie knew about.

"I'm going to go out on a limb and guess it was anonymous," said her mom, finally.

"Naturally."

"What did Prince Hugh say?"

"It's okay to just call him Hugh, Mom. I didn't tell him."

Karen's voice was incredulous. "But why not?"

Jennie took a deep breath. "When he, you know, *punched* that photographer in Birmingham . . . he has these really bad memories of people being mean to his mom. If he does something like that when someone just calls me a name . . . I hate keeping things from him, but I have to be strong for him, too. He's under so much pressure all the time anyway, just being him."

"Well, when you told security or whoever, what did *they* say?"

"That threats are pretty common, unfortunately."

Karen's voice got suddenly sharper, warier. "Who's in the car with you now?"

"Rodney and Ian."

"Should we even be talking about this on the phone? Pretend we're talking about something else."

"Got it. And I agree, I don't think you're ever too old to start trying sex toys."

"Jennie!" said Karen, aghast.

"Sorry. I thought we could both use a laugh."

"Listen to me. Now that you're living in the palace, you can talk to the people who knew Penelope. I'll bet Princess Cecilia knows all kinds of stuff that never made it into the tabloids. And, of course, Kitty Crowden was her best friend, although I seriously doubt you'll run into *her*. She pretty much disappeared from royal circles after Penelope died. Some people say she was paid to keep quiet."

"Mom," groaned Jennie. "Too much."

Four thousand miles away, the Jensen garage door rolled up with a familiar shudder, and Scooter, the family's Airedale, started barking in the yard. He'd been a puppy when Jennie was a junior in high school and leaving him behind was the hardest thing about putting Peoria in the rearview mirror. At that moment, Jennie would have given almost anything for a slobbery dog kiss, despite Scooter's legendarily bad breath.

"I'm just saying you might want to ask around," said Karen, raising her voice over the dog and putting her phone on speaker. "Everybody over there has their own agenda. Princess Penelope learned that the hard way."

With promises to talk again soon, they ended the call.

"Rodney, would you mind pulling over when you get a chance? I think I have the munchies."

"Of course, Miss Jensen."

Her mom's grocery run and mental images from home had induced a sudden craving for junk food. Of course, she wouldn't be able to go in and pick it out herself—that small pleasure had been off the table ever since a quick raid on the convenience store turned into a photo spread under the headline HUGH'S SWEETHEART CRAVES SALTY SNACKS, complete with a detailed breakdown on her fashion choices (yoga pants and a T-shirt on that particular day) and dietary choices (was she still even a vegan?). Bad lighting and a strange camera angle made the bag of "crisps" she was carrying look big enough to feed a family of four—and when she'd escaped the cell phone cameras to finally enjoy her plunder, she'd been crestfallen to discover she'd accidentally purchased roast beef flavored chips. While the amount of meat they contained could probably be measured on the head of a pin, she'd thrown the unopened bag in the trash.

Swallowing a sigh, she spoke to Rodney again. "On second thought, skip it. I'll just wait until we get back."

Princess Penelope

11 AUGUST 1985

Penelope could hardly wait for Hugh to see the lop-eared bunnies, baby goats, miniature pigs, and tiny quail in the makeshift petting zoo that had been set up in the south garden. Hugh adored animals, loved to be around other children, and, like his father, relished being the center of attention. But if he took after her at all, his first taste of cake was going to blow his mind.

Truth be told, she was probably more excited about Hugh's first birthday celebration than he would be. *Progress*, as her therapist would have said—had she not sacked him for sharing her progress reports with the palace.

Cece appeared beside her on the terrace with two cups of coffee.

"Where's our little birthday monarch-to-be?" she asked, handing one to Penelope.

"Fashionably late."

She'd called the party for ten o'clock to allow ample time for play and a birthday luncheon between Hugh's morning and afternoon naps. The weather had cooperated with a bluebird day. The guests, too, had arrived promptly, and now family, close friends, and trusted staff with young children were scattered about the garden enjoying the various amusements. If only Hugh hadn't thrown a spanner in the works by slumbering past his normal waking time.

"That's a bit cheeky," said Cece.

Penelope assumed she was referring to Hugh until she realized Cece was looking up at the banners strung across the trellises. Gold-on-white letters proclaimed:

All Hail the Birthday Boy!

You're #1!

A third banner simply featured a baby boy with crowns on either side.

"A bit over the top?" Penelope asked, bracing for a cutting remark.

"No more than hiring a petting zoo, balloon animal artist, and a bubble station for a first birthday."

"When I realized we'd have nearly two dozen youngsters I thought—"

Just then, Pebbles Rock, London's most sought-after birthday party trio, launched into a loud and spirited rendition of "If We Could Talk to the Animals."

Penelope cringed. "Oh, dear. I've overdone it, haven't I?"

"It's all good fun. Just look at dear Princess Alice. She seems quite enamored with the miniature horse," Cece deadpanned.

"You're awful," said Penelope, unable to suppress a giggle.

"If it was good enough for Catherine the Great—"

Cece's son Rex trotted past, his brown locks flopping into his eyes. "Look, Mummy! The clown made us balloon guns!"

"Pow, pow!" shouted his twin brother, Will, following behind.

"Don't shoot any guests, just each other," Cece scolded them. "Over there, where you won't run any of the little ones over."

She pointed them to a patch of open grass. Nearby, Edmund was teaching Eleanora Osborne-Webb's daughter Anabelle how to play croquet.

"The secret to raising boys is having them do their monstrous little deeds off to the side," confided Cece.

"I'll have to keep that in mind."

Penelope was certain her angelic, blue-eyed, inquisitive Hugh would be nothing like his raucous cousins.

Cece looked both ways before reaching surreptitiously into her blouse and removing a small silver flask. "And here's my top parenting tip."

"But it isn't even eleven yet," Penelope protested, as Cece poured whiskey into both their coffees.

"Late in the day, but we'll have to make do."

"I don't know that this is—"

"Isn't Queen Al scheduled to make an appearance?"

Penelope nodded, unable to refer to their royal mother-in-law as Al, Allie, Alex, or Lexie despite how amusing it was when Cece did. "Her Majesty will only be popping by. I hope Hugh is finally up and about when she arrives."

"Cheers." Cece touched her coffee cup to Penelope's.

Penelope had always hated the taste of whiskey, but the coffee and cream tamped down the old-shoe flavor enough that the extremely Irish coffee slid smoothly down her throat. Even since she'd stopped breastfeeding, she hadn't consumed anything more than the occasional half glass of wine with dinner, and the tingling warmth did feel good in her belly.

She felt even better when the door to the service stairs opened, and the nanny stepped out carrying a well-rested, bright-eyed Hugh. Adorable in his customary "uniform" of navy shorts, white shirt with matching piping, and buckle shoes, he saw the commotion and squealed in delight. The guests on the terrace and in the garden clapped and whistled.

"Here's to the birthday boy!" called Jeremy Legrand, whose son and daughter were somewhere in the petting zoo.

The nanny set Hugh down on the grass and the crowd *ooh*ed and *ahh*ed as he came toddling toward Penelope.

"Darling!" Penelope said, sweeping him up in a hug.

Hugh wriggled out of her arms and stared at the musicians, fascinated. Then, to everyone's delight, he began bobbing to the beat.

Kitty Crowden touched Penelope's arm and smiled wistfully. "Could he be any more precious?"

"I expect I'll be saying the same thing to you before long."

Her best friend had recently gotten married, and Penelope hoped they would have children close enough in age to be friends.

Finished dancing, Hugh began toddling in the direction of the soap bubble machine.

"And the chase is on!" Penelope's favorite pink suede Escada flats sank into the grass as she followed behind.

Hugh stopped in the midst of a group of children. After watching his older, more experienced peers for a moment, he reached his chubby hands to the sky. A glistening bubble landed on his right index finger, quivered, and then burst. Penelope was worried he might cry, but instead, he seemed delighted.

"Pop!" he said, clear as a bell.

"Nicely done!" Penelope said.

"Pop!"

"A new word?" Eleanora Osborne-Webb asked, standing just outside the scrum of children.

"I'm so excited," said Penelope, knowing she was gushing. "He's only said *Mum* and *Da* until today."

"Graham didn't say a word until he was almost two," said Eleanora, turning to watch her daughter swing wildly at a croquet ball. "Anabelle started early, however, and continues to share her every opinion."

"Pop, pop, pop!" chortled Hugh.

Penelope lifted her cherubic son into her arms and started across the lawn. "Want to tell Daddy your new word?"

Maybe she was overdoing things a bit, but the party was obviously a great success, her son was in utter bliss, and everyone was besotted by him and his abilities. It was the birthday party she'd dreamed of. On the croquet pitch, her husband was lining up a shot as though he were on the eighteenth green at St. Andrew's. Knowing better than to interrupt, she waited for him to tap the croquet ball with his yellow-striped mallet before she spoke.

"Edmund, our Hugh is absolutely loving his party. He's run and danced and broken bubbles. He's even got a new word!"

"Good man!" Edmund patted Hugh on the head before returning his attention to the game. "Now, Anabelle, you'll want to get through the hoop in order to take another shot."

"Can you say *pop* for daddy?" Penelope prompted.

Hugh stuffed three fingers into his mouth.

She tried another tack. "Want to learn to play croquet, Hugh?"

"I can't wait until he's old enough," Edmund said.

"It won't be long, given how coordinated he is. Everyone is so impressed that he is already walking and dancing."

"When Mr. Clifford and his son Sebastian join us, you must

try to make your ball hit one of theirs," Edmund coached Anabelle, still keenly involved in the lesson. "It earns our team two
extra shots and really is the fun of croquet."

"Before you start, maybe you'd like to watch Hugh pet the
animals? Anabelle, have you had a chance to see the baby bunnies or the Pygmy goats?"

Edmund sniffed dismissively. "Animals are no novelty to
Anabelle. She lives in the country."

"We have lots of babies in the barn right now," added Anabelle, in a notably similar tone. "They're very cute except they
poo everywhere."

"I was just hoping we might get a family photo before Hugh
is covered in birthday cake."

Edmund's expression softened. "Oh, yes, of course. I see."

It had taken time to learn how to approach Edmund effec-
tively, but she was learning how to go about it.

Then Digby Clifford shouted, "Shall we make it more fun
with a friendly wager?" as he and his son approached.

Before Edmund could inform his friend about the brief
delay, a hush rippled through the garden. Every adult and
school-age child noted the change in the air and stopped what
they were doing. Even the band quit playing midsong. The only
sounds were chirping birds, a braying donkey, and one crying
baby as the Queen joined the gathering wearing her casual,
family-only outfit of a blouse, slacks, cardigan, and of course,
pearls. She nodded at the partygoers on the terrace, all of whom
hastily set down coffees and pastries to bow or curtsey. With a
wave, she gave the musicians their cue to resume.

"Mum will want her grandson's undivided attention and
that of the baby animals, not necessarily in that order," predicted Edmund.

As if proving his point, Her Majesty beelined toward the

petting zoo, hardly pausing to greet the guests, urging them to carry on *as you were.*

Edmund was already withdrawing. "I'll be over after Anabelle and I hand the Clifford men a stinging defeat."

Penelope was disappointed but knew it was futile to press him further. "Want to go see Gram, Hugh?"

"Gram!" Hugh exclaimed.

"Brilliant." Edmund pecked him on the cheek and turned back to his game.

Penelope made her way across the garden and greeted her mother-in-law with a curtsey made awkward by Hugh's weight. "So lovely to see you."

As she reached for Hugh, the Queen wrinkled her famously sensitive nose. "Are alcoholic drinks on the menu this morning?"

"Would you like one?" Penelope asked, willing her cheeks not to color.

While protocol did not forbid an occasional morning Buck's fizz, the Queen's tone made it clear that morning whiskey was a poor choice for the wife of the future king and the mother of the heir.

"That won't be necessary," the Queen said. "I don't have long and I would like to spend the time I do have with the birthday boy."

With that, Penelope's mother-in-law, the monarch, turned peremptorily and carried her most important grandson toward the animal enclosure.

Her hopes for a family moment now firmly dashed, Penelope excused herself and walked swiftly inside. *Alcohol on your breath* was a lecture she didn't care to endure from Edmund, or worse, one of the Queen's gray-suited surrogates.

Bypassing the lavatory in the entry hall, Penelope climbed the stairs to her private loo. There, she used the toilet, touched up her makeup, and then brushed her teeth vigorously. She gargled with minty mouthwash for thirty seconds, just to be sure.

She had just started down the back staircase when unfamiliar voices echoed up from the first-floor landing, probably the extra staff borrowed from Buckingham Palace for the morning.

"And did you see her hair?"

"Exactly the same shade of brown and just as wavy as his."

"Pretty little thing."

"That she is, but he shouldn't stand so close beside her."

"How else do you teach your bastard daughter to play croquet?"

Penelope swallowed hard as they both laughed.

His bastard daughter?

The words landed like stones in her stomach. In the three years since she'd married Edmund, they'd both been the subjects of vicious rumors: *Prince Edmund's Secret Gay Lover! Was Penelope Really a Virgin?* While they sometimes contained small kernels of truth—an innocent boarding school experiment by Edmund; Penelope snogging her former beau—this claim was as revolting as *Impotent Edmund Will Rely on Freddie to Produce the Heir.* Everyone knew Eleanora Osborne-Webb had always harbored a crush on Edmund. Her husband Jonathan even looked like him, not nearly as handsome, of course, but with the same brown, wavy hair. Certainly, their physical similarities explained this preposterous rumor about Anabelle's appearance.

Penelope's confidence only grew after she rejoined the party and spotted Eleanora herself. Unlike Vivienne, or any of the other beauties who caused Penelope legitimate concern, Eleanora was plain. Even when dressed in her formal best, no matter how plunging the neckline or bejeweled the gown, she looked every inch the dowdy country toff. Today's casual look of riding breeches, leather boots, and a lace blouse only accentuated her generous hips and ample bum.

Not possible, Penelope thought as she accepted a fresh cup of coffee, adding cream and extra sugar. When she looked up, she saw Anabelle and Edmund walking together toward the petting zoo. Their hair, dappled by sunlight, was precisely the same color and texture.

So was their posture.

And their gait.

"If you're worrying about Allie's reaction to your party, don't," Cece said, sidling up beside her. "She said, and I quote, 'What a delightful menagerie of little animals.' From her, that's a torrent of praise."

"Noted, thank you," Penelope managed to say, meanwhile wishing she could ask the Queen's opinion of her favorite lamb's premarital rutting.

Instead, she decided to undo all the work she'd put into brushing and gargling.

"Do you have any of that whiskey left?" she asked.

Chapter Twelve

VERITAS VINCIT

"Taringa whakarongo!"

"Kia rite! Kia rite! Kia mau!"

"Hī!"

From her seat on the sideline at the Quaycentre Arena in Sydney's Olympic Park, Jennie watched, transfixed, as the New Zealand wheelchair rugby team, the Wheel Blacks, faced off against the United States. Leading the haka, a traditional Māori dance with call-and-response chanting, the Wheel Blacks's captain bellowed at his teammates, who pounded their gloved hands against their wheels as they answered in unison.

"Ringa ringa pākia!" he exhorted them. *"Waewae takahia kia kino nei hoki!"*

"Kia kino nei hoki!" came the reply.

Jennie had seen videos of Māori warriors performing the haka and understood that it was more than simply a war dance, but that was about all she knew—and she had never seen one in person. The crowd's rapt attention and the athletes' focused intensity made her shiver.

"Ka mate, ka mate!"

"Ka ora' Ka ora'!"

Jennie wished she could understand what the words meant, but even without knowing, the ritual brought a sense of something ancient, primal, and real into the sterile confines of the arena. The players' taut bodies and ferocious game faces reflected their full commitment to something more than the match they were about to play, and even more than the country they represented. As they roared the final lines in unison, Jennie felt her eyes welling with tears. For reasons she would not have been able to explain, it was one of the most moving things she'd ever seen.

"I rather fancy the one with the topknot, don't you?" said Cecilia, Duchess of York, murmuring her approval. "I know he's in a chair and all, but that doesn't mean anything. I've heard you can't tell whether their wedding tackle works or not just because they're handicapped."

"He's cute," Jennie agreed, startled by the tactless comment but deciding it was probably best to keep her answer diplomatic.

All around them the crowd laughed and applauded after one of the Wheel Blacks rolled forward to aggressively bump the chair of a US player. The Yank seemed slightly confused by the challenge but high-fived the Kiwi anyway to show there were no hard feelings.

"A bit too brawny to be *cute*," said Cece.

Jennie hoped she wasn't going to keep it up through the whole game. Hugh was in Sydney Harbor, presiding over a sailing race from the deck of the royal yacht, so Jennie had been dispatched to lend some sparkle to the land-based events. As Hugh had put it, *We're spread thin as jam on toast.* Cece was supposed to be attending the archery rounds but had changed her mind at the last minute, telling Jennie, "The rugby players are so much more compelling to watch." Jennie wouldn't have dreamed of disobeying orders herself but had learned that Prince

Freddie's silver-haired wife exercised her royal prerogative with a frequency that exhausted her minders.

Truthfully, Jennie was so tired she thought she was about to start hallucinating. After leaving the warm breezes of an English spring, she had flown nearly ten thousand miles in twenty-four hours to arrive in late-autumn Australia. Sydney was nine hours ahead of London, and even after two days, her jet lag was still so bad it would be a miracle if she didn't face-plant onto her dinner plate. The only reason she hadn't yet was the adrenaline boost provided by the Unconquered Games, a competition founded by Hugh for disabled veterans from around the world. The sports and games, which included indoor rowing, weightlifting, cycling, sitting volleyball, wheelchair basketball, and even driving, were fascinating and inspiring. Maybe what had made the war chant so moving was the fact that it had been chanted by actual warriors.

At the referee's whistle, the teams began playing hard, propelling their chairs with pistoning, muscular arms and moving the oblong ball down the court with quick, accurate passes. And if Jennie had been unable to translate the words of the haka, she was even more out of her depth when it came to rugby—she hardly knew the rules of American football. But it was her job to look interested, and cameras could be trained on her at any time, so she watched carefully, taking her cues from the crowd. When they *ooh*ed, she *ooh*ed, and when they applauded, she did too, trying to match their level of enthusiasm.

Cece seemed more interested in the players than the game. She and Jennie were so close to the substitutes that they could have reached out and touched them—and when Cece said, "Excuse me," to the nearest one, Jennie was momentarily afraid that that was what the duchess had in mind.

The long-haired player, who had been focused on the game, turned around in surprise.

"Can you tell me where you got your injury?" Cece asked blithely.

"In the legs," he said with a wink. Then he added, with perfect timing, "In Iraq."

Cece furrowed her brow in apparent concern. "Does it still hurt?"

He grinned. "Only when I salute, ma'am."

"We thank you for your service," Cece told him, her words almost drowned out as the crowd went wild for an early New Zealand goal.

"You're good at this," Jennie told her after the player had turned around.

"To paraphrase one of my forbears, as a member of the royal family, you learn never to be tired and to love spending time in hospitals. But there's no trick to it. People do like to be asked about themselves. Ask a few questions and they'll say you have the common touch."

"I'll keep that in mind," said Jennie.

"Not that you'll have much time to sit and listen to their answers, mind you."

When the US team scored the next goal, the cheers weren't quite as loud as they'd been for New Zealand—the games were taking place in the Commonwealth, after all—but the crowd seemed determined to support both sides.

Jennie and Cece may have been close to the players, but they were isolated from the crowd, enclosed in something that resembled a luxurious penalty box with upholstered chairs and buffed parquet tea tables. The plexiglass dividers behind them rose high enough to ensure that no peanuts could be tossed by the gallery.

"I'm glad you decided to join me today," said Jennie, trying to make conversation.

Cece chuckled and turned her pearl bracelet around her wrist.

"I do prefer the rugby. I do wish Freddie had found the time to come. He's a veteran himself—although his only war injury was pricking his hand on a corkscrew off the Falkland Islands."

Jennie was suddenly reminded of something Karen had once told her about Cece—that she had taught Penelope how to drink whiskey.

That particular lesson didn't end well, her mother said. *Cece has to know all sorts of amazing stuff that never made it into the tabloids.*

Reminders of Hugh's mother were not limited to the photos and pillows and secret messages hidden in her old apartment, Jennie reflected. The people she met carried memories of her inside them, too. Penelope had been a part of the lives of so many people still living: friends, lovers, and enemies. But who was which?

"Were you close to Princess Penelope?" Jennie asked.

"An excellent question," said Cece, watching intently as the Wheel Blacks moved the ball downfield. "See? You're learning already."

"But you didn't answer it."

Cece leaned forward in her seat. "I see my reputation as a gossip precedes me."

Jennie's face felt hot. As usual, she had stepped out of bounds without realizing it. "I'm so sorry, Duchess. It's just, I keep thinking that if I understood Hugh's world a little bit better—"

Cece jumped to her feet, along with the rest of the crowd, to cheer what was apparently a particularly skillful goal by the Wheel Blacks. Jennie hadn't seen it but stood up anyway, trying to mimic Cece's genteel handclaps.

"Lovely, just lovely," said Cece.

"Obviously, I know things can be more complicated than they look," said Jennie, assuming the conversation had reached a dead end.

Cece was silent as they sat down again, her eyes roving the

floor as the New Zealand team restarted play by launching the ball onto the US side of the floor.

Then she said, "Well, it certainly wasn't fair, what happened to Penelope. She had one teeny, tiny affair while they were together—really, nothing more than a romp with the stable boy—and they crucified her for it. Meanwhile, Edmund was behaving as men do. With some vigor, I might add."

So her mother had been right. Jennie didn't know how to respond.

"I'm sure it seems quite bizarre to a young thing like you, but he was the future king and those were the times. Boys were allowed to be boys back then. Still are, actually, but at least girls are allowed to be girls now, too."

"That hasn't exactly been my experience," said Jennie, flushing hotter this time, seeing the headlines as though they had been burned onto the insides of her eyelids.

Cece cocked her head and glanced sideways at her like a rare and royal bird. "No, I daresay it hasn't. Probably Penelope's biggest problem was she was always moaning about how difficult it all was for her. She of all people should have understood what she was getting herself into. She grew up orbiting the royal family and her grasping parents certainly groomed her for the role. She ought to have known the crown is ultimately loyal only to itself—self-preservation being its highest aim."

The more Jennie learned about Penelope's life, the easier it was to imagine her mindset when she hid that unmailed letter in her apartment in Kensington Palace. If she *felt* watched and lied to, that was because she *was* watched and lied to. Her comings and goings were reported by everyone from tabloid hacks to the footmen who were suddenly mute when it came to their future king. In the middle of all that, it would take an iron will to *keep calm and carry on.*

And were the secrets and lies limited to Penelope and Edmund's affairs, or were there bigger secrets being kept?

"What did you mean by 'crucified'?" asked Jennie.

Cece's smile faded. "A poor choice of words on my part. But there are always consequences for misbehavior. I hear you've been called in front of the Right Honorable Jeremy Legrand yourself."

Jennie wished it was only for not wearing pantyhose. Even though she was now, and would always be, faithful to Hugh, she had already created several PR problems for the royal family simply by being herself.

"Not for anything like that," she said.

"When you upset the men in grey, your dirty secrets have a way of tunneling under the palace walls," said Cece. "And that is all I'll say about *that*."

Penelope would have had so few people she could trust. How would she have even known who was a friend?

"You and Penelope were friends, right?"

"Of course."

"What about Vivienne Banfield-March?"

"I recently learned the term *frenemy* from my son. I believe it applies. Penelope was curiously close with our favorite journalist, Kenneth Davies, though I don't know if that qualifies as friendship."

"Is Kitty Crowden still around? I haven't met her."

"She may as well be in the Outer Hebrides, even though she's only living in Devonshire. I understand she's quite happy gardening, throwing pots, and judging the local flower show. The intrigue at court was never that one's cup of tea."

Two players competing for a ball collided and the crowd gasped as their chairs flipped over. The US player quickly righted himself, but the New Zealand player lay still, swearing loudly. As trainers ran onto the floor with a medical bag, the crowd fell into a respectful, uneasy silence.

A minute later, the Wheel Blacks player, his face bloodied, pumped a fist as he was lifted upright again. The crowd applauded. On the other side of the floor, the press photographers stood and clicked their shutters furiously, capturing the moment—except for one, whose long-lensed camera was aimed straight at Jennie, recording *her* reaction to the athlete's recovery.

Jennie's irrational impulse was to flip him off. How dare he take *her* picture when she wasn't the story?

But she knew what to do. She clapped her hands briskly, hoping her face showed her relief that the player was okay.

Because that was how a princess would play it.

Chapter Thirteen

AT THE RACES

"It's like *Mary Poppins* with all these top hats," said Jennie. "I keep expecting Dick Van Dyke to jump out of a chimney and start singing."

"Believe me, even Dick Van Dyke would have had a difficult time obtaining entry, Miss Jensen, and *his* English accent was slightly better than yours," said Poppy. "Now *stop gawking*. As you learned in Sydney, you're one of the attractions."

Jennie tried to model regal serenity as she followed Poppy away from the parade ring at Ascot Racecourse, but it just didn't work. Every time someone in the crowd even glanced at her, she felt obligated to smile back with what one royal watcher had dubbed her "goofy American grin."

Minutes earlier, under low clouds spitting occasional raindrops, they had watched a procession of horse-drawn carriages with red-jacketed drivers whirl the royal family around a small oval in front of an applauding crowd. Legrand had made it clear that, as a mere fiancée, Jennie was not yet assigned a seat next to Hugh, so Sidney had come up with a compromise in which she blew him a kiss from the reviewing stands when he passed—a photo op everyone agreed would be catnip to the press.

It had all gone according to plan. After watching the King and Queen roll past in the first carriage with the King and Queen of the Netherlands, Jennie waved at Hugh to catch his eye before blowing a somewhat theatrical kiss as he passed in the second carriage with Princess Alice, Prince Freddie, and Jennie's new BFF Duchess Cece. His charming wink made her feel only slightly less ridiculous. The third carriage contained Rex and William, Freddie and Cece's sons, and their respective spouses. Poppy had whisked Jennie away before the carriages containing nonroyal VIPs completed their circuit. A far more important meeting awaited in the royal box overlooking the racetrack, where photographers would record a "five-minute standing audience" with Edmund and Eleanora before the first race of the day.

When discussing their June calendars weeks earlier, Hugh had mentioned the Royal Ascot, and Jennie had asked, "Is that some kind of hereditary neckwear?"

He had been flabbergasted. "You really don't know, do you? That's a bit like me thinking the Indianapolis 500 is an American terrorist group."

From Hugh, Poppy, and Wikipedia, Jennie had since learned that the racing grounds were dedicated by Queen Anne in 1711, and dozens of other facts she quickly forgot. What struck her most was the stratification of the various spectator "enclosures": the Royal, with a dress code of "morning dress" (top hat and tails) for men and "formal daywear" (tea-length dresses, big hats) for the women, required applications and character references before earning an invite from His Majesty; the slightly less stuffy Queen Anne allowed men to dress down in regular suits and women to wear smaller hats; and the Windsor was open to the public with no dress code whatsoever. At this most traditional of British events, the most celebrated tradition was class structure.

"Do keep up, Miss Jensen!" urged Poppy, leading the way through the Royal Enclosure toward the main stands, which were draped in massive Union Jacks.

Jennie quickened her step. There were no shrieks or signs today, and only a few surreptitious selfies capturing her in the background. But no matter how much everyone pretended to focus on their champagne flutes, lobster rolls, and betting slips, the elegant racegoers were clearly aware of her presence. Rodney, looking uncomfortable in his top hat and tailcoat, trailed at a discreet distance as the crowd parted for them like a black, gray, and navy blue sea.

Not to say that Jennie wasn't photo ready. Underneath a sun hat as broad as a saucer sled, she was dressed like a sexy schoolmarm in a dress with lace bodice detailing and sheer, cuffed sleeves, knotted at the throat with an extravagant bow. The tulle skirt ended at her pantyhosed midcalf, showing periwinkle pumps that had been flawlessly dyed to match.

Before setting out, Jennie had texted a picture to Hugh, who replied with a bare-chested selfie. *You're overdressed.*

That had made her bite her lip. And press her knees together.

"I hope nobody expects me to know anything about horse racing," said Jennie as they entered the grandstand below the rippling flags. "What do I say if the King asks me about horses?"

"What every man wants to hear: What do *you* think?"

Jennie laughed. For someone who knew her curtseys to the inch, Poppy was wonderfully down to earth.

Now striding ahead, Rodney escorted them through a security checkpoint and stood guard as they stepped into a cozy private elevator staffed by a liveried operator. Moments later, the doors opened and two policemen, looking just as uncomfortable in their top hats and tails as Rodney, stepped aside so they could enter the royal box. A footman was waiting with a drinks-laden silver tray. Poppy lifted a tall glass and handed it to Jennie.

"Are you sure you can't stay to watch the race with me?" Jennie asked.

Poppy grinned. "Alas, no, milady. Once the King makes his appearance, I'm off to meet friends in the Windsor Enclosure."

"Oh. I'm sorry."

"I'm not. You're lovely company, but I'll be having much more fun. You'd be surprised at what goes on down there—fist-fights, some years!"

As they made their way out to the veranda, Jennie examined her drink. It looked like ruby-colored iced tea stuffed with a fruit salad and topped with sprigs of basil.

"Pimm's cup," Poppy explained. "Also quite popular at Wimbledon."

"Is that . . . cucumber?"

"Our national fruit. Drink. It will settle your nerves."

Jennie took a gulp and almost spit it back into the glass. It was light and bubbly, slightly herbal, and far too sweet for someone who did her best to avoid sugar.

"Can I just get a beer?"

"Not with cameras en route. We want the headlines to be about your amazing outfit, not your plebeian taste in drinks. Would you prefer champagne?"

"That works."

While Poppy hurried off to replace her glass, Jennie stepped outside and caught her breath as the scene below came into view. Throngs of exquisitely costumed racegoers lined a racetrack covered in a carpet of greenest grass—the complete opposite of the hoof-churned mud she had pictured. The inner part of the oval was tented with pavilions and still more spectators, and beyond them all, the tree-covered British countryside rose gently toward the horizon.

Poppy returned with her champagne. "Jeremy just texted. The King and Queen Consort are entering the secured area."

A photographer and his assistant appeared as if from no-where, avoiding eye contact as they prepped their cameras. Her casual encounter with the King and Queen had been planned with military precision. Although Jennie would not be watching the actual race within camera frame of the royal family, this "off the cuff" chitchat was considered the next battle in the ground war for Operation Public Acceptance.

Jennie gulped champagne as Poppy gave her last-minute instructions. "Try not to think of him as a monarch but your fiancé's slightly stuffy dad—only you do have to curtsey to him and call him 'Your Majesty.' Once your five minutes are up, make your way to your seat and cheer for your horse like the world is watching."

"How will I know when it's been five minutes?"

"Trust me, you'll know. Do you need a refill?"

Jennie looked at her glass. It was two-thirds empty.

"In the photos, you should either have a full glass or be empty handed," said Poppy.

"I don't want to spill when I curtsey," said Jennie, surrendering her glass. "Are you sure you can't stay?"

She was feeling flushed and flustered, despite all of Poppy's careful prep and attagirls. Her previous meetings with the King had all been private. Why did every encounter have so much riding on it?

Poppy pressed a full glass of champagne into her hand.

"Can't hurt," she whispered. "Make sure you don't curtsey too deeply."

Then she slipped away as a footman announced, "His Majesty, the King!"

Jennie waited outside, along with the photographers, watching the bubbles rise to the surface of her glass and resisting the urge to swallow it all. Her hand was shaking slightly, and she wouldn't have put it past herself to drop the delicate flute just as the King and Queen arrived. It seemed to take a long time for the royal party to make its way through the well-wishers inside—but kings rushed for no one, she supposed.

Finally, he stepped out with the serene air of a man who knows the world truly does revolve around him. He was accompanied by Queen Eleanora, the King and Queen of the Netherlands, a tall balding man with a hawkish nose, and Hugh, who was lurking in the back with a sheepish grin.

Jennie astonished herself by executing a perfect curtsey without spilling a drop of champagne. "Your Majesty."

"Lovely to see you, Miss Jensen," said King Edmund, barely moving his mouth. Jennie wondered, not for the first time, whether a *stiff upper lip* was a literal British affliction.

"Your Majesty," said Jennie, curtseying again to Eleanora.

"May I present King Willem and Queen Maud of Netherlands," said Eleanora. "Miss Jennifer Jensen, Prince Hugh's fiancée."

"Your Majesty, Your Majesty," said Jennie, wobbling on the fourth curtsey and wondering if her luck was about to run out.

"You are perfectly lovely," said Queen Maud, stepping forward and warmly kissing Jennie on both cheeks. "We are so pleased to meet you."

Jennie was grateful for her warmth, but before she could say anything in return, King Edmund was introducing the tall man.

"You should know my dear friend, Marquess Felix Hill, MP."

"Your Lordship," said Jennie, offering her hand.

The fact that she had remembered what to call him, and not to curtsey, surprised her again. Maybe Poppy's training was finally paying off. Although she could have been imagining it, she thought she saw approval flicker across King Edmund's face.

Lord Hill bent at the waist and grazed her knuckles with paper-dry lips. "Charmed, I'm sure."

"Darling," said Hugh, sliding in beside her without kissing her or putting his arm around her waist.

"Well, don't you look lovely today, Miss Jensen," said Eleanora.

"Two kings and two queens—we almost have a full deck," blurted Jennie.

In the silence that followed, she wasn't sure what had come over her, other than bottled-up nerves colliding with a sincere desire to break the ice. Fortunately, King Edmund and Lord Hill laughed, giving everyone else permission to do the same.

"I like this one, Edmund!" said Lord Hill, before asking Jennie, "And do you have much horse racing in Illinois?"

The reference to her home state caught Jennie off guard. Then again, a million people who had never heard of her a year ago now knew lots of mundane facts about her.

"I saw a race at the state fair when I was in second grade. All I remember is that my dad lost his bet and one of the horses pooped before the gates opened."

King Edmund chuckled. "You must have had a good seat. Now tell me, which horse do you fancy today?"

Jennie blanked before remembering Poppy's advice. "Oh, I'm not sure, Sir. Which one do you think will win?"

The King took her question seriously, and she listened for the next few minutes—bobbing her head until she felt a little bit dizzy—as he expounded uninterrupted on the strengths and weaknesses of all ten horses in the field. Just when she was strategizing her next conversational gambit, he wished her a pleasant afternoon and it was suddenly over. Only the camera's sudden silence made her realize how rapidly it had been firing.

Felix Hill nodded at Jennie as the kings and queens headed for their velvet-upholstered chairs. "I'm sure we'll be seeing each other again soon, Miss Jensen."

Hugh led her inside, where they stopped in a semi-private area on the other side of a massive pillar. After making sure no one was watching, he kissed her on the lips.

"You were brilliant," he said.

"Really? I felt like a talking mechanical doll."

"Letting the old man go on about horses was a masterstroke. He'll tell me later you're a brilliant conversationalist."

Even though Hugh was wearing the same old-fashioned getup as everyone else, he made it look movie-star sexy. She badly wanted to wrap herself around him but couldn't risk messing up either of their clothes.

"Listen," he said, giving her hand a squeeze. "I'm supposed to chat up our visitors, so make yourself comfortable and I'll come see you as soon as I can. You look good enough to eat, so fair warning."

After another kiss—this one so lingering it almost drove her crazy—he was gone. She watched as he joined the royals in conversation, his effortless manner proving he'd been born to the role.

As Edmund flashed a surprisingly flirtatious smile at Queen Maud, who was almost twenty years younger than him, Jennie recalled what Cece had told her in Sydney: *Meanwhile, Edmund was behaving as men do. With some vigor, I might add.*

Had Eleanora fared any better than poor Penelope? Or was she just better at grinning and bearing it? If Hugh felt awkward about making nice with his stepmother, he never showed it, and their relationship appeared neither warm nor strained. Despite his occasional flashes of temper, his diplomatic nature was one of the traits that made most Britons agree he was well-suited to the throne.

Over the PA, or *tannoy* as she was trying to remember to call it, a voice announced that betting on the first race would close in ten minutes. Despite the party vibe, serious money was still being gambled on the outcome.

Jennie sipped her drink and scanned the room as a familiar-looking woman in her late thirties emerged from the elevator. She'd seen photos of Eleanora's tall, square-shouldered daughter on the mantel. In person, it was clear that the handsome, almost masculine features had become softer and prettier in the second generation.

Caught looking, Jennie smiled, and Anabelle walked over. "We should have met long ago. I'm Anabelle Osbourne-Webb."

"I recognized you," said Jennie.

Anabelle smoothed a wrinkle on the inverted pleat of her otherwise flawless dress. "I can't believe they've left you by yourself. Who else do you know here?"

"Nobody, really, except for Hugh's family."

But almost as soon as she said it, it was no longer true. Turning toward her was Imogen Banfield-March, once again looking like the stunning ex-model she was.

Anabelle followed her gaze.

"Ah, the other Gennie. I hope you show her mercy. After all, you're the victor."

"I was never in competition with her," said Jennie, marveling at the ridiculous phrasing.

"We don't always know who we are fighting against." Anabelle lifted a Pimm's cup from a passing tray. "Her mother Vivienne was the bookmakers' favorite for our dear King before long-shot Penelope suddenly emerged with the bit between her teeth."

"Did Edmund and Vivienne's affair continue?" asked Jennie bluntly.

Anabelle raised an eyebrow. "In the royal box, one doesn't speculate on the King's indiscretions."

"I'm sorry. I'm an idiot."

"With excellent intuition."

"But your mom also . . . emerged victorious."

"True love finds a way," murmured Anabelle. "Enjoy the races."

As Anabelle headed outside, Jennie felt a hand on her arm, turned, and was suddenly staring at slender, ash-blond Vivienne herself. Had she heard anything? She couldn't have—Anabelle would have seen her if she'd been close. Was it possible she'd intended to be overheard?

Vivienne's smile didn't quite reach her eyes. "Jennie! How lovely. I don't believe I've seen you since Birmingham."

Jennie exchanged her glass for a full one, promising herself she would sip it slowly. She was drinking faster than she wanted to, but she needed something to do with her hands.

"Anabelle was just talking about your daughter," she said.

"She does talk," said Vivienne opaquely.

Jennie couldn't help remembering what Vivienne had said in Birmingham. *Imogen will find her prince someday . . . It's much harder for people my age to move on.* Maybe it was due to her third glass of champagne, but suddenly her head was spinning. Were any of these smiling faces sincere?

"Can I ask . . . Imogen is happy, right?" asked Jennie. "I mean, she's not upset with me or anything, is she?"

Vivienne smiled again, still without showing any of her teeth. "Whatever would give you that idea?"

"Well, I know they were very serious. And Hugh's wonderful . . . I just know how I'd feel if . . ."

"Do get a hold of yourself," said the older woman, patting Jennie's arm. "You'll want to pace yourself if you hope to go the distance."

Why did her words sound so much like an echo of, *Penelope couldn't survive here, and neither will you*?

Shaken, Jennie mumbled, "Excuse me, I need to find my

seat before the race," before turning abruptly and practically stumbling outside.

The fresh air helped steady her as she allowed a footman to guide her to her seat. Glancing over at Hugh and his family, she reminded herself she was on camera and couldn't cry, no matter how much she wanted to.

As a girl playing with her dolls, her idea of being a princess was that when she snapped her fingers, other people would have to do what she said. But the royal reality required obedience, an existence of watching from the sidelines—and being *watched* while watching from the sidelines. With so little ability to act freely in public, it was no wonder there was so much scheming behind the scenes. She had stumbled by blind luck into a seat the Banfield-Marches had coveted for two generations. Vivienne had lost her place to Penelope, and Imogen had made way for Jennie. Did mother and daughter have reasons to want both of them gone?

Jennie logged on to the Instagram account she'd recently created and named with a random string of letters so she could look at what other people were posting. Pictures of her at Royal Ascot were already exploding under the hashtags #princessjennie #royalascot #windsorroyal.

At least her outfit was getting good reviews.

From the Private Diary of Princess Penelope

9 OCTOBER 1986
I'm not pregnant again and it's not for lack of trying.
Dr. Smythe has pronounced me fully capable of bearing more children. He says I need to be patient.
I wish he'd say the same to Edmund.
Edmund is to blame for my current situation.

He was the one who urged me to wear something, "with a bit of give at the waist," to the Phantom of the Opera premiere at Her Majesty's Theatre. "It will give the Commonwealth something to be hopeful about," he said.

When I argued against misleading the public, even in such a subtle way, the row that followed was probably heard on Bayswater Road. I was so furious that I gave Edmund more than he'd bargained for by wearing an empire-waist Givenchy gown I'd bought just after we announced my pregnancy with Hugh. The dress is a truly lovely shade of lavender, with a bias-draped bodice and flared sleeves, but I had never worn it precisely because it felt too much like maternity wear.

I had one glass of white wine to calm my nerves whilst I dressed for the evening. One could argue that I should have nibbled on cheese and crackers, but I'd had a late lunch in anticipation of an after-theatre dinner and I wasn't hungry.

I felt fine during the first half of the performance and the intermission, where I drank a single glass of champagne and ate two puff pastries whilst holding a strained conversation with Vivi.

It was in the second act when I began to feel dodgy. Just as the Phantom appeared on the grand staircase wearing the death's head mask to present his new opera, I had to rush out of our box. I was sure I was going to be sick all over the carpet, but Rodney quickly ushered me over to the rubbish bin outside the ladies' WC.

The headlines in the morning tabloid were predictable:

EVENING SICKNESS

IS PRINCESS PENELOPE PREG- GERS?

Edmund was pleased. Delighted really, about the suspiciously convenient bug, bout of food poisoning, or whatever it was that overcame me so suddenly.

Far too suddenly.

I recovered, but questions continue to plague me.

We made no comment on the incident, of course. But as we jetted off for our scheduled holiday in Mustique, the tabloids quoted an anonymous source with first-hand "knowledge" of my "reckless boozing" that evening.

As a result, I have spent the past two weeks trying unsuccessfully to swat mosquitoes, hide from the paparazzi's telephoto lenses targeting my midsection, and ignore the tabloid headlines.

UP THE DUFF AND ON THE BOTTLE

PISSED AND PREGNANT

And the worst:

HAS SHE LOST IT?

Now I am guzzling—strawberry daiquiris— although the alcohol does little to dull my mortification over what Edmund insists is my fault, "for going overboard by wearing that damned dress."

I honestly don't know whether he's referring to the paparazzi, my skewering in the press, or the behind-the-scenes scheming I suspect led to my current predicament.

Was something slipped into my drink? If so, by whom? In addition to Vivi, Felix, Digby, and Clark were all there, although it's not as though any of them were serving. But they could have ordered it done.

Every possibility is more disturbing than the last.

Chapter Fourteen

TAKING THE CAKE

Jennie's phone buzzed with a polite reminder—*Your car is waiting, Miss Jensen*—as she gave herself one last look in the mirror. Her MAC lipstick struck her as just a little bit too nightclub-sexy, so she quickly wiped it off and reapplied a Poppy-approved Charlotte Tilbury matte pink. Fixing an earring that was only halfway in, she skated across the marble floor of her bathroom in slippery panty-hose, then walked into her dressing room and found the clutch and the silk shawl that complemented her cap-sleeved sheath. Slipping into four-inch heels, she stepped carefully into the parlor; despite near daily wear, her mastery of heels was still a work in progress.

She came to a complete stop when she saw what was waiting on the coffee table: a square, gift-wrapped box.

Despite being ten minutes late already, she couldn't resist detouring to inspect the package. Wrapped in royal blue paper and crisscrossed with red and white ribbons, viewed from above it was a perfect Union Jack. There was no card, but she had a pretty good idea who'd had it delivered.

The bow came undone easily when she pulled the ends. Be-neath it, like the Hallmark movie her life had become, the lid was wrapped separately, which allowed her to lift it off the box without tearing the beautiful paper. Inside, cushioned by sparkly white cotton batting, was . . . a cake topper.

But not just any cake topper—a *Hugh and Jennie* cake topper.

Only then did she spot the folded scrap of paper.

Jennie,

Sidney found this action figure in a shop off Tottenham Court Road and thought we should have it. Soon we'll be joined at the hip as well! Looks like lots of people are looking forward to our wedding. But none more than me.

All my love,
Hugh

P.S. Better hang on to this. Someday it will fetch a large sum on eBay.

Public excitement for their July fifteenth wedding wasn't at the fever pitch Karen described when talking about Penelope and Edmund's ceremony, but it had long ago overwhelmed Jennie's naive expectations. Likenesses of herself and Hugh were appearing on T-shirts, hats, aprons, tea towels, drinking glasses, shot glasses, commemorative plates, napkins, lunchboxes, banners, buttons, stickers, party favors, and even underwear. Unbelievably, even the adult film industry was capitalizing on the moment with a video titled *Royals Come Together*, which thankfully did not advertise a threesome. Jennie made a mental note to ask Hugh whether the royal family took a cut of the licensing—not for the porn, obviously—but she knew from experience that merch could be a significant source of income.

The molded plastic groom on the cake topper looked a lot like Hugh, but the most that could be said of the bride was that it also had dark hair. It didn't exactly look like her, but it didn't *not* look like her, either. Had the manufacturers made the bride generic on purpose just in case the wedding didn't come off? Or, worse, had the original model been a different Gennie altogether?

Stop thinking like that, she told herself.

Jennie set the topper on a shelf next to a silver-framed photo of her and Hugh in Botswana. Then she hurried out the door, texting the driver, *On my way*.

Rodney had the night off, and Ben, his baby-faced substitute, hardly looked old enough to have a driver's license. Still, Jennie easily spotted the gun under his jacket and knew he would be just as highly trained as any of the other Met officers assigned to protect her.

"Sorry to pester you, Miss Jensen," said Ben. "But we do want to have you there in time to welcome Mr. Haugen and his family."

"No, I'm sorry. I hope we can still make it in time," said Jennie.

Ben grinned. "Buckle in and we'll find out."

The next thing she knew, the tires were spitting gravel as they headed for the gate. Her first official solo appearance as a "working royal" was a bad time for a late start. With Hugh dedicating a new Royal Navy training facility in Portsmouth, she had been dispatched to represent him at a dinner for the Norwegian Prime Minister Christoffer Haugen at Buckingham Palace. She wasn't the host—Freddie and Cece had that duty—so she didn't have any real responsibilities, but she still didn't want to screw up. Hugh had assured her she'd do fine, but that didn't do much to stop her from imagining the many different ways things could go wrong.

Her phone vibrated with an incoming text. It was Karen this time.

> And how was Royal Ascot?

> I'm not sure who was competing
> harder, the horses or the people.

Her mom sent the laughing-crying emoji.

> I met Anabelle Osborne-Webb

> What did you think?

> She seems nice. Ish.
> She congratulated
> me on my "victory."

Three dots pulsated in the speech bubble as Karen composed a longer reply. Outside her window, the street was a blur. Ben was driving so quickly and confidently that she wondered for a moment whether he had been behind the wheel at Stirling Lines. Fortunately, nobody was shooting this time.

> You probably don't know the rumors.
> People have been saying forever that
> Anabelle is really Edmund's. From before
> he was married to Penelope.

NO!

> Who knows? But where there's
> smoke, usually someone or
> something is on fire.

Despite her all-caps answer, Jennie didn't feel as surprised by her mother's gossip as she probably should have been. If this kept up, the only thing that would shock her would be hearing that people believed something was exactly what it seemed to be.

Buckingham Palace was already coming into view. Despite the usual creeping traffic, Ben had made the two-mile trip in record time. As they rolled through the gate, Jennie wrapped it up.

> Speaking as someone who's been
> burned, the subject of the gossip
> isn't always the one lighting the
> matches.

> I'm just saying. This one has been
> going around FOREVER.

> Gotta go, Mom.

Jennie had seen pictures on the walls of state dinners during the reign of Queen Alexandra, with more than a hundred guests in ball gowns and bow ties lining two impossibly long tables in the Buckingham Palace ballroom. But to her immense relief, this was a more intimate affair. Prime Minister Haugen turned out to be a handsome, fortysomething man with swept-back black hair, prominent teeth, and an adorable family. His wife, Emilie, looked like all she needed to transform into a Viking maiden were a breastplate and shield, and their blond daughters, Ottilie and Grethe, would have made adorable woodland sprites. The only other guests were the Norwegian ambassador and his wife and the British ambassador to Norway and his wife. As the not-quite-dozen guests proceeded into the red-flocked, red-carpeted State Dining Room, Jennie saw they would all fit quite comfortably at a single round table.

"How old are your girls, Prime Minister?" asked Jennie, as they all took their seats.

"Please, call me Christoffer," he said warmly. "And please, ask them."

"My apologies, Ottilie and Grethe. How old are you?"

After some giggling and conspiratorial whispers, Ottilie answered for both of them. "I'm twelve years old and she's ten."

Getting further information out of them proved impossible, but the girls were well-behaved and clearly knew which utensils to use as the meal progressed from soup to fish to beef (Jennie made do with a baked tofu entrée that didn't quite succeed), to cheese and nuts, and finally to a flourless chocolate cake that was so good and so thinly cut that Jennie couldn't help asking for seconds.

Freddie and Cece guided the conversation expertly, and with the ambassadors making opaque comments about North Sea oil, platinum, and cod, Jennie felt more like an ornament than a participant. But when her impending wedding was mentioned, Freddie suddenly pushed back his chair, rose to his feet, and called for champagne, which was uncorked and poured with almost military efficiency by the red-jacketed footmen.

Even though his face was flushed from three or four glasses

of wine—the attendants always filled his first, she noticed—
Freddie didn't sway or slur his words as he raised his goblet in
Jennie's direction.

"I wish to propose a toast to the lovely American singer
Jennie Jensen, who has played a tune to enchant our future
king. Although she may indeed be a rebel from the colonies,
I believe their matrimony represents the very best sort of soft
power. Indeed, prospects of bringing the colonies back to the
Commonwealth have never been brighter!"

"Oh, *Freddie*," said Cece, laughing. Then, to the rest of
them, she added: "There's a reason his diplomatic efforts are
limited to the dinner table."

Christoffer chuckled. "Contrary to popular belief, we Nor-
wegians do appreciate a sense of humor. To be serious, however,
although we no longer make alliances through marriage, weddings are good for any country."

"He is only saying that because my father was quite prominent in the Socialist Party—Christoffer is Labor, so you could
say our family is its own little coalition," said Emilie.

"How did the two of you meet?" asked Jennie, wishing she
had paid more attention to European politics.

"It's very boring, I'm afraid," said Christoffer. "I first became
aware of Emilie when I was in parliament, and she was leading
a protest outside my office!"

Which, of course, led Emilie to ask Jennie to tell how she
met Hugh, a story she hurried through because it had been so
widely reported.

After dinner, as everyone lingered over cups of strong
coffee—and Freddie knocked back a second glass of port—
Christoffer turned to Jennie.

"Miss Jensen, I have a gift to give you and a favor to ask."

Jennie felt suddenly all too present. Side conversations died, and everyone watched as the prime minister's assistant stepped away from the wall and presented her with a poster-sized framed document. She recognized it right away as a family tree, although it didn't sink in for several moments *whose* it was.

"Someone in my office became intrigued by your family surname, Jensen, and wondered whether you might have Norwegian ancestry. When they suggested we commission a genealogist to perform the research, naturally, I agreed. It turns out that your father David's great-great-grandfather emigrated from Trondheim via steamship and settled in Chicago, where he found work in a lumber warehouse. His family was quite large, and his siblings scattered across what I believe are called the midwestern states, from Illinois and Iowa to Minnesota and North Dakota. We wish you to have this family tree to remind you of your ancestral connection to our country."

Jennie admired the beautifully calligraphed chart, where connecting lines had been artfully drawn as slender branches with soft green leaves. Daniel and Jennie were both drawn as equal descendants of Dave and Karen, centered at the bottom of the document, as though all preceding generations had procreated with the single-minded goal of producing them.

Well, Daniel anyway. Surely the genealogist had discovered she was adopted. Or had everyone involved in the family tree's creation been unaware that she was not related to any of these people by blood? Or had they simply decided, in their enlightened European way, that it didn't matter? If so, she wished royals like Princess Stuart would take a cue.

Jennie's own feelings were complicated. In her heart, she was every bit as much of a Jensen as anyone who had been born into the family. But in a nagging, dark part of her mind, she still wondered about her *real* family tree. She knew some adoptees got upset by clumsy handling of their complex parentage, but she had also learned from experience never to take offense when intentions were sincere.

"Thank you," she told Christoffer. "This is thoughtful and just so amazingly beautiful. I know my father is especially proud of his family heritage, and I hope you won't mind if I share your generous gift with him."

Across the table, Cece gave Jennie a nod that could only mean one thing: *Well played.*

Maybe diplomacy wasn't so hard, after all.

Just as she was wondering what to do with the massive rectangle resting on her lap, a footman appeared by her side and carried it away as though they had all known exactly what to do.

"You mentioned a favor?" she asked.

Suddenly, Grethe and Ottilie's fair cheeks blushed scarlet and they started squirming as if they literally had ants in their pants.

Even the prime minister looked uncharacteristically awkward. "I know this is a breach of protocol, Miss Jensen, but my daughters are passionate fans, and I fear I will lose standing in my household if I don't convey their request. Would you please favor us with a song?"

Earlier, neither of the girls had been able to look at her. Now they were both staring, their eyes bright with anticipation. Their fan status most likely began and ended with The Song—the teen romance in The Movie had played well with teens and tweens, and found lasting life on Netflix—but who knew? With Spotify, all things were possible. Of all the things Jennie had expected this evening, singing was dead last on the list. She didn't have a problem with it—even the ambassadors were murmuring favorably—but there was one little problem.

"I'd be happy to, but I didn't bring my guitar. And I'm afraid I'm not very good a cappella."

As the girls' faces fell, Freddie banged the table hard enough that his spoon jumped.

"Surely we have a *guitar* among the treasures at Buckingham Palace." Waving his arm at the head butler, he commanded, "Mr. Shaw, fetch us a guitar!"

It took ten minutes, during which the conversation zigzagged awkwardly from topic to topic: the World Cup, for which Norway had again failed to qualify; an environmentalist's memoir that Emilie recommended highly; and which instruments everyone at the table played, had been forced to play, or wished they could play. (Jennie got a good laugh when she admitted she had been first-chair clarinet in fifth grade.) But finally, a white-gloved footman strode into the room, bearing a Martin acoustic as though it were a holy relic.

The moment was extended even further when Freddie insisted they all adjourn to the gilded, chandeliered Music Room, with chairs and couches hastily arranged for "a proper concert." Sitting on the edge of a chair that had probably seen its share of royal bottoms, Jennie tuned as quickly as she could. It wasn't easy—the instrument was an antique, and the stiff, corroded strings were so old she half-believed they were original—but the guitar did have a wonderfully bright sound.

But finally, Jennie was ready to perform. She had already decided which song to play first, and when she strummed the first notes of "I Can't Even," Grethe and Ottilie shrieked in delight. Like typical tweens, they produced phones they had somehow been hiding inside their dresses, held them up to record, and watched her through their screens.

Given the production required for the "concert," she felt like she owed them more than one song, so she followed up with "Peoria, Illinois." The light and bouncy backhanded ode to her hometown had the adults tapping their feet and the girls bouncing in their seats. The less complimentary lines about Peoria would go over their heads, she hoped.

Despite the prime minister's awkwardness in asking, Jennie was enjoying it as much as everyone else, and maybe more. It had been so long since she performed that it was a joy to have an audience, even an audience of ten dwarfed by the vastness of the reverberating room. A joy, and a relief. Singing always just felt damn good. Most people didn't know it, but singing was an aerobic exercise that released endorphins into the bloodstream, which was why Jennie so often left the stage feeling happy and right with the world.

"Brava!" said Emilie, a cheer quickly taken up by her daughters. "You must play an encore!"

"I'm warning you, this one isn't finished," Jennie said after the applause had died down.

She missed Hugh. So what else could she play?

"*I've got a prince, he's a heck of a guy,*" she sang. "*They don't know that I'm planning to steal him . . .*"

———————

After she got home and closed the door behind her, she called Hugh.

"And how are you, my love?" he asked, his voice just a little bit hoarse from his day.

"Floating on air," she said, slipping out of her shoes so she could carry them. "That's a weird expression. Where else would you float?"

"Water. But it doesn't have quite the same magic, because one *can* actually float on water."

As she climbed the wide staircase to the second floor, the deep wool carpet felt wonderful on her feet—and would have felt even nicer if she wasn't wearing pantyhose.

"Floating on champagne sounds even nicer. Which is where

I suspect Freddie is floating at the moment. Anyway, it went wonderfully. Christoffer and Emilie are super nice, and their girls are ridiculously cute."

"So now we're on a first-name basis with heads of state, are we?"

"We are. I hope I'm allowed to use the royal *we*."

At the top of the stairs, Jennie turned down the hallway toward their private rooms, padding past a long line of British paintings in ornate frames.

"I'll allow it. You're obviously my secret weapon. Well, not so secret anymore."

"And how was your day?"

"It seemed routine at first. I cut the ribbon, I shook the hands, I made the speech. I even got to play in a game of five-a-side football with the enlisted men. You would have been quite proud of me: I scored a lovely goal."

"*So* proud," Jennie teased him. "But what happened after 'at first'?"

Hugh groaned. "Sidney got the word from a friendly reporter that the *Daily Mail* sniffed out an embezzler at the Prince's Trust. Worse, it's someone with a hand in the Unconquered Games."

"I'm so sorry."

"We've already sacked the offender, and she'll be brought up on charges. I'm actually quite grateful to the paper for catching the crook—except for the part in their article where they make it out to be all my fault."

Jennie knew how much Hugh's charities really meant to him, and knew he put in more work behind the scenes than anyone realized.

"I miss you," she said. "I wish you were here so I could make it better."

"Miss you, too. I'll be home tomorrow still, but later than planned."

Jennie walked into their comfortable sitting room. Seeing the empty box, she smiled and raised her eyes to the shelf where she'd placed his gift.

Then she froze. The cake topper had been snapped in half. And while the little plastic Hugh remained intact and standing, the Jennie side was . . . gone.

"Hello? Are you there?" asked Hugh.

"I miss you, too," she said absently.

"Is something wrong?"

"I just realized . . . I forgot to say thank you for the cake topper."

Hugh laughed. "I was afraid it wouldn't reach you in time! Sidney's with me, so he had to find someone else to deliver it. He may have reached out to Legrand for help."

Jennie didn't know what to do. An irrational pang of guilt at seeing his ruined gift was quickly replaced by the more rational thought that it would be hysterical to panic about it. Household staff were in and out all the time. Probably it had been broken accidentally. But Hugh had enough on his mind. There was no point in worrying him if a maid was rushing back with the missing piece and a tube of glue.

"I'm so sorry, but I need to crash," she told Hugh. "I feel like I'm falling asleep on my feet. But I can't wait to see you tomorrow."

"Fair enough. I'm exhausted as well."

After they exchanged goodnights, making corny kissing sounds into their phones, she put down the phone. First, she searched the neighboring shelves and the floor, then every surface in the adjoining rooms. For good measure, she even opened a couple dozen drawers, but the missing half of the cake topper was nowhere to be found.

Lifting the palace phone, she asked for the household manager, who answered promptly.

"Has anyone cleaned our private rooms this evening?" she asked.

"No, Miss Jensen," came the reply. "No one's scheduled until the morning. Do you need service?"

"No, thank you," she said, hanging up.

Standing in the middle of the room, Jennie shivered and hugged herself.

Chapter Fifteen
TAPE DELAY

Jeremy Legrand plucked the remaining half of the cake topper off the shelf and examined it from all angles as though it were an interesting seashell. Seeing his fingers on the tiny plastic Hugh made Jennie feel even further violated in a way she wouldn't have been able to explain—she hadn't yet been able to bring herself to touch it.

"Are you one hundred percent certain this was on this shelf when you left for the evening?" he asked, sounding as though he didn't believe it.

"I put it there right before I left," she insisted.

"And you are also certain it was not handled by a maid?"

"As I've already explained, I talked to housekeeping and they told me no one came in while I was gone."

Jeremy put it back on the shelf and looked at her like he pitied her for accepting this reasonable explanation at face value.

"You don't think it possible they were misinformed? Or that perhaps someone from maintenance stopped in, broke it accidentally, and then became too embarrassed to report it?"

"Why would they take half of it with them?" asked Jennie,

impatient with his obtuse questioning. "Someone came in here, snapped the cake topper in half, and left the Hugh part of it behind. It's obviously a message to me."

Legrand frowned.

Last night, immediately after ending the call with Hugh, Jennie had told Ben, who was still on shift as her PPO, what happened. Ben had taken her seriously enough to call Grant Mc-Cutcheon, who stationed an additional PPO outside the front door. Before she knew it, Rodney had interrupted his evening out and rushed to the scene with beer on his breath but genuine concern in his eyes. Rodney and Ben methodically searched all twenty rooms of the apartment without finding anything out of order. Sensing Jennie's distress, Rodney insisted on spending the rest of the night in a chair outside her personal quarters.

And now, under the pretext of personally delivering her mail pouch, Legrand had appeared at the door, seemingly determined to make her believe nothing was wrong.

"Can't you fingerprint it or something?" Jennie asked as she watched him brush his fingertips against the fine blue wool of his suit pants.

"I imagine we'll find quite a collage of them: yours, Hugh's, mine, Sidney's, Ian's, and Poppy's, as well as every tourist who fondled the item in the shop before it made its way to the palace," he said, in a tone that left no need for an eye roll.

Jennie was determined not to rise to the bait. "Then how about video evidence? There are cameras covering every door from outside. Can't you review the footage?"

"I believe Mr. McCutcheon is one step ahead of you there. And that is his department, not yours or mine. If I might, I'd like to move on to the matter I came here to discuss, which is your behavior at Buckingham Palace last night."

Jennie was so surprised that she sat down in the nearest seat, an overstuffed club chair Hugh liked to read in. In her mind, she pored over her ever-growing inventory of etiquette, wondering which box she'd somehow forgotten to cross off. She couldn't think of a single thing she'd done wrong.

"What is it this time?"

He frowned again. "I'm honestly surprised you don't know. It is, as they say, all over the internet."

All over the internet meant . . . what? More accusations from Lindsey Peters? Nude pictures she didn't know she had taken? Something even worse? Jennie's stomach hollowed as she waited for the latest disaster to land in her lap.

Legrand removed his phone from his jacket pocket, unlocked it, and tapped and swiped clumsily until he had what he wanted. Then he aimed the phone down at her.

Jennie's first thought was: *Jeremy Legrand is on Instagram?*

Then she saw herself, playing a vintage Martin acoustic. In the cap-sleeved dress she'd worn last night in the Music Room at Buckingham Palace.

As Legrand unmuted the video, she heard her own voice, compressed and tinny from the phone's tiny speakers, as she sang, ". . . *they don't know that I'm going to steal him.*" It was posted to the account of @Ottilie_H. There were over three million views already, and the likes and comments were coming in too fast to count.

Her skin tingled with a thousand tiny pinpricks as it slowly dawned on her that her spur-of-the-moment decision to share her love song to Hugh had been a colossal blunder. She hadn't even finished it. Hadn't even played it for Hugh. And now it was being shared with the entire world. She'd assumed the children of a prime minister would have been too well trained to share it publicly. Jennie knew better, and she had only been in training for a few short months. They had been born into this life.

But Legrand wasn't worried about her feelings.

"Needless to say, His Royal Highness King Edmund is most displeased," he said intently, studying her face for what—signs of weakness? "And the lyrics of your little ditty have the Royal-watching press in a tizzy at the notion that you are 'stealing' our prince and plan to 'hold him for ransom.'"

"You have *got* to be kidding me," she said. "It's a *song*. A love song. Not a kidnapper's note."

"Not all of His Majesty's subjects are as sophisticated as you or we might wish, Miss Jensen," he said pityingly. "The communications team is currently preparing the wording of your apology, which I will present for your review shortly."

Apparently, *never complain, never explain* did not apply in this situation. Jennie wholeheartedly believed in making apologies when they were actually necessary, but this situation was obviously being used by Legrand to remind her that she was not yet one of them. Incredulous, angry, and done letting him loom over her, Jennie stood up, forcing him to take a step back.

"I won't apologize for singing a song about how much I love Hugh."

"You may think of it as a clarification, if you prefer."

"This is bullshit."

Seemingly unruffled by her language and her tone, Legrand nonetheless took another step back and straightened his tie.

"If you are indeed to become a member of the royal family, it would behoove you to remember that under no circumstances are you to record and broadcast another unsanctioned music video, Miss Jensen. I have served the Crown long enough to recall the difficulties caused by the attention-seeking activities of Princess Penelope, and I have no wish to see Prince Hugh suffer anything like that again."

There it was. Never mind the fact that she neither recorded

nor broadcasted the video, it was now abundantly clear how Legrand saw her: *difficult*. She knew from her mother how *difficult* Penelope had been as her marriage to Edmund fell apart. For someone like Legrand, whose first instinct was always to deflect, suppress, or make problems disappear, the inability to maintain control of Penelope must have been painful.

"It's a different world now," said Jennie. "Look at the comments on the video. People like it! No, I didn't mean to put it out there, but it's good for the royal family. People don't want to see us as cardboard cutouts or plastic figurines. They want to see us as real people. And I think they love that we're in love."

"As for what is good or not good for the royal family," Legrand began hotly, "I think I—"

There was a knock at the door as a weary-looking Rodney let himself in. If he realized he'd walked into the middle of an argument, he didn't let on.

"Bad news," he said. "We don't have a minute of video from any of the Kensington Palace cameras last night. The cameras were on, but the breaker powering the hard drive was tripped, which means they didn't record. The man on duty says he was watching the screens and didn't see anything unusual."

"Thank you, Mr. Whyte. Please give us a moment to conclude our meeting," said Legrand curtly.

Rodney looked at Jennie with an unspoken question in his eyes. She didn't know how to respond. With a nod, he left, pulling the door closed behind him.

"The video didn't record? Doesn't that seem suspicious to you?" Jennie asked.

"The wiring in this palace was first installed one hundred and forty years ago, and not all of it has been replaced. Power surges are quite common. A technical malfunction is not the same thing as a sinister conspiracy."

"You just don't believe me, do you?" Jennie felt exhausted.

As he turned and headed for the door, Legrand spoke over his shoulder. "I understand this is all unfamiliar to you. Do not infect the prince with your paranoia. It will only create more problems for you both."

The door did not hit him on his way out, as much as she wished it would have. She wasn't being paranoid. The cake topper wouldn't have broken from a simple bump and fall—and if it had, it wouldn't have separated Jennie and Hugh neatly in two. Someone had made an effort to snap it in half. More than a dozen people routinely entered the apartment, and even more than that had access. But few of them also had access to her schedule and to the video room. And although Legrand worked for the King out of his office at Buckingham Palace, he held the master keys, and there was no one more familiar with the byzantine workings of all the royal households. No one more able to make something disappear.

He obviously wasn't on Penelope's side. Had the princess caused him so much trouble that he had finally decided to take her out of the picture? Had he acted on his own behalf, or someone else's? Or a group of someones?

What would happen if he wasn't on Jennie's side, either?

She took the broken cake topper down from the shelf, hardly looking at it as she carried it to a rarely used closet, stood on tiptoes, and pushed it to the back of a high shelf.

Then she messaged Poppy.

> Can you pick me up one of
> those cute Hugh-and-Jennie
> cake toppers they're selling?

Chapter Sixteen

TWO SURPRISES

Jennie had hoped to learn all she needed to know about Princess Penelope from Hugh over time and from his perspective. She could ignore some of the gossip, but the threatening notes, the broken cake topper and Legrand's dismissive reaction, combined with the missing surveillance footage, all made her wonder if there was more to the story than her son could possibly know. For the past hour, she had found herself sitting at a desk that had once belonged to Penelope, staring at a computer screen and skimming articles by hangers-on, friends of friends, conspiracy theorists, and even some legitimate journalists. The sheer volume of confirmatory conjecture only made Penelope look less paranoid and made Jennie more scared.

What she really needed to do, she decided, was to look into the people who had been around during Penelope's tumultuous final years and were still in the picture.

Few people had been more intimately involved, then and now, than Jeremy Legrand. She couldn't very well google him—or anyone else of note—from the palace server, where erasing her search history meant nothing. Instead, she grabbed her phone and laptop and moved into the walnut-paneled first floor library, where she connected her personal hotspot. Before she had even read the results of her first search (*jeremy legrand princess penelope conspiracies*), she found herself wondering if their personal quarters really were free of hidden cameras. She moved outside to the garden, where the buzzing insects, thundering jets, and distant din of London traffic somehow made her feel safer.

She was halfway through a sketchy subreddit ("Why is there so little information about jeremy legrand?") when she felt a hand on her shoulder.

Her reaction was pure instinct. She was half-stumbling, half-falling out of the wicker chair before she had even decided to move.

Hugh was standing there, his arms laden with two dozen of her favorite peach-colored roses, the laugh on his face already fading to dismay.

"My God, I'm so sorry. Are you all right?"

Jennie looked down at her laptop, which thankfully was splayed face-down in the grass.

"I'm . . . fine."

"You looked at me just now as though I were a knife-wielding maniac," he said, smiling wanly.

She shook her head. "You just caught me off guard. I should have been expecting you."

Hugh set the roses on her chair and circled around it to wrap her in a hug. "It's my fault. You looked so lovely that I just stood there watching you for several minutes. And when you didn't notice me behind you, I had the bright idea to give you a surprise."

Jennie buried her face in his shirt, nuzzled his chest, and inhaled deeply. "I'm just really on edge today."

"About the song?"

She nodded. "Mister Legrand came over this morning and chewed me out. Apparently, trying to entertain important guests is only the latest of my fatal flaws. Doesn't he know I'm trying?"

"Bollocks to Jeremy. I love it, and so do millions upon millions of others, both in Britain and beyond. I listened to it on repeat the whole way home. I've been given some remarkable gifts, but no one has ever written me a song."

"Not a whole one. All I've got is two verses and one chorus. It still needs a bridge, a better intro, and a—"

"It's perfect."

She closed the laptop and allowed him to lead her across the grass to a shaded marble bench where they could sit side by side. A tiny bird twittered away in the branches above as Hugh pulled her half into his lap and rested his chin on top of her head. She could feel his heart beating under her cheek.

"I just feel so dumb for not seeing this coming, and I'm mad at myself because I wanted to finish the song before you heard it," she said.

"That's not why you jumped out of your skin just now."

Finally the tears came. Tears of fear. Tears of relief at being with Hugh again, and of frustration because she was so tired of feeling like she always did everything wrong. Guilty tears for keeping the broken cake topper from Hugh. Yet another secret to add to the sorry pile. She hated going along with Legrand's shady tactics, but she had a nagging feeling he was right about one thing: Hugh shouldn't have to rise to her defense every single time something went wrong. She promised herself she would tell him as soon as she got to the bottom of it.

"I'm just stressed out of my mind," she confessed. "Every single thing has the potential to blow up in my face. And it's completely exhausting having people watching me all the time. Now I can't even have privacy in the palace: something I did at dinner is out there in the world and I can't take it back. I just don't know how you do it—I don't know how I'm going to do it. Sometimes I feel like I can't breathe, wondering what will happen next."

For a while, Hugh didn't say anything. He just held her close and kissed her hair until her sobs became sniffles.

"There's nothing wrong with you for feeling this way," he finally said. "Trust me, I know. I wish we could be together without all the rest of it. And I hope you're not having second thoughts, because I don't want to go through it without you."

She raised her head and kissed him, tasting her own salty tears. "No second thoughts. Not about marrying you."

"I can't tell you how relieved that makes me."

Hugh leaned back and looked at her. "I do have another surprise, but after what just happened, I'm not sure it's a good idea to spring anything else on you."

She laughed, finally feeling her body start to relax a little. "I think I'll be okay if I know the surprise is coming."

He grinned. "Then you'd better pack your bags. And don't forget your swimsuit."

Princess Penelope

6 OCTOBER 1989

Penelope needn't have worried about Hugh on this, his first official trip as a working royal. From the moment he'd stepped onto the platform at Paragon Station, smiling shyly, and offered his hand to the local dignitaries, he'd been brilliant. He stood patiently for the inspection of the East Yorkshire Regiment. And at the Sailor Children's Society, he'd not only helped a girl build a sailboat from ice lolly sticks but spread his napkin across his lap without prompting at the casual luncheon that followed.

As they drove past Guildhall and wended through the narrow streets of Old Town, Hugh nodded along to Edmund's history lesson. "Hull was once a wool port operated by the monks of Meaux Abbey and was renamed Kingston upon Hull in 1299 by your great-great-great-grandfather, Edward the First."

Hugh lowered his window and waved to the well-wishers crowding the sidewalks along George Street. "And it's fun here, too!"

"Hull is also known for one other thing I think you'd like to see."

Penelope had assumed they were headed back to the train to relax and regroup, as there was nothing printed on their schedule until five o'clock when they were slated to open something called KUHFF. When she looked at Edmund for a clue, the corners of his eyes crinkled with uncharacteristic mischief.

"It's just past the stadium," said Jeremy Legrand from the passenger seat.

The morning had been cool, cloudy, and drizzly. As they exited Holwell Road, however, as though bending to Legrand's insistence on clockwork precision, the gloom magically began to lift.

Hugh yelped. "I see a big wheel!"

A field crowded with striped tents, concession booths, and colorful rides appeared before them. Penelope finally twigged to the acronym when she saw the banner above the front gates.

"Kingston upon Hull Funfair!"

"Care to pop in?" Edmund asked.

Hugh was bouncing so hard the entire back seat vibrated. "Yes! Yes! Yes!"

He tugged on the door handle as the Range Rover turned into the car park.

"Please wait until we come to a full stop, Highness," said their driver, PPO Andrews.

"Do you think they have a rocket ship ride?" asked Hugh, reluctantly letting go of the handle. "And what about a fun house? They're sure to have a roundabout, right?"

"And much more," Edmund said.

Penelope gave his hand an affectionate squeeze. Going to a funfair was a rare treat, made that much sweeter by his fore-thought. "What a grand surprise."

"You have an hour and forty-five minutes before it's time to open the gates and welcome the people in the queue," said Legrand.

Hugh waited until he received a nod from Andrews and then threw open his door. "I want to stay forever!"

Additional protection officers and staff were already stand-ing by, awaiting their arrival. As she climbed out onto the gravel, Penelope was glad she had dressed for the day in a split skirt, a cotton top beneath her blazer, and black ballet flats, making her well prepared to chase her son around the fair. Edmund, however, was still in his usual uniform of white shirt, red tie, and crisp blue blazer.

"I'll catch up," he said, as Jeremy and Andrews snapped to-gether the portable privacy drape that was always kept in the boot for on-the-go wardrobe changes.

"Last one to the roundabout's a rotten egg!" she challenged Hugh, who was already several steps ahead of her.

With their security detail trailing behind, they raced along the fairground and passed through an unmanned turnstile to the roundabout. The startled operator, who had been lounging against a carved wooden centaur, dropped his newspaper and cigarette, grinding the fag end beneath his heel as he bowed from the waist.

Hugh wended his way through the carved menagerie, trail-ing his hand along the flanks of the various beasts.

"I call the *h*ebra!"

"*He*bra?"

"The zebra," he panted, stopping before the life-sized creature. "Is a boy."

"Then I call the *she*raffe beside your *he*bra!"

Once they were astride their chosen beasts, Hugh summoned the members of their detail. "Matt, Rodney, Estelle, Mr. Clay—climb aboard!"

PPO Matt Leahy remained alertly on watch, but the others scrambled into the saddle. The roundabout began to turn, the calliope hooting, and moments later, the striped gaming tents, shuttered ticket booths, and darkened rides of the funfair were whirring past.

"Yee haw!" yelled PPO Rodney from the back of a brightly painted camel.

As Hugh whooped and hollered along with him, Penelope's mind went back to the funfair in her hometown of Norfolk, where she and her mates would spend the day eating burgers and toffee apples, attempting to win tiny cuddly toys and trinkets, and standing in neverending queues for the Dipper, Waltzer, and Scrambler. While having the fair to oneself might be every child's fantasy, she felt a sudden pang upon realizing her son was indeed the only child present; his companions were adults whose job it was to trail his every step. He would know neither the agony of waiting in a queue nor the elation of finally reaching the front. Then again, he would never have to worry about having his pocket money pickpocketed, either.

Edmund appeared at the railing as the roundabout slowed. Now dressed in a cornflower blue jumper, pressed khakis, and brand-new trainers, he looked like an advert for a posh dad at a family weekend. The thought made her smile—until she saw Mr. O'Malley, the photographer, trailing along behind.

"What is he doing here?" Penelope asked Edmund after she had dismounted.

The photographer had been working busily in the background all day, capturing their every move and gesture, but she had assumed this private time wouldn't be recorded.

"I know you fancy casual photos and O'Malley's been kind enough to take a few snaps. We might use one for our Christmas card this year."

Mr. O'Malley was already walking backward in front of Hugh, firing away.

Penelope tried to remember when she'd expressed a wish for any casual family photos since Hugh's first birthday—a day she'd done her best to forget—or when they'd used one for a Christmas card.

"How very thoughtful."

"Off we go," said Edmund, taking Hugh by the hand and leading him toward a pavilion shading a jumble of brightly colored minicars. "Time to test our mettle on the dodgems!"

"Dodgems?" Hugh asked.

"Cars with tires surrounding them instead of underneath," Penelope explained.

Hugh broke free from Edmund and ran ahead. When they caught up to him, he was gazing over the barrier with a mixture of awe and caution. "They do look awfully dodgy."

Edmund chuckled and rested a hand on their son's shoulder. "You drive them all around and crash into each other."

"On *purpose*?"

"It's all in good fun—you're going to love them."

Edmund helped Hugh through the gate, then motioned for Mr. O'Malley to get situated. Once inside, Hugh went from car to car, trying to choose the best one.

Boys and cars, Penelope thought. She liked to drive her own car when she had the chance but had never quite grasped the appeal of motorsports.

"I want this one!" Hugh announced, climbing behind the wheel of a blue car with a black racing stripe.

PPO Matt shook his head. "Sorry, mate. Not quite tall enough to go on your own."

Hugh's wide smile faded.

Edmund climbed into a red car and patted the side. "Come over here, Hugh. You can sit on my lap and steer."

"Edmund, you love red cars . . ." Penelope began, scenting trouble.

"Because they go faster," he said with a wink.

" . . . but Hugh loves blue cars."

"I see," Edmund said. "Well, perhaps I can make an exception."

"Mum loves blue cars, too," Hugh added stoutly. "I want to drive with Mum."

Edmund cleared his throat. "Well . . . I suppose that's that, then."

He looked away as she folded herself into the blue dodgem. She'd barely seated Hugh between her legs and fastened their seat buckle before Edmund signaled the operator to begin. When he flipped the switch, the electrified grate powering the cars began humming, the poles attached to the back of the cars crackling and sparking as Edmund drove away.

"Blue cars are most definitely faster," Penelope told Hugh.

Once Hugh realized he truly was driving, he started giggling, and instantly crashed them into a parked dodgem. O'Malley clicked away while they learned to work together with Penelope controlling the accelerator and Hugh swerving in quick, sharp turns.

Suddenly, Edmund came barreling toward them.

"Tally-ho!" he cried, just before he rammed them so hard her teeth rattled.

"Bloody hell," Penelope muttered.

Thankfully, Hugh took it in stride. "Mum, that's what you're supposed to do."

Give us whiplash because he's cheesed off? she wondered.

"Press the pedal," Hugh said, turning the wheel.

They sped toward Edmund, who was now showboating for the camera. As they passed him, Hugh quickly cut in and caught his father's red car broadside. The look of wounded vanity and suppressed fury on Edmund's face was worth any further petulance she might have to put up with.

"Nicely done, Hugh!" Penelope whispered.

———————

The table in the center of the picnic area on the Walton Street side of the fair had been set with a fluttering tablecloth and a colorful floral arrangement. It fairly groaned with platters bearing hot dogs, kebab, popcorn, chips, and more—every kind of food Penelope had ever consumed at a fair.

Edmund rubbed his hands in anticipation as he led them to the feast. "And now it's time for tea!"

"Not hungry," grumbled Hugh.

Penelope wasn't particularly hungry either, after she spotted picnic baskets under the table and realized all the food had been prepared at Kensington Palace—safety-approved, chef-prepared facsimiles of actual fair *fare*. Still, she encouraged Hugh, if only to avoid a headfit from Edmund.

"Darling, they have loads of things we never get to have at home."

Hugh hugged his arms to his chest. "I'm still full from lunch with the sailor kids."

Edmund glanced at the concession stands nearby. "Come

on now, dig in. We don't want to offend the people who made this lovely tea possible, now do we, Hugh?"

Penelope struggled to hold her tongue, wondering why on earth he felt the need to pretend the food had actually come from the fair when its sole purpose was as a prop in another photo op.

When Hugh didn't budge, Edmund grabbed his hand, strongarmed him over to the picnic table, and forced him to take a seat. An oblivious O'Malley was still dutifully capturing it all on film, even though these particular pictures were destined never to see the light of day.

"Just take a few bites and you can run along and play," Penelope told Hugh quietly as she sat down beside him.

Defeated, he reached for a cheeseburger as Edmund unwrapped the red and white checked paper from a kebab.

"Let's see who can take the bigger bite, Hugh. Are you ready? One, two, three—go!"

Hugh nibbled disinterestedly while Edmund took an enormous chomp.

"Poor sport," he said, after he'd swallowed.

Hugh shrugged and put down the burger. Then he ate exactly two chips, which he washed down with lemonade. "That's three. May I play now?"

"No," said Edmund.

"I made an agreement with him," Penelope said.

"And I did not. A future monarch cannot be rewarded for blatantly manipulative behavior," Edmund said.

"I couldn't agree more," she said, wondering if the irony was as lost on him as it seemed.

"Then you will agree he needs to stay and eat. Hugh, *eat your tea.*"

As Hugh began to eat, his eyes welling with tears, Edmund finally had the presence of mind to wave off O'Malley.

"For goodness' sake, he's only four years old," Penelope protested.

"And already a mama's boy."

"Are you still angry because he wanted to ride in the car with me instead of you?"

"How utterly daft."

But he wouldn't meet her gaze.

They ate in silence. Penelope's palace-prepared falafel was so devoid of flavor and fun that she was half tempted to join Hugh in a hunger strike. But, somehow, she got through it, and even Hugh managed to eat enough of his burger and chips to please his father.

"Good man," said Edmund in a falsely chipper tone. "And now you've earned yourself a special treat."

As if to demonstrate that he, not Penelope, would dole out both punishment and reward, he waved down a fresh-faced teenager pushing a candy floss cart. The startled girl pushed her cart up beside them and dipped into a full curtsey.

"Your Highnesses."

"Perhaps you'd be so kind as to demonstrate how you make candy floss," said Edmund, his eyes lingering on her ample cleavage.

"I'd be delighted," she said with a giggle. "What flavor would you like?"

Penelope couldn't help but laugh. "He seems to fancy all the flavors."

Edmund glared. "Forgive Her Highness. She's a little potty from all the good food and fun."

"I want rainbow!" piped Hugh.

"That's my favorite, too."

The girl seemed too overwhelmed by their presence to take notice of their spat. Her hands shaking slightly, she showed

Hugh how to gather the strands of brightly colored sugar until the paper cones were overflowing with multicolored candy floss.

Hugh was first, then Penelope, then Edmund. When Edmund took his paper cone, his hand touched hers for a full two seconds.

"This looks lovely," he said, his leer infecting his voice.

After the dumbstruck girl had moved on, Penelope could hold her tongue no longer.

"And here I thought Eleanora Oxbum-Webb was bottom of the barrel," she hissed.

Hugh giggled with delight. "Oxbum!"

"Bloody hell!" thundered Edmund.

Rodney appeared as if from nowhere, took Hugh's hand, and led him away from the table. "They're opening the gaming booths on the midway. Bet you a quid they have a fishing game."

"We'll follow on straightaway," Edmund called after them, straining for equanimity. Then, to Penelope, he snarled, "*How dare you.* In front of Hugh! If your little temper tantrum finds its way to the tabloids, I'll—"

"You'll what? Be forced to confirm Anabelle Osborne-Webb is your daughter?"

Edmund's face flushed a deep red. "What did you just say?"

"You heard me," she said.

She had held it in for so long, trying to avoid even thinking about it, that her own voice scared her.

The silence of the empty fair was deafening.

"I suppose they might also like to know about your habit of pouring your first glass of wine at noon and then drinking until you pass out at eight o'clock. If they're wondering why we haven't had a second child, it's because my bloody wife is in a snoring stupor by the time I come to bed."

Perhaps she *did* drink too much, but it was his fault for not loving her more, for leaving her alone too often, for expecting her to embrace him lovingly whenever he happened to be in the mood. She really only drank to excess on the days when she lost hope that anything would ever change. When it felt like there was no other way to cope.

"I haven't had a drop today," she said weakly.

"The day is still young."

"Not as young as the candy floss girl."

Edmund pursed his lips. "Now you're being melodramatic."

"Says the man who nearly pitched a wobbly because his four-year-old son wanted to sit in his mum's lap. I honestly can't imagine why you'd want another child."

"I love Hugh," Edmund said.

"More than Anabelle?"

"I refuse to play this game."

"Don't row, Mum and Dad."

Hugh was suddenly beside them again. Rodney, looking sheepish, was several steps behind.

"We're not rowing," said Penelope, praying he hadn't heard the worst of it.

"Your mum was just explaining how much she loves to play games," Edmund added, for once fast on his feet.

Hugh peered at him worriedly. "But not you, Dad?"

"I want to do whatever you want to do, son."

"Then the fun house. It's right there!" he said, pointing. "The sideshows aren't open yet."

The tears Penelope had been choking back threatened to erupt at the mere thought of navigating shifting floors, tilted walls, and a claustrophobic hall of mirrors.

"You two go on without me," she said.

After they were gone, she reached inside her blazer pocket

for her slim silver flask and took a quick sip of whiskey. The warmth it provided was so instantaneous that she immediately felt guilty.

But that didn't stop her from having another.

Chapter Seventeen
DEEP WATER

Startled by a cool drop of liquid on her thigh, Jennie opened her eyes, lowered her sunglasses, and peered up at the sky. The cerulean blue was still unbroken all the way to the hazy horizon. Beneath her, the boat rocked softly in the gentle swell. Although her armpits were damp from the Mediterranean heat, she couldn't possibly have dripped sweat on herself while lying down. *Please don't let it be bird poop*, she thought as she raised her knee to inspect the mysterious moisture. Fortunately, it was clear and completely innocent-looking. Sunglasses back up, she lowered herself, closed her eyes, and luxuriated in the penetrating peace off Porto Heli, on Greece's Peloponnese Peninsula, on board a yacht worth more money than her family would earn in their entire lives.

Hugh's surprise vacation was the best gift he'd given her so far, after the engagement ring: no responsibilities, no crowds, no reporters, and best of all, no Jeremy Legrand. With only a month until their wedding, she couldn't have needed it more. At first, flummoxed by the fact that their host was none other than Imogen Banfield-March—whose family owned a nearby

villa, Aegean Oaks, and kept a yacht, the *Somerset*, on standby—
Jennie had wondered how she would possibly be pleasant to
her supposed rival for a week. But she'd been completely won
over by the end of the first day. Not only was Imogen obviously
going out of her way to be welcoming, but she had brought
along her latest beau, Tom Pressley, an MP's son who worked
in e-commerce and dabbled in Formula 1 racing. The pair's
chemistry wasn't exactly red-hot, but Hugh had provided Jennie's only experience of aristocratic courtship, which she had
to assume wasn't typical. Courts, flying solo, had been forgiven
by Hugh and finally welcomed back into the fold after admitting and apologizing for petulantly leaking their relationship to
the press. And while Jennie still wasn't sure she trusted him, it
was easy enough to be friendly—after all, he had played a brief
but important role in her first meeting with Hugh. Rounding
out the group of seven were James Delashay, a school friend
of Hugh and Courts, and his girlfriend Arabella Foxton. Both
of them were so quick-witted and wryly funny that she could
hardly believe they were hedge fund managers.

Naturally, all of them but Tom had been coming here for
years. Away from what Hugh kept referring to as "civilization"
and the pressure to perform for cameras and peers, they behaved
a lot like her own friends with running jokes, goofy games, and
oft-repeated stories she was sure would have cracked her up if
only she had been there herself.

Another mysterious raindrop splashed her neck, undoubtedly carried by some stratospheric wind, as she reflected on one
key difference between Hugh's friends and hers: their insistence
on playing practical jokes. Some were truly stupid, like the time
James filled the sugar bowl with salt before Hugh and Jennie
sat down for breakfast, or the way Courts short-sheeted the bed
before their arrival the previous night.

"Legacy of the British public school system, I'm afraid," a laughing Hugh had explained as he sent back his ruined oatmeal and strawberries. "The masters are so sadistic that the pupils can't help but take it out on one another."

"At least no one's getting buggered in the night here," James had observed.

"Much to the everlasting regret of some," said Arabella, rolling her eyes.

Drop. Drop. Drop. Now they were landing all over her body, even on the book splayed beside her sweating glass of kombucha.

Jennie had heard of freak weather, even tiny fish dropping from clear blue skies, but this was truly baffling. Then she heard a bare foot drag on the decking and she knew. Craning her neck, she saw Courts standing just behind her, holding a large natural sponge dripping seawater. Behind him, everyone else was watching, highly entertained, while James recorded the prank on his phone.

All righty then, thought Jennie.

Calmly, grinning at Courts, she climbed out of the chaise longue. "You totally got me!"

Then, as he laughed and shook the dripping sponge at her, getting water everywhere, she shoved him over the railing into the crystal blue waters of Heli Harbor.

Hugh laughed the loudest. "Well *done*, Jennie!"

That night they dined on the deck, a casual meal of grilled seafood with vegetables, fresh baked rustic bread, and cheap but delicious local wine. The air was so still that the candles on the table barely flickered, and the full moon shining on the glassy sea made a path so bright Jennie found it hard to believe she couldn't follow it to shore.

Imogen was not only smart and beautiful but also the perfect host. Every time Hugh, Courts, and James threatened to get lost in nostalgic stories about grueling hikes or equally grueling pub crawls, she would change the subject and then, at just the right moment, say, "I want to know what *Jennie* thinks." She actually listened, too, as though she found the midwestern perspective simply fascinating. As the conversation hopscotched from TV to movies to music to food, occasionally landing on politics or climate change, Jennie found it all so *normal* that it was hard to believe everyone at the table sat within arm's length of England's levers of power.

The third night, after a perfect day of swimming, napping, and eating, broken only by a noisy hour-long excursion on jet skis, Jennie and Hugh traded back rubs in their cabin. Jennie, relaxed from head to toe after a generous half-hour rubdown, was doing her best to stay awake long enough to return the favor.

"I'm so happy you're here," murmured Hugh, his face in the pillow.

She kissed his left shoulder blade, then the right one, tasting salt on his sun-warmed skin. "Me, too. Can we stay?"

"For the rest of the week, anyway. I hope you won't get tired of my friends."

"I doubt it. They're super nice."

"They absolutely adore you."

"Is that why they keep playing these stupid pranks?"

Hugh chuckled. "It means you're in the club. They've all told me how wonderful you are."

She hesitated to believe it. But as a warm feeling flooded her stomach, she decided to take him at his word. Was it so crazy to think that, given enough time and enough practice, she could fit into Hugh's world after all? Enduring the 24/7 public scrutiny would be easier knowing that, once in a while, they could escape like this.

"But there's one thing bothering me," said Hugh.

"What is it?" Jennie stopped kneading as he rolled onto his side and looked up at her, gently stroking her arm.

"The whole world's heard my song and you haven't yet played it for *me*."

She laughed. "It wasn't finished. I never meant to play it for Ottilie and Grethe, either. It just kind of came out."

Hugh nudged her with his hip. "Well, when will it be done?"

She had been writing and rewriting lyrics on her notes app but the end result never felt like what she had imagined it would be. But that was usually the case with her songs. Maybe it was close enough to call it done.

Giving Hugh a squeeze, she crossed the cabin, feeling very airy with her top off, and opened her guitar case. Hugh leaned against the headboard and pulled the sheet up to his waist as she sat down on an ottoman and quickly checked her tuning. Tapping her foot on the carpet, she imagined a gently brushed snare keeping the andante 4/4 beat as she began plucking the cords.

Then she sang:

I've got a prince, he's a heck of a guy
They don't know that I'm planning to steal him
I've got his heart and the rest of him, too
Says the note that I'm holding him for ransom
But the joke's on you
Cause I won't give him back
For all the tea
In England
There's nowhere to run, and there's nowhere to hide
But I always feel safe when he's near me
They're counting the spoons but they're on the wrong
track

The treasure I took has been buried
But the joke's on you
Cause I won't give him back
For all the jewels
In the Tower of London
Princesses will come, and princesses will go
Some find the door while some lose their way
But if they won't let me take my Prince Hugh
Then I guess that I'll just have to stay

When she finished, his eyes were shining.

"I love you," he said.

"And I love you, too."

"Come here."

She dropped the guitar without bothering to put it back in its case.

Chapter Eighteen
SUNSTROKE

On the fourth day, Jennie and Hugh were sitting together at the back of the yacht, their muscles pleasantly sore from swimming and their brains half-baked by the sun. Neither of them had said much of anything for the past half hour. But when a water taxi arced out from behind the breakwater and began motoring through the chop toward them, Hugh suddenly climbed to his feet.

"Right, that's my cue. I'm off."

"Where are you going?" asked Jennie.

But Hugh had already disappeared belowdecks. Did he have some errand to run on shore? Jennie watched the small boat approach. It seemed fairly full, which probably meant it was bringing local cleaning staff for the second shift. Toweling her hair, she walked to the small bar amidships and requested a cold sparkling water from the bartender, then drank half of it standing in place.

As the water taxi rang its bell to signal its arrival, a couple of deckhands hurried over to the side of the ship to help it tie up. Hugh reappeared, wearing Bermuda shorts, a polo shirt, sunglasses, and a Cheshire Cat grin. Courts, James, and Tom were right behind him, all dressed for town.

"All right, what's going on?" Jennie asked.

"We're under strict orders from Imogen to spend the day ashore," said Hugh.

Jennie wondered if the whole thing was yet another practical joke or just an excuse for a bro-down. She wished she were invited, too, because as nice as Imogen and Arabella were, she still didn't want to spend the whole day with just them.

Then Karen's head popped up above the side of the boat.

"*Mom?*"

"Surprise!"

Her mother kept climbing, carefully watching her footing, until she was standing on deck. "Prince Hugh kept calling it a 'hen do,' but I believe what he means is that we're here for your bachelorette party."

As Hugh started laughing uncontrollably, a shocked Jennie could only ask one question: "*We?*"

There were five of them in all: Karen; her younger sister, Jennie's Aunt Kelly; Amy Bensen, Jennie's high school best friend; Leaf, Jennie's tour drummer; and Diego, her bass player, who apparently made the cut as "one of the girls." The reunion was hectic, with heartfelt hugs, breathless explanations, and wide-eyed wonderment on the part of the guests at their surroundings. When Vivienne Banfield-March appeared as the last of the boarding party, there was already so much commotion that Jennie's stomach flutters hardly even registered. Hugh, Imogen, and Vivienne had teamed up to plan the surprise, and although they all tried to refuse the credit, clearly each of them had played an active role, the collaboration made easier by their long familiarity.

Jennie was too overwhelmed to know what to think. After the water taxi had unloaded the rest of its passengers, whose

purpose she was soon to discover, the pilot jangled his bell again
and Hugh, Courts, Tom, and James hurried over the side. As
the small boat cast off and headed for shore, Hugh put his hand
over his heart and called, "I promise not to hurry back!"

"Surprised?" asked Karen.

Jennie could only nod.

"I'll bet. Probably about as much as I was when the caller
ID said *Kensington Palace* and that Ian fella told me I was flying
first class to Athens. Now, let's get this party started."

As a steward passed around a tray of bubbling champagne
flutes, Imogen, archly playing cruise director, laid out the schedule to everyone's delight. Jennie was getting used to pampering,
but this ended up being like day camp in heaven. First, everyone got a massage, followed by facials and mani-pedis. This
was followed by high tea, where the tea and finger sandwiches
were complemented by caviar, more champagne, some kind
of crab/lobster cocktail, and equally elegant vegan options for
Jennie. Karen, Kelly, Amy, Leaf, and Diego were all drinking
with gusto, and she didn't blame them—this was a bachelorette party, after all—but she was careful to moderate her own
consumption. Not only had she never been much of a drinker,
but she had been in the sun all day, and she wanted to savor
and remember every moment.

Her resolve was tested when, much to her horror, Karen
lugged out two whole photo albums and went through them
page by page, not sparing any of the embarrassing stories, from
the time she got lost at the mall to an epically bad first date.
Imogen seemed rapt and delighted, and although Jennie could
tell Vivienne was faking it, at least she was gracious doing so.

For once, dinner was not the world's freshest sushi, or even
local seafood or English beef brought by courier—it was crispy
chicken supreme casserole, her favorite dinner in grade school,

with tofu standing in for the chicken but otherwise prepared according to Karen's recipe. Her friends from home dug in with gusto, and the younger English women politely cleared half their plates. Vivienne only managed a few bites before pushing it away, excusing her lack of appetite as a byproduct of travel.

After dinner, they all insisted on giving speeches, delivered in reverse order of who had known Jennie the longest. Arabella's was brief and wickedly funny, and Imogen's and Vivienne's were short and respectful. Those from her friends and family were heartfelt but unpolished, making it hard for Jennie to avoid monitoring her hosts' reactions.

Leaf, like most drummers, wasn't a gifted orator. She kicked off with: "I mean . . . holy shit, Jennie! Look at us! We're on a boat, dude!" before moving into a hilarious story about the time they had bonded after being locked out of their hotel in Osaka.

Diego was probably Jennie's closest friend in the music world and also the most honest: "I have to say, once I got over the idea that I was going to be best friends with, like, an actual princess, which makes me an honorary queen"—he held expertly for laughter—"I have to admit that I got worried about you. I don't personally know any genuine, A-list famous people, but I know that it can mess with people's heads. I feel a lot better having seen the way Hugh treats you and the way you two really feel about each other. And, honestly, the fact that we all got invited to this yacht party goes a long, long way toward bribing me. So, here's to you and Hugh."

Jennie did take a drink, with a tear in her eye, after that one.

She had not remained as close to Amy, but from grade school through high school, they were almost inseparable, and they had always kept in touch. Amy seemed both overwhelmed and possibly to be angling for a call-up as maid of honor.

"Even though you and I were never the kind of girls who

really dreamed of being princesses—we were too busy skinning our knees for that—there was always something about the way you carried yourself," she said, misting over. "Something noble. Something—even though I didn't have the words for it—regal."

Aunt Kelly told a bawdy story about the time she tracked down and scared the shit out of the sophomore who got to second base with Jennie and then broke her freshman heart. She concluded it by saying, "I thought I should tell that one now, since they probably don't want to hear it at the Buckingham Palace reception—assuming I'm actually invited after this."

Despite all the laughter, when it was Karen's turn to talk, she suddenly got so overcome with emotion that she could hardly read her notes on the page she'd unfolded from her purse. She called Jennie "my baby girl"; she sobbed about "losing you"; and she said, "I don't care if Hugh does become King of England, if he doesn't treat you right, he's going to have to answer to me"—the last statement finally cracking their uncomfortable hosts' genteel reserve and making them visibly cringe.

Not that Jennie cared. But by the time her mom had finished, she was crying, too.

"I can't get my head around the fact that you are now one of the most famous women in the world," said her mother. "And it's not that you don't deserve it, but when I really get down to it, it doesn't mean anything to me. Maybe I even resent it a teeny, tiny bit, because it makes it harder to see you. But I loved you when you were a colicky baby with poop in your diaper, so I guess I can love you when you're world famous, too."

———

Hugh returned at midnight, slipping into their cabin with a sunburned neck and beer on his breath. He, Courts, Tom, and

James had spent the day in a taverna garden drinking Mythos beer, he explained—possibly more than one taverna.

"But don't worry, Rodney made us leave before Courts made an ass of himself," he reassured her.

"I'm glad," she said, kissing him. "Now go shower."

He did, then passed out immediately.

The next day, an elaborate brunch was laid out for all the guests. Everyone was staying for another night, which delighted Jennie. The yacht was so big that they all had their own cabins, even Karen and Aunt Kelly. Feeling relaxed and happy, Jennie drank not one but two bellinis, letting the bubbles go to her head and knowing that she could just take an afternoon nap if she wanted. Why not live it up?

She had just finished eating a big plate of food when suddenly something was wrong. She had never felt anything like it before. She had only seconds to push her chair back and stagger over to the rail before everything—two bellinis, six pieces of vegan maki, three crostini with rustic olive medley, several grilled asparagus, and a bite of flourless chocolate cake—were forcefully expelled into the glittering blue waters below. Heaving, catching her breath, and wondering whether anything else would come up, Jennie was forced to contemplate the disgusting snail trail down the immaculate white hull of the *Somerset*.

Hugh was at her side instantly, holding her gently, stroking her back. But no one else spoke or moved until, with perfect timing, James asked, "Was it something I said?"

―――――――――

Jennie let Hugh help her back to their cabin, where she spent the rest of the day in bed. She threw up two more times in the wastebasket, then once more in a towel—fortunately, that one was almost a dry heave now that her stomach was empty. Feverish and foggy-brained, she felt completely confused by this sudden turn of events.

"I didn't even drink that much," she told Hugh as he solicitously rubbed her shoulders that night.

"It was definitely food poisoning," said Karen, who had stopped in to check on her. "All that fish sitting out in the hot sun? *Please.*"

"I didn't have any fish," Jennie reminded her.

"Well, something was off. Even a hundred-and-eighteen-pound girl doesn't puke like that after two belugas."

"Bellinis," murmured Hugh.

"I might have had three," said Jennie.

"I want you to go to the hospital," said Karen.

"Your mum's right," said Hugh. "We should have taken you directly."

"That's the last thing we need," protested Jennie. "We'll never be able to keep that secret."

Hugh squeezed her shoulder hard enough to make her wince. "Your health is more important, darling."

"I'm probably just seasick. Or maybe it's sunstroke. I never spend this much time in the sun."

Or maybe it was sun, sea, and a second Bellini. Jennie still couldn't believe she'd thrown up and ruined her own party when no one else had shown any effect from drinking other than a little excess good humor.

"If it *is* food poisoning, then maybe she doesn't need the hospital after all," said Karen, apparently reconsidering her position. "A doctor would just tell her to rest and drink lots of fluid. When Dave ate some bad deviled eggs at the company picnic, his doctor told him to sip ice-cold Gatorade every five minutes until he felt better."

Hugh didn't say anything for a minute. He seemed to be wrestling with the decision. Then he stood up.

"I'll be back soon," he said. "If there's no Gatorade on board, I'm sure they'll have something in the shops."

After he left, Jennie submitted to Karen's mothering, and the washcloth soaked in ice water did feel wonderfully soothing once it was laid across her forehead. After a while, though, she told her mom to go back to the party.

"I'm fine right here, Jennie," she said, leafing through a magazine.

"*Go*. And don't pretend you get to be on a yacht all the time. This is a big deal. I want you and everyone else to have a blast."

Karen smiled and put it down. After changing the washcloth, she kissed Jennie on the forehead.

"Thanks, sweetie. I hope this doesn't ruin the whole day for you. If it helps, you're not the first bride-to-be who upchucked at her bachelorette party."

───────────

She was dozing when Hugh quietly let himself into the room. She sat up as he unscrewed the top of a bottle of antifreeze-blue Gatorade, poured it into a cut-glass tumbler, and brought it over to the bed. His expression was grim.

"What's wrong?" she asked. "Don't tell me you're getting sick, too."

"It can wait."

He handed her the glass and watched her swallow, then set it on the bedside table.

"No, tell me."

Hugh gave her his phone. Jennie stared until she made sense of what she was seeing: a grainy photo, unmistakably shot from far away with a telephoto lens, that showed her hanging over the rail and spilling her guts down the side of the boat.

The headline screaming across the home page of the *Daily Mail* was even harder to process:

PUKING PRINCESS-TO-BE PARTIES ON YACHT WHILE MANCHESTER BURNS

Part Three

PRINCESS CHARMING

Chapter Nineteen

THE THRONE ROOM

Jennie just needed a moment alone—maybe several long moments. But she couldn't have stumbled into a more inappropriate hideout. Rather than making her way to Hugh's private car, halfway down the train, she had walked along a short passageway and opened the nearest door, only to find herself in Edmund's private bathroom. It was like a palace on wheels, with a marble sink, gleaming brass fixtures, and filigreed wall sconces on either side of the mirror. Staring at the brown calfskin toilet seat bolted to the commode, she knew she wouldn't be sitting upon the King's private throne.

Most of the royal household was still gathered in the King's lounge—Edmund and Eleanora, Freddie and Cece, Alice, Prince and Princess Stuart, even Hugh's cousins Rex and Will—all of them sitting stoically in stiff-backed chairs as the train ground its way to its final destination. Edmund wanted everyone present, probably to send his family a message that if his subjects were suffering, so should they.

While Jennie puked her guts out under the bright Mediterranean sun, fire and rescue investigators had been sifting through the smoking ashes of a veterans' home in Manchester. Their working hypothesis was that an unauthorized, uninspected air conditioner had overloaded the fifty-year-old wiring and sparked a fire inside the walls. Because the smoke detectors and the sprinkler system were both on the same failed electrical circuit, the flames spread undetected and unextinguished until twenty-two men were killed and sixty-one had been injured. They were veterans who had served in Yugoslavia, the Gulf War, the Falklands, and even Northern Ireland.

Hugh took the loss personally, blaming himself alongside the officials whose neglect had actually allowed it to happen. Jeremy Legrand's response was more calculated as he predicted—accurately—that the royal family would be condemned by the media due to their longtime support of the charity operating the home. The most visibly involved royal veteran, Hugh made an easy target for public outrage. Jennie's stomach was still churning as she, Hugh, and Karen were rushed onto an overnight flight to London. By the following day, while her mom remained behind at Kensington Palace, Hugh and Jennie joined the rest of his family in a show of force to demonstrate their concern for the victims.

The paparazzi photo hadn't been her fault, obviously. The *Somerset* was not the only boat in Heli Harbor that day, and it would have been relatively easy for any photographer to use a telephoto lens without being noticed. And while the timing of the photo and the fire was a coincidence that would only be linked by a hack headline writer, it really could not have been worse.

The second story—the one that broke in the early morning while they were still flying west across Europe—wasn't her fault, either. But it felt even more incriminating, somehow.

JENNIE'S REAL MUM STEPS FORWARD, blared the headline.

Below that, the subheadline summarized the story with disgusting simplicity: *"I WAS HOOKED ON DRUGS," CLAIMS
EX-ADDICT. "NOW I WANT MY DAUGHTER BACK."*

Cedar Rapids, Iowa, USA—Drug-addicted Diane
Danforth was seventeen years old when she gave
birth to a baby girl she loved too much to try to raise.
She didn't know the father, for starters. And she was
living hand to mouth on the streets of Davenport,
Iowa, where she slept on friends' floors or in abandoned cars.

For cash, she says simply, "I did what I had to do."

Desperate to avoid the responsibilities of motherhood, junkie Diane left her defenseless baby girl
at the Davenport fire station less than twelve hours
after giving birth. Then she scuttled away into the
night.

For twenty-six years, she had no contact or knowledge of her daughter's whereabouts.

But over the past year, media coverage has made
the now clean-and-sober supermarket cashier aware
that Jennie Jensen, fiancée of Prince Hugh and a future princess, is none other than the Baby Doe she so
long ago abandoned.

"I have tried a million times to get a message to
her," Diane told the *Star-Express* in an exclusive interview. "But her people just won't respond. I don't want
money or anything like that. I just want to tell my
baby girl I'm sorry. And if she can forgive me, I want a
second chance. I want to be in her life."

At the time of publication, Kensington Palace has
not answered requests for comment.

On the plane to London, Jennie and Karen had talked and cried together until finally falling asleep an hour before landing. A grimly efficient Legrand met them on the tarmac.

"Don't worry, it's been taken care of."

Jennie didn't find his tone very reassuring. "Has she been trying to contact me?"

"We haven't been able to locate any letters, but it's possible they were discarded. She obviously didn't go through proper channels. The royal family is the subject of outlandish claims every day."

The pain and anger Jennie felt at the tabloid's use of *real mum* in its headline made her want to dismiss Diane Danforth as easily as Legrand did, but she still had nagging doubts. She couldn't even say for sure if she even wanted Diane to be "taken care of." If she hadn't still been half sick and exhausted, she might have asked whether Diane Danforth had been paid to go away or the tabloid had been threatened with legal action by the Crown. It was just too much to think about. And it was hard to imagine when she would feel collected enough to decide how she felt.

"What if she is my birth mother?" she asked.

"Don't be so naive," he said briskly. "Do you think she gave that interview for free? Do you think she's going away simply because we asked politely? Is that the behavior of a remorseful parent?"

"I can't answer that until I talk to her."

"*Don't* talk to her. If this situation had presented itself differently, the reunion might have been useful. But it's quite clear what's happening. She's merely the first one to step forward and won't be the last."

Useful. That single word said everything else she needed to know.

Karen had hugged her tightly before separate cars whisked

her to Kensington Palace and Hugh and Jennie to King's Cross station. "Just take it one crisis at a time. If this woman is real or phony it doesn't change anything about us. I'll be waiting here for you, and we'll work through it together."

"I love you so much, Mom."

―――――――――

In King Edmund's loo, Jennie squeezed eye drops into her travel-weary eyes before bending over to wash her face in the sink. As she toweled dry, she heard raised voices in the next room— Edmund's private suite, she thought. It certainly sounded like Edmund and Eleanora talking. And he didn't sound happy.

"Honestly, it's just one thing after another," Edmund snapped before his sentence disappeared in an unintelligible murmur.

" . . . certainly awful timing . . ." said Eleanora.

"How long must we . . ."

The royal tooth glass, spotlessly clean, was nestled securely in a wall-mounted brass ring. Jennie lifted it and pressed its mouth against the wall. She leaned closer until her ear touched its base. The voices became easier to understand.

"Have you seen her picture?" Eleanora was saying. "It's certainly plausible."

"I don't suppose she'll submit to DNA testing," said Edmund.

"One could have it done without her knowing."

"Unless it's best not to know. What if we discover my grandchild, heir to the throne, is truly descended from a drug-addled supermarket cashier? For all we know, the father was a genuine milkman."

Eleanora laughed. "Don't joke, Eddie."

"I'm quite serious. The genetics could be a nightmare."

"The nippers could all get your nose, for example."

"Stop it. Ancestry aside, my greater fear is that we have yet another one who's simply not cut out for this."

Another one? thought Jennie.

Then the train lurched. Thrown off balance, Jennie banged the glass against the wall. Edmund and Eleanora stopped talking. Had they heard her? The engine's whistle tooted and a shudder rippled through the cars as the train began slowing down.

Jennie quickly wiped the glass clean and put it back. She checked her face in the mirror and then let herself out of the bathroom. She was still hurrying toward the lounge as Edmund's door opened behind her.

Hugh, who was now sitting alone, stood up and hugged her. "How are you feeling? Everyone's gone back to spruce up. We've got ten minutes before we disembark at Manchester Piccadilly."

"I'm fine," she said. Telling herself it was just a temporary lie.

She followed Hugh back to their private car. While Hugh scrolled the latest Twitter takes using his anonymous account, she inspected the black-and-gray designer mourning outfit Poppy had selected for her in the full-length mirror. She wiped off and reapplied her eyeliner before brushing some color back into her cheeks. She looked fine, but she felt terrible.

The buildings had been getting larger and closer together as they glided into the city center. Now, as the train finally pulled into the station, Jennie saw through tinted glass dozens of police securing the area while passengers on the platform gaped at the sleek black cars. Crowded behind a thin cordon, press photographers waited for their chance to shoot them stepping off the train.

Something in her body language must have told Hugh how she was feeling.

"If you're not up for this, just say the word," he said, putting his phone away.

Jennie couldn't meet his eyes. "I don't think I can do this."

He stiffened but recovered quickly. "Then you can wait right here while we make the appearance. I'll explain to my father you're still not feeling well. Jeremy will explain to the press that you're ill."

Even though they both knew her absence would only fuel the false narrative. *Hungover Jennie Snubs Veterans.*

"That's not what I mean," she told him. "I can get through today. And tomorrow. Next year I'm not so sure about."

Worry showed in Hugh's tired eyes, and Jennie could see him choosing his words carefully. The thought that she was forcing him to make her feel better yet again only made her feel worse. Did he really want to spend the rest of his life picking her up, dusting her off, and defending her?

For once, he didn't rush over and hug her. He sank into his chair and nodded to himself. There was a discreet rap on their door—"Five minutes, please"—but he ignored it. He stared at his shoes.

"I can't blame you. The pressure on us is simply unbearable and it will never stop. And I'm not blind. I know it's even worse for you. When they wrote stories about my girlfriends at uni, or the women I dated when I was in the service, the press was always brutal. To them, rarely to me. Boys aren't at fault. Mum was a victim of that, too. The rumors and fabrications . . . once they started, they didn't stop. And then when she did try to find love after separating from my father, they all but called her a whore."

Jennie sat down, too, her eyes brimming with tears. "I don't want you to have to go through it again with me. It's about to get worse and I have no idea where it will end."

"That's quite beside the point because you're the only one I want." He looked up at her. "It's difficult for me to say this, but I think you're rather stronger than my mother."

She laughed hollowly, not knowing how to respond.

"No, I mean it, Jennie. You're amazing. You don't even know how impressive you are. But you just have to keep showing them day by day. Some people will never understand but don't listen to them, it's only noise. All that matters is how the two of us feel about one another, and I know how I feel: I love you and I believe in you. And if you leave, they will win and I will lose. And in the unlikely event that I ever recover from my broken heart, they'll treat the one after you just the same."

Jennie's chest was heaving. She was crying with sadness, with love, and maybe even a tiny bit of hope. She walked over to him, raised him up, and wrapped him in a fierce embrace. It wasn't the right time to tell him that the press was not her only enemy—and may not have been his mother's only enemy, either—that could wait just a little bit longer. No one would ever love her like Hugh. And she would never love anyone the way she loved him. That would have to be enough.

Chapter Twenty

SMALL GESTURES

Jennie was alone. As she explored the side hall in the convalescent wing of the Manchester Royal Infirmary—peering around corners, peeking through doorways, and listening to the quiet echo of her own footsteps—not a single minder had bothered her for one whole minute.

As soon as the royal party arrived at the hospital, it quickly became apparent that despite all their years of training, no one but Hugh knew quite what to do. Even on the occasions when royals stepped out of receiving lines to visit the bedridden, encounters were brief and tightly scripted. But here, with 61 injured veterans and 105 unhurt but homeless, all of them housed together "in hospital" simply because there was no other place for them to go, no script was equal to the scale of the need. Legrand's original plan had been for the entire royal family to be photographed leaving the train, entering the hospital, and receiving ambulatory patients in the cafeteria. Edmund and Hugh would visit the bedsides of veterans carefully vetted so their injuries would not horrify viewers (eliminating all victims of the fire who had actually suffered burns). Then, at a brief "press encounter," Edmund would assure all Britons that nothing could be more important to him than the safety of those who had served King and country.

Before Legrand's plan could be put into action, and even before they had all left the train, Hugh had argued for a different approach.

"There are so many of us," he'd told his skeptical father. "Let's just all spread out. We don't have to rehearse everything. Let it all happen as it will. The more veterans we can speak with, the better."

"We still must have photos, of course," Edmund insisted.

"Of course," said Hugh.

To Jennie's amazement, Edmund okayed it. He must have been seriously freaked out to agree to something that broke so badly from protocol and precedent.

Deciding to go off script was one thing. Actually doing it was another. Flanked by photographers, videographers, favored reporters, and the usual phalanx of secretaries and assistants, most of them still moved in a pack. Shadowing Edmund and Eleanora, Freddie and Cece made a show of poking their heads into adjoining rooms while Prince and Princess Stuart conferred with each other, and Rex and Will seemed somewhat distracted by their phones. Only Hugh and Princess Alice acted truly independently. Determined to help them, Jennie headed off on her own, too. A visit from her would never mean as much to a veteran as one from Hugh or any of the real members of the royal family, but she wanted to do what she could.

And miraculously, no one followed her.

The first room she checked was empty. The bed was stripped, and the furniture and floor reeked of disinfectant. Jennie hoped the room was empty simply because it hadn't received a patient, but it still took her a beat to move on because she also knew that the patient could have died.

In the second room, a bearded man in his late thirties made eye contact almost as if he had been waiting.

"Christ, it's actually you," he said in astonishment, adding, "Pardon my language."

Jennie stepped through the doorway and smiled. "I don't have a royal title yet, so you can still swear like a sailor around me if you want to."

His eyes—bright blue and oddly bloodshot—flickered. "Thank you, ma'am. As it happens, I *am* a fucken sailor."

It felt good to laugh with him, even though his own chuckle quickly turned to coughing, then an alarming hacking that lasted so long she almost ran for a nurse. He motioned for her to sit, though, so she wheeled a stool over to his bed and looked him over while he collected himself. She wondered why the still-young man had been living in a veterans' home until she noticed voids under the sheet below both of his knees.

"Were you injured in the fire?" she asked.

"Smoke inhalation," he croaked. "Not too much worse than I used to do to myself with two packets of fags a day."

"It must be miserable being in the hospital."

He shrugged. "No worse than anywhere I've been. Haven't lived in a proper house since I was sixteen. Two years in reformatory, then I spent thirteen in the army as a transport driver until I got lucky and an IED wrecked my transport in Helmand Province. I'm used to cells, barracks, hospital rooms, you name it. The real reason I'm stuck in this bed is when the firemen pulled me out of my room they didn't bring my prosthetics along. Expensive buggers, too."

"Oh," said Jennie, not knowing what else to say.

"Name's Trevor," he said. "I know who you are, of course.

Nurse told me we were getting a royal visit, but I never thought I'd actually see one of you for myself. Is the King here as well?"

She nodded. "Almost everyone. I can't promise you'll see him, unfortunately."

"That's all right. Don't know what I'd say to His Royal Arse, anyway, especially if I can't get *my* royal arse out of bed. How'm I supposed to bow when I'm flat on my back?"

"I don't think you have to bow if you're a hospital patient."

There was an awkward silence as Trevor's eyes searched hers.

"How're you getting on with them lot?" he eventually asked. "How's life in the palace?" .

Jennie was so taken aback she again didn't know how to answer. He waited until she choked out, "It has its challenges."

"I hear you, love. I wouldn't want *my* fucken life on every Tom, Dick, and Harry's phones, either. I didn't know my real folks, but at least no one's making me feel shite about it, either."

"I thought I was the one supposed to be cheering *you* up," said Jennie, liking him a lot.

Trevor reached down and flattened the sheet, bringing the outline of his amputated legs into horribly clear relief. "I used to live for fucken football. Following Milwall, playing what's basically pub league at military bases. When I lost my legs it was a blow knowing I'd never make another tackle. But I survived that and I'll survive this, too."

Jennie took his hand and gave it a squeeze. "Can I bring you anything?"

Letting go, he picked up the handset on his bed and pressed the call button three times in a row. "Nurses don't answer this thing half the time. I'd love a cup of tea."

Jennie couldn't find a nurse, but she did locate a staff beverage station with an electric kettle, clean mugs, and bags of tea. She brewed Trevor a cup and delivered it, returning once again to fill his request for milk and sugar. Then, wanting to see as many people as possible, she said goodbye and moved on.

In the next room, a very old man sat in a chair playing solitaire on his bedside table. Seemingly uninjured, he was wearing pajamas and a dressing gown and had a tartan blanket draped across his skinny legs despite the summer heat. He looked up when he heard her voice.

"Hi! I'm Jennie Jensen. Can I come in?"

"Yes, of course, young lady," he said in a light Scottish brogue. "Captain Alastair McGinn, Gordon Highlanders."

Jennie found a chair and pulled it closer, noticing a tremor in his gnarled, spotted hands as he continued turning and placing cards from a deck that looked soft from constant use. She had no idea if he recognized her. Maybe he thought she was a social worker or some other civil servant checking up on him.

"Can I ask whether you were hurt in the fire?" she inquired.

Captain McGinn shook his head. "I still walk well and I sleep poorly. Fortunately for me, my room was on the ground floor and close to an exit, so I was able to escape quickly. I watched from the car park as the flames ate up my room. After my curtains burned, I could see the picture of my late wife curl and turn black."

Although he continued playing solitaire on autopilot, his eyes were brimming with tears. Jennie's were, too.

"I'm so sorry."

The old soldier kept talking as though he hadn't heard her, as though she wasn't even there. Turning and sorting cards, he deftly built column after column.

"The fire took everything. All her letters. My clothes, my books, campaign souvenirs. The journal I kept in the war. Even my service uniform and my decorations. Eighty-seven years old and all I've got left is my pajamas and bathrobe. They say you come into the world naked and alone and you die the same way, but you never really think it will happen to you."

"Have you had any family visit you?" asked Jennie, sniffling.

"My wife's dead, my son's dead," he said with a rueful shake of his head. "Grandkids don't know me. My daughter comes twice a year, at Christmas and at my birthday, like she's carrying our Lord's cross up to Golgotha. She's only just been for my birthday and it's half a year 'til Christmas, so I don't suppose I'll see her soon."

Jennie suddenly felt completely inadequate to the task. What could she possibly do or say in the face of a lifetime of pain and suffering? What possible help or hope of healing could she offer? All she could think to do was to be present and listen, which was what she did. She sat by Captain McGinn's bedside for another half an hour while he spoke, almost rotely, about the hardships he'd suffered.

When he finally seemed to run out of steam, she asked, "Can I do anything for you?"

Finally, the cards stopped moving—except for the one in his gently shaking hand.

"Would you give an old soldier a hug?" he whispered.

Jennie rolled the table to one side, leaned over, and wrapped her arms around him. Royals did not *hug*, she knew. But she was not a royal. She was Jennie Jensen of Peoria, Illinois, with no special rank or authority or anything at all except the wish to make this lonely old man feel better.

She squeezed him gently, almost worried about cracking his birdlike bones. He smelled like old age: unwashed hair, musty clothing, sour breath, menthol, and medicine. She willed herself not to recoil but to hug him even tighter. Captain McGinn was right. The same thing did wait for everyone, from commoner to King.

Timidly, he reached for her sides and hugged her right back.

She held him until she felt his tired hands fall away, then plucked coarse, industrial-grade tissues from a nearly empty cardboard box so they could both wipe their shining eyes. She went through two tissues before she could see again.

"I'm the world's worst card player, but if you'd like to deal me in, I'll try my best," she said.

The faintest hint of a smile twisted the old man's thin blue lips. "Ever played gin rummy?"

"I haven't. Is it hard to learn?"

"A wee bit. And it takes a while to play. I've a better one. It's called Scabby Queen."

His hands had already collected the cards from solitaire and formed them into a deck, which shuffled and bridged so quickly her eyes had a hard time following.

"Easier?"

Captain McGinn winked. "Aye, it's dead easy. We'll leave just one queen in the deck and do our best to avoid her. He who holds the queen loses the game."

Maybe he knew who she was, after all. But either way, she liked him.

"Deal," she said.

From the Private Diary of HRH Princess Penelope

17 NOVEMBER 1990

There are things I shouldn't write, but I'm feeling drunk with possibility (and tipsy from champagne), so here, as they say, goes nothing.

Tonight was the Friends of Animal Husbandry gala. Notorious for being a snooze-fest, it is typically attended by yellow-toothed toffs in dandruff-flecked

tuxedos and their overperfumed wives, all of whom
know far too much about far too little. This year
threatened to be even duller than usual due to the
absence of Freddie, Cece, and a few of the more tolerable
FOEs, all of whom sent their regrets (due to "conflicts of
schedule") before the date was even announced.

I've bowed out in the past by "accidentally" agreeing
to a conflicting event and even an "untimely" upset
stomach, so Jeremy Legrand was dispatched in advance
to remind me of the charity's economic relevance to the
Commonwealth, Princess Alice's personal involvement,
and Her Majesty's fondness for the cause. Legrand
assured me the gala had been updated with a more
lively format—which I took to mean a chocolate
fountain or silent auction had been added—and I had
no choice but to promise I'd be there.

The evening began as usual with Edmund, cocktail
in hand, glaring irritably at the glass of wine on my
dressing table, nodding listlessly when he saw my dress
(a gorgeous red Victor Edelstein I hated to waste on the
event), and repeatedly checking his watch to remind
me how slow I am. Despite his watchful eye, I fortified
myself by finishing my chardonnay before we set out.
The last time, at dinner I had been seated beside the
chief benefactor, Lord Atherton, whose fondness for
describing bovine birth ("I was inside her up to my
elbow, trying to wrest her little calf free") had proven
detrimental to my appetite. The gentleman to my right,
whilst a more interesting conversationalist, nonetheless
grazed my breast no fewer than three times with his
elbow. After the meal, Edmund and I opened the
dancing with a waltz, which he soon broke off to cut

*in on couples with the best-looking wives, leaving me
to cha-cha and chat up their codger husbands. The
night had ended with sex and my lingering uncertainty
whether I was the actual object of his desire.*

*My dread of a repeat evening lasted only as long as
the drive to Buckingham Palace.*

*As soon as we'd ascended the Grand Staircase
and started down the hallway, we were greeted by the
thumping bass of disco music. I was certain it was a
figment of my imagination until the footmen opened
the double doors to the Ball Supper room. The space
had been transformed—to the extent any room at
Buckingham Palace can be—into Regine's or Tramp
nightclub circa 1978. Café style seating had been set up
around a circular dance area, overlooked by a DJ in
a metal booth, and a mirrored ball dangled from the
centre chandelier, bathing everything in a shimmering,
otherworldly glow.*

The whole scene was bonkers! Utterly, fabulously so.

*Princess Alice greeted us with kisses, wearing a
form-fitting, gold lamé dress she wouldn't have been
caught dead in back when it was in style. Her latest
beau—the tall, dark, and charmingly Italian Count
Lorenzo Albizi—wore a bell-bottomed tuxedo.*

*"I was unaware this was to be a costume party,"
Edmund shouted over the music.*

*"Only for those of us who planned it," Alice
said, pointing to a small group of similarly "groovy"
partygoers standing nearby.*

*Edmund, who hates more than anything to be caught
out, began fault-finding, insisting the music was too
loud, the seating was too crowded, and the strobe lights*

*were liable to provoke seizures in the elderly guests. Alice
held her ground and insisted the novelty would make it a
smashing event and profitable for the charity.*

*"Lighten up, dear brother," she said, swaying to the
music. "Or, as they say, turn the beat around."*

*I truly wanted nothing more than my husband
to take my hand, lead me out to the dance floor, and
in a scene that would have become legendary, do the
hustle with me. It was, after all, our duty to kick off the
dance portion of the evening. But whilst Edmund had
certainly been in nightclubs, I had no idea whether he'd
actually disco danced before.*

*"I was quite good at the electric slide in primary
school," I told him. "I'll show you, if you'd like."*

"Pass," he said, sauntering away.

*"Wanker," muttered Alice. "Why don't you two kick
off the dancing whilst I try to sort him out?"*

*The Count (as Alice calls him) kindly offered his
hand and we made our way to the dance floor. The DJ
quickly cued up "Dancing Queen" as the two of us tried
out our best disco moves.*

*"That dress is utterly magnificent," he said as we
bumped one hip and then the other.*

*(For the record, I like the Count. He not only says
the right things at the right times, but is clever, kind,
funny, and enables Alice to loosen up. She is under
increasing pressure to marry and I believe they make a
good team, although I do strongly suspect that, in the
absence of obligations, their gender preferences in terms
of intimate partners would be quite different. But who
am I to opine upon marriages of convenience?)*

I went on to mostly enjoy dances with Sir Roger

*Jameson, Clark Thompson, and Cornelius Owens. I
even found myself doing a lively version of the hustle
(and, thankfully, not the funky chicken) with none other
than Lord Atherton, who was clearly enjoying himself
much more than Edmund. When he jokingly suggested
that next year I should consider leaving the prince home
entirely, I was all too serious in my agreement.*

    *Then, from behind me, a lovely deep voice asked,
"Would you do me the honour of the next dance?"*

    *I turned and found myself looking into the (blue,
I think) eyes of a trim, sandy-haired, man in military
dress. Neither elderly nor doddering, he bowed
his (approximately thirty-five-year-old?) head and
introduced himself as Captain Anthony Heald. His
name sounded familiar, but I didn't think we'd met, as
I was sure I'd have remembered. As I wondered who he
was, how he'd made his way to the gala, and whether
Edmund would like me dancing with such an out-and-
out hunk, Captain Heald explained that he was the
guest of the Marchioness Livonia Devereaux.*

    *Livonia isn't a day over ninety-three and is decades
past being able to waltz, never mind disco.*

    *Good for her, I thought, hoping he wasn't one
of those men who made profitable friendships with
vulnerable older ladies.*

    *Before better judgement could prevail, I had
been won over by Captain Heald's dimpled smile and
allowed him to take my hand. I couldn't help but notice
his firm, assured grip, or how smoothly he stepped, or
his cedar-y scent. We chatted a bit. Mostly I just enjoyed
being in the company of a fanciable bloke who was more
or less my age.*

*I rather wanted to continue on with him, so much
so that I did the opposite, accepting an offer from Bryan
"Hands" Holcombe for the next song. As the stocky
reptile was thoroughly pickled, I did my best to keep him
at arm's length during the slow portion of "Last Dance."
Even so, he left me with the pungent aroma of hair oil
on the shoulder of my dress.*

*Knackered and sweaty, I stepped off the dance floor
and helped myself to an ice water with a lime wedge at
the bar.*

*Then Edmund appeared beside me. "Guzzling
cocktails, I see."*

*"Actually, all this dancing has left me quite thirsty."
Emboldened by the jolly time I'd been having, I decided
not to tell him I was drinking water.*

*"You're making an absolute spectacle of yourself on
the dance floor," he said, through his stiff-lipped public
conversation smile.*

*I fake smiled back. "Then so is the esteemed Lord
Atherton, and so are our other honoured guests. All
of whom are kind enough to dance with me when my
husband refuses."*

*"I was coming over to do just that when I saw you
hanging all over Hands Holcombe. Of all blokes."*

*"If you don't fill out my dance card in advance,
how will I know who's allowed and who's not?" I asked,
flagging down a waiter for a glass of champagne I now
very badly needed.*

*Edmund waved him away. "You've already had
more than enough."*

"Yes, I suppose I have," I said.

Holding back tears, I turned and walked in the

*direction of the loo. Before I got there though, I detoured to
a balcony where I could get some fresh air. I was slumped
over the chilly marble railing, gazing out at the barren
trees in the garden below, when I heard my name.*

*Captain Heald was in the doorway. He asked if
he could join me. When I nodded, he stepped out and
asked what no one ever does anymore: "Are you okay?"*

*What could I possibly tell him? That I'd been
dressed down by my flirtatious husband for flirting with
a man I found revolting, when a man I might very well
like to flirt with was now standing right in front of me?*

"Better now," I murmured.

*His eyes (which were in fact hazel) radiated
kindness. "I was concerned you might have got the
wrong impression of me during our brief conversation."*

"How's that?" I asked, genuinely puzzled.

*"The Marchioness Devereaux is . . . well, she's like a
grandmother to me."*

*He looked so earnest that I couldn't help but smile.
"So you're trying to say you're not an item?"*

*His laugh was deep and genuine. "I'm merely a riding
instructor with the good fortune of working for a large,
lovely family that's taken me in as one of their own."*

*I suddenly realised why his name sounded so familiar.
"You are the Anthony I've heard so much about."*

*"I trained Felix Hill and Eleanora Osborne-Webb
just this week, so I suppose I may just be the Anthony of
which you speak."*

*"Anne Claxton-Murray gave me your name a few
years back, but—"*

*"You never contacted me," he said, looking as
disappointed as I felt.*

"I became pregnant with Hugh."

I had to wonder if Edmund's discouragement of my riding lessons had less to do with risk to the pregnancy and more to do with the risk of allowing his wife to learn to ride from Captain Anthony Heald.

He leaned against the railing, close enough that I could feel the heat of him.

"I hope I'm not stepping out of line, but there's no time like the present," he said.

I wanted to say it was impossible for me to take riding lessons until I'd produced the long-anticipated spare. Or that I shouldn't be so near a man who wasn't my husband, especially one who looked and smelled so delightful. But Edmund has no such scruples, so why should I have maintained mine for so long?

Going forward, I will have to keep this diary somewhere more secure than the locked drawer of my writing desk, because what happened next was that I leaned in and kissed Captain Anthony Heald.

And he kissed me back.

Chapter Twenty-One

HUGGING THE THRONE

"Have you *seen* the headlines?"

As Poppy swept into the living room with an armload of newspapers, Jennie was so startled she splashed black coffee all over the tea table. Hugh had already gone to his office and Karen was reading silently with her feet up on an ottoman. Jennie hadn't even had a chance to catch her breath since their hurried departure from Athens, and after returning from Manchester late at night, she planned to spend the day doing nothing until a late afternoon "premarital counseling" meeting with the archbishop of Canterbury.

"I haven't, actually," she said, lifting that morning's mail pouch out of the way of the spreading puddle.

"*Jennie,*" tsk-tsk'd her mother. Without missing a beat, Karen dropped her book, shucked tissues out of the nearest box, and blotted the spill.

Jennie hoped her tone of voice didn't reveal her irritation to Poppy, but the daily media reports on her latest shortcomings were getting hard to take.

Then it finally registered that her minder was *smiling.*

"So sorry to startle you both," said Poppy. "But honestly, it's *good* news this time!"

While Karen carried sodden tissues to the nearest waste-basket, Jennie leaned forward and lifted a tabloid from the top of the stack.

JENNIE YANKS HEARTSTRINGS OF HURT VETS, announced the *Sun*.

SHE'S GOT THE ROYAL TOUCH, proclaimed *Metro* underneath it. Below the headline was a grainy photo of Jennie hugging Captain McGinn. The angle and the intruding door frame made it clear a photographer had followed her down the hall.

In the middle of the page, the veteran was quoted in large print: **SHE WAS KINDNESS ITSELF. NO AIRS AT ALL. SHE SPOKE TO ME LIKE I WAS HER UNCLE.**

Jennie kept flipping. All the tabloids seemed to agree. Even the so-called quality papers, their pages folded back to reveal columns and smaller stories, noted her visit to the Manchester Royal Infirmary with brisk approval.

Yes, the news was all good. But even then, relief was slow to come. Once again, even though she should have known better, she felt ambushed. Her actions had been documented without her knowledge and were now being discussed and dissected at breakfast tables, and undoubtedly on TV programs, across the country.

"I know, right?" said Poppy as Karen plopped down on the couch next to Jennie and patted her hand comfortingly. "It's a lovely change."

"It doesn't change anything for those poor veterans," Jennie observed.

"You leave that to Hugh," said Karen. "The important thing right now is that, for once, they've seen the real you. And they're not talking about . . . anything else."

Poppy folded her arms. "She's right. And if you need even more of a pick-me-up, it's even safe to go on Twitter—trust me."

Jennie pushed the papers aside. As Karen began digging through them, she sat back and sipped her half-full and rapidly cooling mug of coffee.

"Has the King weighed in? I'm sure he's found something wrong with my performance. I mean, we're not supposed to hug, right?"

Poppy appeared to be resisting an urge to roll her eyes. "I'm not privy to His Majesty's thoughts, but don't jump to conclusions. As an American royal-in-training, I believe you enjoy more leeway. This is what the pundits call a win, and I doubt anyone, in either palace, is displeased with that."

"I hope you're right."

"Anyway, I'm off," said Poppy, standing up. "Don't look so *glum*. This is good news, it really is!"

After she had left, Jennie leafed through the newspapers again. Only *Metro* had the actual photos of her private conversations with the veterans, but all of them had managed to pad their accounts with staff interviews, anonymous "insider accounts," and images from the official photo ops at the train station and outside the hospital. And Poppy was right: it was all good. But something still felt a little bit off.

"I was just trying to be a human being and they're covering this like it's a well-executed publicity campaign," she complained.

"You're overthinking it," said Karen.

"Maybe," Jennie conceded, deciding not to share her deeper concern: that the stories were all about *her*. She didn't feel comfortable being the face of the royal family even for a day and wondered if that fact alone would be irritating to Edmund—no matter how well it had been received.

She got her answer a few minutes later when her phone vibrated with an incoming message from Jeremy Legrand, texting like he was dictating a telegram.

> Morning headlines all good. Want
> you to interview with Kenneth Davies
> to capitalize. Will make necessary
> arrangements. Very well handled,
> Miss Jensen. May not have given you
> enough credit.

She showed Karen her screen.

"A compliment from that man?" said her mom. "It even sounds like he might be trying to apologize."

Jennie felt the weight lifting from her chest. "Maybe he's not president of the Jennie Go Home Society after all."

———

Jennie felt relatively relaxed as Rodney piloted the car east toward the Thames through rush-hour traffic. She had spent the day reading, napping, and teaching herself a tricky Richard Thompson song on guitar, and it had done a lot to soothe her jangled nerves. She had only seen Hugh for a hurried lunch at home, but they would be reunited soon at Lambeth Palace for their counseling session with Mason Weller, also known as the archbishop of Canterbury and the man who would perform their wedding ceremony. Hugh had assured her the meeting was merely a formality and promised her a late dinner in a private room at Soho House.

Rodney popped a hard candy into his mouth while they waited at a stoplight just past Wellington Arch. "If you don't mind my saying so, I saw today's papers, Miss Jensen."

"I don't unless you're describing the Page Three girl," she told him.

He took it as she'd hoped, chuckling and raising his warm brown eyes to meet hers in the rearview mirror. As he did, she suddenly realized that her image of him was distorted by the backseat view. He was middle-aged handsome, like a tougher-looking Martin Freeman, but if she closed her eyes and pictured him, she would only see kindly eyes with tired creases under steel-gray eyebrows badly in need of a trim.

"What I mean to say is that, as veteran, I appreciate what you did in Manchester," he clarified.

Jennie felt embarrassed by the suggestion that she *did* anything. "I just showed those men common, ordinary kindness. I'd like to think anyone would do the same thing."

"One would," agreed Rodney.

"And I'm glad if it focuses people's attention on them. It's bad enough that they were injured serving their country, but to get hurt in a place where they're supposed to be safe is just horrible. I can't imagine surviving a war only to die in a fire."

Rodney put the car in gear and returned his eyes to the road. "Well, you couldn't have done anything about those things, and you deserve credit for the way you handled yourself," he insisted.

"I feel guilty that people are making it about me. But I'm grateful it's not another story about my birth mother. Or a picture of me puking."

Her PPO fell silent while he gave his full attention to the suddenly snarled traffic. Double-parked delivery vans on both sides of Lower Grosvenor Place had created a pinch point, and horns blared and tempers flared as shouting drivers jockeyed for position. Pedestrians, taking advantage of the pause to cross in the middle of the block, only made matters worse.

But after they passed the bottleneck, he suddenly spoke again.

"After Princess Penelope was seen vomiting at *Phantom of the Opera*, she became convinced she was poisoned," he said matter-of-factly.

Jennie flinched, startled. "She thought someone was trying to kill her?"

Rodney's eyes flicked upward and met hers in the mirror again, then resumed diligently scanning the street.

"Her beliefs about what happened were rather . . . convoluted. She believed someone had slipped her something to make her vomit, leading the public to believe she was drinking whilst in the early stages of pregnancy. Which would make her look bad, because she was under pressure to provide the Crown with another heir."

Jennie still couldn't get her head around the fact that Rodney had so much first-hand knowledge of Hugh's mother. But she didn't feel starstruck as usual, because this was the first time he had ever shared something about the emotional torment Penelope endured. Something she could relate to. The theory sounded just outrageous enough to be delusional—and just familiar enough to be plausible.

"I apologize if I've spoken out of turn, Miss Jensen," said Rodney, apparently reading her silence as offense. "It's just that the incident in Greece reminded me of—"

"Did she say who poisoned her?"

Rodney signaled and smoothly turned the wheel. "Again, I can't speak to the truth of any of this, but I heard plenty of gossip over the years that Vivienne Banfield-March wanted Edmund for herself until Penelope got in the way. I hope you won't think less of me for sharing this. I never concerned myself with sorting fact from fiction. It was my job to keep the Princess safe and I did the best I could. My life's regret is that I couldn't stop her getting on that plane."

As he finished, there was a quaver in her stalwart body-guard's voice.

Once upon a time, Penelope's poisoning theory would have sounded ludicrous to Jennie. That was before she found herself heaving her guts over the side of the yacht. Before she knew just how dangerous her world was and how far the people in it would go to get what they wanted. Before she had given any thought to the people connecting her to Penelope: Edmund and Eleanora, Vivienne and Imogen, even Jeremy Legrand. The royal family and its hangers-on had been simmering with grudges and ulterior motives for centuries—certainly before Hugh had turned up at Jennie's gig in Ibiza.

If Penelope was poisoned, she wondered, *was I poisoned, too?*

Chapter Twenty-Two

MAKING CONFESSION

Rodney drove past the public entrance to Lambeth Palace, turned across oncoming traffic, and stopped at a nondescript wooden gate in the imposing red-brick wall. The gate opened as if by magic, but after they pulled through, Jennie saw it had actually been operated by two boilersuit-clad gardeners. A somber, suited man waiting at a side door introduced himself as the archbishop of Canterbury's chief of staff. She followed him into the medieval-looking structure while Rodney waited with the car.

Several hallways and one flight of stairs later, the chief of staff showed Jennie into a long, high-ceilinged room with large paintings of long-dead clergymen hanging between leaded-glass windows. He withdrew, closing the doors behind him.

Hugh looked up from the ancient leather-bound book he was examining, closed it, and sprang to his feet to cross the room.

"His Grace will be with us momentarily, I'm told," he said, giving her a kiss. "Hope you've swotted the Book of Common

Prayer—or at least the Church of England Wikipedia page. Your answers will determine the fate of the monarchy."

Still dazed by Rodney's revelations, Jennie was feeling further overwhelmed by the ancient strangeness of Lambeth Palace and the fact that the man they were meeting had a title that sounded like the punchline in a Monty Python sketch.

"Kidding, my love," said Hugh, seeing the look on her face. "It's strictly a formality. They'll bring in tea and we'll chat before he confers his blessing."

"We need to talk," she said urgently.

Hugh cocked his head. He opened his mouth to speak and closed it again before ushering her over to a white linen couch.

"It's an awkward time for second thoughts," he said, sitting down next to her. "Or third thoughts."

Jennie gripped his hand, wondering where to start. She'd been dancing around things for too long, afraid of upsetting Hugh and his family. He needed to know what she did.

"When I melted down in Manchester, it wasn't just about all the hits I'm taking in the media, or being afraid of public appearances," she told him.

He looked at her cautiously. "I don't understand."

"I mean, yes, it's all those things. But there's something I should have—"

Her words failed like she'd suddenly run out of air.

"*What?*"

She breathed deeply until she felt dizzy. "I wish I'd told you sooner. But you have so much craziness to deal with already, and I guess I didn't really believe it until now. I didn't trust myself. First, I got a handwritten note saying your mother couldn't make it here and neither would I."

He shook his head. "We all get crank letters."

"This one was handwritten and hand delivered by someone

inside the palace. No stamp, no return address. I found it in my mailbag. Then the cake topper you gave me got snapped in half, and the *me* side disappeared."

"But it's still there," he protested. "I see it every day."

"Because I replaced it."

"Why on earth would you do that?"

"Because I couldn't decide if it was a sinister message or a stupid fluke that would make me look paranoid. Because I didn't want to worry you. Because I really, really wanted to believe things were all right."

Hugh sighed and let go of her hand, turning to face her. "Jennie. I'm genuinely sorry you felt you couldn't come to me. I would never want you to think my problems are more important than yours, or than the two of us."

Hugh watched her so intently it was hard to meet his eyes.

She didn't look away. "I think someone is trying to scare me into not marrying you."

"Unfortunately, with the attention that is focused on us, we are bound to have our detractors, people to whom we become overly important. But—"

"People who poison us?"

Hugh flinched like he'd been slapped.

"No one else had food poisoning on the yacht," she continued. "And I wasn't drunk. I kept trying to find excuses for these things, and ways to rationalize them, but I kept coming to the same conclusion."

"Who on that boat would have wanted—"

"Imogen."

"My God, Jennie!"

"Maybe. Possibly. I don't know," she backtracked, hearing how crazy the words must have sounded to him as they spilled out of her mouth.

"Imogen is one of my oldest friends," he said flatly.

"And an ex-girlfriend."

"We patched things up long ago. We're *friends*. What would she possibly have to gain by hurting you?"

"Or maybe Vivienne did it. She wanted to marry your dad, after all."

"And didn't. That's ancient history."

"Vivienne told me Imogen would 'win her prince eventually.' She even told me it was hard for her to move on from your breakup!"

Hugh put his fingers to his forehead and massaged his temples. "But you can't really believe this."

Jennie slowed down, knowing she was stepping onto dangerous ground. "Princess Penelope—I mean, your mom—thought Vivienne poisoned her years ago. Not to kill her, but to make her sick, so the press would find her puking and think she was drinking when she shouldn't have been. When she should have been trying to get pregnant. It was a huge story, wasn't it?"

Hugh didn't answer as his shoulders slumped.

"What are the odds that something so similar would happen to me?"

"We've been through this before," he said distantly, staring out the window. "My mum was under enormous pressure, more than even you can realize. When she was in the grip of depression, she saw things that weren't there. She thought the world was out to get her. The sad truth is that what did her in was random shitty luck—a pilot's incompetence—and not some cooked-up conspiracy. I couldn't bear it if you . . ."

"But what if she *wasn't* paranoid? If people really were out to get her and she tried to tell someone, she'd sound crazy, right? Sometimes people actually are gaslighted. You saw the note where she talked about needing to see someone even though it was dangerous."

"It didn't necessarily mean mortal danger. It could have been danger to her marriage. Danger to her public image."

"I didn't tell you, but I found another note. She came right out and said your father wanted her dead so he could remarry."

Hugh's face hardened. "And where is this note?"

"I put it in a safe deposit box in Buckingham Palace."

"Leave it there. That's the best place for it."

"You still think this all sounds crazy, don't you?"

"Of course not," he lied unconvincingly.

"I don't want to be one of those conspiracy theorists making connections that aren't there. But I think these connections are real. There's no reason I should have been the only one who got sick on the boat. *Imogen's family's boat.*"

The more she proclaimed her sanity, the more paranoid she sounded to herself. But if she could only convince him, then maybe she could finally convince herself.

"Please believe me, Hugh," she begged.

Finally, for the first time, she saw anger flicker across his face. "Even if I did believe you, no one would believe me, either. The two of us can chase all the shadows we like and then what? One of us has to keep both feet firmly grounded in reality, because honestly, Jennie, my love, none of this makes sense. If you keep watching for signs and portents, it will be just one thing after another."

Jennie shuddered, hearing the echo of Edmund's words on the train: *Honestly, it's just one thing after another.*

If she was becoming Penelope, was Hugh going to become his father? Were they destined to replay a doomed romance?

The doors opened and a slim man with closely cropped silver hair walked in. He wore a simple black suit with a clerical collar, wire-framed glasses, and a large cross of nails.

Jennie heard her own thought as a page's announcement. *The archbishop of Canterbury!*

"Good morning, Your Highness," he said with a warm, gentle smile. "And to you, Miss Jensen."

"Your Grace," said Hugh, rising.

Jennie did the same thing.

Archbishop Mason Weller closed the doors behind him and crossed the room. "Shall we begin, lovebirds?"

CONFIDENTIAL

Metropolitan Police Royalty Protection Command Daily Report

Personal Protection Officer: Declan Andrews

Date: 12 February 1991

0729: Arrived at Hyde Park Barracks (Knightsbridge) with HRH Penelope for horseback riding lesson.

0730: Interim security of HRH transferred to riding instructor Captain Anthony Heald confirmed verbally. Despite some concern about Heald's overly friendly manner with HRH, he has extensive military training and HRH has made clear she feels safe and comfortable in his hands.

0731–0900: Observed HRH's lesson from riser on south side of indoor ring. At approximately 0815, HRH's horse startled and reared. CAH was off his mount and caught HRH as she fell. HRH and CAH waved me off and assured me HRH was uninjured so I returned to my seat. HRH received a comforting embrace. Lesson continued without further incident.

0925: Arrived back at KP. HRH in unusually high spirits despite her near tumble.

1000–1130: Conducted security reconnaissance in advance of HRH's Friday visit to Central Ballet School.

Security challenges to be addressed include courtyard visible from surrounding high rises and lack of a suitable secondary departure route.

1150: Arrived at San Lorenzo Restaurant in advance of HRH's lunch date with her friend, Mrs. Kitty Crowden Stone. Lone paparazzo observed outside.

1200–1315: Lunch. HRH ordered gamberi salad, Pellegrino, and crème caramel. Fellow diners buzzing but well-behaved. Stopped an American tourist from taking a candid.

1330–1430: Drive to Slough Community Health Centre.

1500–1630: Ribbon cutting ceremony. Larger than anticipated crowd and many eager but polite subjects all looking to greet HRH. Local police assisted capably. No specific incidents to report.

1630–1800: Traffic delays. HRH anxious, checking her watch, and called KP from the mobile to check in with Hugh about school day and have a light dinner prepared. HRH reported feeling tired and said she was looking forward to an early night.

1805: HRH safely home at KP.

1815–1930: Prepared reports for next week's recces.

1930: Debrief by relief PPO Whyte, who shared concerns about unaccompanied comings and goings by HRH after hours. Decided to stay and investigate further.

2100: Wearing a baseball cap over a curly blonde wig, HRH exited security gate in her silver BMW. I followed in Kindall's Vauxhaul Astra. (HRH has not only ridden in my MG but attempted to borrow it in the past.) She turned left onto Bayswater Road, left again on Kensington Palace Gardens, and left again on Kensington High Street. Now on the south side of Hyde Park, she wound her way onto Sterling Street, where she passed up a well-lit parking space and proceeded around the corner, reverse parking in a dimly lit area adjacent Montpelier Square.

Stopping at a safe distance, I cut the lights and engine in time to witness a male figure approaching the BMW from the direction of the square. I watched in some shock as HRH released the boot of her car and the man proceeded to fold himself inside. She then got out of the car, checked to see whether anyone was watching, and closed the boot.

I tailed the BMW until confirming HRH was heading directly back to KP, at which point I passed her car, raced back to the empty space in the employee car park, and was readmitted onto the palace grounds. Taking cover behind a boxwood hedge, I was able to observe as HRH parked in the NW corner outside her apartment, out of view of security cameras 5 and 6. When she opened the boot, I was able to identify the passenger as HRH's riding instructor Captain Anthony Heald.

INCIDENT REPORT
Sussex Police
College Lane Police Office
East Grinstead, West Sussex
15 March 1991

15 March 1991: At 1630, Anthony Martin Heald, aged 30, was traveling westbound on High Street at a rate of approximately 55 KPH when the 1986 Ford Cortina in which he was a passenger was struck broadside by a lorry emerging in reverse from a blind alley on the south side of the street located between 81 High Street and 79 High Street. The lorry's lift gate was still in a low-ered position and struck the Cortina approximately six inches above the door frame, shearing off the top of the car and beheading Mr. Heald.

The driver of the Cortina, Patrick Robert Quigley, also 30, was taken to hospital for treatment of lacerations, a fractured left wrist, and possible concussion. In the judge-ment of medical staff, confirmed by blood analysis, Mr. Quigley was not impaired by drugs or alcohol.

The driver of the lorry, Shay Owen, 37, was uninjured. Owen told responding officers he was unfamiliar with the operation of the lift and had been unable to restore it to full upright position after making a delivery of beer barrels at the nearby Dorset Arms. Mr. Owen, who was hired for the day as a casual laborer, was cited for operating a vehicle in an unsafe manner and failure to yield the right-of-way and referred to the Kent, Surrey, and Sussex Magistrates' Court.

Mr. Heald and Mr. Quigley are both officers in the Royal Household Cavalry currently stationed at Knights-bridge Barracks. Quigley told the investigating officer the two men were en route to a "country pub-crawl."

The crash area is not covered by CCTV. Canvassing produced two credible eyewitnesses.

Ladyblossom Grace, aged 42, a cleaning woman, was driving behind the Cortina and braked to a halt as the ac-cident unfolded. She said Quigley did not appear to be operating his vehicle in an unsafe manner. She added, "The lorry just come from nowhere."

The other witness, Robin Ossian, aged 55, was walk-ing toward the accident site, having just exited the Dorset Arms. Said Mr. Ossian, "The poor chaps never saw that lorry coming. The whole thing was one in a million."

Submitted by Detective Sergeant Pamela Powers, Sussex Police

CONFIDENTIAL
Cellular Phone Call Intercept
Date: 15 March 1991

"Thank God you answered. I'm so scared."

"Penelope?"

"They destroy everything that matters—" [static]

"What are you talking about? I can barely hear you."

"I have to whisper. There are ears all around."

"Aren't you in Majorca?"

"Yes, at [REDACTED]. Edmund just told me on the way down to dinner. I couldn't react so I went into the loo. I don't know what to do."

"Slow down, Penelope. Told you what?"

"It's horrible. The poor man. I never believed they'd go this far."

"I'm not a mind reader."

"He's gone."

"Who's gone?"

[inaudible] ". . . you'll see it on the news."

"How will I know what on earth I'm looking for?"

[knocking] "Penelope, everyone is waiting for us before they begin. Are you going to be much longer?"

"Just a minute! I'll be right out. Dear God, how am I going to get through this evening?"

"Penelope, pull yourself together and tell me what's going on!"

"I must go."

[End of recording]

HRH The Princess of Wales

23 MARCH 1991

All Penelope could think about was Anthony. The terror forever frozen in his lifeless eyes. His lifeblood matted into his sandy hair. His head—his beautiful *head*—severed from his body, lying on the roadside like a piece of refuse.

Feeling only half alive herself, and deep within enemy territory at the home of Lord and Lady Banfield-March, Penelope clutched her wine glass and took a long pull of chardonnay. The cocktail party, a thinly veiled excuse to show off recently completed renovations, should have been canceled out of respect. Vivienne—whom Anthony had coached to multiple ribbons in dressage—had been at yesterday's funeral. So, too, were a number of his other pupils. All of them had shed crocodile tears but were now gossiping, laughing, and carrying on as though he hadn't been . . .

Beheaded.

Penelope drank again.

Historically speaking, wasn't that the preferred method of punishment for men who dared trespass on the property of a king or king-to-be?

What would become of an errant princess?

Penelope drained her second glass, trying to wash away the image of her own head rolling onto the infamous lawn at the Tower of London, her blood seeping into soil enriched by that of the heretics who'd preceded her.

"Ghastly," she muttered.

Misunderstanding her, Digby Clifford's wife Caroline forced a smile and tried to defend their hostesses' choice of decor. "The russet-tinged walls are a bold choice to be sure, but the faux paint technique is marvelous for hiding imperfections."

"I have to admit, I tend to agree with Her Highness," said Anne Claxton-Murray, ever auditioning to be a lady-in-waiting. "Although I do adore the Schnabel above the fireplace."

Penelope was in no mood to let it rest. "I was not commenting on Vivienne's taste, but the horrific loss of Captain Anthony Heald."

"Such a tragedy. I've thought of little else since it happened," said Caroline, waving at Sybil Branscombe, who'd just entered the foyer.

"I don't know when I'll be able to ride again without shedding tears," added Anne with a dramatic sigh.

Felix Hill appeared beside Caroline. "They say it happened so quickly the poor chap had no idea. Probably didn't feel a thing. When you think about it, we should all be so lucky."

None of them cared about Anthony now that he was no more use to them. How could they be so callous about his horrifying demise?

"I should think one would prefer to die in old age," she said pointedly. "In one's sleep."

"Preferably liquored and loved up," Felix added with a wink, clinking her empty wineglass with his tumbler. "How about I fetch us a refill?"

"I don't want any," Penelope lied. Since the *Phantom of the Opera* incident, she'd been watching who handled her food and drink. Her first two glasses had been plucked from a tray carried by a passing waiter. She would never accept a cocktail from the likes of Felix Hill—or any of the Friends of Edmund, for that matter—ever again.

"I just adore that man's gallows humor," Anne said, as they watched him leave for the bar.

The utter lack of irony only made Penelope's need for a drink more urgent. As they began prattling on about the gold-plated fixtures in the powder room, she excused herself.

After working her way into the vestibule, she waited behind

a newly installed colonnade until Felix exited the bar area. Once he was safely out of sight, she made her way over to the ornate teakwood wet bar Vivienne had told one and all was the only real "splurge" in her remodeling.

"Uncork a fresh chardonnay for me, please," she told the bartender.

"Yes, Your Highness," he said with a bow.

Penelope watched him tear off the metal foil, plunge and twist the corkscrew, and pull the cork. As he reached for a wineglass, she offered him the one in her hand.

"Wouldn't you like a clean glass?"

"It's not necessary. However, I would like the bottle."

"The whole thing?"

"For safety reasons."

It came out sounding like *satiety*, but she couldn't worry about that, any more than she could care about how flustered she'd left the poor man when she took the bottle by its neck and disappeared through the nearby French doors.

Outside, in the dimly lit interior courtyard, she could finally breathe. Conversation swirled from the open doors surrounding her as Penelope set the bottle on a wrought iron table and sat down to drink a third glass of wine.

She was halfway through a fourth when her uneasy reverie was broken by the sound of Edmund's deep laughter, followed by a distinctive guffaw that could only be Eleanora Osborne-Webb. Just inside a drawing room on the south side of the house, Eleanora was regaling Edmund with an apparently hysterical story.

Hot tears rolled down Penelope's face.

She had known her relationship with Anthony couldn't go on indefinitely without someone in the palace finding out. But, like Edmund and Eleanora, she believed it wasn't in anyone's best interest for the details of any indiscretion to come to light.

Eleanora laughed again.

Eleanora, whose daughter looked more and more like Edmund every time Penelope laid eyes upon the girl. Eleanora who was alive and well, while the man who'd made Penelope smile for a mere three months had been . . .

Beheaded.

Furious, Penelope stood up. She was less steady than she'd expected.

Stay where you are and let the moment pass, said the angel on one shoulder.

And then Edmund placed his hand on the small of Eleanora's back.

What are you waiting for? said the devil on the other.

She took a big swig for courage, grabbed her bottle, and wobbled into the drawing room.

"Penelope, join us," said Eleanora, flashing her best fake smile. "We were just—"

"Pretending no one we knew was decapitated this week?" said Penelope, enunciating as clearly as she could.

"Bloody hell. You're completely pissed," snarled Edmund.

"Not yet, I'm not," she said, even though she sounded slurry to herself.

Eleanora cupped her hand around Penelope's elbow. "Let me get you a coffee. Perhaps something to eat?"

She shook it off. "I don't want to be poisoned!"

"What on earth are you talking about?"

"This party should not be happening." Penelope's dismissive wave at the people present was a wild flail. Her arms were hardly hers.

Edmund's expression was one of unadulterated disgust. "Your invitation was simply a matter of form and could have been tactfully declined. *Should* have been. I suspect we'd all have been much happier if you'd chosen to carry your wine bottle around at home."

Keeping her eyes locked on his, Penelope raised the bottle to her lips and drank from it, feeling the room-temperature white wine dribble down her chin.

"It would be safer for everyone if you went home." Edmund motioned to PPO Rodney, posted in the corner of the room, telling him, "Get her out of here."

"For my *safety*," she mocked him, swaying.

But Edmund had already turned his back.

And she was being pulled away into darkness.

Chapter Twenty-Three

HARMONIC DISTORTION

Jennie strummed and slashed the strings of the Fender Stratocaster, losing herself in a fog of sound that filled the room. The volume knob of the small amplifier was already at ten, and Jennie would have turned it even higher if she could, even though the crunching chords were so loud they almost hurt her ears. After getting nowhere with a new song for far too long, she had finally put down the acoustic and plugged in. Making a lot of noise made her feel better, both because it brought back the all-but-forgotten feeling of being onstage and because it took her mind off the fact that she and Hugh had hardly spoken since she'd told him everything at Lambeth Palace. But she knew from experience not to rush him when he was processing anything related to his past.

Then, through the noise, she heard a voice. Someone was shouting her name.

Jennie muted the strings, then turned down the guitar's volume to kill the squeal of feedback. She had to squint through the sun beaming through the skylight of her music studio before she saw Hugh standing in the doorway.

"I thought you were at the office," she told him.

"And I thought you preferred acoustic guitar," he said, removing his fingers from his ears. "Are you planning to open for Metallica?"

She shrugged. "It felt like a metal morning."

"You do realize you're bleeding."

Glancing down, she saw blood spatters on the white pick guard of the cream-colored Strat. The knuckle on the end of her right ring finger was split, an injury that seemed too small to have produced so much blood.

"I did *not* realize."

"Good thing I was trained as a battlefield medic," said Hugh, ducking out the door.

Jennie put the guitar on a stand and stuck her finger in her mouth until Hugh returned with a linen hand towel.

"Thanks," she said, holding the cloth tightly against the cut. "Earlier you said you had a full schedule today."

"I've rescheduled my meetings because we need to talk." Hugh sat down on the piano bench with the warm sun between them. He gently pressed a few random keys and then stared at the keyboard. "Yesterday I told you that I didn't want you to keep things from me. And then I gave you every reason to do just that by getting angry and refusing to believe you."

Jennie lifted the towel and inspected her finger. "*Do* you believe me?"

Hugh pressed more keys, accidentally arriving on a diminished minor. "Something His Grace the Archbishop said stuck in my head: If ours is to be a marriage of equals, then neither of us stands before or behind the other. Any concern of yours must be an equal concern of mine."

"So you accept the possibility that someone put something in my drink?"

"I can accept it intellectually, if not emotionally."

"Are you apologizing?"

Hugh stood up. "I am. I'm sorry, my love. I will stand by you no matter what."

They met each other in the sunlight and hugged until the warmth had thawed everything.

"I accept your apology," said Jennie. "Now what?"

"The standard cure-all for any crisis," said Hugh. "Tea."

After the tray had been delivered, they sat together on the couch and began playing with theories—calmly, rationally, the way they should have in the first place.

"I'm aware I'm hardly unbiased," said Hugh, spooning sugar into his mug. "But I honestly can't imagine a person on the planet who wouldn't love you. Not once they've met you."

"It probably doesn't have anything to do with liking me as a person," said Jennie. "Someone in the palace, or someone in our circle, might want me out of the picture. For all the reasons, starting with the fact that I'm American. Because I'm adopted. Because I messed around in college. Because my dad sells bulldozers for a living and my mom gets her hair done at the mall."

He sighed. "Maybe I'm just too trusting. My forbears would have assumed the worst motives of all parties at all times. The ever-present possibility of the axe must have keenly sharpened one's senses."

Jennie sipped her black tea and felt her tongue tickle at its tartness. She added oat milk and a small squeeze of brown rice syrup and stirred.

"All you have to do for proof that not everyone loves me is to go online. But Twitter trolls don't have access to my mail or my food. Or anything to gain if we break up. I already told you about Imogen and Vivienne—"

"And we don't have to see them if it makes you uncomfortable."

"I also feel uncomfortable thinking I might be making a false accusation. I want to *know*. Is there anyone else who wouldn't want us to be together?"

Hugh took a bite from a biscuit and crunched thoughtfully. "Courts certainly preferred life before you came along. But even assuming he prefers I would remain a bachelor—hardly realistic on his part—it's hardly something one poisons someone over."

"But what if it was part of a campaign to make someone feel unhappy and unwanted?"

"If there's a connection to my mum, as you suggest, then whoever doesn't like *you* wouldn't have liked *her*," he said, shaking his head. "Courts was a child then, like me, and his parents played no part in palace life."

"Poppy's uncle is Digby Clifford, right?"

"You're reaching. And Poppy wasn't with us in Greece."

"Neither was Legrand, but he seems to hate me more than anyone, and he certainly has the ability to make things happen."

Hugh coughed, seeming to almost choke on his tea, and set his mug down. "Jeremy doesn't hate you. He only hates anything that inconveniences the Crown. The man lives for his work."

"And acts on your father's behalf. I know he doesn't love me."

Jennie knew she was once again making Hugh uncomfortable, leading him in a direction he didn't want to go. But he had promised to support her no matter what, so she couldn't hide what she was thinking.

"He would run any girl through the gauntlet," Hugh protested. "He wasn't exactly cozy with Imogen, either."

"And Eleanora couldn't be married to Edmund as long as Penelope was alive."

"But to connect that to *you*, and to think that my father or

Eleanora would have . . ." Hugh seemed to be trying hard to keep an open mind. "The poisoning thing does seem a coincidence for the record books, I agree, but surely it's just that—a coincidence? The notes, on the other hand, *must* be investigated."

It felt good to have finally let go of her secrets. But voicing them aloud had not had the effect of making them feel more real. If anything, it was like telling someone about a dream: the logic that had seemed so inevitable and airtight in her unconscious mind sounded flimsy by daylight. Like one of those dreams where the bullet fell out of the gun barrel and clanked on the floor.

In her heart she *knew* what had happened. But was it really all in her head?

"I'm going to talk to Grant McCutcheon immediately and tell him this is a priority," said Hugh resolutely. "I want a report on everyone who could have possibly handled your mail pouch. I will insist he question everyone again about any irregularities. I don't know what we can do about the food situation, but I suppose he could at least run background checks on anyone involved in the preparation of the food on board the *Somerset*."

"I don't know if I feel embarrassed or afraid. Both, I guess."

Hugh turned toward her. With one hand, he gripped her shoulder, and with the other, he raised her chin. "Listen, no one threatens the bride-to-be of the future King of England. Whoever is behind this should be afraid, not you, and I intend to make certain of it. We will remove all shadows of doubt."

"Thank you," she told him, kissing him on the cheek.

Wondering if even the future King of England could shine a light bright enough to chase away the shadows.

Chapter Twenty-Four
THE CAMERA WINKS

"I interviewed your mother-in-law, you know," said Kenneth Davies as he deftly clipped the lavalier mic behind his lapel. "It was a ratings smash and I'm certain this will be as well."

"No pressure," said Jennie.

The silver-maned BBC broadcaster laughed, flashing crooked but whitened teeth. "Trust me, I want more than anything to put you at ease."

Even though they were in her Kensington Palace apartment, seated in low-backed upholstered chairs that wouldn't intrude upon the camera frame, Jennie felt anything but at home. The formal drawing room had been transformed into a set with stage lights and reflectors, multiple cameras (one each over their shoulders and one off to the side for wide shots), boom microphones, and thick ropes of cable. Wearing laminated lanyards to prove they'd cleared palace security, members of the production crew ringed the room, standing behind cameras, peering into monitors, and leaning against the wall to check their phones. Each one of them had been sworn to secrecy by an ironclad NDA that still probably did little to stop them from sending candid texts or pictures to friends who could, with a click, easily post them online.

Jennie's team, vastly outnumbered, consisted of a smiling, upbeat Poppy; a preoccupied-looking Ian; and, inevitably, a sternly focused Jeremy Legrand.

She liked Davies, the renowned interviewer who had been a welcome guest in British homes for almost three decades, but she knew his likability was also a secret weapon that had led many famous but unwary subjects into candid confessions. And she wasn't naive enough to believe that broadcasters behaved the same with no cameras in the room. But she had been partially reassured by something Hugh told her the night before in bed, when after making love, they had languidly discussed their schedules for the following day.

My mum liked Kenneth Davies quite a lot. She told me she trusted him.

But had Princess Penelope always trusted the right people?

Maybe even Davies's casual mention of her had been calculated to put Jennie off balance before he asked his first question. Even the fact that she was being interviewed by someone she would have liked to ask questions seemed just a little bit too convenient. Was it a setup?

Stay on guard, Jennie reminded herself.

"Recording in five . . . four . . ." said the headphone-wearing producer, finishing the countdown with his fingers.

"Shall we begin?" asked Kenneth Davies.

"Of course!" she said, so cheerfully she hoped she didn't sound deranged.

As the red light on the camera over Davies's left shoulder came on, a very subtle change came over Davies—he was on, too.

"The princess from Peoria, Illinois," he began in a warm, rich, tone, pronouncing her home state with a hard *s*. "The pop singer from the American heartland who has played a tune to capture a prince's heart—can she win the hearts of England, too?"

Jennie hesitated. Was this a question for her? Davies was waiting, so she went for it.

"I can't answer that, I'm afraid," she told him. "But I can tell you that England has won *my* heart, and I hope the love affair will be mutual as its people get to know me."

The glint in Davies's eye seemed to say, *Good answer.*

She hoped, anyway.

"You've faced criticism in the press for errors in royal protocol," he continued. "Even you must admit you're an unlikely choice for a future Queen Consort. How do you respond to the doubters?"

"I'm sure all of the criticism is justified," said Jennie, playing it off with a laugh she hoped sounded sincere. "After all, I'm still learning the ropes. I've made a lot of progress but it's just not possible to master centuries of rich tradition in only a year. So I hope people will judge me by my willingness to learn and trust that I will grow into the role that's expected of me."

"Spoken diplomatically," said Davies.

Poppy was giving her two thumbs up and it was hard not to grin at her. Given the encouraging signals, Jennie decided to expand on her answer.

"I've heard a lot of people say they think I was hunting for a prince. And to them, I just want to say, if that was actually my plan, I would have been a lot better prepared."

Davies arched an eyebrow. Had she gone too far? It was too late now.

"Let's talk about your childhood," he said.

Jennie was able to catch her breath and reset while he detoured into more familiar territory, asking her what life was like growing up, when she started writing songs, about the stupid name of her first band, the Hormones, and other easy stuff. As

Ian had advised during their practice sessions, she tried to keep her answers light and simple, making growing up in the Midwest as relatable as possible to English viewers. When he moved on to her first meeting with Hugh, Davies became downright avuncular as he asked her to share as many details of their romance as "she was willing." They covered so much ground so quickly that the interview seemed destined to serve as a pocket history of Hugh and Jennie's premarital relationship.

She was coasting, and out of the corner of her eye saw that Poppy was nodding enthusiastically at her screen—no doubt skimming the live social media commentary—when Davies surprised her with another hardball question.

"And as the world now knows, you were adopted as a baby. Have you reached out to your birth mother, Diane Danforth?"

Ian had also coached her on this, no doubt relaying orders from Legrand: *Smile, pause, and respectfully decline to discuss it. Tell him it's too personal.*

Jennie decided things were going well enough that she could disregard this particular instruction. Mothers were too sensitive a subject to dismiss, and people might think Jennie was cold and calculating if she refused to talk about it.

Wanting viewers to feel like she saw them, she broke eye contact with Davies and let her eyes be drawn to the glassy, unblinking camera lens just past his ear. The red light stared back at her as she took a deep breath.

"I can only imagine how painful it was for Diane to give away her baby girl, all those years ago," she said slowly, picking up speed as she figured out what she wanted to say. "But the only mother I have ever known is my mom, Karen Jensen. She and my dad, Dave Jensen, raised me and my brother Daniel with more love than I can possibly express. When I was old enough to understand, they explained that I was adopted, but never once did they make me feel like that was a bad thing. Instead, they made me feel special. Diane's desire to meet me only reached me through the headlines. And if she is in fact my biological mother, all I can tell you is that it's going to take me a while to get my head around it and I'm not ready to deal with it yet. As you know, I'm getting married at the end of July."

"Just one month away," said Davies. "King Edmund and Queen Consort Eleanora: Are they feeling like mum and dad yet?"

"I will *never* presume to call them *mum* and *dad*," said Jennie, trying not to snort when she laughed. "And I mean that with only respect. They have been so gracious to welcome me into the royal family and I'll do everything I can to prove myself a worthy daughter-in-law."

Jennie had been realizing that her word choices were getting more and more British as she tried to curry favor: *I'm afraid* and *presume* and *prove myself a worthy*. She only hoped she wasn't accidentally slipping into her *Spinal Tap* accent.

"Lovely, just lovely," murmured Davies. "Miss Jennie Jensen, the BBC thanks you for your time."

"And out," said the producer.

The red light on the camera over Davies' shoulder winked off.

"You were simply marvelous," he chuckled as he unclipped his microphone. "Are you sure you haven't married into the royal family before?"

"I'm not sure I could survive doing it twice."

He paused and looked her in the eye. "I've interviewed my share of royals over the years, and believe me, I know what a challenging part it is to play. Princess Penelope . . ."

"I know she struggled with it," offered Jennie. "That was well documented."

"Some people find the compromises required by royal life hard to accept."

Around them, the crew was already starting to break down. Even though no one appeared to be listening, Jennie didn't know what to say—what was safe to say.

"How has your introduction to the royal family *really* been?" he asked.

And that was when her training finally kicked in. Penelope may well have trusted Kenneth Davies. But was she right to?

"Thank you so much, Mr. Davies," she said, taking off her microphone and rising from her seat. "I'm afraid I have no further comment."

From the Private Diary of Princess Penelope

15 APRIL 1991

I have been banished, sentenced to dry out at Balmoral, where quite ironically, it couldn't be more drizzly, damp, and bone chilling. Even the dust—which the skeleton staff can never whisk entirely from the mantels, picture frames, and priceless bric-a-brac—is cold to the touch. It would be so much easier to "get my shit together" (as Edmund so eloquently commanded) if they would turn up the bloody heat.

In one sense they have, as high as it will go, by vowing to publicly pronounce me an unfit mum and remove Hugh from my care if I don't sober up.

My actual sobriety isn't the real issue. No one ever says a word about Freddie, the Gloucesters, and even Her Majesty, all of whom rely on Gilbey's gin to smooth the sharp edges of this unnatural existence. If my well-being was their primary concern, they'd have arranged for me to spend thirty days at a well-heated treatment facility in the care of licensed professionals. The potential

exposure was too great, or so I was told, even though the
tabloids had to have been buzzing about my absence
from Windsor on Easter Sunday.

The stark beauty of this country is overshadowed
not by the gloomy skies but the utter loneliness I have
always felt when I am here. My sole companion is one
Dr. Ian Davite, or as I secretly call him, Dr. Idiot. Best
as I can tell, his expertise comes from his own stint in
rehab. But, like the fingerless, woolen gloves I found
in a side table drawer in the drawing room and now
wear to warm my hands while writing, I am focused on
finding solutions, not creating more problems.

Officially, I was sent here as punishment for
embarrassing Edmund with my alcohol-induced
public outbursts. My true crime was far more serious:
contacting the BBC TV journalist Kenneth Davies and
arranging an on-camera interview.

How stupid I was to think they weren't watching
and listening. Not to know that any attempt at telling the
truth would be blocked. There are simply too many people
willing to protect my husband and the sanctity of the
crown. Status quo über alles would be the family motto if
we didn't hide the Germans in the Windsor wardrobe.

I now know I hold no power, but there is strength in
realizing that the only person who can lift me up is myself.

I have stopped drinking entirely and follow all of
Dr. Idiot's directives. I make lists of the people I believe
I have harmed. I identify the irrational thoughts
that lead to my negative behaviours. I learn to adopt
healthier, more realistic expectations of the world and
the people around me.

Just as I am instructed.

Of course, Dr. Idiot is reporting everything I say or do to the Firm. Today's assignment was to list reasons I am angry with myself or others.

Here are the answers I gave him:

I am angry with myself for allowing alcohol to interfere with my ability to maintain appropriate control of myself in social situations.

I am angry with myself for compromising my relationship with my child due to my use of alcohol.

I am angry with myself for not grasping the breadth and scope of my responsibilities as the future Queen.

I am angry with myself for embarrassing Edmund, but I'm hopeful he will approve of the changes I am making.

I am angry that I am here, but I am working on myself for the betterment of all.

My real list, which I did not share, also includes the following:

I'm apoplectic that anyone dares to suggest my son should be taken away. I will disappear with Hugh before I will ever let that happen.

I am incensed that my husband has affairs with whomever, whenever.

In fact, I'm outraged that the heir apparent breaks the Ten Commandments at will, sometimes several at once, yet I am always expected to act with dignity and grace.

I am livid with myself for putting up with it.

Most of all, I am disappointed in myself for losing control. I will never allow that to happen again. I cannot win the game they play unless I'm clearheaded.

I will play their game. And I will win.

Chapter Twenty-Five

SECRET HISTORIES

Windsor Castle, with its grounds and gardens, two working farms, and even its five-thousand-acre Windsor Great Park had been closed to the public for the weekend so King Edmund could host what Hugh called a "dine and sleep." Since the death of Queen Alexandra, who'd lived there nearly full time, Windsor had become Edmund's favored weekend retreat. Invites were regarded as golden tickets by England's elite, though not by Hugh, who preferred the homier holiday get-togethers at Balmoral Castle in Scotland. But when the King summoned— even Hugh and Jenny's invitation had been formally worded on creamy Buckingham Palace letterhead—attendance was mandatory.

Because it was Jennie's first visit, Hugh asked Rodney to drop them off a short distance away so she could "properly experience the approach." As they strolled up the aptly named Long Walk toward the stout gray turrets of the castle, the red-gold-and-blue Royal Standard fluttering above to show the King was in residence, she watched in delight as a small herd of red deer walked out of the trees and slowly crossed their path.

"So a dine and sleep is a fancy way to say slumber party?" Jennie asked.

"If you like," said Hugh. "Only don't expect to see the prime minister and the home secretary roasting marshmallows in their pajamas."

"I'm actually picturing liveried footmen hand feeding them s'mores."

"I'd pay a pound to see that," he chuckled. "But seriously, it's a big deal. It means my father is welcoming you in."

The weekend didn't exactly promise the rest Jennie and Hugh needed after what had been an exhausting June, but royal relations had warmed in the wake of her interview with Kenneth Davies. Poppy's reaction during the live broadcast had been prophetic: over the next twenty-four hours, wave after wave of positive responses rolled in. Even some of her harshest critics in the establishment papers grudgingly conceded that she had done a good job, and that if the prince was indeed intent on marrying an American, he might not have chosen as poorly as they initially thought.

Also calming her nerves was the fact that Grant McCutcheon's eighty-seven-page report had failed to turn up evidence of either immediate danger or overarching conspiracy. An exhaustive investigation had followed her food from farm to table and found nothing suspicious. Unless one of her hosts had actually poisoned it during mealtime (Jennie pictured a fake ring with poison drops inside), it just couldn't have happened. Jennie was reassured to learn that, invisible to her, the kitchen had been closely supervised by their PPOs.

The broken cake topper was still a mystery, but a review of the video system confirmed that power outages were a regular occurrence. At McCutcheon's order, the wiring had been replaced and a battery backup ensured it wouldn't happen again.

The biggest unknowns still had to do with the handling of her mail pouch. Letters were delivered to Buckingham Palace by Royal Mail, where they were scanned for explosives and sniffed by dogs before being hand-sorted by junior members of the communications staff. Mail for Jennie's attention was reviewed first by Ian and then by Legrand, who finally authorized what would go into her mail pouch. At Kensington Palace, it was delivered by one of several footmen who had all been questioned extensively. The report hinted that a disgruntled employee still was the most likely source of the notes and said they would be watched closely. Jennie, of course, was the newest member of the household. In other circumstances, she reflected, suspicion may have centered on her.

Last in, first out.

The only remaining step, concluded McCutcheon, was to perform a forensic analysis of the notes themselves. *Would Ms. Jensen kindly place these at our disposal?*

Jennie informed him that she would, just as soon as she returned to London and had the chance to retrieve them from the bowels of Buckingham Palace.

Finally, after who knew how many hundreds of yards, they reached the castle. As they walked through the main gate, shadows cooled the light sweat that had formed on her arms. The cobblestones under their feet emanated a crypt-like chill.

"Welcome to the eleventh century!" joked Hugh.

Jennie kissed him on the cheek. If the royal family had endured almost a millennium, surely she could survive the weekend.

———

They spent the afternoon touring the castle, and Hugh was a funny and fast-moving guide. More than at any other time in their relationship, she felt like she was part of living history as they walked the grounds; visited the graves of Hugh's grandparents, Queen Alexandra and her husband, Prince Magnus, Duke of Edinburgh; viewed the mansion-sized Royal Lodge; rested their legs on pews in the soaring, Gothic St. George's Chapel; and traipsed through room after room of red-and-gold Georgian, Victorian, and Baroque grandeur in the endless castle itself.

Hugh blithely shared mind-blowing facts—the place had been built in the eleventh century to defend London by none other than William the Conqueror—while Jennie *mm-hmm*'d and made mental notes to google things like the Norman Invasion. Because her Aunt Kelly was married to her Uncle Norman, Jennie couldn't help imagining it as an army of beer-bellied men with camouflage baseball caps, mirrored Oakley sunglasses, and sunburned necks.

Dinner the first night was an extravagantly formal, thirteen-piece-place-setting affair. Edmund and Eleanora were hosting Prime Minister Helen Jeffries and her husband Brian, Home Minister Clive Terry and his wife Sarah, and several more dignitaries, in addition to the actor Craig Daniels and piano prodigy Ollie Hsu. Even Poppy's assiduous coaching fell short, and Jennie was thankful she'd studied the etiquette primer that accompanied her invitation.

Men and women were seated alternately, with the King and Queen opposite each other at the center of the long table and views across completely obscured by lavish floral arrangements. The only people Jennie could comfortably talk to were seated to her immediate right and left. While she would have loved to sit next to Ollie Hsu or even Craig Daniels, unfortunately she had been sandwiched between Brian Jeffries (friendly but so boring it was like he'd had his personality surgically removed) and Felix Hill (whose banter veered uncomfortably between flirtation and condescension). She noticed that Edmund alternated conversation partners with each course of the meal, a solution that was either clever or completely lame.

Also unfortunate was the fact that her view of Hugh was completely blocked by the riotous floral arrangements. They were so big that the staff must have had to literally climb up on the table to complete them.

After profiteroles and brandy, Jennie discovered why Ollie Hsu had been invited. The entire party left the State Dining Room and went through to the Crimson Drawing Room for a forty-five-minute performance of Chopin's Piano Concerto Number 1 in E minor. Hsu's virtuoso playing made Jennie realize why she had not been asked to give a command performance of her own—either that, or no one wanted to be reminded of her Instagram accident.

As her eyes drooped from the heavy meal, alcohol, and the long day, the group retired to yet another room, where ties were loosened, tiaras set aside, and guests slouched into the furniture for idle chitchat that seemed to last forever. She nearly nodded off several times before Edmund finally yawned and called it a night. No one, she now knew, along with a million other bits of protocol, could leave before the King.

———————

The following day, the stuffy guests departed and family and friends arrived—only Jennie, Hugh, and Felix Hill stayed. Everyone dressed down. King Edmund in chinos and a button-down shirt shocked Jennie almost as much as if he had worn Bermuda shorts and flip-flops. After impressing no one on horseback (given the most docile horse, she soon was left far behind), Jennie found herself paired with her future father-in-law for a surprisingly competitive game of croquet.

"Unfortunate," said Edmund, watching her ball roll wide of the first wicket. "But I believe we can play this to our advantage."

When Eleanora left her shot just short, Edmund pounced, deftly hitting her ball and taking advantage of his second stroke to knock her off the playing field into a flowerbed.

"*Really*, Edmund," she said, her voice flat with resignation.

The King was already squatting, lining up the angle of Jennie's next shot, even though it was now Hugh and Cece's turn. "The objective of the game is to win."

"Make way, old man," said Hugh, getting ready to swing.

Despite Jennie's inexperience, due to Edmund's deadly accuracy they went on to win the game, with Hugh and Cece coming in a close second. The game hinged on a miss by Cece that was hit so badly Jennie half wondered if she had muffed the shot on purpose.

Cocktail hour was held on the lawn, with drinks and canapés ferried back and forth by the usual army of footmen. Jennie enjoyed hearing a dirty joke from Princess Alice, even if it took her a long beat to get it. ("What do you call the useless bit of skin on a willy? A chap!") They did dress up for dinner, ditching the black ties and evening gowns of the previous night for sport coats and simpler dresses. The menu was simple but satisfying, with King Edmund twice reminding them, "Everything but the Dover sole comes from our own farm here at Windsor!"

After dinner, everyone retired to the King's private sitting room to talk, the younger family members discreetly detouring en route to vape or scroll on their phones. Yesterday, Jennie had been dazzled by the history of the castle. Today, she marveled at the sight of Hugh's family acting like normal people.

Suddenly Freddie spoke up. "Yar or nar!"

"*Nar*," said Edmund.

But everyone else cheered, "Yar, yar!"

Jennie turned to Hugh on the couch. "Please translate?"

"An old family game," he explained. "Each person tells a story and everyone else must guess whether or not it's true. Usually played when new people come around. We've all heard each other's tales so often it's difficult to pass off a false story."

"Oh, all right," relented Edmund. "But I really hope some of you have brought fresh stories. None of your bloody military exploits, Freddie."

"Don't believe for a moment you've heard all of them," said his younger brother.

"We all know about the corkscrew," said Edmund.

"It was *shrapnel*," insisted Freddie.

"Jennie guesses first!" cried Cece to appreciative murmurs.

Jennie waved her hands, trying to ward off the dubious honor. "But I'll fall for anything!" she protested.

"That's exactly the point," said Hugh.

Princess Alice rose from her gilded Louis the Somethingth chair and glided over to the massive, ornate mantlepiece. "I'll tell the first story, because I'm much nicer than the rest of you."

"Bollocks!" said Freddie.

She smiled blandly and ignored him. "When I was a girl of fourteen, a horseman of the guards pledged true love to me. He courteously explained that he would never lay a finger upon me, because he was married and knew that I would someday be also, yet he wished me to consider ourselves *spiritual* man and wife. He insisted that I must keep his platonic love forever a secret and promised he would never speak of it again. But, he said, I would know his devotion by the white rose he would wear in his lapel."

"Oh, for fuck's sake," stage-whispered Freddie as Cece shushed him.

Princess Alice turned to Jennie as she concluded her story.

"Before this day, I told only one person of this extraordinary approach: Great-Aunt Margot. I believe I expected her to have him shot or exiled or something, but she just smiled and said, 'I should keep him around if I were you. He is the perfect husband. He neither speaks to you nor you to him, and neither must you take him to bed.'"

"NAR!" roared Freddie. "Nar! Nar! Nar!"

As the rest of the family weighed in with yars and nars, *nars* were clearly in the majority.

"Nar," said Hugh. "Don't fall for it."

But Princess Alice's clear gaze and steady voice had worked a spell on Jennie. The story just seemed too *specific* to be false.

"What say you, Jennie?" asked Edmund.

"Yar?" she said tentatively.

There was a sudden silence. Everyone looked expectantly at Alice. She locked eyes with Jennie, gave a quiet nod, and took her seat.

"I still say bollocks," muttered Freddie. "What utter rubbish."

"Surely you're pulling our legs?" said Edmund to his elderly aunt.

"I'm not," she said. "It's all true."

The King shook his head. "Extraordinary. Well, this game is off to a roaring start. Miss Jensen, by tradition, the guesser tells the next story."

Jennie's heart beat faster.

Hugh gave her hand a reassuring squeeze. "Don't feel obligated to outdo her. You could tell them you once had a pet iguana named Harold."

As Jennie stood up and walked to the cold fireplace, she still felt pressure to perform. After Alice's amazing story, she didn't want to disappoint everyone by making them guess whether she'd ever had an exotic pet.

The eyes on her were unnerving, so she focused on a painting of Queen Alexandra across the room. The former monarch's mild expression made her an easier audience.

"After I was left at a fire station when I was just a few days old, the firemen took me to the hospital," she began. "Then child protective services gave me to a foster family. I lived with them for five months until my parents, Karen and Dave, found me through an adoption agency. It took another half a year for the whole process to play out, so by the time I was officially adopted, I was almost a year old."

Out of the corner of her eye, she saw Hugh beaming at her. Squaring her shoulders, she raised her voice and continued more confidently.

"Davenport, Iowa, where I was found, is about a hundred miles from Peoria, Illinois, where my parents lived. My parents met the foster family at a rest stop in between, and they took my big brother Daniel along with them. He was four years old, so even though they explained to him what was happening, he didn't totally get it. He thought Mom and Dad found a baby on the highway and brought her home."

That delivered a few chuckles, along with a reassuring feeling that, despite the risk, she had picked the right story to tell.

"My parents told me the real story when I was old enough, but Daniel still believed they had randomly found me on the road—I mean, it wasn't *that* far from the truth. But that gave me an idea. And one summer, I made him spend day after day riding bikes all over the neighborhood, supposedly looking for a new baby to bring home to Mom. She made us stop when she found out . . . and I'm still not sure he's forgiven me."

After the laughter died down, Edmund nodded and voted, "Yar."

Eleanora echoed him, and so did almost everyone else. Hugh, of course, already knew the story was true.

Only Freddie was a *nar*, despite conceding, "She's a good storyteller, I'll give her that much."

"All true!" said Jennie, once the votes were in.

As she took her seat, she felt good. Hugh's family had laughed, just as she'd hoped. But more than that, their smiles told her they were seeing her in a new light, as a person with a story. It was hard to believe she had ever suspected Edmund and Eleanora of being anything more than parents who wanted the best for their amazing son.

Chapter Twenty-Six

SPILLING THE TEA

Jennie stepped out of the bedroom suite and quietly closed the door, blinking against the brightness of the hallway. Like a hotel, the lights in the common areas of Windsor Castle stayed on all night. Given that this was just one castle of a large collection, she tried not to think of the electric bill.

The night before, she had been dead on her feet and desperate to go to sleep, but tonight she was wired for some reason. Maybe she was still feeling the adrenaline surge of having the whole royal family's attention. Even though it had gone better than she could have possibly expected, she still hadn't been able to "get off," as Brits hilariously called drifting off to sleep, even between the high thread count Egyptian cotton sheets of their ridiculously soft four-poster bed. Hugh was slumbering peacefully, so instead of turning on a lamp, she had grabbed a book and her phone, planning to find a private place to read.

It should have been easy. After all, there were over a thousand rooms in Windsor Castle.

She followed the winding hall to a small sitting room where the door was open and several lamps were turned on. It looked empty enough, but when she flopped down in a wing-back chair in front of yet another cold fireplace, she almost screamed. Freddie was slouched in the chair next to hers, still as a corpse, his glassy eyes fixed on the tumbler of whiskey resting on his stomach.

Then he blinked to life like an animatronic prince in Disneyland Paris's Hall of Royalty and asked, "Come here to raid the whiskey, too?"

She held up her book. "Couldn't sleep."

"Then I'll tell you a bedtime story," he said, struggling to an upright position. "Though I can't guarantee sweet dreams."

Her first instinct was to bolt. She wasn't sure she wanted to hang out with Freddie when he was this drunk. He was funny and irreverent, true, but even sober he was often just a little bit too much. But now that she was in the chair, it was hard to make a graceful exit.

"What are you drinking?" she asked, just for something to say.

"The tears of my enemies," he said. "Which taste rather like thirty-year-old cask-strength Lagavulin."

"That's funny, because I always thought the tears of *my* enemies would taste like cucumber water. But I haven't had a chance to try any yet."

"If you are still by Hugh's side when he ascends to the throne, you'll be able to bottle crates of them."

Freddie's voice was so thick Jennie wanted to ask him to clear his throat. But when he swallowed more scotch, it cleared up.

"You shouldn't have told that story," he said, sounding more alert.

Giving up hope of getting any reading done, she put her book down. "Why not? I thought everyone liked it."

"Of course they liked it, girl. They liked it because you made yourself *vulnerable*. Have you ever known any of us to reveal anything personal?"

She thought about it and had to shake her head.

"That's right. Because the moment you do, it will be used against you. Like my fucking *corkscrew* in the fucking *Falklands*."

Jennie was tempted to ask him if it was true but decided against it. "I've always thought the opposite," she said instead. "That when I'm honest with people, they're more likely to be honest with me and to treat me like a human being."

Freddie drained the glass and put it on his side table. "That's because you're American. You're programmed to believe things will always turn out for the best. If you had been born here, you'd know differently."

She was starting to wish she had a glass of whiskey, too.

Freddie leaned forward, started to speak, then thought better of it and picked up his glass and climbed awkwardly to his feet. He tilted across the room to a sideboard holding a crystal decanter.

"Let me give you a piece of advice, Jennie Jensen of Peoria, Illinois," he said, sloshing more amber liquid into the tumbler. "You need to watch yourself. Watch what you say."

"You mean I should be less personal?"

When he replaced the stopper in the decanter it made a *boonk* sound. "For a start. You're like a . . . like a little mouse . . . a little mouse in the grass who doesn't know she's surrounded by owls and foxes and weasels. And my brother the King is the worst of the lot. He's a conniving bastard and he always has been."

She expected him to punctuate his insult with a barking laugh, like usual, but Freddie truly seemed to be in a dark place. Which gave her the idea that he might be willing to spill some tea along with the whiskey.

"I know he wasn't kind to Penelope," she ventured.

That brought the laugh. "Wasn't kind? Wasn't . . . *kind*? Good God. I was no admirer, always thought she was a bit daft, but Edmund was a poor husband to that girl. Everyone raved about the so-called passion between them, but as far as I could tell his only passion was his mad desire to control her movements, her body, her *thoughts*. If she defied him he went completely mad. After she shagged that stable boy her days were numbered, and meanwhile he himself was chasing every piece of fanny that caught his eye."

"Did she know?"

Freddie returned to his chair, carrying his too-full glass as carefully as if it were an egg on a spoon. "He had dozens of lackeys covering his tracks. Felix Hill knows where all the bodies are buried. I'll wager Digby and Clark could tell you stories from boys' weekends, too, if they weren't sworn to carry them to the grave. But she knew. How could she not know?"

"About Eleanora? I've noticed the two of you aren't exactly close."

"Eleanora will smile at you"—he fell into the chair, somehow not spilling a drop—"while slipping the carving knife between your ribs."

"I've heard that rumor about Anabelle being Edmund's," said Jennie, wanting to see how far he would go.

"They may have tested that checkout girl who claims to be your mum, but I promise you dear Anabelle's DNA is off limits. Though there is a strong resemblance," he chuckled. "Ellie was Eddie's most regular sport fuck, even before he met Penelope. Quite ironically, sexual experience was disqualifying for the job of producing heirs at the time."

"And once Penelope did her job, Eleanora could leave her husband for Edmund," said Jennie, wondering why no one had told her that Diane Danforth's DNA had been checked. Or if they were planning to share the results.

"After a great many years had passed. Games like these are not played over a weekend."

Jennie tucked one leg underneath her and turned sideways in her chair so she could observe him more closely. He looked old and tired, the gin blossoms in his cheeks an inflamed purple.

"You told me not to reveal anything to anyone, but here you are, telling me all this," she said.

Freddie arched his eyebrows. "Did you hear me say one thing about myself? Still, you're right. You shouldn't trust anyone. Even me. Especially me. After all, we're all out for ourselves and always have been. That's the British Empire in a nutshell. But as the empire shrinks, we turn increasingly on each other. Searching for new people to destroy."

Jennie was drained and wanted to leave, but something was bothering her. "Does Hugh . . . know as much as you do?"

He shrugged. "I can't say for certain. He's always been a little bit golly-gee-whiz. A bit American. Which is maybe why he likes you so much. His mum's death was truly a tragedy. I believe we've all tried to keep certain painful facts from him. Though at times I wonder if the real truth is that he doesn't *want* to know any more than he does."

They both fell silent, contemplating the neatly cut logs stacked in the immaculately swept fireplace.

Jennie had feared a threat from someone in the royal orbit, like Vivienne or Jeremy Legrand. Or even a mailman with a grudge. But Freddie's fierce takedown of his own brother had her wondering if the people in this particular solar system were behind everything. What if Edmund and Eleanora themselves had conspired against Penelope after she'd served her purpose?

To what lengths would they go if they thought Jennie wasn't even fit to pop out an heir? She and Hugh had hardly even talked about kids. They both wanted them eventually, but he'd assured her there was no rush.

What if his father saw it as a much bigger priority?

"I think I'd better turn in," she told Freddie.

With a shudder, she grabbed her things and practically ran for the door, wanting only to nestle next to Hugh.

"Sleep tight," he slurred.

She wondered how much he would remember in the morning.

But she knew she wouldn't forget a word.

HRH The Princess of Wales

16 FEBRUARY 1994

Penelope sat across from Kenneth Davies in the Blue Drawing Room at Buckingham Palace. Behind them, a carefully tended fire flickered in the ornate, white marble fireplace, even though their "fireside chat" was being filmed at half-noon to maximize optimal natural light. It was a far cry from the live, cover-of-night confessional she had planned, back when she'd mistakenly believed such things were still possible. Today's interview was even sanctioned by Queen Alexandra herself.

Or so Penelope had been told.

All she knew for certain was her strategy of playing nice— obeying all rules, meekly following her palace minders, and never stepping even a toe out of line—was paying off. Hugh was a happy and well-adjusted ten-year-old with a fully present mother. Edmund trusted her enough that she once again enjoyed the kind of freedom she hadn't seen since the early days of her marriage. And her busy calendar of engagements and patronages enabled her to live ever more publicly, free from the constant surveillance she endured behind palace gates. Her own desires be damned.

"I can honestly say I'm thankful to have stumbled the way I did," Penelope said, focusing on Davies as if they weren't surrounded by minders, assistants, makeup artists, BBC producers, and cameras documenting her every blink. "The experience not only forced me to look inward and examine my weaknesses but enabled me to be a better mum and, I hope, a more effective, empathetic public servant."

She didn't add anything about being a better wife, which technically she was, if being a better wife meant pretending everything was peachy while her husband played castle with the newly divorced Eleanora Osborne-Webb.

"Your ability to handle difficult circumstances with strength and grace is inspiring," said Davies with a kindness she was unaccustomed to.

Penelope smiled with sincere appreciation. "Yesterday morning, I had the opportunity to help hold wee ones at a homeless shelter so their mums could fill out job applications. The women I met there have been through so much, but still approach the future with hope. They are the true inspiration."

Kenneth Davies was approximately her age, and to her knowledge, it was his first visit to Buckingham Palace, but he wasn't tongue-tied in the least. She had no doubt he'd been offered the interview because of his discretion during what the palace called her *fleeting instability*. Savvy enough to stick to the questions penned by Jeremy Legrand, he hadn't pressed her to divulge the details of her drinking problem or which particular demons had driven her to the bottle. But he had also peppered flattering commentary throughout—*deeply committed to your son, entirely rehabilitated public image, dazzling do-gooder*—that no one at the palace could refute. As a result, Penelope not only trusted him even more than she had when she'd tried to initiate contact, but recognized that he, too, was a *star on the rise.*

His only uncomfortable question came at the very end of the hour-long interview.

"While there's nothing more endearing than a successful come-back story, I would be remiss if I didn't ask you about one of your few detractors, Marquess Felix Hill. As reported in several tabloids, he was recently overheard at a club dinner telling other diners that your rehabilitation is 'all for show.' How do you respond?"

Penelope's first inclination was to blurt, *Felix Hill is a complete wanker.* Edmund's best friend was an undisputed, unrepentant arsehole. Unfortunately, he was also an astute judge of character—hers, anyway. She would indeed have already drunk herself to death if not for her fear of losing Hugh, a threat so cruel that only Felix himself could have suggested it to Edmund.

But she had learned to suppress such instincts. Instead she said in a measured tone, "The Marquess, whom I've known for years, is a royalist in the strictest sense of the word. As such, he never hesitates to speak his mind or act to ensure things continue exactly as they have for centuries. He is one of Prince Edmund's closest friends and most trusted advisors, and I admire his loy-alty. But by bettering myself and helping others, I've learned to focus on the important things and hope the truth of my ac-tions will show in time. "

Davies nodded approval. "Thank you for being you, Your Highness. And for everything you do."

"It's been my pleasure," she told him, holding her smile until the lights on the cameras went dark.

While no one was to touch her without her tacit approval, Kenneth Davies blithely disregarded protocol by reaching out to pat her shoulder. "Brilliantly done, Your Highness. The world is going to love you even more for your honesty and vulnerability."

Penelope was touched. "I truly appreciate how easy you made this for me."

"The pleasure is all mine," Davies said, his warm off-camera smile fully revealing his crooked, nicotine-stained teeth. "I will admit it's quite difficult to conduct an authentic interview while remaining within the parameters set by the palace."

"Imagine trying to conduct an authentic life while remaining within those parameters," she said, lightening the remark with a chuckle that was not particularly genuine.

He waited until a nearby cameraman had finished rolling a length of cable and carried it away toward an equipment crate. "If not for the red tape, I certainly would have asked you some follow-up questions."

Penelope hoped he didn't notice her hand had begun to tremble. "About what?"

"Well, I couldn't help but notice you said very little about the royal family. And even less about your relationship with Edmund."

Across the room, Jeremy Legrand rose from the powder-blue silk chair from which he'd been watching. He'd instructed her to smile, pause, and respectfully decline to discuss anything she felt was too direct or too personal during the interview.

But the interview was over . . .

"Everything is pure bliss, of course," she said loudly.

Davies raised an eyebrow at her tone. "Of course."

Then, as Legrand began making his way toward them, she lowered her voice. "And if you believe that, I have a bridge to sell you in Brooklyn."

"I don't yet own any property in the States," he said gamely.

"Nor do I," she said. "Although a book is considered a property, correct?"

"Indeed so," he said, the light in his eyes showing he understood where she was headed.

"And there are many book publishers in the States?"

"Very many."

"Then perhaps property across the pond is a good long-term investment," she concluded.

Legrand reached them, arm extended to shake Davies's hand, just as her private secretary Sophie Jones, newest lady-in-waiting Anne Claxton-Murray, and Rodney Whyte converged and began to bestow reserved *nicely dones*.

"Nicely done, indeed, princess," said Kenneth Davies.

Penelope couldn't have agreed more.

Chapter Twenty-Seven

CATS AND DOGS AND DRAGONS

Jennie stumbled into the living room with water dripping from her hair, trying to remember the last time she'd been caught in the rain. It had seemed like something that could never happen again. She rarely even opened doors for herself anymore, and the people who did that for her always seemed to have large umbrellas handy, ready to shield her from the elements. But no system was foolproof.

After returning from Windsor the previous day, she had been required to spend her morning shopping for clothes—now that she needed different outfits every day, it was amazing how much time she spent in private fitting rooms—and after dropping Poppy at Buckingham Palace for her biweekly check-in with Legrand, Rodney had delivered Jennie to Kensington Palace with the windshield wipers working overtime in a sudden summer storm.

Parking on the brick-paved inner courtyard, he hustled around the car and opened an umbrella before opening her door. But as she climbed out of her seat, a sudden gust of wind turned the umbrella inside out and the bucketing rain had soaked them both before they could reach the shelter of the entrance portico. Fortunately, a footman had promptly fetched her a towel, and she was still drying her hair as she entered her private quarters.

Seattle, she suddenly remembered. She and Diego had been exploring Queen Anne Hill the afternoon before a show when drizzle from the ever-present gray clouds began falling on their uncovered heads. But that rain had almost been pleasant. And most Seattleites, she noticed, simply pulled up their hoods.

When her hair was as dry as she could make it, she lowered the towel—and let it slip out of her fingers to the floor. She had seen something that made her muscles go limp.

A tiny, plastic Jennie Jensen, jagged on the side where it had been snapped away from a tiny, plastic Hugh, was neatly centered on the marble-topped coffee table.

She looked at the shelf where she'd put the replacement. It was still there. Still fully intact. She crossed the room and had almost picked up the broken one when she stopped herself.

Fingerprints, she thought.

Jennie lifted the household phone and asked for Rodney. He arrived in less than a minute, still soaked, apparently still searching for a towel of his own.

"What is it, Miss Jensen?" he asked.

She pointed at the coffee table. "I need to know who put that there."

Rodney appeared startled but controlled himself. Familiar with the contents of the room, he looked up at the shelf, just like she had. He nodded. He didn't need an explanation.

"I'll be right back," he said.

Only after he left did she think to check the other rooms. Nothing else had been disturbed. She texted a picture of the broken cake topper to Hugh.

Look what just showed up

Call security immediately

Rodney's already on it.

Hugh's next text took longer.

We both need to remain calm until
we learn more.

OK.

Was she calm or was she in shock? She was moving so slowly
it was like she was wearing lead boots. But her heart was beating double time.

Rodney returned twenty minutes later, looking relieved.
"Mystery solved, Miss Jensen. We have it all on the video. While
you were out, workmen came in to clean behind the radiator
covers, just as they are scheduled to do every summer. One of
them found the broken cake topper in an odd little corner and
knew it wasn't right to take it with him. It must have fallen
behind and taken a funny bounce."

"Oh," said Jennie as she sat heavily in the closest chair.

"I've been assisting Grant McCutcheon with the investigation," Rodney said gently. "I know this little mystery has
been weighing on your mind, but I'm sure it must make you
feel better to know there's an explanation. Just a freak occurrence. Probably couldn't get it to land like that again if we tried
a thousand times."

Jennie didn't feel better. She just felt confused.

"Will there be anything else?" asked Rodney.

Realizing he was probably as desperate for dry clothes as she was, she shook her head. "No, thank you."

After he left, she sat there, still damp, until she was shivering in the air-conditioning. Someone was messing with her. Even if it was plausible that the broken piece of cake topper had fallen from the shelf, bounced on the carpet, and somehow lodged out of sight under the radiator—and she had gotten flat on her stomach the first time she looked for it—there was no way in hell the chunky plastic cake topper would have broken apart in the first place unless the maid had been dusting it with boxing gloves.

But with this innocuous explanation, insisting that something was wrong would only make her look unbalanced. She needed to provide evidence that was less open to interpretation. And she had already promised to provide it to Grant McCutcheon.

She texted Rodney.

> After you dry off, please
> bring the car back around.

> Very good, Miss. Where will we be
> going?

> BP.

————————

The Yeoman of the Gold Plate, Ellis Swainscott, looked surprised to see her. In the few months since her last visit, the strands of his combover seemed to have grown slightly longer and thinner.

"How may I be of service?" he asked, inclining his head with the ghost of a bow—habit, she guessed.

"I need to retrieve something from my safe deposit box," she told him. "And I'll need to do it in private."

"Naturally," he said.

Ellis ushered her into the same small sitting room as before and she waited while he descended into the vault. She wished she could go with him. Once again, she pictured him climbing into a narrow little elevator and descending deep into the earth, tiptoeing past the sleeping dragon, and using a large iron key to open the safe. He was gone longer this time—maybe the dragon had fallen asleep with its head against the door.

She hadn't told Buckingham Palace she was coming and knew the odds of running into Edmund, Eleanora, or even Legrand were remote. What would she say if Eleanora suddenly decided to pop down and pick up some diamonds?

Fortunately, she didn't have to come up with any lame excuses. Ellis returned, apologizing for the delay without specifying what had caused it, then placed the large steel box on the table in front of her. She waited for him to leave, thinking she would take pictures of the notes just in case she didn't get them back from McCutcheon.

But when she lifted the lid, the box was empty.

The anonymous note to Penelope telling her that, *Despite the danger, we must find a way to be together*, was missing.

So was Penelope's note saying, *I must be very careful or they will kill me, too.*

"Mr. Swainscott!" she called.

He opened the door so quickly it was like he'd been waiting with his hand on the knob.

"Are you sure this is the right box?" she asked, hoping but not believing it could be true.

"I know it's the right box," he insisted. "You see, it's numbered. I took great care to record the number and I always double check."

She looked. There was indeed a metal number stamped on the box. But she hadn't noticed it before, so she had no idea if it matched.

"If it's the same one, then why is it empty?"

Looking ashen, Ellis grabbed the lapels of his blazer like he was trying to steady himself. "I . . . don't know. This—this has never happened before. I assure you, no one has handled this box but myself. Are you quite sure—?"

He stopped himself before suggesting that she might have been mistaken.

Jennie knew the notes hadn't vanished into thin air. They had been taken. She had been told that no one except the Yeoman of the Gold Plate had access to the vault. But rules like that obviously didn't apply to the King of England. He could order an exception or break the rule himself. He probably had his very own key. And his very own motive for stealing his ex-wife's notes?

Princess Penelope's paranoia about always being watched didn't seem so far-fetched anymore.

"I'm so terribly, terribly sorry," gushed Ellis. "I simply don't know what can have happened. I assure you, I will inform my superior and we will perform a thorough search for the missing item or items. If you could perhaps tell me what we might be looking for . . . ?"

Jennie closed the empty box and stood up.

"It wasn't anything valuable, just sentimental," she forced herself to say, not trusting him any more than she did anyone else at this point. "Please don't go to any trouble at all. There's no need to tell anybody. And there's definitely no need to do a search."

Ellis paused, seemingly torn between his duty to help, his hunger for absolution, and his role as a cog in the golden wheel. "You're quite sure?"

"I won't tell anyone if you won't," she said.

She meant it, too. Because it was finally obvious that there was no safe place and no one she could trust in Buckingham Palace . . . not if she didn't want to disappear, too.

Chapter Twenty-Eight
SOUTH BY SOUTHWEST

Why did Hugh's Range Rover have to have a stick shift? Were they really that much more common in Europe, or was it some kind of a guy thing? Maybe it was an anti-theft device to ensure his car wasn't stolen by a clueless American. If so, it hadn't worked, even though Jennie had ground the gears and stalled the car so many times that she hoped Hugh wouldn't have to replace the entire transmission. At least the three floor pedals were in the right place. Shifting with her left hand, she had made it out of London without crashing and burning. And the separated lanes of the M4 and the M5 allowed her to stop flinching at oncoming cars on the wrong side of the road. She had gotten used to that only as a back seat passenger. Taking the wheel was a different experience, and reminded her how she had never loved driving, even in the good, old USA.

She was headed southwest, where the skinny finger of Devon and Cornwall pointed toward the open Atlantic. A while back, the M5 had become the Devon Expressway, skirting the edge of Dartmoor National Park. Prompted by Siri, she downshifted and took the off-ramp turning due south onto the A3121, passing a roadside sign for the oddly named towns of Ugborough, Bit-taford, Loddiswell, and Ivybridge.

Now on two-lane roads again, she tightened her death grip on the wheel and glanced down at the screen in the dashboard, where the blue dot of her car blithely followed the blue line of the road. Turns came more quickly—thankfully traffic was thin—and she soon lost track of lefts and rights as the roads got narrower and narrower. Finally she found herself on an over-grown dirt track where the overgrowth was so heavy it brushed the car. Could this really be the way? All she remembered about her final destination was that it had been near something called the South Devon Area of Outstanding Natural Beauty.

Her decision to burst out of the royal bubble that morn-ing had been pure impulse, a simple realization that there was nothing besides privacy and security forcing her to stay inside it. She found Hugh's car keys easily enough, and even though the security officers at the gate seemed startled to see her drive up, they'd promptly lowered the road blocker to let her pass.

The biggest downside to driving herself was that she couldn't get out of the car. After more than four hours without a break, her fingers were cramped on the steering wheel and her blad-der was bursting. But she was not going to allow herself to be caught on cell phone video coming out of the loo at an Esso petrol station. Thankfully, the Range Rover's tank had been as full as her bladder.

She hadn't played a podcast or even music so she could focus on the task of driving. Which also gave her plenty of time to think about what she was about to do.

She may as well be in the Outer Hebrides, even though she's only living in Devonshire, Cece had said. *I understand she's quite happy gardening, throwing pots, and judging the local flower show. The intrigue at court was never that one's cup of tea.*

Did Penelope's best friend know something that had made her disappear? Or would she be completely clueless?

"You have arrived at your destination," announced Siri as the car came out of the trees and its wheels bumped onto paved road.

Jennie slowed to a stop next to a low stone wall with an open gate. Below her, a gray stone estate sat halfway up a hill with green fields falling away below. The main house was old, but not ancient, its walls covered with bushy climbing ivy. Around it were several outbuildings and terraced gardens with slender palm trees, spiky bushes, and other completely unexpected tropical plants. Apparently Devon caught subtropical breezes.

Birds chirped and fluttered in the foliage as she got out of the car, but otherwise there was no sign of life. As she walked through the gate to the door—it looked like she had arrived at a rear entrance—she heard a sound like a crate of teacups falling onto a sidewalk. Leaving the heavy brass knocker untouched, she followed the source of the sound around the side of the house.

Next to a small shed, a sixtyish woman was dusting off her hands near an empty wheelbarrow and a pile of broken pottery. She wore a dusty white smock, baggy men's pants, and a crumpled sun hat.

"What happened?" asked Jennie.

"Bloody readout on the kiln timer," said the woman in a tone of exasperation, seemingly unperturbed by Jennie's appearance on her property. "The numbers are so fiddling small. Thought I'd fired it for fifteen minutes, not fifteen hours. Only a week's work, though, not to worry."

"I'm sorry to show up unannounced. I'm Jennie Jensen. I was hoping you might have time for a cup of tea."

Kitty Crowden nodded. "I know who you are. I was wondering if you might search me out before you went through with it."

Jennie realized her mouth was hanging open and clamped it shut.

With one last look at the broken crockery—the size of the pile suggesting it wasn't her first mishap—Kitty strode toward the house. "Good job we don't need to drink out of any of *those*. Let's get the kettle on the hob."

"Can I use your bathroom first?" asked Jennie.

———————

By the time Jennie came back from taking the world's longest pee and washing up until she felt alert and refreshed, the kettle had already whistled. She helped herself to a stool and watched Kitty spoon tea and pour water into an attractive handmade pot. The rambling farmhouse kitchen was pleasantly messy, and sunlight from the window illuminated breakfast crumbs and a drop of congealed strawberry jam next to a half-sawn loaf of bread.

Following Jennie's eyes, Kitty swept the crumbs into the sink. "The cleaning lady comes every so often, but the B&B down the road keeps her much busier than I do."

"Do you live here by yourself?" Jennie asked.

"I do. My parents have passed, my husband died of cancer, and here I remain, frequently reminding my children they can stay as long as they like. My granddaughters will spend part of their summer holidays here, one of the highlights of my year."

While the tea steeped, Kitty busied herself with taking down teacups, arranging crackers and cheese on a plate, slicing an apple, and washing a small bunch of grapes. Her hair was dry and wispy, her face was free of makeup, but her eyes were sharp with deep laugh lines.

"Well, are you going to make me drag it out of you?" asked Kitty with a chuckle.

"I wanted to ask you some questions about Penelope. Because nobody else will give me straight answers."

"Not even Hugh?"

"I'm not sure he knows them. People say you were her best friend, but that you kind of made yourself disappear. I just wondered if there was a reason for that."

"Well, I was her best friend largely because we grew up together," said Kitty, deftly cutting a bruise out of an apple with a paring knife. "We weren't much alike, but we were in the same year at school, the same classes, the same little social circle. I loved her, but I never cared for most of our peers. Angling for position never suited me. I certainly never wanted to live in London. My parents thought the world revolved around Buckingham Palace and never understood that they had raised a country lass."

"It is beautiful country."

"And a far cry from where we grew up," said Kitty. "Follow me."

She carried the tea tray out to a flagstone patio shaded by a mix of palms and native trees. Waving away a bluebottle fly, Kitty pushed a small plate in Jennie's direction.

"I should have told you I can't eat the cheese," she said apologetically. "I'm vegan."

"Of course you bloody are," Kitty huffed, playfully put out. She went back into the house and returned with a tub of hummus. "My bloody favorite neighbor is a bloody vegan, too."

Jennie liked her. And, on gut instinct only, trusted her.

"I found a note in Penelope's things," she said, dipping a cracker into the hummus as Kitty poured out the tea. "It was to Penelope and said, 'Despite the danger, we must find a way to be together.'"

Kitty grimaced. "Anthony Heald, most likely. Her riding instructor."

"I know they had a brief affair."

Kitty stirred milk and sugar into her tea, then turned her iron patio chair sideways. It was either so she could enjoy the admittedly beautiful view or so she wouldn't have to look Jennie in the eye.

"She loved Edmund, the poor girl, she really did," she began. "I'm honestly not sure how he thought about her—when he did think about her. He was a billy goat through and through, before, during, and after. She tried so hard to make him love her, but he was never going to change. He had so many lovers I quite lost track. There was Vivi, of course, who badly wanted to marry him. And Sherry Rowland. He was on and off for years with a stage actress who was forever trying to break into film, Joanne something or maybe it was Valerie something. And then of course there was Eleanora, who waited in the wings until she could make her comeback."

"Prince Freddie said she plays the long game," Jennie said with a laugh.

"To be sure. And when Penelope finally realized she couldn't change Edmund," she continued, "I suppose she decided that what was good for the gander was good for the goose. She convinced herself she was quite serious about Anthony, but you must remember he was exceptionally good-looking."

Jennie had been so transfixed that she almost forgot her follow-up. "And then Anthony Heald died."

"He lost his head, quite literally. A bizarre and unthinkable road accident. No one could have seen that coming," Kitty added archly, her knife clinking on the plate as she sliced off a thick piece of hard cheese.

"Oh my God," whispered Jennie.

"I was the first person Penelope called. It was horrible. She and Edmund were staying in Mallorca as guests of the King of

Spain. Poor thing, she was out of her mind with sadness and fear and Edmund was in the next room so we couldn't talk. She never even got to grieve properly because she couldn't admit she'd been seeing him. And he was such a minor figure in the circle hardly any of the FOEs even went to his funeral."

"Foes?"

"Friends of Edmund. That was Penny's term for the prigs he surrounds himself with. Not just Eleanora but Vivienne, Felix, Ann, Digby, and that lot."

"You didn't sound completely convinced when you said no one could have seen his death coming. Is there any chance it wasn't an accident?"

Kitty placed the slice of cheese on a cracker, chewed it deliberately, and swallowed tea. "Penelope firmly believed it was murder. It would have been difficult to choreograph. But it certainly solved the problem of making him go away."

Despite the long drive and her growling stomach, Jennie didn't feel hungry anymore. "I also found another note that Penelope never sent. She said they were going to kill her so Edmund could marry someone else."

"No surprises there. That was right before they sent her to their version of rehab."

"I'm starting to understand why Penelope always felt like she was in danger because I've been getting threats of my own. I think I might be in danger, too."

"And, like Penelope, you're quite popular with the public," said Kitty. "We can't have you getting more popular than the King, now can we? What does Hugh say about all this?"

"Hugh is supportive and trying to be helpful but I can't prove anything. And the notes from Penelope just went missing, so I don't even have evidence that what happened to her might be happening to me."

Kitty looked off into the distance. "You wanted to know why I left court. You've answered your own question. These are the people you spend a lifetime dealing with. I could have made a more advantageous marriage, could have ingratiated myself. I chose not to. My late lamented father likely went to his grave wishing I had been pretty enough to dangle in front of Edmund—and thank Christ for that." She shuddered. "I've always felt strangely responsible for Penny's fate because it was my father who put the whole idea in her parents' head. He knew how to read the royal tea leaves."

"But Penelope did find love again, right? With Scott Corbyn?"

"He was much more suave and worldly than Anthony. Rich as well. He didn't have to plead for Penny to meet him in midnight assignations—he just spirited her away on his private plane."

They both fell silent, pondering Penelope's final flight.

Hundreds of yards away, a drone ascended into the sky and began buzzing along in an unnaturally straight line, like a robotic bird.

"Awful things," said Kitty. "The B&B owner is always taking aerial footage for his website and social media. If I still had ammunition for my husband's birding guns I'd shoot it out of the sky."

"I wouldn't blame you. It's creepy."

"What are your plans for tonight? Surely you're not driving straight back to London. That's much too much for one day."

The very idea did sound exhausting. "I hadn't thought that far ahead," Jennie told her.

"Well, you can't check into a motor inn, not with your famous face. Stay here."

"I couldn't put you out."

Kitty waved off her objection. "I won't take no for an answer. I make a tofu stir-fry that will neither delight you nor kill you.

And besides, I have something you might like to read. I always meant to give it to Hugh one day but one's protective instincts remain strong. You can read it and decide for me."

"What is it?"

"Penelope's diary."

From Princess Penelope's Private Diary

18 NOVEMBER 1994

I've long thought it would be smashing to work the celebrity phone bank for the BBC Children in Need telethon and help them raise heaps of money. Of course, I never pursued it, because senior royals are expected to avoid fraternizing with the media.

Especially this senior royal.

But my chat with Kenneth Davies was such a huge ratings success, the BBC invited me to come on this year. I assumed I'd be forced to decline, but public approval of yours truly has apparently risen to an all-time high—second only to Her Majesty, it seems—and in order to capitalize upon my popularity, it was decided my presence at the telethon would be a boon to the royal brand.

I like to believe everything happens for a reason. Had I succeeded in speaking with Kenneth Davies the first time I tried, it would indeed have done damage to the royal family, but the personal cost would have been catastrophic. This was a far better moment. Kenneth and I met up backstage, and with only the furry, brown Pudsey Bear costume as witness (the mascot's wearer being on a quick fag break before escorting me onstage), I was able to pass along the list of names, dates, and incidents that will form the basis of a book he has now

*unofficially agreed to pen. He promised not to publish
a word until I've given him the go-ahead. Unless I die
first, that is—then anything goes.*

*Shortly thereafter, I was live on camera with Pudsey
(fully reanimated and smelling like an ashtray). Our
skit went off without a hitch and raised double the
donations anticipated. I was then escorted to a raised
dais to answer a "royal red" phone. Although my
preference would have been to sit with the other celebrity
phone-bankers like Rowan Atkinson and Robbie Fowler
(!), my line was connected to a speaker so my chats with
unsuspecting callers would be heard live.*

The evening only got better.

*At the VIP cocktail reception during the break for
BBC News at Ten, I was sipping sparkling water and
trying to pretend I didn't hear Terry Scott berating the
waiter for putting two olives, not one, in his martini.*

*"I hate it when someone I admire turns out to be
a prick in private," said the less publicly recognized
celebrity standing next to me.*

I couldn't help giggling.

*"Your Highness, I do apologise for my language,
but I just can't bear that kind of rubbish behaviour," he
said, turning to offer a respectful bow. "That's no way
to treat someone who's only doing their job."*

"I quite agree," I said.

"Scott Corbyn," he said.

"Yes," I said.

*I have been aware of Scott Corbyn's existence for
years—he owns half the retail chains on High Street,
after all—but our paths had never previously crossed.*

He smiled wryly. "May I say that you, however,

are every bit as charming and kind as advertised. The way you set those gobsmacked callers at ease was quite touching."

"I try my best," I said, feeling my cheeks warm.

In photos, Scott Corbyn is always well-dressed (as one would expect) but appears quite average in the looks department. In person, he exudes a charisma that somehow enhances everything about him, from his shiny brown brogues to his wavy brown hair.

I found myself quite unable to stop talking, going on to say, "I know it's grand for ratings, and of course, everyone calls in hoping to chat with someone famous, but I'm sure none of the viewers actually expected the likes of me to pick up the phone."

"Lucky them," said Scott.

"Why have we never met before?" I asked.

His explanation—that he generally doesn't like glitzy social events unless they are for very worthy causes—struck a chord. So did his admission that he'd offered to answer phones because a charity he supports, Willow House, was a beneficiary of tonight's donations. But his final reason threw me for a loop.

"As an avowed anti-monarchist, I tend to avoid royal circles," he said. "Present company excluded, of course."

I believe I have fallen in love.

19 NOVEMBER 1994
I sent my lady-in-waiting Anne Claxton-Murray on a mission to discover what, if anything, the palace has on Scott Corbyn.

It may sound downright barmy to engage Edmund's eyes and ears on such a sensitive task (she really thinks

I don't know she rifles through my desk drawers on the regular, although she has no idea I leave keys out so she can) it's actually a stroke of brilliance on my part. I couldn't possibly snoop around without arousing suspicion. Sending my very capable right-hand FOE, however, signals a legitimate need for information— which I told Anne was to assess any risks if I were to become involved in his charities.

Which is the official reason for my plan to meet with Scott Corbyn next week.

Anne returned from the depths of Hades (or wherever such information is stored) with a thick file folder—further confirmation that palace intelligence gathering is as detailed as I believed.

Scott Corbyn was even more impressive than I thought. A middle-class boy from Croydon, he'd borrowed money to start a jeans import business at age twenty-two and then parlayed it into a chain-store empire within a decade. He now holds interests in various industries and owns property across the globe. The Willow Foundation, his charitable trust, has a charter to dispense much of his fortune. Among the recipients I noticed Willow Academy, a school in Leeds which is primarily funded by the foundation and serves children with mental health needs.

Before I allowed my heart to flutter out of my chest, I read through the section which noted the anti-monarchist statements he'd made:

"The monarchy is archaic and does not serve the needs of a changing Britain."

Which I agree with, although I do what I can personally.

"Anti-monarchy protestors should not be arrested."
I also agree, so long as they are peaceful.
"The Queen herself is a revered institution, but
Edmund has little to offer. When his mother dies, he
should renounce the throne."
To which I couldn't agree more.
I knew everything I needed to know about Scott
Corbyn in advance of our meeting except for one thing,
which I found near the top of the page in the personal
information section:
Marital status: divorced.

28 NOVEMBER 1994
The Willow Foundation, which I learnt today was named
in honour of Scott Corbyn's sister, who died from leukemia
when she was a girl (one of the few facts overlooked by
palace intel) is headquartered in a charming five-story
brownstone on Lumley Street in Mayfair.
Whilst the staff were as warm as the décor in
the reception area—pale greens, tans, and goldenrod
furnishings set against walls papered in a willow bough
print—I felt nervous. As I boarded an old lift which
slowly chuffed and clanked toward the executive offices on
the top floor, I began to wonder if I was about to be made
a fool of. Scott's success, after all, has been predicated in
large part on his ability to charm his way into getting
what he wants. Was his interest in me, a member of the
monarchy he so abhorred, based only on what I could
help him accomplish? As the doors slid open, I girded
myself for personal disappointment with the promise of a
professional association that could help so many others.
Scott was waiting for me in what turned out to be

a combination office and sitting area that spanned the entire top floor of the building.

"Welcome, Your Highness."

I didn't urge him to call me Penelope.

I sat in one of two butter-coloured leather chairs, and he took the other. As he poured tea from the pot on the table between us, I had to stop myself from admiring his strong hands. The tea was a truly delicious ginger-green variety he said he discovered in Ceylon and now imported exclusively. Whilst we sipped, he proceeded to fill me in on everything I already read—the irony didn't escape me—from his lack of formal education and dashed dreams of being a professional footballer to the success that allowed him to, in his words, "pay the rent and give the odd pound away."

According to the palace, over a million annually.

"I confess I'm a bit nervous," he told me. "At our last meeting I'd taken a couple of drinks first."

"There's no need for that," I said, even though I was feeling the flutters myself.

He took a deep breath and proceeded to ask two questions. The first, which I expected, was whether I would work with the Willow Foundation, in a capacity yet to be determined.

To which I answered yes.

The second he asked with a steady gaze, as though he was looking at me, not Princess Me.

"Is there any truth to the rumor that you and Prince Edmund lead separate lives?"

"He is in love with someone else," I answered.

"I'd like to say I'm sorry, but I'm not. Because I would very much like to ask you on a date."

His directness terrified me. The answer, of course, had to be no. I couldn't even speak.

"Being involved with me is dangerous," I finally said.

His smile was luminous. "I certainly hope so."

6 MAY 1995

With Anthony, my impulse to have an affair came from my need for attention and wanting to feel as though I mattered. I confused excitement, and of course lust, with love. Now all I feel for him is grief and immeasurable guilt.

Scott inspires me to be a better version of myself. For the first time, I've met someone who treats me as his equal—neither putting me on a pedestal nor pushing me off one—someone with whom I am forming a deep and lasting bond.

And the sexual spark between us is unlike anything I've ever felt before.

I feel loved and appreciated. I feel safe.

I feel so . . . alive!

19 MAY 1996

Because Hugh will be off to Eton in the fall, because gorgeous weather was forecast, and because I don't need a reason to spend quality time with my son, I spirited him away for a mini-holiday in Pembrokeshire.

We spent an afternoon on a fishing skiff, hiked in Pembrokeshire Coast National Park, and had an all 'round lovely time knocking about outside Haverford West as guests of Cadoc Hughes, a downright tolerable school chum of Edmund's.

Whilst everything on our agenda had been planned,

*I did arrange one surprise stop in Canaston Bridge.
Hugh and I rarely get a chance to indulge in our love
for thrill rides, and as luck would have it, one of Scott's
companies has just purchased the amusement park there.
I knew Hugh would be chuffed to ride the brand-new
rollercoaster before it opens to the public next week.*

*Scott and I have been cautious and will continue
to be so. Neither of us has revealed our personal
association to anyone, and I had never even mentioned
Scott Corbyn's existence to Hugh until today, when
I introduced him as "Mr. Corbyn, the owner of this
amusement park."*

*Scott escorted us over to the ride to confirm with
the operators that all was in working order. Hugh could
hardly stand still as we waited for the go-ahead—I
think he imagined himself as some sort of daredevil test
pilot, putting his life on the line to ensure the ride was
safe for the public.*

*It was indeed a thrill to be the only riders, but
after three exhilarating but extremely twisty, stomach-
dropping goes on the bumpy wooden coaster, I was
green at the gills whilst Hugh was just getting started.
Thankfully, Scott was kind enough to switch places with
me and they rode four more times together.*

*As we started back to London, a still buzzing Hugh
said, "Dad would have hated that. Vom. Spew. Look
out below!"*

*I laughed, but then my heart broke when he added,
"I wish he was fun like Mr. Corbyn."*

25 MAY 1996
My least favourite charade is the one in which I

*accompany my husband to a ball where we dine, dance,
and pretend we aren't in love with other people.*

*Halfway through our first spin on the dance floor
this evening, as I breathed through my mouth to avoid
his nauseating cologne, he dipped me dramatically. As
he pulled me back up, he leaned close and whispered.
"You'll live to regret bribing my son with a trip to Scott
Corbyn's shit amusement park. I've allowed this little
dalliance to go on for far too long."*

*It wasn't easy, but somehow I maintained my own
fake smile whilst I recovered from the shock. "There's
nothing little about Scott Corbyn. Or our dalliance."*

*His eyes were dead as he said, "Put an end to it. Or
I will."*

15 NOVEMBER 1996
Scott proposed to me today.

*Instead of giving me a ring, he got down on one
knee and shared the plan he came up with during
the six unbearable months we've been apart at my
insistence.*

*It is a crazy, romantic, hopeless gesture, but I love
him madly and can't bear to live without him for
another day.*

*He's got hold of information exposing Edmund's
many affairs, including a secret recording of what he says
is an embarrassingly lewd exchange between Edmund
and Eleanora. (God forbid I ever have to hear it.)*

*I will leave on his jet, bound for Dagon Island in
the Caribbean, which he owns, where no one can touch
either of us whilst the rest of it plays out.*

Once I'm safely out of reach, he will contact

Edmund to demand a quiet and civil divorce in which I gain equal custody of Hugh. Otherwise, the dossier will be released to the media.

The idea of blackmailing the Crown terrifies me, but Scott maintains excellent security and seems to have no fear for his own safety.

I told him no. I reminded him of every conceivable thing that could go wrong. But he wouldn't budge.

"Let me secure your safety and your future," he said.

Finally, I said yes.

Chapter Twenty-Nine

BURNING QUESTIONS

Jennie was glad Hugh had texted her instead of calling. That way, he couldn't hear the uncertainty in her voice as she struggled with the urge to tell him where she really was and what was really happening.

How are things at KP?

> I'm getting a lot of
> reading done.
> How's Paris?

Am I in Paris? I'd quite forgotten.

> That's what you told me, anyway.

Meeting rooms look the same the
world over, alas. But wrapping up
shortly. Home tonight.

Can't wait. Love you.

Love, love, love you, too.

Since she was answering via Siri, he also couldn't hear the huge truck that had just roared past her on the M4 as she re-traced her path to London. She had promised not to withhold anything from Hugh and even temporary omissions made her feel like a liar. But although she trusted him, she no longer trusted his family or the people working for them. She couldn't risk having him say the wrong thing to the wrong person. It was also possible her phone was tapped, just like her mom had always feared. She needed to call Karen and tell her she was right but couldn't do it until she got her hands on a disposable phone. Hugh's Range Rover probably had a tracking device, but there wasn't much she could do about that now.

Jennie glanced over at Penelope's diary on the passenger seat, wondering if she should have stowed it in her suitcase or at least put it in the glove compartment. It felt like she was car-rying a bomb in broad daylight.

Calm down, she told herself.

It was hard to get her head around what she had just read—and reread—the night before in Kitty's guest room. Seeing it all in Penelope's own looping cursive had made Hugh's mom more painfully human than ever before. The erratic entries, sometimes pausing for weeks or months, detailed the whole course of her doomed marriage and Edmund's relentless attempts to control her. Jennie had been almost unable to breathe as she turned the pages, watching Penelope's transformation from moon-eyed in-nocent to out-of-control wreck to battle-scarred veteran who had learned to play the game by keeping her guard up and watch-ing what she said. Her brief, doomed fling with Anthony Heald left her heart broken until she met Scott Corbyn. In her final days, Penelope had finally found the true love that had always eluded her, and died hoping she might live happily ever after, after all. That she might be finally safe.

The diaries didn't prove anything except for Penelope's own paranoia, but the consistency of the details and her own haunting voice made them almost impossible to disbelieve. Most damning was Scott Corbyn's plan to blackmail Edmund. It said a lot that he and Penelope thought it had been needed to keep Penelope and Hugh safe. It said even more that it hadn't.

And what happened to the secrets she passed along to Kenneth Davies?

But it had been Corbyn's plane that crashed. Not one owned by the royal family.

There were still so many questions left unanswered.

And one man who seemed most likely to answer them.

The clerk at the Selfridges perfume counter gave a horse laugh when Jennie asked where she could find Scott Corbyn. But when Jennie lowered her oversized sunglasses and lifted her Chicago Cubs baseball cap, she paled, stammered an apology, and rushed off. Less than a minute later, a man with a blue blazer and a squawking walkie-talkie hustled her into a private lounge.

"A thousand apologies, Miss Jensen," he said. "Otherwise we would have greeted you properly. I'm sure the miscommunication about your arrival is on our end. Mr. Corbyn doesn't maintain an office in this building."

"Oh," she said, feeling foolish. Of course he didn't.

"But if you'll be so kind as to wait here, I'll see if I can discover where you might find Mr. Corbyn today."

He closed the door, leaving Jennie in a windowless room with plush furniture and a basket of gourmet snacks. Suddenly starving, she devoured a bag of almonds, two tangerines, and a nutrition bar that wasn't vegan. Under the circumstances, she decided she could survive trace amounts of egg.

She was an idiot to show up unannounced and expect Corbyn to be there. In addition to Selfridges, he owned several high-fashion and fast-fashion clothing chains, a portfolio of hotels, controlling stock in Sainsbury's, and probably his own small planet. To expect him to be prowling the floors of his flagship store was ridiculous. But for the past year, other people had made her appointments, chauffeured her everywhere, and guided her to private entrances. On her own, she once again felt as clueless as when she'd just arrived in England.

The security guard returned with an even larger colleague. "Mr. Corbyn will be delighted to receive you at the Willow Foundation."

One of them walked in front of her and one of them behind as they moved through the store quickly enough that if any shoppers did recognize Jennie, she was gone by the time they had opened the cameras on their phones. The guards escorted her outside, across Oxford Street and into narrow Lumley, where she was ushered into a five-story brownstone. A creaky private elevator took her to the executive office on the top floor.

Scott Corbyn was waiting for her when the door opened. The expansive room with a desk in one corner was expensive-looking but cluttered and dated—all pale greens and goldenrod—exactly the same as Penelope had described it in her journal. Behind him, floor-to-ceiling windows offered a sweeping view of London rooftops. Corbyn was himself impeccably attired in a blue chalk-stripe suit, a tightly knotted tie, and handmade leather shoes. His expectant expression was just as warm as the previous time they'd met.

"Welcome, princess," he said, smiling.

"Please don't," she told him.

He waved away her objection. "The formalities will be concluded soon enough."

Her chest tightened and her eyes suddenly filled with tears as she realized how little time lately she'd spent thinking about her future with Hugh. How few moments she'd even had to feel happy and in love. How worried she was that their wedding day might never arrive.

Corbyn's forehead wrinkled with worry when he saw her expression. "Please sit down."

Once she was seated in a heavily worn, butter-colored leather chair and had sipped from a bottle of sparkling water, Jennie was able to regain control of herself.

"Tell me why you came to see me," said Corbyn, sitting down across from her.

Jennie took Penelope's diary out of her purse and put it on the glass-and-brass coffee table. "Do you recognize this?"

"I'm afraid I don't."

"It's Penelope's private diary."

Now it was Corbyn's turn to falter. His lips parted as he slumped slightly in his chair. "You've read it, I assume?"

"I feel bad about reading something that I know is so personal to you. But this was given to me so I could learn more about threats that have been made to my safety."

Corbyn stared at her, questioning.

"I think Penelope was murdered and I think the palace covered it up. And Mr. Corbyn, I'm honestly terrified that whoever was behind it might be after me, too."

He looked at the diary with longing but also fear, as if he was afraid it might blow up in his hands.

"Do you want to read it?" she asked.

"Not because I believe I'll learn anything I don't already know, but because I still miss her. I *know* she was murdered. And I've spent nearly twenty years trying to get the world to believe me. Immediately following her death, journalists at least spoke to me and reported what I said, even if they were only humoring me. But the official version won out. Now, outside the fringes of the internet, everyone thinks I'm mad as a March hare."

"Not everyone," she said.

He stood up abruptly, as if it was too painful to sit any longer. Stepping to the wall of windows, he stared out like he was looking into the past.

"They tried to pin it on me, you know, by waiting until she was on board my personal plane," he said. "I'm convinced that was done both in order to make me look guilty and to twist the knife. Three days before it happened, I told her I had compiled a dossier on Edmund's own indiscretions that would serve as an insurance policy should he try to retaliate against either one of us. The following day she agreed to leave the country with me. I urged her to bring Hugh because I knew she would miss him desperately. I also knew they would never, ever dare try anything so long as he was with her. She argued that was too risky—if there was any suggestion she was kidnapping the future king, Edmund would order them both forcibly returned. But once she was safely out of the country on Dagon Island, out of royal reach, I was going to help her sue for divorce."

Corbyn's way of talking had gradually changed from conversation to recitation. His flat, clipped words sounded like they'd been shaped by repeated tellings. Even though it had not come to pass, Jennie felt nauseated by his calculated willingness to use Hugh as a human shield.

"What happened the day she left?"

"A week earlier, my usual pilot quit, telling me he'd had a better offer of employment. These things happen, and I didn't find it suspicious because I hadn't yet informed him of the flight plan. I will go to my grave blaming myself for not looking into it more closely. The palace must have found a way to eavesdrop on my private conversations with Penelope. I sourced a replacement . . . and then of course you know what happened. Princess Penelope was assassinated for daring to love—I always say *me*, but it could have been anybody."

"But how do you *know*?" asked Jennie, feeling unsettled by his intensity.

He chuckled and shook his head. "Three and a half million pounds buys quite a lot of information, as it happens. Come see."

He turned and started walking away, forcing Jennie to jump out of her chair and hurry after him. She followed him out of the spacious office and down a hallway hung with framed photos of Scott and Penelope beaming as they posed together inside hospitals, community centers, and beneath a sign for the Willow School. After using a keypad to unlock a steel door, he ushered her into a room where shelves lined all four walls. Most of them were filled with neatly labeled banker's boxes, but some were piled with books and stacks of papers.

Corbyn walked along the shelves, trailing his fingers along the boxes. "Half of this comes from my private detectives, half of it I gathered myself. Dossiers on every single member of the royal family highlighting all known antipathies toward Penelope. Interviews with former palace staff who have been willing to talk. This whole wall documents the day of the crash itself, proving that, short of sabotage or foul play, there was no reason for the plane to go down. I have aircraft specifications, detailed weather reports, transcripts of the black box and air traffic control, and dozens of interviews with crash-scene investigators and aviation experts."

Jennie pulled a paperback off the nearest shelf: *Fourteen Minutes from Freedom: The Assassination of Princess Penelope.* The cover art superimposed photos of Penelope, Edmund, and Corbyn over a photo of the crash site.

"After no publishing house would touch that, undoubtedly feeling pressure from the Crown, I published it myself," Corbyn told her. "The author suggests the actual takedown was engineered by Mossad agents in a quid pro quo."

"I had no idea there was this much out there," she mumbled.

"There should be even more. Penelope did a series of private interviews with Kenneth Davies on the understanding that it would be turned into a book, but the Crown was the highest bidder for the manuscript. Of course, they have no intention to publish it. Davies is their man now. He told me he burned the tapes and all his notes as part of the bargain. I don't believe him, but regardless, he was not the champion she hoped for."

Penelope had given him power over the document. *Unless I die first, that is—then anything goes,* she had written in her diary.

"I will go to my grave blaming myself," he said again. "But I would feel much worse if I hadn't done everything I could to bring her murderer to justice."

Jennie looked at him numbly.

"King Edmund, of course," Corbyn clarified. "He wanted to kill me, too. I was supposed to be on the plane with her. Only a few people knew I had to change my plans at the last minute. The reason I had to stay behind was actually to make arrangements regarding my dossier on Edmund, but I was going to join Penelope the very next morning, flying commercial. Of course, *they* used my absence to throw more suspicion on me." His voice had risen almost to a screech. "What was my *motive*? That I loved her?"

Overwhelmed by his accusation and everything it implied, all Jennie could think to do was direct the conversation back to known facts. "But the official investigation absolved you of any wrongdoing, just like it never incriminated Edmund."

"They released only half of the truth. Because the Crown ordered the investigation through the Metropolitan Police and supervised every step of it. The public report is a sham document. Buckingham Palace has the uncensored one, and it will never see the light of day."

Jennie suddenly felt claustrophobic, walled in by the tens of thousands of pages of paper devoted to Penelope's death. Did they contain the truth or just more speculation and wild theories Corbyn himself had helped spread? He seemed stuck in a loop, unable to move on from his obsession.

"I need some air," she practically begged.

———————————

Standing on a private balcony with her fingers wrapped firmly around the railing, even London's smoggy summer breeze made Jennie feel better. The distant honks and sirens of the city felt reassuringly familiar. Corbyn stood downwind, smoking a cigarette.

"You said you had blackmail material on Edmund," she told him. "Why didn't you just go ahead and release it after she died?"

He laughed bitterly. "I tried. I packaged up all the most damning and salacious stuff about Edmund and sent it to ITV because I knew the BBC wouldn't touch it. But even they refused to seriously investigate. Many of the details have come out over the years, of course, but only in the scandal sheets. Everyone seems quite comfortable with the idea that the King played Jack the Lad but no one can countenance the fact he's a killer."

Jennie could almost hear Penelope say *I told you so* as she turned to go. "I'd better get back to Kensington Palace. Hugh's coming home soon."

Corbyn tossed his half-smoked cigarette over the railing, a small gesture that made her wonder if she had overestimated his goodness.

"I have copies of all the important materials," he said, following her inside. "I'm quite happy to share them with you."

"Thank you, but I don't have a safe place to keep them. And I probably shouldn't be seen coming here."

He fell in step beside her as she crossed his office to the elevator. "I'll have them delivered to a suite at the Savoy. You can view them at your convenience."

"Don't put it under my name."

"Of course not. At the front desk, just give the name . . . Penny Scott. Only the two of us will know."

Jennie eyed the elevator call button, unable to shake the feeling that he wasn't just doing it for her.

"Why are you doing this?"

"To help you and Hugh. I hope someday you can help me tell the real story."

As the elevator descended, she collapsed against the wall, barely able to stand. Giving expression to his grief had driven Corbyn to the edge. Hugh kept his smothered, but his occasional explosions told her it was still burning.

What was going to happen to her if she kept asking questions? And what would happen when she finally found the answers?

Chapter Thirty
CALLING HOME

After knocking twice, Rodney entered and crossed the room to hand Jennie a vinyl bag printed with the Carphone Warehouse logo. She could feel the edges of a slim cardboard box inside.

"Old habits die hard," he said with a chuckle. "I drove five miles further to save ten pounds."

"I really appreciate it," she told him.

He hesitated as if he was waiting for an explanation, or maybe just further instructions. She wondered if she should make an excuse. Not that she owed him one or that he'd ever even ask. When she pulled into the courtyard an hour ago, Rodney had been outside chatting with the valet. He raised his eyebrows at the dusty, bug-spattered Land Rover, but didn't ask her where she'd been, saying only, "I imagine you'll want that washed."

And when she asked him to buy her a prepaid phone, he nodded and got on with it.

If she wanted to give free rein to her fears, she could speculate that his lack of curiosity came from the fact that the palace had been keeping him updated on her whereabouts. But Rodney was old school and had told her before it wasn't his place to ask questions.

"Thank you, Rodney, that will be all," she said.

"Yes, Miss Jensen." He paused at the door. "It's good to have you back."

"It's good to be back," she said, finally smiling. She knew from reading Penelope's diary that he didn't like it when she'd given him the slip, and now she'd just done the same thing.

After the door closed, she unboxed the Nokia smartphone. It wasn't charged, so she uncoiled the cord and plugged the chunky adapter into an outlet above the baseboard by a bookcase. Then, changing her mind, she unplugged it and took it into her bathroom, closed the door, and plugged it in next to the sink. She sat down on the toilet and waited until the phone came to life.

Then she dialed the only number she knew from memory.

Karen had gone back home until the wedding, saying she needed to "feed your father and water the plants," although Jennie was also sure it had something to do with keeping the neighbors from thinking she'd abandoned their cul-de-sac for Kensington Palace. Her mom always wanted to appear grounded—even though she also loved having details about the grandeur of royal life dragged out of her.

Thankfully, she was also one of the few people in America who still picked up for UNKNOWN CALLER. *What if it's an emergency?* she always said.

Jennie felt terrible for teasing her about that.

"Hello?"

Karen's tone was wary in a way Jennie wasn't used to hearing. But she was so relieved that she almost started sobbing.

"Mom, it's me."

"Jennie! I just got back from walking Scooter. Where are you calling from?"

"I got a disposable phone, just like you suggested."

"What happened?" she asked, suddenly on guard again.

"I think Penelope . . . may have been right that the Firm was out to get her."

Jennie heard the dog's nails clicking on the kitchen floor before the patio door slid open and shut. Then it was quiet again.

"I'm sitting down," said her mom. "Tell me everything."

Even though her bathroom was practically soundproof, Jennie lowered her voice, not liking the way it echoed off the marble. She caught Karen up on the last twenty-four hours, from her visit with Kitty Crowden and reading Penelope's diary to this afternoon's talk with Scott Corbyn—and his conviction that Edmund had Penelope killed.

"Wow," said Karen. "Wow, wow, wow. That's . . . a lot."

"I'm starting to think he's right, Mom," Jennie said, suddenly hoarse. "You tried to warn me, too. I could be in real danger. I'm supposed to get married in three weeks and I'm scared!"

"First of all, where's Hugh?"

Jennie recognized her mom's take-charge mode from bee stings, breakups, and career setbacks and began to feel better almost instantly.

"He's coming back from Paris tonight."

"Do you have any reason to believe you're in imminent danger?"

"No, but I've never felt that way. Everything is just so hard to read. It's like finding my way through fog."

Karen sighed. "I'm not trying to minimize in any way what you're feeling, but I could kick myself now for filling your head with all that stuff. I know I spent too much time watching E! and TMZ. Mostly I found the rumors and theories entertaining. I mean, some people think that Penelope is on an island with Elvis and Amelia Earhart. But honestly? When it comes down to it, it's hard to fake an aviation accident. If you look at the facts, they didn't find one shred of real evidence pointing to foul play."

"If they did, they didn't release it," said Jennie, remembering Corbyn's claim that the real report had been censored.

"Again, that's all speculation."

Jennie wondered if her mom's sudden about-face was just an effort to make her feel better. She thought about Anthony Heald's beheading, another "bizarre and unthinkable accident" for which no evidence of wrongdoing had been found.

"It doesn't change the fact that Penelope and her first lover are both dead," she said. "And the love of her life would have been dead, too, if he had gotten on the plane with her like he'd planned."

"Look, even if I can't really believe Penelope was assassinated, that doesn't mean I don't understand why this is so hard on you and why she got so paranoid before she died. People in the palace really did gaslight her! They covered up Edmund's affairs, they tried to make her feel crazy for asking questions, and they punished her for every mistake she made and smeared her in the press. That would be enough to make anyone snap."

Jennie laughed bitterly. "You sure have a funny way of telling me to go through with it."

There was silence on the other end of the line.

"Mom?"

Lowering the phone, she looked at the screen and saw the call had dropped. She called back.

"Ominous, huh?" she said, after they had reconnected.

Karen laughed. "I probably hung up with my cheek. I'm always doing that to your dad. What I was saying when we got cut off was that I would *never* tell you to do something that doesn't feel right. If you want to call it off and come home, your room is always waiting."

"I'm not—"

"I know you've had a lot of crap to deal with, and your life is insane right now, but there's a massive difference between you and Penelope. She never had a happy marriage. What you and Hugh have . . . it could be like what I have with your father. It's what I always dreamed of for you. The kind of love that only comes around once in a lifetime."

Jennie missed Hugh so much it physically hurt.

"And Edmund loves Hugh, too," continued her mom. "Would he really do anything to his son's wife? I don't think you're wrong to be on your guard. That's probably a good instinct for your new life. But you need to get a hold of yourself and remember why you're in that situation in the first place. Not so you can be Princess Jennie, but so you can marry the man you love."

"No, I know," she murmured.

Karen had a full head of steam and showed no signs of slowing down. "Trust me, the more everyone gets to know the real you, the easier everything will get. The problems you've had in the press are pretty small compared to what Hugh's mom went through. And at least you don't have a drinking problem! The more they love you, the more your problems with everyone—the royal family, the press, and anyone else—will go away."

Now Jennie *was* crying. She'd done more of that in the past year than she had in her whole life. But these were good tears. Her mom might be a little bit naive, but she always knew what to say to make her feel better. And she did make some good points.

Jennie thought of Scott Corbyn, trapped in his mausoleum to Penelope. Then she pictured Hugh waiting for her at the front of Westminster Abbey, his eyes shining as she walked toward him. She knew where her future lay.

She stood up, staying close to the sink to keep the phone plugged in. "Thanks, Mom. *So* much. I have to go."

"Is everything okay?"

"You made me feel a lot better. It's weird, but I really feel like I need to go to the studio and write."

Chapter Thirty-One

DISOBEYING ORDERS

A roar went up as Jennie and Hugh moved to the front of the box, and the crowd hadn't even seen them yet.

The members of Coldplay had just taken the stage at Wembley Stadium, and before they'd even played a note, the crowd covering the field surged toward them like an onrushing tide. High above them, in a luxury box at what would have been the fifty-yard line if they were in an American football stadium, Hugh grinned at Jennie and squeezed her hand.

Then someone below spotted them. Faces turned upward in a rippling motion that reminded Jennie of cards turning over. When she and Hugh waved, the cheering was *almost* as loud as it had been for Coldplay.

In the spotlight, singer Chris Martin, realizing he had competition, bowed in their direction, grinned, and paraphrased John Lennon: "All of you in the cheap seats clap your hands. The rest of you just rattle your jewelry."

"Let's sit," said Jennie, tugging Hugh down, not wanting to steal any attention from the performers.

As the gentle synth wash of "Head Full of Dreams" gave way to

throbbing bass that pulsed through the huge speaker stacks flank-
ing the stage, they settled into their seats. Hugh signaled their server
for a beer and Jennie asked for a sparkling water with lime and a
splash of vodka. Joining them in the box were Rex and Will; Sidney
Reddy, his wife, and twelve-year-old son; Ian O'Rourke and his
nervous-looking girlfriend; and Rodney and Jim, Hugh's latest PPO.

England's national stadium hadn't quite reached its concert
capacity of 100,000, but it must have been close—the only empty
seats Jennie could see were near the very top of the oval-shaped
bowl. The promise of seeing not only Coldplay but Dua Lipa, Ed
Sheeran, Harry Styles, Elton John, and even Adele on the same bill
had briefly crashed Ticketmaster the day the show went on sale. It
all started with a surprising tweet from Noel Gallagher challenging
his brother Liam to reunite Oasis for a concert to benefit the victims of the fire at the Manchester veterans' home. That kicked off
the brothers' feud all over again, so they were out, but Ed Sheeran's
response—*If it happens, I'm in*—gave the idea momentum, and
within twenty-four hours, enough big acts had signed on that all
of a sudden, everyone wanted in.

Concert promoters quickly formed a working group, tick-
eting sites pledged to waive fees, and soon there was only one
venue big enough to stage the event. Projected revenue from
ticket sales, livestreams, and merchandise was so staggering that
organizers pledged to help other veterans' charities—including
Hugh's Unconquered Games—after the needs of the fire victims and their families were met.

The crowd had been baking in the sweltering July heat all day.
Warmth radiated from every surface in the stadium, bringing with
it the familiar festival smells of sweat, sunscreen, and spilled beer.
But with the field and the lower levels cooled by shade as the sun
went down, the energetic fans showed no signs of fatigue.

As the band shifted smoothly into the synthesized strings

of "Viva La Vida"—playing the hits was always a good idea at a charity gig, Jennie knew—Hugh bobbed in his seat, enjoying himself. She noticed that he'd already downed half his beer. But he'd been working so hard, promising her it was all so they could enjoy a month-long honeymoon, that this was a break he badly needed. Jennie wished she could relax, too, but she was a bundle of nerves. She had never, ever seen a crowd this big.

After forty minutes of playing their best-loved songs, the band eased into their gentle, uplifting, "Up&Up." When she heard the first line, Jennie stood up.

"Bathroom," she told Hugh, squeezing his shoulder. "Be right back."

"You can't wait until they're done?" he asked, laughing.

She shook her head. He smiled up at her before refocusing his attention on the stage. He didn't even notice when she walked right past the private bathroom near the back of the suite. Or that Ian and Rodney had peeled off to join her.

Outside the door, four burly stadium security guards were waiting. They quickly formed a phalanx around her as Ian led the way to the elevator that would allow them to bypass both the endless sloping ramps and any concertgoers who might actually have been headed to the toilets.

Three minutes later, she had been waved into the heavily guarded backstage area by a headset-wearing stage manager. The sound there was deafening and boomy. She stood behind the impossibly large video screen, watching Chris Martin's forty-foot-tall face in reverse as he exhorted the sea of fans to never give up. Played live, the song seemed a lot longer than the album version.

A guitar tech rushed up and handed her an acoustic guitar with a pickup and a radio transmitter attached to the strap.

"This is tuned, right?" she asked, as she looped the strap over her shoulder.

"Um." Looking panicked, he took the guitar back and checked it with an electronic tuner.

Good thing I asked, thought Jennie. The last thing she needed was to walk out on stage and hit an F# minor that sounded like she'd just picked the guitar up at a yard sale.

Would her fingers even form the chords correctly? Would she even remember the words?

She couldn't recall time ever moving as quickly as it had the past week. She'd written most of the song in a few hours, but arranging and recording it had taken days, her concentration constantly broken by the dozens of phone calls required to arrange her appearance at the concert while keeping it a closely guarded secret.

Thankfully, her manager was more than happy to run point and had supported her pledge to donate any related profits to the Manchester veterans. The publicity was bound to boost sales of her catalog, giving him a rare and well-deserved payday.

The new song, which she had simply titled "Manchester," was queued up to drop on Spotify right after she finished playing—but only if the response was good.

Coldplay was almost done. Jonny Buckland drew out the last shimmering chords as Guy Buckland played harmonics on the bass and Will Champion played drum fills while the crowd clamored for more.

The tech handed her the guitar again, saying, "Good to go."

Then the band's manager escorted her up a short flight of metal stairs so she was waiting just offstage. She could see the band in profile, their faces blazing in colored light as they raised their arms to thank the adoring crowd.

Jennie was finding it hard to breathe. She'd never had stage jitters like this before. She was shaking so badly she didn't know if she could stand, never mind walk out on stage.

Why was she doing this? She hadn't cleared it with the

palace, so she was directly disobeying Legrand. She had been warned. If this backfired, she wasn't just going to get hauled into his office again. Something much worse would happen.

Breathe, she told herself.

Chris Martin looked her way, clearly wondering if she was ready to go on. The manager gave him a thumbs-up.

And just like that, Jennie felt better. Because she didn't care what anybody thought. She didn't care what happened. Because this was who she was. This was nothing like her song for Hugh escaping into the world. This song was her choice, and it wasn't about her—it was about the people who really deserved the world's attention.

She wished Diego and Leaf were there with her, but the concert organizers had insisted she use one of the bands already scheduled to play. So why not Hugh's favorite one?

Jennie chuckled to herself, picturing him wondering why on earth she was taking so long in the bathroom.

There was a brief lull in the cheering. The audience seemed puzzled why the band wasn't leaving the stage.

"We've got a treat for you, a special guest who's written a new song to benefit the victims of the fire," said Chris Martin. "Please give a very warm welcome to . . . Jennie Jensen!"

During the beat while the crowd processed this information, someone gently pushed her forward. And then suddenly she was walking into the heat of the night, the glare of the lights, and the warm embrace of the crowd.

Jennie started to play.

———

Hugh wrapped his arms around her in the back seat as they inched through the crowded streets toward Kensington Palace.

Both of them were still glowing and neither of them had much to say. At the wheel, Rodney tapped his fingers to a Rod Stewart song playing softly on the dashboard radio.

A DJ started talking over the fade. Jennie wasn't paying attention until Hugh suddenly said, "Turn it up."

Rodney raised the volume.

". . . festival organizers estimate the event will raise well over twenty million pounds for the victims of the Manchester fire and associated veterans' charities. If you've been watching the livestreams, you'll know that some of the performances were absolutely mesmerizing. And in the biggest surprise of the day, the American singer Jennie Jensen, who is engaged to marry the Prince of Wales later this month, took the stage with Coldplay as her backing band to play a song she wrote called 'Manchester.' The lyrics are simply extraordinary. It's just dropped on Spotify and I'll be sharing it with you now."

Jennie felt a tickle down her spine as her finger-picked chords, including the squeaks she'd decided not to edit out, filled the car.

"Brilliant!" said Hugh.

"Buckingham Palace is going to hate everything about this," she reminded him.

"Bollocks to them. We're winning the ground war thanks to you. How can they criticize a song that raises a million pounds for charity?"

As they listened, Jennie could still find problems with the recording—she wasn't as good a bass player as Diego, and the drum track was Drum Machine 101—but the lyrics made her points poetically and the melody, she had to admit, was inspired.

Then, suddenly, the sound got wonky. There was a wobbling echo like it was out of phase. Had something gone wrong in the mastering process en route to Spotify?

"Rodney, turn that off, please," she said as her stage fright surged back.

"Jennie—" Hugh protested.

Rodney turned off the stereo. But the song persisted. Where was it coming from? Jennie rolled down the tinted, bulletproof window and heard her own voice spill in with the smoggy air. There—the car ahead of them was playing the song with its windows down.

"Even better," said Hugh, kissing the top of her head.

Then the volume surged and got louder, discordantly, like someone changing stations and finding the same song at a different part as a young man weaved through traffic on a scooter, playing the song on a Bluetooth speaker dangling from his backpack.

Then it was blaring from the open windows of a corner pub, spilling out into the night as the patrons saw her looking and spilled out onto the sidewalk.

"There she is!"

"Nice one, Jennie!"

Three men in England soccer shirts started singing like they were at a match:

One of our own, she's one of our own
Jennie Jensen, she's one of our own

Hugh gave them a wave, then squeezed her even tighter. "Why don't we stop by Buckingham Palace for a nightcap and see if my father wants to celebrate with us?"

Part Four

WILD CARD

Chapter Thirty-Two

PASSING NOTES

Jennie looked down the long table in the crowded 1844 Room at Buckingham Palace, where members of every possible constituency had been assembled for the official presentation of the wedding day schedule. There were only ten days to go. She and Hugh sat at one end, with Sidney next to Hugh, and Ian and Poppy next to Jennie. King Edmund and Queen Eleanora commanded the middle of the table, both flanked by their personal secretaries, and their secretaries' secretaries—Jeremy Legrand had not one but *two* assistants. Across from them were representatives from the mayor of London, the Greater London Authority, the London Fire and Emergency Planning Authority, the Metropolitan Police, and several other departments Jennie had already forgotten. Minor functionaries lined the walls on blue-and-gold chairs set between the marble columns, either taking notes or killing time on their phones. Only one chair was empty: Grant McCutcheon had not yet arrived. At the far end, Felicity Welburn, the celebrity wedding planner who had also coordinated Edmund's second nuptials, was presenting at a large video screen.

Jennie had attended, performed at, and stood up in more than a dozen weddings, from an informal ceremony on the banks of the Illinois River to a big Jewish wedding in Queens to a full-blown Catholic mass in a downtown Chicago cathedral. She'd worn a sundress, a suit from the Macy's clearance rack, and thanks to her Aunt Kelly, a mauve bridesmaid's dress with dyed-to-match pumps and velvet hairband. She'd eaten at backyard buffets and catered banquets. All told, she'd probably been present at seven or eight wedding rehearsals.

Not one of them had required a ninety-two-slide Power-Point presentation.

Felicity clicked through the plan with the crisp dispatch of a battlefield general, covering the timetable of events in fifteen-minute increments. Hugh and Jennie's movements were marked on detailed maps where both of them were represented by cartoonish crowns.

"Mine's bigger than yours," Hugh whispered.

"Size isn't everything," she said, gently elbowing him in the ribs.

Karen and Dave were in another wing of the palace, trying to stay awake and fighting jet lag after their overnight flight from O'Hare. Karen had wanted to come to the meeting but had been turned down by Legrand. Apparently, even the bride's mother didn't qualify for security clearance.

"All cars will proceed down the mall past St. James's Park at a speed of no more than twenty miles per hour," pronounced Felicity. "We want to give onlookers an opportunity to see the guests en route to Westminster whilst following the Met's security protocol."

Hugh would be waiting at the church with roughly two thousand guests while everyone else made the two-kilometer ceremonial journey from Buckingham Palace. Karen would be in the first car, a black Audi, guided by a cop on a motorcycle.

Then six silver Volkswagen vans would ferry all invited Jensens and Windsors to the church before black Rolls Royces delivered Edmund and Eleanora, and then Jennie with Dave, the father of the bride. Black Range Rovers full of PPOs would follow each of their cars.

As Felicity advanced the slide, Hugh scribbled something on a piece of paper and slid it over to Jennie. He kept his face expressionless while she read it.

Still not too late to get hitched in Las Vegas.

Without cracking a smile—Legrand just happened to be looking her way—she wrote her answer and showed it to him.

Are you trying to get both of us locked in the Tower of London?

Even though the magnitude of the event was more than she could really get her head around, truthfully, Jennie couldn't wait to finally wear the dress. She'd had the semifinal fitting the day before and had admitted to both Saskia and Poppy that the corseted satin dress—with its long-sleeved, high-necked, hand–embroidered and beaded tulle overlay—made her look like a princess. She felt beautiful and almost prepared for the title that would soon be bestowed upon her.

"Remember, the return from Westminster Abbey to Buckingham Palace for the luncheon reception will be made via open-topped carriage, and it is assumed that most onlookers will stick around to cheer the happy couple," continued Felicity.

The door opened and Grant McCutcheon came in with Rodney close behind. Without pausing, he walked around the table and stopped by Edmund's chair. He bowed and then stepped forward to whisper in the King's ear.

Edmund frowned, then cut Felicity off mid-sentence. "We'll pause for fifteen minutes. Clear the room."

Without hesitation, the forty or so attendees picked up their things and headed for the doors. The slide frozen on the screen read: *eliminate the unexpected.*

"What's going on?" asked Hugh.

"Wait," said Edmund.

Jennie's stomach churned as she and Hugh pushed back their chairs and walked down the table to the King and Queen. Soon they were all standing expectantly around Mc-Cutcheon and Rodney. Only Legrand had stayed behind. The head of royal security waited patiently until all the doors had clicked shut.

"Well, what is it?" asked Edmund curtly.

"It's quite serious, I'm afraid," said McCutcheon. "The Marquess Felix Hill, MP, was apprehended inside apartment 1A. We have determined that he entered with threatening intent."

Jennie reached out for Hugh as Edmund, seemingly flabbergasted, asked, "What—*Felix?* How could you possibly know what he intended?"

Grant nodded at Rodney. "Officer Whyte, please make your report."

"Your Royal Highness," said Rodney, bowing slightly. "Since the localized threats to Miss Jensen were first reported, I've made it my business to perform extra patrols of apartment 1A. As she traveled here to Buckingham Palace with Prince Hugh's PPO, I visited the residential wing and did my usual walk-through, top to bottom. I was coming down the stairs from the first floor when I saw Lord Hill entering the private quarters. Obviously, this was most unusual. When he saw me, he quickly put something in the pocket of his coat. I questioned him but he refused to answer and attempted to leave. I contacted my

superior, who ordered me to detain him. A search of his lordship's pocket revealed a note, written in red marker, with the
words: *you will die.*"

"This is, quite frankly, too fantastic to believe," said
Edmund, looking uncharacteristically rattled.

"The search and questioning were recorded on video," said
McCutcheon. "Lord Hill maintains his innocence and claims
he was en route to visit Prince Stuart. He says he was merely
confused and entered the palace through the wrong door. But
without question the note was in his pocket."

Hugh put his arm around Jennie, which even Legrand ignored given the more serious issues at stake.

"Can I see the note?" she asked.

Everyone leaned forward as McCutcheon showed them a
note in a sealed plastic bag. The block letters looked exactly
like the ones that had spelled out *Penelope couldn't survive here
and neither will you.*

"Obviously, Lord Hill was trying to disguise his handwrit-
ing, but this is identical to the previous threat," said Rodney.

"But Felix is my best friend," said Edmund, his voice un-
certain for once. "Why would he do such a thing?"

"It's quite obvious. He is a rabid royalist and she is American," snapped Hugh.

"He's always told us he liked her *spark*," offered Eleanora,
seemingly coming to the defense of both Edmund and Felix.

"Well, why would he admit he hated me if he was secretly
trying to drive me out?" Jennie asked.

No one said anything, probably because the answer was all
too obvious.

"So he denies it completely, even though he was caught
red-handed?" Hugh asked McCutcheon.

The security chief touched his tightly knotted tie. "I'm afraid he does *not* deny disliking Miss Jensen. He had some . . . unsavory things to say about her."

"Don't beat around the bush, man!" ordered Edmund.

McCutcheon passed the buck to Rodney, who blushed uncomfortably.

"Lord Hill called you an . . . 'oversexed tart' and . . . questioned your bloodline," he said apologetically. "I believe the word he used was 'mongrel.' I'm so very sorry, Miss Jensen."

"At least now I know," she said, feeling sorry for Rodney.

Eleanora let out a whooshing sigh and squared her shoulders. "This all seems quite far-fetched. What would he have hoped to accomplish by sending nasty notes like a schoolboy?"

"We have only begun our investigation, ma'am, and I'd hate to rush to judgement," said McCutcheon. "But it seems so far that the Duke may have thought he was acting in the best interests of the monarchy. Believing Miss Jensen unfit to become part of the royal family, he would have wished to scare her off in order to spare the Crown the embarrassing drama Edmund went through when he was married to Penelope."

"*Spare me*," said Edmund, in a tone that was hard to read.

"What do we do now?" asked Hugh.

"We've placed him under house arrest to ensure he won't harass Miss Jensen," said McCutcheon. "We can't rule out the possibility he might wish to physically harm her. But we have to keeps this quiet—"

"As well you should," interrupted Legrand.

"—until we know whether Miss Jensen wishes to prefer charges."

"The Crown does NOT wish to prefer charges," said Edmund.

"That's Jennie's decision," said Hugh, turning to her and taking her hands in his. "What do *you* want to do?"

"Before you answer," said Legrand, "consider the story you

wish to be told about your wedding."

It was hard to think with everyone staring at her. She wanted to go for a walk with Hugh and talk it over. But people would be coming back into the room any minute. It still made her feel shaky to think that Felix Hill had actually been in her home, but now that she knew, she almost agreed with Eleanora: it seemed borderline comical that the aging playboy had been there to leave a mean note. He was pathetic, really.

What if Legrand was right for once? Did she need Felix Hill to be publicly shamed, or did she just want him to stop? Did she want the headlines during the week of her wedding dominated by his sad little plot, or did she want them to be about the happy start she was making with Hugh?

Maybe the choice wasn't so hard, after all.

"If you can guarantee that he won't get near me again, then I don't want to do anything until after the wedding," she told McCutcheon.

"You have my word on that," he assured her.

Then, turning to Rodney, she took his hand and squeezed it with both of hers. "Thank you for looking out for me."

"Just doing what I've always done, Miss Jensen," he told her.

Edmund stepped away from the group, shaking his head. "I hope there are no more unpleasant surprises on the agenda. Can we carry on and get this meeting over with?"

Hugh looked at her, asking the question.

She nodded.

"Yes, we can," she said.

HRH The Princess of Wales

18 NOVEMBER 1996

No one ever recognized Penelope in the curly blond wig, baseball cap, jeans, trainers, and jumper she wore when she snuck out of Kensington Palace to visit the shops or catch a new movie. Just as tonight, no one seemed to think anything of the woman getting into the back seat of the black Mercedes on Kensington High Street in the drizzly dusk.

To make absolutely certain she hadn't been spotted or followed, Penelope walked past the sedan and circled back before opening the door and sliding into the back seat. The driver said hello, but his eyes didn't linger on the rearview mirror, nor did he indicate he had any idea who she was. He simply pulled away from the curb and disappeared into traffic.

Exactly as planned.

Penelope had been caught trying to sneak out in the past—once by an overzealous new guard and once by a groundskeeper who appeared from behind a hedge as she was skirting around it. The consequences then had been inconsequential, merely that she'd been saddled with a PPO when she'd hoped to fly solo.

But today she'd made no mistakes.

At exactly 4:45 p.m., in the presence of a housekeeper, she'd been "overcome" by a sudden, severe migraine and retired to her bedroom after saying she was not to be disturbed. At 5:00 p.m. sharp—when the daytime security shift clocked out, the nighttime crew signed in, and no one was watching—she made her swift, silent exit through a series of not-so-secret doors.

Penelope took her first steps of freedom carrying only a Chanel tote (a "bon voyage and welcome" gift from Scott) containing her wallet, her passport, two tampons, a pack of Airwaves gum, a Dior lip gloss, and her diary. Once the divorce was granted, she hoped to retrieve her clothes and a few treasured items: a framed photo of her and Hugh, her grandmother's crystal perfume bottle, her cassette collection. If that proved impossible, she would ask to have everything auctioned off for charity. All the jewelry, including her engagement ring, wedding band, everyday diamond studs, and the string of pearls given to her by the Queen as a wedding gift, awaited Edmund in the safe. She knew he would look there first once he was notified she was gone for good.

Her first stop on the way east and now south toward Blackbushe Airport was Kitty Crowden's house, where she gave Kitty her diary as added insurance, a way to back up everything Scott had uncovered. Kitty already knew most of the stories inside and was the only person Penelope trusted to safeguard the book until she returned. In the meantime, she planned to start a new volume, writing not as the Princess of Wales but a princess rescued from her years-long slumber by the prince of her heart.

Penelope's nerves hadn't allowed herself to feel too hopeful, but as the driver turned onto Royal Windsor Way, the rain stopped and the moon appeared from behind the clouds. It felt like a good omen about her journey away from all things royal and Windsor.

Except for Hugh, of course.

Parents did not show up unexpectedly at Eton College. But she wasn't just any parent, not yet anyway, and the staff didn't hesitate to locate Hugh for her. He appeared in the administrative offices flushed and damp, sweating through his gym kit, seeming slightly off-camber about her sudden appearance.

"We're playing against Walpole House," he said in greeting.

"I won't keep you but a minute," Penelope said, too brightly. She always let Hugh know when she left the country, and not telling him was unthinkable, but she obviously couldn't have given him advance warning. And she still couldn't reveal where she was going, or why. "I'm off to the airport so I thought I'd pop in and say hullo."

"Hullo then," he said, warmly, while gazing longingly in the direction of the all-weather pitch.

"I'll be back as soon as I can. I promise."

"Sounds good," he said, not asking where she was going.

"Love you," she said, both hurt and grateful that he hadn't.

"Love you too, Mum, but they're going to call the game soon so we can shower before supper and I'm playing outside center."

"You'd better run along then," she said, her voice hitching.

At the thought of how long it might be before she saw him again, she wondered if she would make it out of the office without breaking down. Thankfully he was happy and engaged at school. She hoped his cloistered existence would shelter him from the media onslaught.

"Toodle pip," he said, trying to be funny, before giving her a cursory hug.

As she pulled him in closer than he surely preferred, Penelope savored the still boyish smell of him—like a sweet, wet puppy. "I'll phone as soon as I can, darling boy."

He'd undoubtedly be half a head taller next she saw him, but that would happen whether she was sleeping with one eye open at Kensington Palace or safe and sound on Dagon Island.

Just half an hour later, she spotted the flashing lights atop the control tower and then the sign for Blackbushe Airport. She wished Scott was with her. He'd planned everything, checking and rechecking every detail right down to the departure from this obscure airfield. At the last minute, however, he'd told her he needed another day to make the final arrangements to secure their future. It was disappointing but irrelevant in the grand scheme of things.

Although she was flying solo tonight, she'd never felt less alone.

The driver pulled up to a metal gate. They were waved

through, and the Mercedes rolled onto the smooth tarmac toward Scott's gleaming new white Citation jet.

"Here we are, ma'am," the driver said.

"Indeed," she said.

Penelope exited the car and walked into the clear, cool autumn evening. She climbed the metal staircase and boarded the plane. She settled into a pillowy soft white leather seat feeling buoyant and happy.

As the flight attendant sealed the cabin door, she was filled with an overwhelming sense of peace.

Chapter Thirty-Three

DOWN THE AISLE

Jennie felt the bass pedals of Westminster Abbey's massive pipe organ in her belly as she waited just inside the Great West Door. She had expected to walk down the aisle accompanied by "The Wedding March" (singing *Here comes the bride, all fat and wide* in her head) until Felicity Welburn had disabused her of that notion. Royal weddings were different. Instead, the organist was playing a lofty hymn called "I Was Glad When They Said unto Me," a psalm set to verse for the coronation of King Edward VII in 1902. Jennie couldn't really argue with the choice. The song definitely checked both boxes: pomp and circumstance.

Behind her, one of the two heavy doors opened to admit a sheepish wedding assistant—frowned at by Rodney—and a gust of cool, damp air. After baking London for weeks, the English summer had reverted to form. The wind caught Jennie's train and made it billow like a sail until it covered her like a ghost.

Hugh, barely visible through the jewel-box structure of the Quire, almost a football field away from her, saw it and cracked up. So did her parents, watching from a nearby pew.

"Cut!" said Felicity from the scaffolding above, her voice crackling from a dozen walkie-talkies. "Start from the beginning."

The music stopped. Saskia and Adalberto helped reset the piece of muslin standing in for the real ten-foot train so Jennie could get used to walking without stepping on it.

Her dad slid closer, watching them work. "We could weigh that down with a couple of sinkers," he suggested. "I didn't bring my tackle box, but I'm sure there must be a fishing outfitter somewhere in London."

"*Should* we add some weight?" asked Adalberto worriedly, raising an eyebrow at Saskia.

She looked up at Felicity, who shook her head.

"Trust me, that door will *not* open after Ms. Jensen comes through."

Everyone took their places again, from camera operators to Edmund and Eleanora's seat-fillers, as Jennie prepared to rehearse her *stately, dignified* walk down the endless aisle of the 750-year-old church.

With one week to go, the popular tourist attraction had been closed for the day to allow a run-through in situ, as Felicity relentlessly called it. Even without the small trees, bushels of flowers, and red carpet that would be installed before the coming Friday, the soaring nave was breathtaking. Delicate Gothic columns supported an impossible weight of stone. The ancient grandeur of the place conferred a solemnity she hadn't expected to feel.

And that was despite the snaking cables, multiple camera setups, and heavy equipment cases that would be artfully hidden on the actual day.

"Do you need anything? Water? Tea? A biscuit?" asked Poppy, appearing at her elbow.

"Vodka soda, hold the soda," said Jennie, kidding along even though she felt absolutely fine.

"Coming right up," said Poppy with a wink. "*After* you mock march down the mock aisle. Until then, it's mocktails for you."

Jennie felt light and airy, unlike the dress she would soon be wearing. Today, for the rehearsal, she had on a corseted silk day dress Saskia had created to approximate the feel of her wedding dress without giving away the cut or styling to lurking paparazzi.

Though the week had been busy it had been surprisingly relaxing, even fun. The official events would start next Thursday with a gala dinner for foreign dignitaries and other VIPs at the Mandarin Oriental, kicking off a wedding day so long she had been warned by Felicity to think of it as a marathon and to pace herself accordingly.

Felix Hill's betrayal had been kept from the headlines, but for Jennie, knowing that the source of the threats was a bitter old man who just wanted things to be like they were in the old days—when future kings married the right sort of person—made everything feel a lot less menacing.

He probably did Penelope dirty, too, after he decided she needed to be cast out of the royal family, but a man who waged war with a red Sharpie didn't seem capable of bringing down a plane. It seemed safer to trust the known facts instead of wallowing in endless speculation: the crash had to have been an accident. With the Marquess Felix Hill, MP, safely watched by the Metropolitan Police at his Belgravia pied-à-terre, she could enjoy the run-up to the wedding without worrying about creepy notes and symbolic messages.

Edmund and Eleanora eventually accepted that their friend had acted like a stalker, and both of them had separately asked how she was doing—which was as close as she would get to an apology. They might not ever love her the way Karen and Dave loved Hugh, but she could survive that: even in Peoria people had problems with their in-laws. She would always have detractors, but the people of Britain seemed more than okay with the idea of an American princess. Many of them were begging her to go on tour (#FreeJennie was trending on social media). Legrand had even grumpily agreed to "reconsider it in due time."

Which felt like a win.

"Feet getting sore!" called Hugh from the front of the church, his voice echoing off the vaulted ceiling.

"Suck it up, buttercup!" she shouted back, to appreciative laughter from the dozens of helpers and minders.

Felicity's voice crackled again through the walkie-talkies. "Cue the music!"

As the organ chords climbed triumphantly to the heavens to announce her entrance, Poppy whispered, "Go!"

Jennie began walking, careful to keep her steps measured, her pace even, her chin up and her eyes on Hugh. Things would feel different once the pews were packed with the world's most important people, but now that she had performed in a packed Wembley Stadium, she was less worried about keeping it together. Even if the wedding—also broadcast live around the world—would have a hundred times as many viewers.

She crossed the worn, gray flagstones, detouring around the grave of the Unknown Warrior, to the jewel box of the Quire, a small but ornate structure where the church's choir sang daily but on her wedding day would be filled with family: his on the right, hers on the left.

Passing inside, she could see ahead the narrow stalls for singers and the famous black-and-white chessboard floor facing the high altar where kings and queens had been crowned. Where she would be married. On the day, she would have the Maxwell family tiara, a touching loan from Hugh's maternal grandparents, carefully pinned to her head.

Still half a football field away, Hugh grinned broadly at her and said, "At last!"

She glanced up at the gold-starred blue ceiling, briefly distracted by its beauty.

There was a flash of light and a deafening bang.

Jennie felt herself thrown into a wall. The air had been punched from her lungs. She gasped for breath.

Everything went black.

Chapter Thirty-Four
RECKONING

Below on the river Thames, a white tour boat glided under Waterloo Bridge, its deck packed with tourists raising their camera phones as they turned south toward the London Eye, Big Ben, and the Houses of Parliament. Then there was a high-pitched whine as it was overtaken by a blue ThamesJet speedboat, its speakers blasting the twangy opening notes of the James Bond theme. The speedboat's life-jacketed passengers screamed in delight as their driver swerved toward the bigger boat and sprayed it with a rooster tail of water.

Jennie closed the window, leaned back in her chair, and plugged her ears, trying to tell if they were still ringing. The high-pitched whine was so faint she almost couldn't hear it. She had finally stopped coughing: the smoke she'd inhaled was no more than a tickle in her throat. She reached for her phone out of habit before remembering she had left it in the drawer of her nightstand so she wouldn't see the lock screen filled with pleading notifications from Hugh.

Even though the day was warm, with fluffy clouds scooting across a sunny blue sky, she pulled her bathrobe closed and shivered.

"Do you need a blanket?" asked Karen from the couch across the room, still watching her like a hawk.

"I'm fine, Mom."

Someone was at the door of their suite: *knock-knock*— pause—*KNOCK*.

"There's your father." Karen jumped up unlocked the double doors to admit Dave, carrying a big bag of Krispy Kreme.

"I figured you were probably tired of scones and tea," he said, lifting it to show her.

Jennie's eyes teared up with gratitude. Her near-death experience had left her raw and emotional and ready to cry at a moment's notice. Gratitude for the way her parents were taking care of her had made her heave with sobs in the shower. They were doing an especially great job of making it look like it was no big deal, from the coded knock to the fact that they were avoiding room service. Her dad excused his trips to random fast-food joints by telling her he knew she would want as many tastes from home as possible. Which wasn't wrong.

Nobody needed to say out loud that it was really because she had just survived a bombing and they wanted to make sure she wasn't poisoned.

Again.

"Thanks, Dad," she said. "Love you."

"We love you, too," Dave and Karen said quickly.

Her mom ended the awkward pause that followed by saying, "I'll get some plates."

Dave followed her to the kitchen.

Jennie had regained consciousness in the ambulance with Hugh gripping her hand while a paramedic squeezed a bag to force air into her lungs. In the front passenger seat, Rodney was screaming at the driver to go faster. Doctors at the emergency department quickly decided her injuries weren't life-threatening.

Miraculously, she'd been shielded from the blast by a heavy equipment case that the bomber couldn't have anticipated— if he or she had waited until Jennie's wedding day, she would have been killed instantly. The Quire was so badly damaged that it would probably have to be demolished. Hugh, watching in horror, hadn't been touched.

Still, as she came out of shock, the pain was intense and they'd dosed her with some serious painkillers. Everything hurt. Bruised from head to toe, she also had a concussion, two fractured ribs, and lungs full of smoke. The ringing in her ears reminded her of the time she'd stood in the front row at a Metallica show, and she was so confused she might as well have been high.

Hugh didn't leave her side for a minute.

Grant McCutcheon and a Detective Chief Inspector Shaw from Scotland Yard had made their report that evening, and despite admitting there was a lot they still didn't know, they concluded that the bomb had been meant for Jennie. They also strongly suspected the bomber had been present in the church—meaning he or she could have been any one of five dozen people—but cautioned against jumping to conclusions. They were still searching every inch of the cathedral for hidden cameras or transmitting devices that could have been used to trigger its detonation remotely.

"What about Felix Hill?" she'd croaked.

"We have his house under twenty-four-hour manned surveillance, and his ankle monitor indicates he has not left his home," said Shaw. "But he may be working with persons yet unidentified."

Even in her fog Jennie knew the bomber was a palace insider, someone who had seen the rehearsal schedule and had access to the church when it was closed. And whoever it was, they were still out there.

The doctors, Hugh, and Legrand all wanted Jennie to stay in King Edward VII's Hospital overnight. The Windsors assured her it was safe, but Jennie still felt exposed. She didn't want to be around anyone but her parents. And she definitely didn't want to go back to Kensington Palace. Karen had been busy pricing hotels on her phone when Jennie realized she knew where they could go. Hugh was distraught as she climbed into a cab with her parents, begging her to tell him they were still getting married. All she could tell him was that she didn't know.

When Scott Corbyn told her he would reserve a room for his files at the Savoy, his five-star flagship hotel, Jennie had assumed it would be a standard room, not the two-bedroom, four-bathroom Royal Suite that ran the length of the fifth floor. After they checked in, a shocked Karen had googled the price and learned it usually went for fifteen thousand pounds per night—and yet it was sitting empty, just waiting for Jennie to review Corbyn's files in privacy. Neither he nor Jennie could have guessed she would actually need to hide out there.

Three days after the blast, her ribs still ached and her right hip was sore as hell. Her split lower lip looked bee stung and she had two black eyes that were turning yellow-green. Carefully, clenching her jaw against the pain, Jennie got up, crossed the room, and sat down on the couch by the coffee table where they'd been eating all of their meals. The elegant oval table in the dining room next door was covered with Corbyn's papers and even more boxes were stacked underneath it. So far, she hadn't been able to bring herself to touch a single piece of his obsessively collected evidence.

"Dough-nuts!" sang Karen, doing her Oprah impression as she swept back into the room with a pyramid of Krispy Kremes on a plate of Wedgewood bone china. "Your dad tells me these are ve-gan!"

"Coffee," grunted her dad, doing a perfect Dave impression. One big hand carried a box of coffee and the other cradled three teacups like they were eggs about to hatch.

Jennie tried not to wince as she leaned forward for a caramel-frosted doughnut. She took a big bite and chewed slowly, savoring the intensity of the sugar rush.

"So, how are we feeling today?" chirped Karen, pretending not to notice her discomfort.

"Sore, but basically fine."

"On a scale of falling off your water skis to totaling your Corolla?" asked Dave.

"Definitely closer to a car crash. But I don't feel like my head is filled with helium anymore."

"And what are you thinking, now that your mind is clearer?" asked Karen, raising an eyebrow over the rim of her coffee cup.

Wondering if she should have milked the concussion longer, Jennie took another bite and washed it down with weak black coffee before answering.

"I want to go home," she said. "I really, really want to get out of here. Go back and sleep in my old room for like a month, then get a place that's not New York or LA, maybe Chicago so I can be close to you guys. Then I just want to do nothing. Take long walks and write songs, start being myself again. Play some open mics."

Karen was staring out the window while her fingers pulled her uneaten doughnut into little pieces. Dave watched Jennie impassively while he munched an apple custard crumble, the ends of his mustache getting coated in custard and crumbs. They were both waiting her out.

She sighed. "But I know I can't. Even if I flew home today and never came back, it's all going to follow me forever. Because even after the reporters give up, there will still be people aiming their phones at me. Every person I meet is going to want to know the details and I'll suspect everyone's motives for the rest of my life. I'll probably be physically safe, because whoever is doing this wants me to leave, not die. I think. I obviously don't know. So maybe they'll try again."

"You'd also be living without Hugh," said Karen matter-of-factly.

"I know, Mom."

"And you'd have to live with yourself, knowing you gave up on true love and let them—whoever *they* are—win."

Jennie saw Hugh's anguished face and heard him saying, *If you leave, they will win, and I will lose.*

"I *know*. But if I can't go home, I can't go back to Kensington Palace, either. And I can't stay in this hotel for the rest of my life, because at some point, Scott Corbyn is going to start charging us."

Karen still hadn't eaten a bite and her doughnut was now just a pile of crumbs. "I want you to be safe," she said, finally making eye contact. "And Lord knows, I want you to come home. I couldn't care less if you never became Princess Jennie. But I've always said I only want you to be happy, and what you're describing doesn't sound like a very happy solution."

Dave wiped his mustache with a napkin, getting half of the frosting and crumbs, then reached for a glazed. Jennie knew from experience he wouldn't weigh in unless asked.

"What do you think, Dad?"

"I think you should listen to your mother."

"And you think I should go back to Kensington Palace?"

He nodded in the direction of the dining room, where Corbyn's evidence archive waited. "I think before you make a decision, we should at least take a look."

CONFIDENTIAL

Interview Report

Hunter & Associates Investigations

Date: 13 May 1998

Case Number: C1450-25

Client: Corbyn, Scott

Report Submitted by: Denis Hunter, Hunter & Associates Investigations

Nature and Scope of Assignment: This report is filed as part of the ongoing investigation into the 18 November 1996 crash of Mr. Scott Corbyn's Cessna Citation V near Blackbushe Airport, Camberley, Surrey, which resulted in the death of pilot George Gallagher (age 38), flight attendant Dominque Azan (29), and Her Royal Highness, the Princess of Wales (37).

Relevant Background Information: Due to reports of pilot George Gallagher's erratic behavior during preflight check and an autopsy report showing .02 BAC, I was directed by client to discover when and where Gallagher had been drinking. After independently verifying the widow Jane Gallagher's assertion that George had spent the night of 17 November 1996 at home with no drink taken (see Jane Gallagher interview transcript), I canvassed local establishments until I obtained positive identification at Cricketers, Cricket Hill Lane, Yateley, Hampshire. This pub is regularly frequented by off-duty Blackbushe employees due to its convenient location on the outskirts of Yateley, just 2.25 kilometers from the airport. I spoke with several patrons who confirmed seeing Mr. Gallagher inside the pub with an alcoholic beverage prior to departing for the airport and assuming controls of Mr. Corbyn's Cessna Citation V to fatal effect.

Witness: Michael Jenkins

Occupation: Head Bartender, Cricketers Pub

Age: 42

DOB: 20 August 1954

Residence: Charles Street, Camberley GU15

Length of Current Employment: 5 years

Summary: I met with Mr. Michael Jenkins at Cricketers Pub on Tuesday, 12 May 1998 at 10:00 a.m. Per his statement, Mr. Jenkins came on shift at 4:00 p.m. Monday, 18 November 1996, and worked until 12:00 a.m., when the establishment closed. He described the crowd as sparse but not out of the ordinary for a drizzly Monday night. Jenkins positively identified Gallagher's photo and confirmed seeing him from approximately 5:00 p.m. to 6:00 p.m. He stated that Mr. Gallagher was not a regular and couldn't remember serving him at Cricketers in the past.

Transcript of Recorded Conversation:

Please note Private Investigator Denis Hunter will be referred to as Investigator and Bartender Michael Jenkins will be referred to as Witness for ease of identification.

Investigator: Thank you for taking the time to meet with me this morning. I am conducting an in-depth investigation into the circumstances surrounding the aviation accident at Blackbushe Airport on 18 November 1996.

Witness: I figured someone would be by to talk with me sooner or later. Only surprised it took you so long.

Investigator: Why is that?

Witness: The papers said the pilot was drunk when he crashed the plane. I have no idea what he consumed before he came in or after he left, but I can assure you, he wasn't overserved here. He ordered a half-pint of lager and didn't ask for a refill.

Investigator: You didn't think of coming forward?

Witness: Would you? I need this job, mate.

Investigator: So I am the first person to contact you about his visit to Cricketers.

Please note that the witness nodded in the affirmative.

Investigator: Please speak into the recorder.

Witness: Yes, I only wish it didn't bring back the memory of that night. We all heard the whine of hydraulics as the plane decelerated and then the crash. I went out to the car park and saw the orange glow of flames in the distance. The sirens went on all night.

Investigator: It was a terrible tragedy. Had you seen the pilot before?

Witness: Never in my life. Seemed like a regular bloke. We exchanged a few words and an hour later he was gone. I honestly didn't put it all together until the following day. Dominque, the stewardess, used to drop by on the regular. Beautiful eyes. Had she been five years older and me a year or two younger I'd have asked that lovely bird out. And Princess Penelope . . . my lord . . .

Investigator: Would you like to collect yourself, Mr. Jenkins?

Witness: I'll muddle through. You have questions that need to be asked. If my answers somehow help them find out what happened, maybe it will help me, too.

Investigator: Describe Mr. Gallagher's demeanor. Did he seem like he had been drinking already?

Witness: If he had, he was a pro at hiding it. When I brought the drinks to the table, I kidded him that pilots in uniform shouldn't be seen in pubs. Mr. Gallagher laughed, thought that was funny. I got the impression his mate was egging him on. He said they needed to celebrate.

Investigator: His mate?

Witness: The two of them were sitting together at the high table right there. I can't imagine how the poor bloke is feeling given how thrown off this has me.

Note that witness pointed to the table situated closest to the short end of the bar on the north side of the dining area.

Investigator: Did Mr. Gallagher appear well-acquainted with this individual?

Witness: If I had to guess, they were old chums.

Investigator: Can you describe the other man?

Witness: Dark hair, short back and sides.

Investigator: Any other defining features?

Witness: I'd say he was of similar age as Gallagher.

Investigator: So roughly forty?

Witness: Sounds about right. Nothing else really stood out about: average height and build. I wasn't paying enough attention to tell you about his eye colour or if he had a mole or anything like that.

Investigator: You are describing a very generic British male.

Witness: That's pretty much what he was. Just another punter. Wait a minute, I do remember one thing.

Investigator: Which was?

Witness: His order. First time I can remember anyone drinking two pints of bitter while they ate a sticky toffee pudding with extra ice cream.

Note to Client:

Mr. Corbyn,

I think we can both agree that my next step is to locate George Gallagher's companion.

DH

Chapter Thirty-Five
CRASH LANDING

Jennie's hand was shaking so hard the words blurred on the page. She dropped the piece of paper like it was on fire.

Her parents hadn't noticed. On the couch, Karen frowned at the comb-bound manuscript splayed in her lap. Dave was visible through the open doors as he dug through another box of evidence at the dining room table. Every surface in the Royal Suite was covered with piles of documents, each one of them topped with a sheet noting who reviewed it and what they had found. Multicolored sticky notes fanned out from the sides of the stacks, flagging everything that seemed important.

For three days, Jennie, Karen, and Dave had been reading Corbyn's archive from top to bottom. And for the first two and a half, Jennie had wondered if they were wasting their time. The tens of thousands of pages weren't organized in any meaningful way. Within them—as she suspected the first time she saw them—science rubbed elbows with speculation, and official accounts jockeyed for position with crackpot theories. The sheer volume of material was absolutely overwhelming. Thick dossiers had been compiled for everyone with any possible motive to kill Penelope, from Edmund and Eleanora (who wanted her out of the way so they could get married) to Jeremy Legrand (acting either for Edmund or for reasons unknown) to Vivienne Banfield-March (who simply wanted Edmund all for herself). There were also a dozen files on fringe candidates like Peter Benatti, a "stalkerazzo" who'd hounded Penelope until his behavior landed him in Wandsworth Prison. Released the morning of her death, he would hardly have had time to arrange her assassination despite his questionable alibi.

Then today after lunch, Jennie discovered the boxes of files submitted to Scott Corbyn by Denis Hunter, a particularly dogged private investigator. For two and a half years, Hunter had dedicated himself to tracking down expert testimony and eyewitness reports from a staggering number of people with an equally staggering number of connections to Penelope's last day on earth. Some of them were obvious choices, like Kensington Palace staff, although the only people willing to talk were the ones who'd left royal service. Some of them were so random— like a dog walker who claimed to have seen Penelope ride out of Kensington Palace on a bicycle—that Jennie couldn't help suspecting Hunter of running up the bill on his wealthy client.

The box labeled BLACKBUSHE AIRPORT contained files, carefully indexed, on every single employee who had worked a shift during the month before Penelope's death, and CD-ROMS that apparently held recordings from every airport security camera during the forty-eight hours before Penelope's fateful departure. Hunter had conducted exhaustive interviews not only with the airport staff but with attendants at nearby service stations, regional air traffic controllers, members of the Hampshire Constabulary, and on and on and on. Still more folders contained extensive background reports on the pilot, George Gallagher, and the flight attendant, Dominique Azan, as well as interviews with their friends, families, and significant others. Their separate journeys to work on the fatal day had been meticulously documented with maps and timelines.

The official inquest into the crash had been conducted by the Metropolitan Police and then edited by the Crown before public release. The copy Jennie found in the files was indignantly annotated in almost illegible cursive—Scott's, she guessed—with most of the ink on the pages noting the airport fueler's famous claim that Gallagher had been "acting drunk" while performing his preflight inspection. The summary findings of the autopsy, however, noted that when tested, his remains showed a BAC of only .02 percent, which was not only legal but seemed unlikely to impair an experienced pilot.

The Met's investigators had left it at that. But Hunter, presumably at Scott Corbyn's direction, had taken it upon himself to find out where Gallagher consumed the small amount of alcohol in question. He retraced the pilot's journey from home to the airport and discovered a midafternoon stop at Cricketers, a pub in Yateley, just off the M3 and just over a mile from the airfield.

True to form, the PI interviewed every patron he could find who'd been in the pub that day—only eight, given that it had been a Monday. Most of them had noticed the uniformed pilot and some of them recalled a glass of beer in front of him. Only the barman, Michael Jenkins, seemed to know he was the pilot who crashed the plane that killed himself, the flight attendant, and the People's Princess. And only Jenkins recalled Gallagher's drinking companion.

Jennie searched the box until she found a file labeled *GALLAGHER—UNKNOWN FRIEND.*

The folder was empty.

———

Ninety minutes later, Jennie stood outside a heavy oak door in Buckingham Palace, fiddling with her phone. She was wearing yoga pants and an oversized hoodie with earbuds dangling from the collar—a look she knew would probably trigger Jeremy Legrand.

Which was fine by her.

Her parents, waiting in a taxi in the courtyard at her insistence, hadn't wanted to let her out of their sight. Karen, in particular, fretted as though her only daughter was about to walk into an ambush. But Jennie knew by now that wasn't how things worked. No one would ever touch her while she was in any of the royal family's castles—the bad things only happened after you left.

Besides, Legrand would never answer Jennie's questions with her parents staring at him.

"Come." He answered her knock curtly, but the look on his face when she opened the door made it clear she was the last person he expected to see at the end of his workday. He stood up as she closed the door behind her. "Miss Jensen. I'm pleased to see you are—"

"I know Penelope's death wasn't an accident," she told him. "And the person who killed her is the same person who tried to kill me, too. Of course, you already know that."

His jaw literally dropped. Ever the pro, he quickly recovered.

"You must still be feeling unwell. I can't imagine how you could think such a thing, let alone make such a baseless accusation," he said tightly.

Jennie sat down in front of Legrand's desk, wanting to make sure he didn't throw her out before she said what she had to. He sat back down, too, eyeing her warily as she reached into her tote, like he thought she was about to pull out a gun. As her fingers closed around the document, she realized it was a different kind of smoking gun.

"I don't think it was you—at least, not literally," she explained.

"Imagine my relief," he deadpanned.

She pushed Hunter's interview of the bartender across his desk. "Scott Corbyn has always felt responsible for Penelope's death. After all, he hired the pilot and it was his plane that crashed. He believes she was targeted because the Crown didn't approve of their relationship. In the twenty years he's been investigating what happened, he's accumulated more evidence than the official police investigation ever did."

Legrand studiously avoided looking down at the papers. "I'm aware of his obsession. It might surprise you to know that I have kept up on the case."

"Then you also know that the official report was either incompetent or incomplete. Why did the police do such a rush job? Why didn't they follow up on the pilot?"

With a sigh, he finally picked up the papers. His eyes flicked back and forth as he began to read.

"You know why," Jennie insisted.

"I'm afraid I don't."

"Because the powers that be—the government, the royal family, *you*—don't want to have to explain why one of your own met with the pilot the day the plane crashed."

"I don't follow."

"Rodney Whyte."

Saying his name aloud made her so queasy she almost wanted to throw up. How would she convince Legrand when she still couldn't believe it was true?

Legrand looked up at her in surprise. He seemed to be resisting an urge to issue a rebuttal. What looked like worry clouded his eyes before he turned the page and continued reading.

"I wasn't aware of such an encounter," he finally murmured.

"But there are many possible reasons for it. Perhaps, as Princess Penelope's PPO Whyte was merely doing his job and performing due diligence."

Jennie shook her head in disbelief. "*He didn't know she was leaving that night.* At least, he wasn't supposed to know. But you knew, didn't you? Edmund knew. Even though Scott and Penelope did everything they could to keep it secret."

"I'm afraid we're not as all-seeing as you might think." He turned back to the first page but didn't return the report. "What makes you believe this identifies Mr. Whyte? All I see is that the barman claims the pilot had a few swallows of beer with an unnamed person."

"Who ate a sticky toffee pudding with extra ice cream while he drank two pints of bitter ale."

"*That* is your damning evidence?"

"I have Penelope's diary. She wrote about Rodney's sweet tooth, and I've seen it myself, plenty of times. Bitter ale and a pudding is a weird combination. But all that detail really did was make me realize that Rodney was with Princess Penelope in 1986 when the papers reported she was stumbling drunk at *Phantom of the Opera*, but in her diary, she wrote that she only had a couple glasses of champagne. And Rodney was also there this year on the *Somerset* in Greece when the same thing happened to me: I had a couple of bellinis and felt like I had been poisoned. And now here he is again, meeting up with a pilot who looked like he was stumbling drunk before he climbed into the cockpit—when even the official report admits there was hardly any alcohol in his system. I'd call that a pattern of poison."

The muscles in Legrand's face had gone slack. He was corpse gray. It looked like he was hardly even breathing.

"Slow down," he said thickly, shaking his head. "Just . . . slow down. I would like to see the diary."

"No. I'm not going to let that disappear like the notes I was assured were secure in the Buckingham Palace safe deposit box."

"I don't know what you mean."

Did he mean it?

"I'll admit that Princess Penelope was ill-treated," Legrand said, collecting himself. "By the media, yes, but also by the royal family. Her husband. And, I'm sorry to say, by me. But the gears of the system must turn smoothly and she was a cog with too many teeth. We wanted her to go away."

"So badly you arranged for her to be killed."

Jennie pictured her phone in the front pocket of her hoodie and saw the seconds racing past the square red RECORD button as it captured everything through the microphone on her earbuds. She leaned forward, wanting to make absolutely sure it caught his next words clearly.

"I assure you," he continued, his voice strengthening, "that although we did withhold some details from the final report, nothing was done that would have harmed a hair on her head. Can you imagine the risk to the monarchy if it were to actually . . ."

He didn't finish his sentence.

As Jennie looked around Legrand's office at the decades of tidy clutter, the plaques, trophies, and tokens of royal appreciation, she remembered something Hugh had once told her: *Pieces are taken and replaced but he always protects the board to ensure the game will go on.* She had always seen Edmund's private secretary as loyal to Edmund in all things. But if Hugh's instincts were right, maybe some things were even more important to Legrand than Edmund himself.

"If you know anything more, you have to share it," she told him. "My life is at stake and so is your precious monarchy."

Legrand peered at her warily. "Why would I give the keys to the castle to someone who might burn it down?"

"I don't want to burn it down. I want to live in it with Hugh. But we both need to be safe. If the monarchy is brought down, it won't be by me, but by the secrets you're keeping. You have to let the light in."

Legrand fiddled with an old-fashioned skeleton key in a small dish by his pen cup.

Jennie put her hands on the edge of the desk and waited until he looked up. "Even if you don't think I deserve the truth, or your country deserves the truth, don't you think Hugh deserves to know what happened to his mother?"

The only sound that broke the silence that followed was the scraping of the key in the dish. Finally, Legrand stood up.

"Wait here."

He left the room through a narrow door at the back of his office. While he was gone, Jennie checked her phone to make sure it was still recording. She hoped to convince Legrand to come clean on his own—but the audio file would give her leverage if he didn't.

He came back, sat down, and opened a manila folder with bent corners and wire prongs holding the pages in place. "A fact that has always bothered me is that the pilot, Gallagher, was known to have served with Mr. Whyte. They served together for several years when the pilot was seconded from the RAF to Whyte's SAS squadron. They performed a number of missions together before Whyte left the military and joined the police. After some years, Gallagher became a commercial airline pilot. Rodney told our investigators they lost touch long ago. I couldn't imagine at the time it meant anything significant, as former military people pop up in many lines of work. But if, as you suggest, Rodney had met with Gallagher on that very day . . ."

There it was. In a way, they had known all along but hadn't known what they'd known. How much information had Legrand hoarded, not knowing what it meant or how it could be used? How many other mysteries went unsolved due to indifference and neglect?

If he was telling the truth.

"Help me make the connection," Jennie pleaded.

Legrand closed the folder and tapped it against his chin. "I would be a fool to serve the king if it cost him his crown. I'll have Commander McCutcheon bring Mr. Whyte in for questioning."

"I want to read the uncensored report. And I want to be there when you arrest Rodney."

"I'm afraid the latter is impossible."

Jennie took a deep breath and looked him in the eye. "We'll see what my future husband, the prince, has to say about that."

Chapter Thirty-Six

OPEN QUESTIONS

"Rodney?"

Even in the flickering twilight, Hugh's expression was in-credulous.

"I almost couldn't believe it myself," she said.

They were treading water in the middle of Buckingham Palace's century-old swimming pool, which was located in a conservatory at the northwest corner of the building. With the overhead lights off, the underwater lamps projected rippling shimmers on the sloped glass ceiling. Jennie hadn't wanted to risk telling Hugh in Kensington Palace or anywhere else Rodney might be listening. Feeling paranoid that he could even have hidden a tiny microphone in her purse or her clothes, after leav-ing Legrand's office and sending her parents back to the hotel, she texted Hugh to meet her at the pool.

I'll be right there, he'd answered.

On arriving and seeing her, he hadn't said anything about the choice of location, just shucked off his clothes and slipped into the water, instinctively understanding it was anything but a romantic invitation.

And now that she'd told him everything, he was struggling with it, just like she had.

"Your mom trusted him," she continued. "They went everywhere together. He would have overheard so much and he could have learned the rest by spying. I think he was the one tapping her phone and he probably bugged her apartment, too. You learn how to do stuff like that in the SAS, right? That has to be how he knew she was planning to leave the country with Scott Corbyn."

Hugh dipped his chin in the water and regarded her seriously. "Which is why we're meeting in a swimming pool."

Jennie nodded. "He has access to our apartment and goes in there without us all the time, so he could have broken the cake topper. It would have been easy to drug my food on the yacht because I was the only one eating vegan. And he knew every detail of the wedding rehearsal, so he would have known where to put the bomb. The only thing he couldn't anticipate was that massive equipment case being left in the way."

"And thank Christ for that." The look in Hugh's eyes had slowly changed from bewilderment to fury.

"He's even tried to make me suspicious of other people. After he poisoned me, he dropped a hint about Vivienne, saying your mom always thought Vivienne had poisoned her at the opening night of *Phantom of the Opera* to make her look like a drunk. Rodney could have done that, too, or who knows? Maybe your mom just had a stomach bug and he knew I could confirm that story—which I did, after Kitty gave me the diary."

Jennie had passed it along to Hugh, who'd put it aside unopened, telling her he wasn't ready to read it. He'd relied on her to tell him what was inside.

Jennie's arms were getting tired, so she swam toward the shallow end until she felt her feet touch the bottom.

"So you truly believe . . . he killed my mum?" Hugh asked as he followed her.

"Yes."

"But why?"

"I don't know. Legrand told me he asked to be assigned as my PPO, and that at the time he assumed it was because Rodney loved you and your mom so much. Everything connects through him but none of it makes sense."

Hugh shivered, even though the water was almost bathwater warm. "Mum *was* a problem. But even supposing that was reason enough to try to kill her—why would Rodney possibly try to kill you? You weren't running away. We were about to get married, for heaven's sake."

Jennie found his hand underwater and squeezed it. He pulled her closer until they were inches apart. Her whole body ached for him.

"If he was spying on me, he would have known I was starting to get suspicious about what happened to your mom. But I stopped after Felix Hill got caught. So I honestly don't know why."

"And what about Felix Hill?"

She shook her head, frustrated that she didn't have all the answers yet. "That's why Rodney has to be questioned, and we have to be there to hear what he says, even though Legrand doesn't want us to."

Leaving unsaid for now that Rodney could have been working for Felix Hill . . . who could have been working for Edmund . . . and that Jennie couldn't help wondering if Legrand was giving up Rodney to protect himself and others.

Hugh let go of Jennie's hand and put his arms around her waist. When he pulled her closer, she put her head on his shoulder and almost melted into him.

"Trust me, you and I will both be there to hear what Rodney has to say," he murmured. "But you haven't even mentioned the biggest question that needs answering."

She looked up at him. "What's that?"

"Are we still getting married?"

Chapter Thirty-Seven

UNMASKED

The four-car caravan sped east out of London just before dawn with no lights or sirens. At the wheel of his Range Rover in the rear, Hugh carefully maintained his distance from the car in front of him.

"One of my mates at school called this the whitest borough of London," he said. "I suppose he would know. Even though he wanted to be a DJ, behind his back, everyone called him the whitest bloke in London. As though any of us could talk."

He had been monologizing the whole way, filling the car with trivial conversation despite Jennie's lack of response. She appreciated his attempts to distract her but all she could think about was what was waiting at the end of the journey. She had never seen Rodney's home but had asked him about it and all she could remember him saying was, "Oh, Hornchurch is nice and quiet. Suits me down to my bones."

A nice, quiet place for keeping secrets.

Grant McCutcheon, DCI Shaw, and Jeremy Legrand were in the lead car. Two senior members of the Royalty and Specialist Protection Branch were in each of the second and third cars. And Hugh and Jennie followed in the fourth.

Negotiations with Buckingham Palace and the Metropolitan Police had gone on late into the night. Speaking for the King, Legrand insisted Rodney be detained when he arrived for work at Kensington Palace and questioned on the premises by Legrand himself before the police took him into custody. McCutcheon wanted to arrest him at home and then hold a formal interrogation at Scotland Yard. Hugh brokered a truce by suggesting a third way: arresting Rodney at home and questioning him on site, with both Hugh and Legrand present, before the police hauled him off to a holding cell at Scotland Yard, where he would await charges. Jennie didn't really care how it happened as long as she got to hear with her own ears what Rodney had to say.

She and Hugh were supposed to wait in the car, behind tinted windows, until McCutcheon called them inside. Besides the potential danger from Rodney—who was armed with his service pistol—the story would explode if any early risers saw the Prince of Wales assisting an arrest on a quiet suburban street.

The purple sky was brightening as they left the A13. Minutes later, they passed the Hornchurch tube station, heading for the center of town. The neat, semidetached houses gradually gave way to shops and storefront businesses. Ignoring traffic signals on the nearly deserted roads, McCutcheon led the convoy onto a residential street, turned left and then right, and suddenly they were there: Rodney's house was a single-story mock-Tudor with a steeply pitched roof, set behind a low brick wall.

Jennie felt like she had a pill in her throat she couldn't swallow as McCutcheon braked to a halt with two wheels on the curb. The cars behind it blocked the entrances, sealing Rodney's personal car, a blue Nissan Qashqai, into the brick-paved forecourt. Instantly, all six policemen were out of their cars. Two of them raced around the side of the house into the backyard while

McCutcheon and Shaw approached the front entrance. All of them wore bulletproof vests and were armed with pistols; the final two men lugged a heavy battering ram, which might have seemed like overkill if the man inside hadn't planted a bomb in Westminster Abbey.

Nothing moved on the block as Hugh stopped across the street.

"Charming neighborhood," he said, still trying to lighten the mood.

She tried to play along. "The neighbors will have a lot to talk about over breakfast."

McCutcheon pounded on Rodney's front door. While he waited for Rodney to answer, Jennie couldn't help noticing random details, like the spindly TV antenna rising above the chimney and the neatly squared hedges bordering the narrow lot. She pictured Rodney working with garden shears in the shadow of the newer, larger houses crowding in from both sides.

Apparently, there was no answer. McCutcheon pounded on the door again, listened briefly, then signaled to the men with the battering ram and stepped aside. They took their places on the top step, nodded at each other, and then swung the heavy iron cylinder, hitting the door just next to the lock and handle. Even from across the street Jennie could see the door crack open. The policemen dropped the ram and charged inside, followed closely by McCutcheon and Lieutenant Shaw.

Hugh squeezed her knee. "Quite a wakeup call. Won't be long now."

She tried to smile and couldn't.

Branches whipped and waved in the thick bushes at the side of the house. Then, like something out of a nightmare, Rodney burst out and ran for the street barefoot, still wearing striped pajama bottoms and a white T-shirt.

"Bloody hell," said Hugh, already opening his door.

Jennie saw the flat black gun in Rodney's hand. "Hugh—no!"

Focused only on escape, Rodney didn't appear to have seen them yet. Jennie hardly recognized him. It was like someone else was inhabiting his body.

Hugh streaked across the street, across the grassy boulevard, toward Rodney. Jennie fumbled to open her door. The scream caught in her throat as Hugh launched himself, rugby-tackling Rodney and slamming him into the low brick wall where it curved toward the sidewalk. The gun flew out of Rodney's hand as both of them collapsed in a heap.

Jennie sleepwalked toward them as they began wrestling. Hugh quickly gained the upper hand, straddling Rodney and pinning him to the ground. Shouting, he began raining blows on Rodney's head just as the agents from the backyard caught up and the other men spilled out of the house.

Jennie fell to her knees in the grass.

Hugh landed one last punch before they pulled him off.

"Took you bloody long enough," groaned Rodney.

Rodney glared at Jennie from the middle of his living room, his face red and welted. His hands were cuffed together behind the high back of the wooden chair back and both of his legs were shackled to the chair legs.

Jennie had wondered what his home would look like inside, half-imagining they might find a dirt-floored basement with a wall of crazy snarled in red string—or at the very least, a dartboard with her picture on it. But the small rooms were clean and orderly—surprising enough for a middle-aged bachelor— and remarkably old-fashioned. If it weren't for the oversized TV, the PlayStation, and the charging stations for Rodney's electronics, Chez Whyte—with its heavy wooden furniture, framed black-and-white photos, and tea towels from Queen Alexandra's Golden Jubilee—looked like it could still be home to his parents. Maybe even grandparents.

One officer was guarding the front door while the rest of them searched the house, leaving only Rodney, Jennie, Hugh, McCutcheon, Shaw, and Legrand to attend the interrogation.

While Shaw finished setting up a video camera on a flimsy tripod in front of Rodney, Legrand parted the front curtains and peered outside.

"Any witnesses?" asked Hugh.

"Two dog walkers seem to be finding reasons to extend their conversation," Legrand said, pulling the curtains back into place. "I imagine more will arrive."

"Perfectly normal when police cars appear on a quiet suburban street," said McCutcheon.

"The sooner we move him, the better."

"I agree."

DCI Shaw turned on the camera and popped the viewing screen out of the side. After checking the picture, he turned on a few more lamps to improve the lighting and then gave McCutcheon a thumbs-up.

"Let's begin," said McCutcheon.

Shaw pressed a button and RECORD appeared in the corner of the screen next to a red dot.

Rodney had stopped staring at Jennie and his gaze was wandering from face to face with the resentful patience of a caged predator. She was chilled by the realization that she didn't know him and never had. It seemed impossible that she could have spent so much time with him without having any idea who he really was.

McCutcheon pulled a chair in front of Rodney and sat

down. Jennie and Hugh sat on the edge of a couch off to one side while Legrand paced behind them.

"I would like to remind you that you do not have to say anything," began McCutcheon. "But it may harm your defense if you do not mention when questioned something which you later rely on in court. Anything you do say may be given in evidence."

Jennie wondered what would happen if Rodney refused to speak. She couldn't imagine a worse outcome than silence. After everything, she needed to *know*.

Rodney's chest was heaving so wildly she wondered if he was having a heart attack. If her own pulse didn't slow down, she might have one, too.

"I'm going to save you all a lot of fucking trouble," he said, spitting the words.

"Your cooperation is appreciated and will be noted," said McCutcheon.

Her formerly calm and dependable PPO seemed like he was going to vibrate out of his skin. He answered almost before McCutcheon could finish, his strangled voice an octave higher than usual. "I never meant to hurt her. I loved her—*I loved her.*"

He sounded eerily like Corbyn.

"Then why did you set the bloody bomb?" shouted Hugh, drawing a sharp glance from McCutcheon.

"Not *her*," said Rodney, jerking his head at Jennie in disgust. "Princess Penelope."

McCutcheon broke the stunned silence that followed with a reflexive, "Go on."

Hugh's body was completely rigid. Jennie caressed his hand and found his fingers balled in a fist, his knuckles already swelling from the fight.

Rodney's malevolent gaze lingered on Jennie before slowly

turning back to McCutcheon. "She was my English rose, she was. She should have lived to be queen. And I was so, so determined to keep her safe. Nobody showed any appreciation for the countless hours I put in off the clock, but that never bothered me. Because of my dedication, I was the first one to realize she needed protecting from herself. From the people she turned to in order to make her feel better."

Legrand had stopped wandering and now stood directly behind the camera. "What kinds of people?"

McCutcheon, who seemed to have resigned himself to the group interrogation, waited for Rodney's answer.

"I had to kill her riding instructor," he said matter-of-factly. "That was harder than blindfolded chess, but I pulled it off with no one involved knowing what part they played. I only wish King Edmund had done more to help Princess Penelope be happy in the system. She was a beautiful young woman and she needed to feel loved. To a man like Scott Corbyn, she was easy prey."

"And how exactly did he prey on her?" asked Jennie.

Rodney kept going as if he hadn't heard her, the words spilling out like water over the top of a dam.

"My *colleagues*"—he grimaced—"didn't take my warnings seriously enough. They didn't realize what would happen if the public found out our princess was straying from her marriage. I had to use electronic help to watch her around the clock. And that's how I found out about her plan to sue for divorce and marry Corbyn."

Rodney wasn't even waiting for questions. He spoke and they listened as if they were all in some kind of trance. The idea that *now she would know* kept Jennie frozen in place.

"I had a stroke of luck when Corbyn's pilot left to work for some other rich scumbag. My mate Georgie G was a capable pilot, and I knew he was looking for something. All I had to do was let him know about the vacancy and let fortune handle the rest. He couldn't resist bragging about his moneybags client and how his first day on the job would be flying Corbyn to his private island. I insisted on taking Georgie for a drink to celebrate his good fortune." Rodney's voice faltered, then grew stronger. "He never said one word about Penelope being on board. I guess the stupid shit didn't know, either, and I didn't put it together." Lamplight reflected in his eyes as tears streamed down his cheeks. He rattled his chains and twisted in his chair so violently Jennie thought it would break. "You don't know what it's been like, carrying this for so long!"

"Why couldn't you just have let her go and be happy?" Hugh's voice was as fragile as Jennie had ever heard it.

Rodney looked at him scornfully. "Would you have had me let your beloved mum run off with a man from the rag trade? And have the future King of England raised between two homes like a common child of divorce? She belonged in the palace. *You* belonged there, Your Royal Highness. I knew she'd come around eventually."

Jennie's mind reeled with the knowledge that Rodney hadn't tried to kill Penelope and she had died because Corbyn's plan actually worked—they really had kept her departure a secret. Rodney truly believed only Corbyn would be on the plane.

"She was never, *ever* supposed to be hurt," sobbed Rodney, his chin falling to his chest. "And the worst part is that I got away with it. Part of me always wanted to be caught and punished. I've been waiting for years for this day."

"If all this is true, then you are guilty of murdering not only Princess Penelope and Anthony Heald, but the pilot, George Gallagher, and the flight attendant, Dominique Azan," said McCutcheon. "Whose lives are equally important."

"You think Britain was made great by treating everyone like the King? You and me *aren't* as important. The funny part is that Georgie was an anti-royalist. Got what he deserved, the lousy Mick. Too bad he didn't live to see the irony."

Jennie stood up and walked within an arm's length of Rodney. She saw McCutcheon tense like he expected her to spit on the prisoner.

"If killing Penelope was a mistake you deeply regret, then why did you come after me?" she asked.

Rodney's look was almost reptilian in its coldness. "Because I needed to make amends and because, like Mr. Hill said, you have mongrel blood. Miss Banfield-March should have had your place. I didn't intend to hurt you, either, but you didn't scare easily, and you are fucking nosy to boot. You started getting suspicious about Penelope's death and you're like a child throwing toys out of the pram—stupid enough to bring down the system."

"By telling the truth?"

"I couldn't risk having you blurt it out onstage at some pop concert."

"Tell me how Felix Hill is involved," said Grant McCutcheon, nodding at Jennie to move aside.

She stayed where she was.

Rodney shrugged. "I wasn't doing anything he wouldn't have wanted me to do. I knew he had said negative things about Miss Jensen in private, so I nabbed him and put the marker in his pocket, knowing Miss Jensen would be only too ready to believe. But I was running out of time. It gutted me to damage our precious cathedral, but I knew it would send a message to the world."

Jennie looked at Rodney's tiny, pixelated face on the screen, grateful all his words had been recorded. It was no wonder his sanity was in shreds. He'd accidentally killed the person he'd sworn to protect and spent the rest of his life trying to keep his mistake a secret. Jennie might have felt sorry for him if he hadn't taken three other innocent lives in the process—and almost killed her, too.

Hugh was much less forgiving.

"It's a shame we don't do beheadings anymore," he said.

Chapter Thirty-Eight

I'VE GOT A PRINCE, HE'S A HECK OF A GUY

It sounded like all the bells in England were ringing as the stately organ chords rolled out from the doors of the church behind them.

When Hugh had suggested "the chapel" as an alternate to Westminster Abbey for their rescheduled wedding, Jennie couldn't help picturing a little white country church with a pointed steeple—but of course he meant St. George's Chapel at Windsor Castle. And while it was yet another Gothic church with soaring ceilings, acres of stained glass, and stone beasts crowning the roof, it did have two things going for it. It was half the size of Westminster Abbey, for starters. More importantly, nobody had tried to blow her up there.

Being alive and in love still felt like some kind of miracle. Marrying Hugh was icing on the cake. But what seemed most unlikely of all was the fact that, after negotiation and planning that had dragged on for the rest of the summer, the wedding was going off just the way they wanted it to. Even the weather was cooperating: the late September day was sunny and warm without a cloud in the sky or a breath of wind to disturb the picture-perfect scene.

The guests were making their way along the flagstone path and up the broad stone steps in no particular order. There were no heads of state and no celebrities. No invited guests from the media. Not even a videographer—just a single photographer who, with her assistant, would take pictures for both their private photo album and for public distribution. But the biggest break from protocol and tradition, one that seemed likely to horrify the older half of Britain, was that Jennie and Hugh were standing side by side outside the church doors to welcome guests as they arrived.

"If we're going to do things differently, we may as well let everyone know from the off," Hugh had said.

Karen and Dave reached the top of the steps, her mom looking resplendent in the metallic-knit St. John's dress she'd been so excited to find *on sale.* Her dad's mustache was neatly groomed and might even have been styled with a little bit of product. Despite his obvious discomfort, he was absolutely rocking the morning jacket and ascot Karen had insisted he wear. Her brother Daniel and his wife Amber stood sheepishly behind them, awed by the occasion.

"Oh God, I'm already ruining my makeup," Karen sobbed as she looked Jennie up and down. "If I hug you, I'm going to wreck your dress."

"It's fine, Mom," Jennie told her, grabbing her and squeezing tightly.

Dave shook Hugh's hand. "Congratulations, um, son, I mean, Your Hughness."

"You can count on me, sir," said Hugh, winking at Jennie.

Edmund and Eleanora seemed bemused by the idea of arriving in the middle of the line but were gamely attempting to appear unruffled.

"I daresay I can be grateful you didn't elope," said Edmund, who offered a smile but not a handshake or hug.

Eleanora did give Jennie the lightest brush of a hug before they passed on into the church. "I am so sorry for everything you've endured. I hope we can make you feel more welcome going forward."

"That means a lot," said Jennie.

Poppy had told her that, as the bride, she would not be expected to curtsey.

The line of guests kept flowing. Jennie had worried it would feel backward to have the receiving line first, but standing together felt natural and right as they greeted Courts, Rex and Will, Diego and Leaf (judging by their perma-grins and glazed eyeballs, Jennie was pretty sure both of them had taken something to calm their nerves), and Isabella. Imogen, Vivienne, and Mark Banfield-March smiled warmly but hardly paused. Kitty Crowden gave Hugh a lingering hug.

After Rodney's arrest, there had been intense disagreement about what to do with his confession about Penelope's death. McCutcheon argued it should all become part of the public record at trial, while Legrand, reverting to form, insisted it was better to cover it up and let the secret lie. Hugh had remained silent on the subject for days while he processed it all with a therapist— one he made certain had no connections to Buckingham Palace.

Learning the truth had brought him a strange form of relief. It validated Penelope's so-called paranoia and proved she had been perfectly sane in her suspicions. The fact that Rodney had acted alone, driven by grief and madness, removed any suspicion Hugh attached to Edmund and Eleanora, who may have wanted Penelope out of the picture, but certainly didn't want her dead. But Hugh's grief at reliving his mother's final moments had taken a toll on his usual sunny disposition. How could it not? His mom had not died in an accident but was *murdered*.

Jennie still didn't trust the King and Queen entirely.

Who else had the authority to remove the notes from her safe deposit box?

The only thing everyone agreed on was that revealing the true story would ignite a firestorm of media scrutiny as the story of Penelope's death was exhumed and examined forensically by millions, if not billions—when all Hugh wanted was for his mother to rest in peace.

Jennie assured him she would support whatever decision he made, and she meant it. But finally, Hugh realized he had no choice: his mother would have wanted the truth to be known. Edmund shocked everyone involved by agreeing to release the full story, with the caveat that the announcement be made at "an appropriate distance" from the wedding. He had even drafted a history-making statement to accompany the news, writing that while the House of Windsor had nothing to do with Penelope's death, the way she was treated was his greatest personal regret.

He made no promises of change, but at least, Jennie thought, he showed an ability to adapt.

Somehow, Jeremy Legrand was followed by Scott Corbyn in the receiving line—the two of them may even have been talking. Legrand offered his respectful congratulations. Corbyn's eyes were bright as he kissed Jennie's cheek and told her, "We've won!"

Hugh smiled at her after they had passed. "What's next? Dogs and cats living together?"

The Peoria contingent, led by Aunt Kelly, was almost last, and loudest—laughing at their shrieking, Jennie posed for a few quick selfies.

Then Freddie and Cece sauntered up, Freddie in full morning dress and Cece in a pale pink cape overlay midi-dress. When Jennie told them how wonderful they looked, Cece said, "You can't throw away *all* the traditions."

Freddie kissed Jennie's cheek. "And now you've got to the top of the ladder. Mustn't step on any more snakes."

It was like the tiniest cloud had slipped past the sun, a reminder that they still didn't know who had taken the notes from the vault.

But maybe it didn't matter. Even if Edmund himself was responsible, it didn't necessarily mean he was guilty of anything other than spying.

Right?

Finally, Hugh and Jennie stood alone on the top step. Two new PPOs grinned up at them from below. The organ paused and the expectant murmur inside the church hushed.

Then Jennie heard the chords of a familiar tune. A stately, if baroque, rendition of the song she'd written for Hugh.

Her chest fluttered. She hadn't been expecting it.

"Seriously?" she asked Hugh.

He shrugged. "If you're going to break with tradition, may as well go all the way."

"I love it," she said, kissing him. "I love you."

"I love you, too. Shall we?"

He offered her his arm and she laced hers through it. They walked through the doors together, side by side.

ACKNOWLEDGMENTS

We are grateful to Joelle Hobeika, Josh Bank, and the entire team at Alloy Entertainment for bringing us this project and helping make it so much fun to write. Thanks also to Addi Wright and everyone at Blackstone Publishing for taking a chance on two crazy kids in love (That would be Jennie and Hugh.). And, as always, deep gratitude to everyone at HG Literary, but most of all, Josh Getzler, the most loyal agent and the best friend we could ever ask for.

A special, extra loud shout-out goes to Javier Ramirez and Kristin Enola Gilbert at Chicago's Exile in Bookville. Your friendship and support mean the world!